Praise for *A Free, Unsullied Land*

Maggie Kast's searching, intelligent novel is a page-turner. Few novels have so powerfully evoked the longing -- and the hope -- of individuals at the juncture in which their culture's delusions are crumbling. In the most surprising and most wonderful ways, it is an epic novel.

—Kevin McIlvoy, author of *58 Octaves Below Middle C, The Complete History of New Mexico: Stories, Hyssop, Little Peg, The Fifth Station*

Through Kast's descriptive powers and her creation of the brilliant and thwarted Henriette, a young woman's striving to realize herself is as magical and terrifying as Alice's adventures in wonderland.

—Sharon Solwitz, author of *Blood and Milk* and *Bloody Mary*

A Free, Unsullied Land

Maggie Kast

Fomite
Burlington, Vermont

ISBN-13: 978-1-942515-21-0
Library of Congress Control Number: 2015947755

Fomite
58 Peru Street
Burlington, VT 05401
www.fomitepress.com

Cover painting: *Remembering* © August Burns

For my parents

Thanks to the editors of publications in which some of these chapters originally appeared, in different form. "Sleeping with Men" was included in *Seek It: Writers and Artists Do Sleep* from Red Claw Press, and "The Hate that Chills," 3rd place winner of the Hackney Literary Contests, appeared in the Birmingham Arts Journal. I'm grateful to the many friends who helped bring this novel to birth, especially the members of my writing group: Rosellen Brown, Garnet Kilberg Cohen, Tsivia Cohen, Peggy Shinner, Sharon Solwitz and S. L. Wisenberg. Writing teachers Fred Shafer and Kevin McIlvoy contributed insightful critique at crucial points along the way, and Polly Rosenwaike did careful copy editing. The Ragdale Foundation provided me with nurturing space and supportive community during the final stages of revision. Special thanks to Marc Estrin and Donna Bister of Fomite Press for intelligent and generous editing and detailed attention to design and production. And for support in putting the "public" in publication, I'm grateful to my fellow Fomite authors: Jan English Leary, Ilan Mochari and Lynn Sloan.

Part I: 1927-1930

Chapter 1

Sweaty in the hot summer of '27. An execution is imminent, and the family has been dreading it for years. Henriette wakes to the sound of feet hurrying along the hall outside her second-floor bedroom, then down the stairs and back up again. A thin, keening sound. Coughs and sobs. It's her older brother Carl, plagued by a nightmare.

Henriette was eight in 1920 when Nicola Sacco, a shoemaker, and Bartolomeo Vanzetti, a fishmonger, were convicted of robbery and murder in South Braintree, Massachusetts, and she's grown up with this wound to her sense of hope and possibility. Wisps of adult conversation drifting above her head taught her the story. Now she lies rigid in her bed, as though her stillness could stop time, standing by while others face what may already have become disaster.

Father first assumed the two Italians were guilty. As followers of the anarchist Luigi Galleani, the men could be expected to plant bombs and murder anyone they considered a class enemy. Mother feared the jury was prejudiced against immigrants, workers, and all victims of the Red Scare then roaring to life. The Attorney General had recently embarked on a round-up of those considered Red, chaining five hundred men together and marching them through the streets of Boston, then holding them without trial and eventually deporting them. Mother's dear friend and mentor, Jane Addams, had been attacked as disloyal for her opposition to war.

Henriette sat silent through many dinners while her parents argued, her shoulders rigid, focused on spooning her soup "as little boats go out to sea…away from me." Late at night, roused by fighting voices, she'd stand in her bedroom in the dark, aching for calm, while angry words curled under and around her door like smoke. She'd bite her swelling lip and strain to hold her parents together while Carl ran through the house, trying to outrun bad dreams. Here he goes again, panicked at midnight. His identical twin, Russell, is used to the sound and does not wake.

Sacco and Vanzetti protested their innocence for seven years following their conviction, supported by the likes of Albert Einstein, George Bernard Shaw, and H.G. Wells. By the time Henriette was twelve, the case was famous all over the world and awakened her own sense of justice. Ordinary people in London, Paris, and Tokyo demonstrated against the impending executions. The judge's refusal to admit eye-witness testimony by Italians persuaded Father that the trial had been unfair, and the whole family awaited the outcome of motions and appeals with trepidation. Each time Henriette learned of another failure, her stomach opened onto a dark space of apprehension. Maybe the world was really not a good place.

As she entered adolescence she felt energized to protest. Her favorite poet, Edna St. Vincent Millay, wrote to the governor of Massachusetts in a letter widely publicized, "I cry to you with a million voices: answer our doubt." Her poem, "Justice Denied in Massachusetts," was published on the front page of the New York Times. Millay was arrested along with Katherine Anne Porter and Dorothy Parker for demonstrating against the execution. Then a convict named Celestino Madeiros confessed to the crimes, and the protest continued to spread. Henriette read the papers and learned about the IWW, International Workers of the World, a leader of the movement to free the two men. She rolled the organization's nickname around in her mouth, "Wobbly, wobbly," and read about anarchists and Bolsheviks.

Now she lies in bed, hot, moments before hope is lost. She pictures Carl sparking as though he were a live wire, as though his own body felt the deadly current that could at any moment zip through all three convicts: Sacco, Vanzetti, and Madeiros. She refuses to think about what it's like to know the moment when you will die, to be strapped into a chair and wait for someone to throw a switch. She murmurs Millay's despairing lines: "Forlorn, forlorn/ Stands the blue hay-rack by the empty mow/We shall die in darkness and be buried in the rain."

Just before her thought of execution can defeat her refusal to imagine it, her parents step out into the hall across from her bedroom. The running stops. The cry subsides, and voices speak soothing, grieving words. It's shortly after midnight, and the radio has just announced the execution. Henriette tenses, squeezes out tears, and thinks of Vanzetti's words, written when his last appeal failed: "The taking of our lives — lives of a good shoemaker and a poor fish peddler — all! That last moment belongs to us. That agony is our triumph." She knows that this disaster can never be undone. Opening her bedroom door, she stands there, helpless, seeing the shame in her parents' eyes, shame for their country and the rule of reason in which they've put so much faith. Mother's arm encircles Carl, who pants and drips sweat, his face pale, while Father's stony face for once does not melt at the sight of Henriette.

Huge crowds follow the funeral cortege through the streets of Boston, and people wear black armbands reading, "Justice crucified." Vanzetti's final words, spoken to the warden as he walks to the electric chair, are publicized. "I wish to say to you that I am innocent. I have never done a crime, some sins, but never any crime. I thank you for everything you have done for me. I am innocent of all crime, not only this one, but of all, of all. I am an innocent man. I now wish to forgive some people for what they are doing to me."

The words chill Henriette with their dignified generosity, their tragic failure. They stay with her as she grows up and goes to college, popping up at odd moments to remind her of the world beyond family, classes, and boyfriends. Maybe she will not remain a bystander forever.

THE YOUNG WOMEN OF FOSTER Hall hurried from dark, wood-paneled dorm rooms down polished stairs, meeting each other's eyes with worry and excitement, and then looking away. No one knew just who would have to drop out, their funds for tuition obliterated by the Crash of '29 and the escalating economic disaster. Breakfast smells wafted up the stairs: the rich aroma of coffee and the steamy odor of boiling oats. Chilly and nervous in the food line, the women took small helpings of toast, tea, and coffee and proceeded to the dining room, where the clatter of dishes competed with low-voiced introductions.

Henriette stepped lightly into the line, having finally arrived where she'd wanted to be for a year and more. All through high school and the year she'd spent at home after graduation, when Mother insisted she was too young for college, she'd yearned for the South Side and its university. Meetings of Wobblies and Trotskyites. Jazz playing in the nearby clubs. The intellectual life of the classes, where students debated whether homosexuality was illness or social deviance. Though money was tight at home, she was confident of staying in school, for Father was a pioneer of advertising — the man who'd invented the Sears Roebuck catalogue and continued to write it. He'd gone to work for Julius Rosenwald when both were young men, shared Rosenwald's philanthropic interest in education for Negroes, and he expected to stay at Sears for the rest of his life. When former Brigadier Gen. Robert Wood began his ascendence at the company, Father adopted Wood's more conservative stance but never gave up on education for all. As floods in Mississippi and the ensuing Northern Migration brought more and more Negroes into the city, both Father and the company thrived. No crash, however devastating, could stop Sears from selling dresses for $6.75, as well as car radiators, musical instruments, brood coops for chickens, and asphalt roofing to families all over the country.

Henriette took a tray and went through the food line, taking black coffee, oatmeal, and a piece of toast. After eating a few bites, she pushed the food away and joined the crowd heading out. Everyone wanted to be on time for the first day of class, even if it might be their last. The sun was out and the day warming as Henriette entered the main quadrangle and walked among students scattered on stone benches and grass, dotting the lawn with bits of color. She wondered which of the boys and girls might become her friends. Younger than most of them, she tasted her freedom. It would be spicy, like the soups her brother Carl liked to make, and smooth, like the swing of her body the year before when she'd danced to jazz with Harold Overstreet at the Sunset Café.

She shifted her books onto one hip, feeling the pull of her sweater against her breasts, and yanked her shoulder-length hair out of her collar. Her shirtwaist open at the throat, she approached the Social Sciences Building, where she found room 122, the lecture hall for Introduction to North American Anthropology, and slid into a seat near the back. Classmates to her right and left would see her long, straight nose and olive complexion in profile, might notice that she looked like Nefertiti. In front of her, curved rows of seats converged on a lecture podium. There the professor, a heavyset older man with a square chin above dewlaps, busily sorted notes. On a small table to one side was an electric slide projector, black and silver and bigger than Father's wooden stereopticon, the viewer through which he displayed his three-dimensional wildflower photos. A white-haired teaching assistant hunched over it, arranging the slides one by one, keeping track of their order. The T.A. raised his head, and Henriette saw his young face. He couldn't be much older than her twin brothers, four years her senior. The contrast between the T.A.'s face and hair was unsettling, and she kept her eyes on him. His prominent forehead and deep-set eyes gave him a sort of animal look that roused her shapeless but intense desire. When he dropped his hands to his sides, his unusually long arms suggested an early primate, but his three-piece suit looked properly academic, and his large head sat comfortably on his slight body. As he rose to arrange papers on a lectern, Henriette noticed his economy of movement, the energy exactly proportioned to the task, and she smiled inside at that sinuous perfection. Fascinating, but so beyond her.

"Welcome to the brand-new Department of Anthropology," said the T.A. He passed out syllabi. "Any questions?"

"The subject of this class will be Indian Culture and Artifacts in North America," announced the T.A. "Any questions?" Henriette raised her hand, eager to be noticed but not yet sure what she would say.

"Why is this class required before Culture and Artifacts in the South Pacific?" The T.A. paused a moment and turned to the Professor, who was still busy, then looked back at her.

"I guess it's just because A comes before P. Some administrator was learning how to alphabetize." Laughter, and she joined in. Sometimes her sassy questions got her into trouble, but this one had produced an interesting result. The Professor began his lecture, spreading a droning blanket over the T.A.'s spiky wit. Unsatisfactory, she noted, and her mind drifted off.

She couldn't believe she was actually here, at the University of Chicago in the South Side's Hyde Park, that she had finally defeated

Mother's determination to tuck her safely away with a bunch of girls at Vassar Female College in Poughkeepsie, New York. Her rebellion had slowly built up steam during her year at home in suburban Oak Park, with her high school friends away at college. She'd read and fretted and killed time at the movies, that dark place where she could weep and laugh without restraint, following detective Charlie Chan as he solved murders — "like potato chip," as he said in his pidgin English, "cannot stop at just one"— or mouth agape at "The Constant Nymph," as orphaned, teen-aged Tessa fell in love with a married composer, ran away with him to Belgium, and finally sickened and died. In contrast to her stagnant life, the movies made everything vivid and real.

Whenever Mother allowed it, she traveled to Chicago's South side to visit her brother Carl, in his first year of medical school at the U. of C. and living in an apartment. She'd climb to the second floor, where the smell of frying garlic and ginger promised some new trick he'd learned from a Chinese restaurant; a yeasty smell meant bread, rising or baking. Everything Carl made woke up her appetite as surely as meals at home suppressed it.

College itself had never been in question for Henriette or her brothers. Their father had lived his first years among the horse-drawn carts, yearning violins and passionate prayer of a *shtetl* in Galicia. His own father's early death had forced him to give up school for work, and he'd sold candles door to door, slept crowded with his sisters in a dirt-floored house, and held his nose at smells of pickling sauerkraut and unwashed flesh. More than this Father did not tell, but Henriette had gleaned the essentials. He'd emigrated at thirteen with his mother and sisters, just in time to escape waves of pogroms sweeping across the Russian Pale, and had worked ever since to support his family. He was proud of all he'd achieved without formal education, but the aim of his hard work was to provide that gift for his children, and the twin boys had already graduated from the University of Wisconsin, Carl in pre-medicine and Russell in business. Now a graduate student at Purdue, Russell was studying advertising and sought Father's legacy and approval. Mother had attended the University of Chicago for a year and a half before marriage, but lack of funds had forced her to drop out, and Henriette's charge was to make up for the unspoken sorrow of Mother's failure.

When Henriette was born, all that disappointed hope circled the infant girl like a chorus of fairy attendants, and when Henriette was two, Mother registered her with Vassar. By age five, Henriette knew about this destiny. Of course she would still have to apply when the time came, but rumor was that those registered got preferential treatment. Henriette accepted Mother's expectation until her last year of high school, when the poets of the Harlem Renaissance stunned her with brilliant images like Countee Cullen's "copper sun and scarlet sea." She had to be where Negroes wrote poems and organized to change the world and were reborn, and in Chicago that meant Hyde Park.

WITH THE VAST DEPTHS OF Lake Michigan on one side and impoverished Negro tenements on the other three, Hyde Park had long wrestled with its anchor, the University of Chicago. As more and more unemployed were evicted from their homes, a Hooverville took shape on the University's green Midway, and camps of cardboard or tin proliferated. Offended by the stench of this invasion, the University called the police, but for every camper they kicked out, two more arrived. The sparks from this collision of worlds lit fires of poetry, protest, and academic debate, and posters all over the neighborhood announced dramatic performances in newly adapted lofts. Readings were held wherever there was heat, light, and a few chairs. Unannounced but rumored, speakers gathered crowds at speakeasies, and drinkers absorbed ideas along with unidentified booze, known as dark stuff and light.

Henriette wanted nothing more than to submerge herself in the thick of Hyde Park. Sick of being the little girl in the living room when her parents entertained Negro leaders, she was determined to enter their world on her own terms. A personal renaissance — that's what it would be. And with men. The only young men she knew were her brothers' older friends, and at the U. of C. half of the student body would be male. Father supported Henriette's desire and was willing to pay for it, preferring her to be closer to home than Poughkeepsie. But he did not confront Mother directly. Each day of her year at home, Henriette had protested the Vassar plan, insisting on her own choice, and after she'd been admitted to both schools, Mother agreed.

THE SOUND OF HANDS CLAPPING brought Henriette back to the lecture hall. She was here and that was what counted. Still seated, she watched the T.A. put on a charcoal overcoat with black velvet collar, pack up the slides, and leave with the Professor. Then she rose and spoke to the student beside her.

"Who is he?" she asked, sotto voce. "The T.A. Do you know?"

"No idea," said the student. "Why? I'm Nadine Abravanel," and she extended her hand. Henriette shook it and introduced herself, feeling dwarfed by Nadine's ample breasts and muscled arms, intimidated by the straight black hair that curved along her face, emphasizing her forthright manner. "Are you here for anthropology?" asked Nadine. "South Pacific?"

"I just asked that to see what he'd say," said Henriette. "I'm more interested in literature."

"Me too," said Nadine. "Especially poetry. Why don't you sign up for American poets? I'm going to. We get to read Edna St. Vincent Millay, Walt Whitman, and Robinson Jeffers too. Have you read him?"

"Millay's my favorite," said Henriette. " I haven't yet read Jeffers."

Nadine moved towards the door, and Henriette turned to another student.

"Have you registered yet?" she asked.

"I can't," said the student, keeping her voice low. "I might have to drop out. You know — money — my father — his job. What about you?"

"Lots of students are in your shoes," said Henriette, wishing she hadn't asked. She felt doubly guilty about her situation: first for her privilege, which seemed undeserved, and second for her need to escape the hands that fed her. She owed so much to her parents, but when she thought of Mother she saw a juggernaut, threatening to crush her, while Father huddled in corners, springing out unpredictably to stand too close and then explode with rage. She pushed the thought away. She wanted to talk about the T.A., but she didn't want to reveal the sudden desire and ambition she'd felt on seeing the white hair, the velvet collar, and the arms so obviously evolved from ancestral forelegs. As she joined the crowd leaving the hall, she turned to the person beside her.

"That T.A.," she said. "Do you think he's foreign?"

"Maybe. He could be a visiting scholar. Or a dandy." Opinions swirled around Henriette. The coat looked aristocratic. Could he be a duke or count from some European country? A linguist, with his unaccented speech, or a Finn, since they all learn English from the cradle? Henriette thought of the dark body hair that curled, escaping from his collar and cuffs, and she couldn't help but imagine hair curling all over his body. "Why don't you ask him?" someone said.

"Me?" asked Henriette. She shrank, timid at the thought of confronting him with a personal question, then reminded herself it was only words. "All right," she said. "Another day."

Suffocating dark and a panicky need for air. A bad dream she couldn't remember must have robbed her of breath. She gulped air and grabbed the rough edge of the blanket, then let go and moved her hands to her body, from breasts to waist and thighs. She was all here, out of the dream world and safely in her bed, but where? In the faint light from the window she saw the hulk of her Secor # 2 typewriter on the desk. Of course, she'd dropped into sleep, tired from the first day of school, in her new dorm room at college. The dark mountain across the room was her roommate Effie, under blankets, and the wheezing that Henriette had thought was her own came from that mountain, a troubled sound that turned the room too small, the bed hard, the blanket scratchy. Looking up, Henriette made out the black line of a shelf where she'd arranged her favorite books. A light might wake Effie, so she stood on the bed and felt the edges of the volumes in the dark: a small book with well-thumbed pages; that would be the poems of Millay; her clothbound Shakespeare; the sleek, slippery dust jacket of *1066 and All That*. But the books weren't much comfort if she couldn't climb into them and travel in their worlds. She plopped down on the bed, realizing too late that she made the springs squeak, and her throat swelled, threatening tears.

She would not cry. There was plenty of air, and she was safe here. She crawled toward the foot of the bed and reached a hand up to the heavy typewriter, the monster that had gotten her through term papers in high school and columns for the school paper, then her valedictory address and letters to her friends at college. The typewriter had been a hand-me-down from her father, and she never used it without remembering how hard he'd worked to teach himself everything he knew. Effie and some of the other girls had new duotone portables, light and efficient, in shades of green, crimson, or orchid, but Henriette preferred her reliable workhorse. She ran one hand over the smooth, hard body of the machine, along the date "1913," the year of her birth, engraved on the front, then found the keys and danced on them with her fingers, the keys responding as though with a little tune.

If only she could funnel all the desires of her mind and body through this machine, the machine that would compose them into a stream of words and speak for her. She imagined her fingers feeding words to the typewriter and the typewriter spitting them out, neat and black, on clean white paper. As long as she could maintain that stream of words, from fingers to machine to paper, she'd be in control of the telling, and there'd be plenty of air to breathe.

Her fingers on the keys brought a flash of a trumpeter's black fingers, fast and accurate, rushing among the valves, playing the late set at the Sunset Café where Carl had taken her the year before. Her eyes had drooped and her chair was hard, but she'd stayed to the end, longing for the trumpeter to notice her, hoping Carl might lure him to their table to say hi to the white kids from the suburbs. That night in bed she'd imagined those fingers playing tunes on her spine, starting on her neck and making their way down.

A memory she tried not to allow seemed to force its way in from the typewriter to her fingers, reversing the tide that put her in control of the story. She lifted her fingers from the keys and felt the smooth rubber platen, the round cases for the ribbon perched high on the frame. But no object, no matter how solid and normal, could obscure the memory that elbowed its way into her mind: a book she'd pulled from her satchel one day after high school; an apple she'd taken from the kitchen; her own body plopped down on the couch to read while she ate; Father, the one who always took her side, unexpectedly home. She squelched the scene before it played itself out. This could not be real, was not true. She knew she was wrong even to think it.

Again her breath felt short, and she jerked her hand from the typewriter and swung her legs to the floor. She felt along the edge of the bed to the wall, then along the wall to the door, where she found the cool handle and turned it. A blade of light pierced the room, and she slipped out, then closed the door behind her. Her pace speeded up as she trotted down the bright hall, her breath coming more easily. She had gotten away; she was at college. No matter how loudly her parents fought, she would not hear them. She could not be found wanting by Mother or disappoint Father.

In the empty bathroom, lights humming, she threw cold water on her face, then returned to her room. As she eased the door open, a slice of light hit the shiny body of the typewriter, and the machine reflected back with bright highlights. It would be her armor, a bulwark of defense against intrusive memory and bad feeling, a piece of home that would help her to keep the story straight as she made her escape.

She eased the door shut, sat down carefully on the foot of the bed and crossed her legs, not yet ready to return to sleep. The thought of playing the keys reminded her of the soothing effect her fingers could have on her body, and her hand slipped to the ankle of her crossed leg and then across the blanket to her crotch. No, she would not forsake the dream of pristine words for the mess of wetness and needy, heavy breath. She would not even begin to think of the night she'd spent with Lucky, the older City News reporter she'd met the year before, and the terrifying vision she'd had of herself on a slab, cold, as she lay beneath him, invaded and stripped of words, plummeted into a Dark Age of wolfish appetite and greed. She curled on her side, and sleep soon washed her body away.

Chapter 2

On the cusp of her teens and wearing her brothers' cast-off knickers, Henriette stopped on her way home from school to buy a five-cent Tango bar, hoping to insulate herself from hunger at tense, rule-bound dinnertime. The family gathered in the dining room as usual, the table sparkling with polished silver, white china, and crystal for resolutely legal water. Henriette took her seat and unfolded her tented napkin, while Mother gave thanks to no one in particular for food, life, and freedom. Spoons clinked on bowls. Carl addressed his father: "You won't believe…"

His twin brother, Russell, interrupted, "Carl actually thinks that Father might be interested in what he has to say."

Then soft and round, a glob of chocolate pudding arced through the air, thrown from its footed glass. Carl still held the goblet, his burst of teen-age anger as callow as the wrist that poked from its outgrown shirt. Five people froze. Father's face turned red, color flooding from neck to ears to forehead. A gasp, and Mother's mouth opened, eyes widened. Henriette sat terrified of what might come next, her stomach knotted. She stepped aside and waited for the explosion of Father's sputtering rage, as unpredictable as the too-fond hands that often made her squirm. The pudding landed across the table on Russell, and thick black curls mixed with chocolate. The glob had found its target, but in

Henriette's memory it flew on, through the years of high school and college and beyond, a great flung gesture of revenge, the unraveling of dinner, the act that would forever tempt her to seek out and admire rebellion while remaining a bystander, an onlooker crouched on a rock with a sea raging around her.

HENRIETTE FINISHED HIGH SCHOOL AT sixteen in June of '29, triumphing with a valedictory address on the new Negro poets. Like held breath, her long year of waiting began. Her close-knit group of girlfriends, all one or two years older than she, went off to college. The joy of her graduation faded, and Mother sought to occupy her with chores she could never execute to Mother's satisfaction. A familiar and dreaded hollow space opened somewhere under her ribs and above her stomach, and she knew that only an escape from the house could save her. She begged Mother to allow her to take the elevated train, the "El," to visit Carl in his South side apartment, but well-armed rum runners roamed the city, and the St. Valentine's Day massacre was fresh in Mother's mind. In late June Henriette turned seventeen, and in the fall Mother finally agreed, insisting that Carl promise to be at home.

At the Austin stop on a September afternoon, Henriette climbed on the El, wearing a wool crepe dress, silk stockings with carefully straightened seams, and heels. Lawns gave way to swampy prairie dotted with farmhouses, then tenements and smoke stacks. Soon these were replaced by abandoned buildings with broken windows and sidewalks where children, dressed in rags, rummaged in garbage cans. It had been just a month since the Stock Market Crash, and it seemed like the world Henriette had grown up in was falling apart. She wondered if the new universal despair would penetrate the tenuous wall around her and join her personal desperation in an apocalyptic finish.

Her mood brightened as she drew closer to the Mecca of Hyde Park.

She got off the train and walked west on 57th Street, sheltered by trees turning red and yellow. From an apartment window came sounds of a violin playing up and down the scale, and she let the cheerful music carry her into the student life inside, imagining a game of chess and a glass of contraband liqueur. As she walked on, the violin faded, giving way to the gravelly complaint of Bessie Smith, and Henriette ached to belong here, breathing air clouded with cigarette smoke, sneaking into a speakeasy or hanging out with the Wobblies, whose posters were plastered on trees and kiosks. First Unitarian Church loomed up on her right, with its pseudo-Gothic stonework, spires and turrets, while the archway of the University's Mandel Hall beckoned on her left. She'd attended lectures and concerts in that hall with her family, and Carl had pointed out the number of seats oddly identical to the date of the Norman Conquest: 1066, proclaimed on a mounted panel.

Now Bessie was behind her, and the intricate trumpet of Louis Armstrong wound its way from a window just ahead, pure and shapely, making her want to wrap her arms around the sweet, sad sound. She entered Carl's building and climbed the stairs. As he opened the door, she wrinkled her nose.

"I made bouillabaisse last night — needed a break from memorizing bones." said Carl.

"I'd gladly memorize bones," said Henriette. "I'm going crazy at home, but they won't let me come down here except to visit you." Carl heated the pot, and they ate the spicy tomato broth redolent of orange and anise, stirring in spoonfuls of rich rouille to make it even hotter. Then they picked the meat from mussel shells and ate the shrimp and fish, spitting out bones and soaking up the last of the juice with chunks of bread.

"Where did you learn to make this?" asked Henriette. "Mother wouldn't let anything this hot in the house."

"She subdues food and then turns it on others," said Carl, and he whacked the table to illustrate. "She'd no more cook a roast gently than let us come to dinner ten minutes late. But in fact I got the recipe from Mrs. William Vaughn Moody, the poet's widow. Mother uses the new Crisco so the house won't smell of schmaltz, but Mrs. Moody uses butter, and so do I." He explained how he'd torn the page out of the cookbook and then called on Mrs. Moody at her Home Delicacies Association, where Rabindranath Tagore was visiting.

Henriette gasped. "Did you meet him?" She'd been reading Tagore all summer, thrilled to discover the poems and stories of the Indian who'd won the Nobel Prize in literature.

"Just shook his hand," said Carl, focused on his soup. "Mrs. Moody showed me how to flavor the rouille with garlic and red pepper. Of course you have to make the mayonnaise first," he finished, smiling and looking down with embarrassed pride. The soup made Henriette's eyes water and nose run, expanding her head. "Wanna go out?" he asked. "I thought you'd like the Sunset Café. It's a swell joint — classy — and we'll get to hear Louis Armstrong, Satchmo."

"You got the moolah?" asked Henriette, skin prickling. "I only brought enough for carfare."

"It's cheap to get in," said Carl. "And we only have to buy one drink." They drove north along Lake Park Avenue in Carl's Tin Lizzie, bought used. Darkened cross streets, run-down bungalows and tenements led them into the heart of Bronzeville, where large brick homes with pillared porches alternated with office buildings and cafés. They turned west on 35th to Calumet, where the bright lights of several clubs illuminated the block.

"Is it OK for us to go here?" asked Henriette, peering out the window.

"Yeah," said Carl. "It's a black-and-tan club — there's lots of them around here. They don't care if you're black, white, or homo for that matter. Come on." Inside the crowd was packed and the air dense with cigarette smoke. Around the bar people stood three deep, and the newcomers joined the standing crowd while getting their bearings. Henriette felt self-conscious despite Carl's words — there were just a few white people and none of Henriette's age. If they were selling liquor the place wasn't even legal, and the thought of real trouble made her armpits wet with nervous sweat. All around her, draped and fringed chiffon floated over breasts and buttocks, and short skirts revealed shapely calves and spike heels. The women laughed, talked, and drank, touching each other, and she stood close to Carl, feeling thin and underdressed. Two white men and a woman stood at the bar, talking to the bartender.

On the bandstand a seven-piece band tuned up. Bright lights made the white ties of the musician's tuxedos gleam, and sweat glistened on their brown faces. Soon Carl spied a couple of chairs near the back, and they squeezed in, then ordered ginger ale. Carl took a flask from his pocket and added some brown stuff to his drink, while a white man in shirtsleeves and open collar entered from behind the bar and began to move through the crowd, shaking hands with everyone he passed. He made his way to the bandstand and embraced several of the musicians, who slapped him on the back. So it was all right for her to be here. The band began an upbeat piece about swing rhythm itself, making her feet tap.

"Swing that music," sang the vocalist, and Carl leaned over.

"That's him, that's Satchmo." The singer looked unassuming, medium height with chocolate-colored skin, but the voice was inviting and the smile, warm and engaging. She had expected a showoff type of performer, but Satchmo put the music ahead of himself. If only she could meet him and shake his hand! Surely it would be different from meeting a Negro at home, like when Dr. Dubois came, and she'd had to be formal and polite, curtsying in her red velvet dress. Here she was a person in her own right, and whomever she met might become her friend. She swayed a little in her chair, happier than she'd been in a long time.

Satchmo began the next piece with a long, slow solo on the trumpet. The sound wound like a vine around a tree, first surrounding her, then finding its way into the hollow below her ribs and putting a floor under it, giving her solid ground to stand on. Maybe she was in the right time and place after all.

After the solo, other instruments began to respond. The piece developed a steady beat but remained slow and sad, sad enough to make you cry, and Henriette held her breath, afraid she might embarrass herself. The music didn't let up; fearless, it just kept probing all the nooks and crannies of a bad, disappointed, feeling, and Henriette let sensations stream through her, unnamed. The music emboldened her, holding her up while she looked hopelessness in the face. The execution just two years back had shaken both her and the world, but this music looked beyond such things and raised her spirits. Carl leaned over.

"Some barrel house jam, hunh?" Henriette nodded appreciation, unable to speak. The band filled in under the melody, the support allowing the sax to cry yet more painfully, and tears streamed down her face, tears of amazement. She found a napkin, dried her eyes and blew her nose. A tall, black man with steel-rimmed glasses and a rounded stomach approached their table, and Carl stood to shake his hand.

"Harold. How are you? My little sister," and he indicated Henriette. "Harold Overstreet — a graduate student in economics at the University."

"How do you do?" said Harold, his careful articulation making a joke of the formal greeting. With a little bow, he shook Henriette's hand. He wore a double-breasted suit and tie, and beads of sweat stood out on his forehead.

"Join us," said Carl. Harold put his glass on the table and sat, and Carl offered him the flask.

"Don't mind if I do," said Harold. He looked a little older than Carl, perhaps thirty, with a sturdy figure, broad nose, and black mustache.

"Harold is studying how economics can help the working guy and not just make the fat cats fatter," said Carl, irony as always in his voice. Henriette thought of the directness of Bartolomeo Vanzetti's words: "Never in our full life could we hope to do such work for tolerance, for justice, for men's understanding of man, as now we do by accident." Such a contrast to Carl's layered meanings.

"I'm interested in justice for working people," said Harold. He leaned back, and his jacket fell open to reveal a bright, white shirt and tie with a sparkling stickpin. "The Soviet Union is a model." To Henriette the Soviet Union seemed more exotic than jazz in a snowy sort of way, with frigid, glistening flakes flying from the hooves of horses as a troika dashed along a road.

"They're in the groove tonight," said Harold, indicating the band. "Would your little sister care to dance?"

"I don't know how," said Henriette. Harold laughed, a deep full laugh with head thrown back.

"There's no 'how,'" he said. "You just dance, baby. Come on." He guided her gently by the elbow through the rows of tables to the floor. "We'll step out and step heavy," he said with a smile. "I'll show you." He placed a hand on her waist, took her other hand and led her around the floor. It was easy to follow him. She simply joined her inertia to his and they moved as one. Now she entered the music with her body as well as her mind, and waves of pleasure lifted her spirits still higher. Her dress swirled against her calves as she turned, and she smiled, knowing the crepe flared to reveal their shape. Harold smelled of a woodsy cologne as well as sweat and tobacco. Her right hand enjoyed the touch of brown skin, the gentle grasp of his adult fingers. At the end, Harold made her a small bow and led her back to the table, thanking both her and Carl in his decorous way before he returned to his table.

She had done it, she had danced, and she looked around, without making it obvious, to see if any of these other Negro men might ask her to dance. Satchmo began to sing again, "I double dare you, to sit over here, I double dare you, to lend me your ear." Henriette pictured herself rising to the bait. "I double dare you to kiss me and then; I double dare you to kiss me again, hot mama." Henriette rolled the last two words around in her mouth, giving them Satchmo's offbeat inflection, "hot mama," and she licked her lips, tasting the person she'd like to be.

The closing tune began with percussion; then the trumpet played a gospel-sounding melody.

"Bye and bye," sang Armstrong, "when the morning comes. All the saints, the Lord is gathering home. We'll tell the story, how we'll overcome; we'll understand Him better bye and bye." Was this a song about death? She thought of Vanzetti, who considered his death a victory. "Now we are not a failure," he'd said. "This is our career and our triumph." Satchmo's song sounded as happy about what was coming "bye and bye" as "Swing that Music" was about swing. After the first verse, he said, "Take it brother Higginbottom," without missing a beat, and the drums took a solo turn, and so on with each instrument. A new language played in Henriette's brain as she and Carl drove home. Another day she would have rested her head on his shoulder, but she'd made a friend at the Sunset Café tonight, and next time it wouldn't matter whether Carl looked back to check on her or not. She would have to find a way to spend more of her time down here.

After that, every time Henriette heard jazz, it transformed the paralyzing boredom in her bones into energy, and Carl's friends were just enough older to intrigue her with worldliness and experience. Carl gave her a key to his apartment, and she learned to lie to Mother about whether and when he was at home. Father didn't ask about what she did in Hyde Park, and she hoped he would support her branching out, experiencing new music and ideas. But politics like Harold Overstreet's were another matter. Sears was firmly anti-union, and Father supported his employer, barely tolerating Mother's work for the Women's International League for Peace and Freedom. Negro education, yes, he favored that, but class warfare, never. Of course Mother didn't believe in anything called "warfare" either. The League had opposed U.S. entry into the Great War, a position made illegal by the Sedition and Espionage Acts, and Father had always insisted Mother stay on the right side of the law. Something akin to war had broken out over that conflict the year Henriette turned five. Now she understood the issues, but only jazz gave hope of freedom from her embattled home.

THE STOCK MARKET CRASHED AT the end of October. As the world spiraled downward in a depression more severe than anyone could have imagined, Henriette was oddly relieved. She no longer had to hide under a façade of celebration but could join her own mood to the general malaise.

SNOW FELL IN LATE NOVEMBER, and the warm smell of fowl roasting greeted Henriette as she climbed the steps to Carl's apartment on a Saturday afternoon. A tall, lanky man in his mid-twenties opened the door. "You must be Carl's sister." A growth of beard darkened his face, and straight black hair came down a greasy inch over his ears and on the back of his neck.

"That's Rick Luckenbach, Lucky," called Carl from the kitchen. He walked to the door, wiping his hands on a towel hanging from his apron. "I'm roasting a duck."

"He's giving it the doggone royal treatment," said Lucky. "Had me working a bicycle pump to get air under the skin and holding it up in front of a fan for an hour. Now tell me, which one of us is crackers?"

"Both," said Henriette. "What's the air for?"

"Let's see how the duck comes out," said Carl. "Then I'll tell you." All three sat down in the living room, Henriette perched on the edge of an overstuffed chair, ankles crossed, wool jersey dress clinging to her legs. Carl poured the two men drinks of whisky and soda, with ginger ale for Henriette. Lucky asked what she was doing.

Henriettte described the Vassar plan with sarcasm, rolling her eyes and changing the cross of her ankles. "The U. of C. is where I've always wanted to be," she said, "and I'm determined to go there. Are you a student?"

"No," said Lucky. "I'm a reporter. I work for the City News Bureau."

"I wrote columns for the school paper in high school," said Henriette, hoping he would ask about them but hesitant to claim the center of attention. "What do you do for City News?"

He rose and paced, pants too short for his long legs and showing an inch of sock above his shoes. His hands chopped the air as he explained how he covered the police, the County Courthouse, and a variety of disasters, hanging out with prostitutes and waitresses — whoever could give him a story. He smelled of smoke, and yellow stained the first two fingers of his right hand. "They tell us if your mother says she loves you, get the evidence," said Lucky, and he gave a loud hoot. Boastful, thought Henriette, but attractive. She wished she could beat him at his own big-talking game.

"What if everything she does contradicts what she says?" asked Carl.

"Kill the story!" said Lucky. Carl went out to the kitchen to suction fat from the pan. The sun lowered in the sky, making leaf patterns on the living room floor, and Lucky turned to Henriette. "I don't go for brunettes, but you're beautiful, you know." Henriette had never been approached by an older guy, a working man who knew his way around cops and, no doubt, women. Carl returned with more drinks.

"Doesn't little sister get any?" asked Lucky.

"She's gotta start sometime," said Carl. "You want a drink?" Henriette nodded, hoping to prove herself. She'd tasted whisky before and didn't much like it. Carl brought her a tall glass with ice and light brown liquid, and she took small sips. "Tell us more about the Bureau," said Carl, as the sunlight turned deep yellow.

"You should have been with me last night," said Lucky. "A girl was passed out on the street in front of a bar. A copper wrote her a ticket for public drunkenness and stapled it to her shirt!" He laughed. "Half of the guys at City News are American Cocksmen, a bunch of loudmouth, boastful despoilers, and half are Honestly Married Men, a bunch of saps. You can guess which half I belong to." Henriette was beginning to feel woozy, and his way of talking tickled her, a kind of lowlife poetry.

"I guess you're not married and you're not a sap," she said.

"You guessed right," he said. "Now what about you? I don't think you're a sap either." Henriette got up and danced unevenly around the back of her chair, conscious of the way her belted dress outlined her figure. She leaned over the chair and addressed Lucky.

"Seventeen years and she kept her virginity," she sang. "Goddam decent for this vicinity." Pleased with her repartee, she reminded herself to write it down when she got home, then wished she could take back, "virginity." Sure, she could say anything, but words might arouse other people in ways she didn't expect, and she glanced at Lucky just in time to see his eyebrows rise and a smile flit across his face.

He reached back and took her arm. "So many little morons in hot pants running around. I can see you're a smart girl," he said. Carl sputtered.

Embarrassed, Henriette disengaged her arm. "Now what about that duck?" she asked.

"The duck will join the party," said Carl, and they all went out to the kitchen. A bird the color of burnished mahogany emerged from the oven to rest on a platter, its skin slightly separated from the flesh and crackling crisp. Lucky took plates and a knife; Carl handed Henriette a bunch of green onions, some kind of sauce, and a stack of thin pancakes he'd bought at a Chinese restaurant, and they marched into the dining room, singing, "Here comes the duck, the duck that we pumped up," and improvising rhymes. Henriette let her voice ring out loud.

Carl wielded a knife with a surgeon's precision and served each person crisp slices of skin and dark meat. Then they rolled up pancakes around meat, skin and sharp green onions, lathering them with the sweet-and-salty sauce, and ate them out of hand.

"They do it in Peking," said Carl, triumphant. "And now I've done it here. It's the air that does the trick. Was it worth the work?" he asked Lucky.

"It's a doozy," said Lucky.

"Just ducky," said Henriette, loving Carl for making food a celebration and loving his duck for covering her faux pas.

"I live nearby, on Blackstone," said Lucky, words a little slurred. "Wanna come home with me?"

"No, Lucky," said Henriette, patting him on the arm. "Maybe I'll see you again here at Carl's." After Lucky left, Carl threw a blanket and some pillows to Henriette, and she prepared a couch for sleep, grateful to be here with her skilled, funny brother. Carl was so unafraid of their parents and so wise in the ways of the psyche. He'd often shared his developing theory of human nature, where he categorized people according to hatred and anger. Mother was the expert hater, Father the angry victim, and all of the children were wacky, he'd say with a laugh.

Deep down Henriette knew there was trouble below Carl's charm and intelligence. She remembered the night when a fatal electrical jolt had ended the lives of Sacco and Vanzetti, and Carl had lit up with terror as though it were he in the chair. And lately Carl had acted reluctant to go out of doors. Her admiration for him would always be tinged with concern and fear that he might wander off, leaving her stranded. Rupture was possible.

AFTER THE NIGHT OF THE duck, Henriette ran into Lucky occasionally in the C-shop, at Carl's, or at a political meeting, where he joined her in raising voices to the drafty rafters, singing the Internationale or the Wobbly anthem about "pie in the sky when you die — that's a lie!" She recognized him as challenging and rather crude, but he was a prize, an older man who found her attractive. She encouraged him with nods, smiles, and flirty little touches on the arm or shoulder, feeling brave but doubting her wisdom.

One night in early spring, she joined both men at a meeting of the Left Wing Workers and Students Alliance, held in a second floor loft where folding chairs were arranged in ragged rows. Copies of the Daily Worker and other publications were spread on tables around the edges of the room. Harold Overstreet, the Marxist she'd danced with at the Sunset Café, called the meeting to order and asked for a moment of silence to remember the martyred workers, Sacco and Vanzetti. Henriette wished the moment had been longer, fearing that the world might forget. Then Overstreet spoke about Negroes starving and freezing to death, protesting with an "indignation rally," where a crowd moved an evicted family's furniture back into their apartment. An older man, short and slight, stood to applaud. Henriette was about to join him when Lucky leaned in to whisper in her ear. "I've interviewed that guy. He's a professor of anthropology, Isidor Daniels." Henriette nodded, impressed that a professor had joined this crowd. Now Lucky's arm was an inch from her shoulder, and he kept sliding closer, so his thigh touched hers. Her heart began to jump around in her chest, and her eyes searched the drafty room for clues on how to behave or feel. You want this, she told herself. This is being free. Should she just sit there? And if she did, did that mean "no" or "yes?" She searched the library of movies in her head that told her what people did, but she couldn't find anything for man approaching girl and getting closer by the minute. An Anarcho-Syndicalist got up and demanded an end to hierarchies, exploitation, and domination, but Henriette was no longer listening. If this moment in time were leading from words to arms, legs, and her unspeakable center, as it seemed to be doing, what would she do? She knew she'd regret it if Lucky thought her a hopeless kid. Just let it happen, she told herself.

"This is getting boring," said Carl to Lucky. "And I have to be up early. Would you bring her back to my place?" There went Carl, disappearing again when she might need him.

"Sure," said Lucky, looking at Carl and sinking his arm to Henriette's shoulder, then patting her knee.

"Bye," said Henriette, knowing her face showed nothing and wishing there were a voice that could speak through that face. "This sweet patootie is going out on a limb," it would say. "She thinks it might break. What advice would you have for a broad-minded seventeen-year-old virgie bewitched by a rakish older reporter who seems to think she's the cat's meow and clearly expects to take her home?" The meeting gradually disintegrated into discussion and then argument, and people drifted off.

"Come on," Lucky said. "It's cold in here. Let's go home, and I'll warm you up."

"OK," said Henriette, numb. They walked on snow-packed streets to Lucky's second-floor apartment, a more grown-up place than Carl's, with a comfortable couch, glass-topped coffee table, and several chairs in the living room. A Victrola and a big stack of records sat in a corner, and Henriette headed for them, concealing her tension and embarrassment.

"You've got wonderful music," she said, and sat on the floor, still in her coat, looking through the records.

"Take your coat off," said Lucky, "and I'll stop calling you 'little sister.' You're a girlfriend now. Want a drink?"

"No thanks," she said, shrugging out of her coat, feeling small and scared. From her armpits rose her personal beef-broth smell of fear. She hoped he didn't notice.

"Come on," he said, taking her hand. He pulled her to her feet and led her to the bedroom. This is losing my virginity, she said to herself, heart pounding. It's OK. I can do whatever I want. But thoughts and words were no match for real live hands that unbuttoned her shirt and unfastened her bra, revealing newly developed breasts. They were private, and he was cupping them. What was she supposed to do? Just stand there, like a statue with its sculptor? She saw herself as if through the wrong end of a telescope.

She crossed her arms in front of her chest, while Lucky slid his hands to her hips. If his touch was molding her, making her into a woman, it should be giving her power, yet she felt like a willow in a chilly breeze. He unzipped her skirt and let it fall to the floor, and she stepped out, then shivered as he pulled down her underpants. He led her to the bed, pulled down the covers and covered her up, then quickly undressed himself. She lay stiff, feeling cold and sweaty. Before he turned out the light, he looked over at her, rubbed her cheek with his knuckles and said, "Hey, girlfriend. Don't worry. It's just a bit of a smooch." Right, she said to herself, glad to be told what she was doing, like hearing her feelings named. Just a bit of a smooch.

Lucky crawled under the covers, and his warmth felt good: hairy skin, belly, and arms. He kissed her and that too felt good, even the surprising tip of tongue. She liked his hands on her back, but when they slipped down under her buttocks, she pushed them away. That part of her was untouchable, veiled in a cloudy miasma of desire and danger, beyond the reach of language. She would not be reduced to appetite, a beggar out of control, placed at the mercy of a man who was after his own satisfaction. A faint smell of apples arose, and her stomach rebelled as it always did at the sickly sweet odor and the way the sweet-sour juice could trickle down her throat and make her choke. She sniffed again, and the smell went away, perhaps a bit of dream or illusion. She wished this were over, a *fait accompli*, one of many things at which she'd succeeded.

As Lucky pressed her closer, she named each new perception, placing it in her world of known things. That's his prick, poking me in my stomach. What's that, brushing my thigh? Good god, must be his balls. He rolled on top of her, and no words seemed suited to the ridiculous situation in which her stony body found itself, invaded. If she felt pain she ignored it, but Lucky's ragged breathing and accelerating pace, his convulsive climax, his collapsed weight on her chest and the slow trickle between her thighs made him seem like an avatar of some ancient creature, a throwback to times before Victrola records or food in the fridge, before art on the walls or books on the shelves, and she thought of her parents' household, imagining its orchestrated meals and verbal quarrels replaced by frantic fights for food and fisticuffs. She curled into a ball away from Lucky and shed a few silent tears, feeling used and unloved, then determined to rise above this primitive level as far as she could go, up and up.

She didn't know if she slept or not, but she woke fully in the chilly dawn. The melody of a Mills Brothers song began to play in her head, and she hummed along. "I'll be glad when you're dead, you rascal you.

I'll be tickled to death when you leave this earth, you dog." Then, with a regal sense of triumph as she rose and dressed:

I'll be standing on a corner high
When they bring your body by.
I'll be glad when you're dead,
You rascal you.

UP, UP, AND AWAY. WITHOUT waking Lucky, she let herself out and hurried back to Carl's. She left the experience far below, naming it "intercourse," and later, when it multiplied, it became "sleeping with men."

BY THE FOLLOWING SPRING, MOTHER had agreed that Henriette could attend the U. of C., but memories of the night with Lucky were turning into visions of her body as detached and lifeless, lying on a slab. Rising above herself became not triumphant but frightening, and she told Carl about moments of panic, where the world receded and left her connected to nothing, though she didn't tell him about sleeping with Lucky. Carl recommended that she see Dr. Catherine Whitson, an up-and-coming psychoanalyst. "She's a good Socialist, like the Viennese émigrés she trained under. I think you two would get along," he said. Henriette felt flattered. Both she and Carl revered psychoanalysis, imported from Europe and just becoming established in the U.S., but Henriette had never considered herself worthy of such intensive care. Carl explained how it could help with feelings of panicky separation, the old threat of rupture that had long haunted Henriette.

Seeking an appointment felt like crossing a moat, the demon-filled gulf that divided her feelings from words. The month before school started, she took the Illinois Central train to Hyde Park and walked along 59th Street to Student Health at Billings Hospital, forcing her feet to keep moving, willing her heart to slow down. To keep panic at bay, she observed and

catalogued her surroundings, fixing her attention on the gray city's pseudo-Gothic spires and gargoyles on her right, while on her left stretched the
broad, green expanse of the Midway Plaisance, populated with cardboard
boxes where the newly unemployed and homeless took shelter. Leaves
would be falling in a few months, and Henriette shuddered to think how
those people in boxes would fare once Chicago's wind started howling and
snow began to fall. She picked her way around a mountainous pile of blankets on the sidewalk, beneath which someone had found warmth from a
grate that connected to the University's underground tunnel system.

Henriette approached a window at Student Health Services. A nurse
sat with a little white cap on graying hair and looked up, unsmiling.
"My brother's a medical student, going into psychiatry," said Henriette.
"He told me I might be able to see Dr. Whitson."

"The doctor is very busy now," she said, licking a finger and rif-
fling through pages. "Many students are upset." Naturally, thought
Henriette, all those forced to drop out and search for work. Guilt for
her privileged status sent a twinge through her innards. Perhaps few
students came in here and asked for a particular doctor. Carl had told
her that Dr. Whitson's recent publications had attracted notice — she
was a rising star and one of the best. Did the nurse find Henriette arrogant, asking for the star, or just out of her mind? She forced herself to
stand her ground. If she could see the admired doctor, it would prove
her worthy of the holy grail of psychoanalysis.

There'd be no monetary charge for a student, but the emotional price for the treatment would still be high. Henriette had layered
concealment and denial of concealment over and over for so long
that her insides felt like geological strata, hard and fixed, overlaid by
an embroidery of words. She could say everything, but she couldn't
feel anything. Analysis would cut through the embroidery and take
a pick to the rocks. The price would be her carefully constructed

private refuge, the island of no feeling to which she retreated when the sea raged at home.

"Dr. Whitson can see you when the semester starts, in a month," the receptionist had said, returning to her typewriter. "Come on the first Monday in October at four."

"Thank you," Henriette said, and she walked out in a daze, both gratified and scared.

Chapter 3

After the second meeting of the Indian Culture class, Henriette took her time gathering her books, waiting for the others to disperse. Then she walked down toward the podium, a bounce in her step.

"Yes?" asked the T.A.

"My name is Henriette Greenberg," she said.

"I'm Diller Brannigan," said the T.A., shaking hands and meeting her eyes, an inch below his. "Can I help you with something?" His tone was professorial and his black brows heavy and serious, but his young face made a joke of his white hair, and she almost laughed, disconcerted. What was supposed to be her opening gambit?

"Some of us have been wondering," she began, "whether field researchers have to speak the native languages," she improvised.

"The best ones do," he said, in a voice deeper and more musical at close range than when he spoke to the class. "At least one language, sometimes more. Studying linguistics helps. That's what I'm doing."

"So you're taking a class?" asked Henriette. "Are you a graduate student?" Diller continued to slot the glass slides into a special case as they talked, and Henriette's nervousness faded.

"Yes, second year. I'm studying North American Indians. You?"

"I might be interested in North American too."

"Not South Pacific?" He looked up with a teasing smile.

"I just asked that to see what you'd say. I liked your answer," and she cocked her head and waited to see what sort of impression she'd made.

"Requirements can be arbitrary," he said. On her side, then.

Their voices echoed in the funnel of the empty amphitheatre, suddenly sounding loud. Diller invited her to the C-shop for coffee, and she hesitated, needing time to get used to him. His thick brows looked primitive, like a rugged mountain too steep to climb, though his manner was perfectly civilized.

"I can't now," she lied. "I've got a class. How about later?"

"How's three?" he asked.

"I'll meet you there at three," she said, then held her books close to her chest, hugging herself. The coat, the white hair, the academic job — so much made Diller out of reach. How different he was from Lucky, tough and utterly confusing, taking her to bed and then treating her with mild interest, as though nothing had changed. Diller was older too, though probably younger than Lucky, but completely different — polite and accommodating. Maybe he might find her attractive, and she would turn out to be desirable in a new way, a way she could enjoy without danger.

By three o'clock she'd changed into a red and black plaid skirt and a soft black sweater that made her feel cuddly. She walked across the main quadrangle to Mandel Hall and entered through a massive, stone portal worthy of a castle. Standing in the doorway of the C-shop, she waited for Diller, shy to meet him outside the context of class. He walked toward her smiling, and she noticed again his fluid grace, so different from her own elbows and ankles that always seemed to get in the way. The noisy room was full of chatting students, and steamy smells of soup and coffee drifted from behind a counter, where workers slammed pot lids and assembled sandwiches. They sat in a corner booth, and Henriette asked about Diller's unusual first name.

"It's my mother's family name," he said. "French. They were French Huguenots. Originally it was d'Ailly. People call me Dilly."

"OK, Dilly," she said, wondering if Huguenots were like Founding Fathers, and what they thought of Jews. She was alert to this question now, but she hadn't even known she was Jewish until another child chased her home in first grade, shouting, "Dirty Jew!"

"Am I Jewish?" she'd asked Mother when she got home, and Mother took her in her lap and wept. Henriette's grandparents had crossed the ocean to escape anti-Semitism, but it had followed them wherever they went and was prevalent in Oak Park. Even Henriette's best girl-friend was apt to make negative remarks about Jews. Her parents had converted to Unitarianism. At All Souls Church they listened with ad-miration to the rationalist, non-denominational lectures of Reverend Jenkin Lloyd Jones, but Jewish identity always hung over Henriette's head, a sword waiting to come down and cut her off from her blond, Protestant classmates.

"I hope you don't get too much of 'silly dilly,'" she said.

"I did as a kid," he said, sounding serious. "And I'd still like to beat up the big guys that teased me."

"Beat up?" asked Henriette, frowning. Reverend Jones preached non-violence above all, and her parents concurred with him as pas-sionately as they fought with each other. "Who beats people up?"

"I do. Any day, if I have to," said Dilly. "I can't forget those beefy guys with peanut butter breath. Merciless and leering. 'Silly Dilly's hair is white, little guy's afraid to fight.'" He flexed his big hands, long, blunt-nailed fingers stretching and curling to fists. "If I'd been bigger, I'd have socked a stomach or kneed a groin. I couldn't wait to be the biggest boy on the block." Henriette was attracted to Dilly's resolve but wary of anger, the sudden release that could provoke hands to actions a person couldn't take back, leaving one alone on a rock, deprived of human contact forever. What would Father think of Dilly? Bitterly she remembered that Father had considered Lucky a "nice young man," merely a friend of Henriette's brothers, when to her he'd been a fink. But a truly nice young man who might one day be a suitor, someone Henriette liked and admired? Maybe it would be the death of Father.

"When my classmates and I saw your coat, we thought you might be Transylvanian." She pointed to his effete-looking velvet collar. He snorted.

"I wear whatever I can get, usually hand-me-downs. This coat belonged to my brother, Finn."

"Oh," said Henriette, hesitating to ask about the brother.

He began to twist one of the buttons. "Where I come from, you wear a coat until there's nothing left but threads. This suit you see is what I have — I get it cleaned in summer, pressed from time to time."

A poor boy, then. Lucky was poor too, but he had a decent job, something that a graduate student might never get. The ambient noise seemed to grow louder. Henriette leaned in to be heard. "Where do you come from?"

"A small mill town called Kitichara," said Dilly, sliding his elbows closer to her on the table. "In Wisconsin. It's Chippewa for Leaping Buck. You?" So he was provincial as well. Then she could teach him something, unlike Lucky, who seemed to know everything about the big, bad world.

"Oak Park, a suburb west of here. Actually a village," she said, trying to make her origins sounds more like his.

Dilly went for coffee, and Henriette imagined life with one handed-down suit. He offered her a little pitcher of cream. "Thanks," she said. "I take it black."

"Have you decided on a major?" asked Dilly.

"I don't know," said Henriette. "I'm crazy about literature, and I like to write. I'm interested in the inside view — how the psyche works — more than in customs of native peoples.

"What kind of literature do you like?"

"Mostly poetry. What about you?"

"I don't know much about poetry. I like to read outdoor stories, like Jack London. Anything adventurous."

"I thought the guy who lectured today was a drip, going on about material culture and kinship systems."

"He's the Dean of Social Sciences," said Dilly, his eyes kind but skeptical. "But I don't think you have to choose between outside and inside views. I have a political science class with Professor Henry Hankton, and he talks about how Freud provides an additional point of view for social science. See, it's like this," and he grabbed two sets of salt and pepper shakers, gesturing with them as though they were puppets. "I can look at you and you and you (one shaker in one hand, three in the other) from the outside and describe how you live — everything from material culture to myth and ritual — or I can interview just you and get to know you in depth."

The room retreated as they continued conversing inside a bubble of assessment and intrigue. Dilly's enthusiasm and inclination to think in compromise pleased Henriette. Maybe he would be interested in her views of civilization. She'd recently read Huxley's novel *Point Counterpoint*, and had adopted his idea that Jesus, Newton, and Henry Ford had "ripped the life out of our bodies." She used that to explain her sense of separation from her physical self and its feelings, her suspension above her body in a cloud of words. She picked up a salt shaker, laid it on its side, moved two others away, and placed a standing pepper next to it.

"What about you?" she asked. "Have you ever been on the couch?"

"Certainly not," he said, shaking his head.

"Everyone needs to be analyzed," said Henriette, and sat back, folding her arms.

"Why do you need analysis?" asked Dilly, sitting back. "It's one thing for social scientists to use the 'insight interview,' as Professor Hankton says, but analytic treatment? I've always thought it was for crazy people. I don't think I'll ever need it." Henriette looked down. She was on her way to see Dr. Whitson now.

"What's the matter with you?" he persisted. She rummaged in her briefcase, feeling trapped. How could she tell him about seeing herself on a slab or about a father who'd once told Mother he liked rye bread and now was reduced to sneaking downstairs at night to eat white? It was all way too complicated, like a huge ball of impossibly tangled yarn.

"I have linguistics next," she said, pulling out a schedule to disguise her lie.

"You're in for a treat," said Dilly. She hoped he wouldn't insist she explain herself, or write her off as nuts from the start. Both alternatives made her cringe, even as his calm confidence and competent-looking hands aroused her desire. "I think you'll be interested to hear Professor Sapir, " continued Dilly. "He's also integrating psychiatry and social science."

Henriette raised her eyebrows and nodded. "See you in class," she said, and they headed out.

HENRIETTE WALKED WEST ALONG 59TH Street towards the Student Health Service, Dilly's words echoing in her head and sending fluttery warmth from stomach to brain and back. He'd pressed her, tough in his own way, but then returned, conciliatory, to her interests. She tucked him away to contemplate later and looked ahead with trepidation. Her nerve had served her well in that encounter with the nurse, but now she would have to produce — what, herself? — and maybe there was nothing there. Something unpleasant moved in her gut, and her mouth felt dry. Last week's mountain of blankets was gone, but the cardboard boxes looked like a permanent encampment, with wisps of smoke rising from flaming cans of Sterno. How could she be so concerned with her troubles when others were cold and hungry? Maybe analysis would strengthen her to take action, to do something worthwhile. She arrived early for her appointment and fidgeted in an empty waiting room with beige walls, sticky seats, and a green plant that seemed too big and prickly. The beef soup smell rose from her armpits, and a drop of moisture ran down her side.

A door opened, and a tall woman appeared in a calf-length navy skirt and fitted jacket. "Miss Greenberg?" the woman asked. "Come in." Henriette entered and quickly took in a couch, a bookshelf, a low table, and a tank with several small, bright fish. She feared meeting the eyes of Dr. Whitson and kept her own averted, standing frozen for a moment, not sure where to go. The couch. If this was going to be the real thing, that was where she belonged. She gestured toward it and looked up, questioning, keeping her head on one side. "Yes," said Dr. Whitson. "Lie down if you wish." On the couch Henriette felt a bit safer, as if her closed eyes hid her from the doctor's sight. Dr. Whitson asked her routine questions about her family, where she lived, and what she studied, and Henriette was relieved if impatient. "What brings you here?" asked Dr. Whitson. Henriette didn't know what to say. It was all just too terrible. Or too perfectly fine. What did she have to complain about?

"I feel guilty about being here," she said, glad she'd admitted at least one true thing.

"Here in school or here in therapy?" asked Dr. Whitson.

"Both, I guess," said Henriette. She tried to remember how Dr. Whitson looked, but she hadn't seen more than the suit. She imagined a warm glow emanating from smiling eyes and mouth. Seconds passed, and the silence grew itchy.

"Say anything that comes into your mind," said Dr. Whitson. Immediately Henriette's mind filled with all the four-letter words she'd ever heard — some of the meanings she knew and some of them she didn't — and she certainly wasn't going to say *them*. More seconds, and the sound of Dr. Whitson uncrossing and crossing her legs, the scratch of her pen on paper. What was she writing? I don't think I can do this, thought Henriette. After what felt like a long time she decided to say it.

"I don't think I can do this." She squeezed out the words and felt her throat cramp with unshed tears.

"Give yourself time," said Dr. Whitson. The silence lengthened. Dr. Whitson cleared her throat, and Henriette wondered when she'd ever be able to give voice to the words in her head, to let her feelings stream from her mouth and trouble the air of this tight enclosure. If she spoke, her story would hover forever in the space between Dr. Whitson and herself, revealing and shaming. And once those words were out, she could never put them back. Even admitting concealment would be the start of revelation. Was she condemned to concealing concealment forever?

Henriette's thoughts began to race through the night she spent with Lucky, details flashing before her. His arm across the back of her folding chair, his leg next to hers, his records, her smell, his hands, apple odor, everything swirling and sucking her down like a maelstrom until she lay as though dead and he just above her, making use of her body. She retreated and watched the scene from on high.

"I see myself as if through the wrong end of a telescope," she said into the air above the couch, and then watched the words float up and back to Dr. Whitson. "I'm small and far away."

"And where is the observer?" asked the doctor.

"Oh somewhere up there," said Henriette, offhand, pointing vaguely up and feeling foolish, for she knew perfectly well she was on the couch, not the ceiling. There was no way she could express what had happened to the person at the other end of that telescope.

"That's all for today," said Dr. Whitson. The fifty-minute hour was up, and Henriette had accomplished nothing. She sat and then stood, looking Dr. Whitson full in the face for the first time. She looked to be about fifty, just younger than Mother. Her nose was hawklike, the eyebrows dark, the glance direct, her finger-waved hair too soft for the astringent face. Her shoulders were as broad as a man's, though that could have been fashionable padding.

She extended her hand and shook Henriette's firmly. "See you next week," she said.

Henriette walked back along 59th Street, replaying the hour in her head, searching for nuance, trying to decide whether Dr. Whitson had glowing eyes and mouth or narrowed eyes and lips. Then she remembered Dilly. If she didn't know herself what she was doing in therapy, how could she explain it to him? The meeting with Dr. Whitson had not been what she expected. Could that be all it was, the long-awaited analytic hour?

Chapter 4

A week later Henriette and Carl were sitting on a stone bench in Hutchinson Court. Water bubbled from a fountain in the center, making cheerful music in the crisp air, and students lingered to chat. Dilly approached.

"This is my brother, Carl," she said to Dilly. Then to Carl, "Diller Brannigan," Carl reached up languidly to shake Dilly's hand as though meeting someone new were hard work. "Carl's studying medicine here at the University," added Henriette, hoping her brother's status would increase her own in Dilly's eyes.

"Going to be a doc, eh?" asked Dilly.

"Actually I hope to be a psychoanalyst," said Carl. His slightly nasal tone seemed to undercut whatever he said.

"So the interest runs in your family," said Dilly. Carl and Henriette exchanged knowing glances. "Something sure runs in our family," said Carl, looking at the sky for answers.

"Screaming mimis," said Henriette. Let Dilly hear it all. See if he could take it.

"Heebie jeebies," echoed Carl, beginning to laugh.

"We're both barmy as hell," said Henriette. "As you can probably tell." She looked directly at Dilly.

"Walking textbooks for psychopathology 101," continued Carl, elbowing Henriette.

"Psychopathology with overdeveloped compensatory verbalization," said Henriette, riding the updraft of her fancy talk.

Carl laughed, and Henriette joined him, watching his words box up her problems and set them aside.

"Can you move over?" asked Dilly, and he wedged himself into a space between them. Carl wiped his eyes and then turned to Dilly.

"What are you interested in?" he asked. "Besides us. I mean what are you actually doing here?"

"I've been working on a dig," said Dilly, "and I'm studying anthropology. Think of it as a rescue operation for dying cultures." Carl leaned back and stretched his long legs, then yawned.

"I need rescuing myself, mostly in the form of food and sleep. That's life in med school, but someday I'd like to look at myth and ritual. Freud did." He yawned again.

"He looked at it from the inside, and we look from the outside, so we have objective evidence. The two work together," said Dilly, turning from side to side to address both. Did this mean Carl and Dilly were going to get along? Or was she once again trying to engineer camaraderie between others, leaving herself in the background, longing for attention? Old habits were hard, maybe impossible, to break.

"Sometimes I'm not sure even medicine is objective," said Carl, his manner again world-weary. "We don't know why people live or die."

"I thought you said you needed food," said Henriette, tapping Carl's shoulder. "Let's eat."

"Come back to my place." Carl included Dilly with his eyes. "I cooked up bossy in a bowl last night."

"You've got an apartment with a stove?" asked Dilly. "I cook on a hot plate or eat in a dorm where meals are cheap." Difference, again. All three began walking towards Carl's place on Maryland Avenue.

"Where do you live, Henriette?" Dilly asked.

"I've been at home — I mean living in Oak Park — the past year, but now I'm in Foster Hall. The parents were driving me crazy. Literally." Henriette hoped Dilly would understand that she was "crazy" without being some kind of wild woman or idiot. She shouldn't have to explain everything.

The three entered Carl's building and walked up to the second floor, taking care not to trip on carpet coming loose from the stairs. Inside the one-room apartment, they threw down books and satchels on a hastily made bed and walked out to the kitchen. Dilly's eyes roved over the gas stove with its white porcelain levers and the small electric refrigerator. "Do you cook all the time?"

"As often as I can," said Carl. "It keeps me sane."

"Jeepers, this is swell," said Dilly.

"Look around. Feel free." Carl took out a pot, and Dilly looked into the refrigerator and opened the oven.

"I'd give a lot to have a stove and electric fridge," said Dilly. We have an icebox at home, of course, for summer." Carl handed Dilly a box of matches and turned a porcelain lever on the stove so Dilly could light it. As Carl stirred, a deep, meaty aroma filled the apartment.

"Smells good," said Dilly. "Like my mother's stew, though we use the venison we hunt."

"You actually shoot and kill animals?" asked Henriette. "You shoot deer?" She pictured frightened doe eyes.

"If we want to eat," said Dilly. "Sometimes we use bow and arrow."

The image of Dilly hunting with any weapon shocked her, but she tried to sound admiring. "Like something from a fairy tale," she said, setting the table with bowls and spoons.

Carl filled bowls with deep brown gravy and chunks of browned beef, round potatoes, and odd-shaped carrots.

"What makes carrots come out like that?" asked Dilly.

"It's called roll-cutting," said Carl. "I'll show you later."

"Where'd you learn to do it?"

"Cooks in Chinese restaurants," said Carl. "We could go together to Chinatown sometime. I like to make friends with the cooks and pick up tips." Dilly and Carl dug into the stew with enthusiasm, continuing to talk about apartments and food. They seemed to take a liking to each other, and Henriette wondered what they could find in common: the short, sensible social scientist from the back woods and her tall, complicated, brother. Yet here they were, chatting with enthusiasm about commonplace things.

Dilly's curly-haired arms and mix of intellect and know-how continued to captivate her, while his status as a T.A. excited her aspirations, but she couldn't imagine the primitive way of life he'd led: hunting, fishing, and farming to survive. She'd gladly give up Mother's three-course dinners, but she couldn't kill to eat. And killing was the least of it. Didn't you have to clean and scale and skin the creatures too? Equally attracted and repelled, she felt goosebumps rise, and she shivered.

AT HENRIETTE'S SECOND ANALYTIC SESSION she lay on the fabric-covered couch, staring at the ceiling. The room seemed to darken and the air to thicken. Henriette squirmed as though lying on nails, breathing hard.

"What are you feeling right now?" asked Dr. Whitson. No one could make Henriette spill herself out all over that too-neat office. She felt the doctor's sharp eyes piercing her, the mind dissecting her, the room holding her prisoner.

"I thought this was supposed to help," said Henriette, hands over her eyes.

"I think it is helping," said Dr. Whitson. "You're experiencing your bad feelings right here, where we can explore them." These words puzzled Henriette, and she lay still a long time, trying to parse and measure her experience and the doctor's interpretation. Her breathing slowed. Surely the problem was Dr. Whitson herself. She must be some sort of evil witch who could evoke panic by a few well-placed words. Unfair and manipulative. And this counted as treatment? Any neurotic would improve if threatened with burning at the stake — that's why they used electric shock — but no thank you, not for Henriette. To herself she said, I'm not coming back, but aloud she said nothing.

"Time to stop," said Dr. Whitson. Had fifty minutes gone by? "See you next week." Henriette did not respond, and she avoided checking the doctor's face for signs of wizardry or succor, afraid of what she might see.

Still, she returned the next week, and on and on, sometimes dreading the visits and always skeptical about their effects. The doctor kept urging her to say whatever came into her mind, and accepted equally Henriette's smart revelations and her trivial, daily drivel. Gradually she realized that she was one of many patients, and the doctor couldn't possibly care two cents about her, with her paltry round of who said this and who did that. Resigned, she barely noticed when the routine appointments began to anchor her week, no matter how strangely. The doctor sometimes gave a barely audible laugh of amusement or approval and sometimes maintained a silence as dark and deep as the unknowable side of the moon, but she always spoke up at the end of the session —"It's time to go. See you next time."— both infuriating Henriette with the immediate dismissal and reminding her that she was not yet abandoned altogether. In that enclosed office it made no difference if she were selfish, angry, silly or smart. It was freedom of a sort.

HENRIETTE HAD SIGNED UP FOR American poetry, and the class began not with Jeffers or Millay but with harder times, with words written by men and women struggling to survive in a new, hostile land. The class included students from every year — Nadine, the girl who had read Robinson Jeffers, and Effie, Henriette's roommate, among them. Henriette found a new model in Anne Bradstreet, the Puritan poet who immigrated to America and survived the poverty, scurvy, and tuberculosis of 17th-century New England to write with devotion of her husband, "If ever two were one, then surely we." Henriette's mind looped and sang with the music of words and churned with the feelings they evoked. With poetry, the lines of others, it seemed that words and feelings ran towards each other for a big embrace, whereas her own words and feelings faced off like enemies. She made a point of saying whatever she wanted, but when she talked about feeling an old wall went up between her heart and voice, so the voice revealed nothing, and the heart was sealed off in a place she couldn't reach. "Flesh of thy flesh, bone of thy bone." She mulled over Bradstreet's words, tapping her pencil as she waited for lunch.

THREE WEEKS INTO THE QUARTER, Henriette, Effie, and Nadine had grown accustomed to eating together in the dining hall of Foster, where they consumed gray meat, damp potatoes, and boiled vegetables while discussing literature, recipes for cocktails, and exotic desserts like baked Alaska. Sounds of conversation mingled with the clink of silverware and china one noon as the three friends chose among vegetables plopped on plates by white-uniformed women, red faces moist from steam. From the serving line, the girls carried plates to a table in the windowless, wood-paneled dining room, lit by round ceiling globes.

"I'd like to know how Bradstreet did it," said Henriette, taking a seat.

"Not just the poems, but her marriage." She pushed some floppy broccoli around on the plate.

"People were used to hardship then. And some are discovering it again, right now. We have it easy," said Effie, pointing first to the food and then to the room full of students dressed in skirts, sweaters, and shoes in good repair. "Some have no warm clothes at all."

"Art depends on life," said Nadine, responding to Henriette with slow assurance. "If you live as fully as Bradstreet did, then you can write like that." She cut the meat and began to eat.

"Is the reverse also true?" asked Henriette. "If you write, then you get a full life?" Nadine was only a year older but seemed much more worldly. She'd already written notebooks full of poems, lyrics in which she hinted at her love for women, and Henriette found them brave and beautiful.

"I don't know," said Nadine, her voice a low hum. "Writing can be a way into feeling, but you have to have real experience too. Look at how Millay's work deepened when she protested Sacco and Vanzetti." She quoted: "'Sour to the fruitful seed/Is the cold earth under this cloud.'"

"Experience can be dangerous," said Effie. "Look at all the unhappy writers. Even suicides." She took a few bites and pushed her plate away.

"I think writers are people who stand apart and observe, bystanders," said Henriette. "I've always felt like that." It was easy to say, but she doubted anyone could know what it felt like to stand on that perilous rock alone, a bystander surrounded by the rising waters of rage.

"Some stand apart and some are engaged," said Nadine, scooping up mashed potatoes. "Jeffers secludes himself in a remote canyon on the California coast, while Wright and Hemingway — all the writers who publish in *New Masses* — they take political responsibility and get involved. You should both visit me in New York. I'd introduce you to the people at *New Masses*, and you could stay with me. My mother loves to feed my friends — it's a Jewish tradition." Henriette moved her plate aside.

"My mother's Jewish, but she doesn't like to feed anybody," said Effie.

Henriette considered whether she should say she was Jewish too, then decided not. After all, her parents were Unitarian. Wasn't she too? The whole thing was confusing. "You wouldn't want to eat dinner with my family," she said. "It's like a steam engine on the brink of explosion, and it goes on and on forever."

"Phooey," said Nadine. "I wouldn't be afraid." She laughed with a loud snort and said she'd love to come, then collected her dishes and carried her tray to the dish window. Henriette and Effie followed.

Chapter 5

Shortly thereafter, a knock on Henriette's door announced a call. As she closed the door of the phone alcove, a bare bulb overhead quivered, casting a shaky shadow of her head on the shiny desk. Fear assaulted her, the eerie feeling that she was more a thing than a person, a thing she could observe from a disconnected distance. Ever since she'd started seeing Dr. Whitson, the feeling had surprised her at the strangest moments, jumping out from behind a casual conversation, a book, or a gargoyle. Apparently therapy had brought to life the very feeling it was supposed to cure. Suppressing nausea, she picked up the heavy black receiver and leaned into the wall-mounted phone.

"Henriette?" said Mother. "When are you coming home for a weekend? You promised."

A visit home would not be good for her, not now. "I just got here," she said, "and I have a lot of work."

"Well so do I," said Mother. "But that doesn't mean you can't take a day to come home. Russell's coming, and I know you'd like to see him. I need your help, and your father wants to see you too. Here he is," and she put him on. His voice was soft and wheedling.

"We miss you, darling. Please come home." Didn't Mother hear the need, the too sweet begging, in that tone? Apparently not. Mother would be angry if she didn't come, but Father would be hurt, even physically hurt if his disappointment precipitated an attack. Despite the danger Henriette always pitied him, yearned to give him what could never be enough. Oh God, she thought, how can I squeeze a month's worth of college experience back into my Oak Park self?

Her thoughts turned to Dilly, so far beyond her in years and knowledge, so fascinating and so different. Growing up poor, he might never have been to a suburb like Oak Park. She'd have to hold him inside her if she went home, her secret sweetening the oppressive tedium of meeting expectations. Her other secret wasn't so sweet. She certainly wouldn't discuss her analytic sessions, with their unspoken four-letter words and sense of failure. Still, she couldn't say no to her parents, and she agreed to come the following weekend.

AT THE SIGHT OF THE screen porch a lump pained her throat, and a surge of regret washed over her, as though the house offered a return to a golden age when all was right with the world and her skin fit neatly and comfortably on her body. After a month of new challenges, home tempted like a bed full of stuffed animals. She opened the screen door to the porch, and the porch swing creaked, moving in the wind and reminding her of lemonade on summer evenings, homemade ice cream, and Mother sitting with her on the swing. Then her mind tunneled back to the happy days when her brothers had sat her down with the telephone book to teach her to read. She was five years old.

"Read these names," said Russell. "See, they all start with 'A'. The first one is 'Abel.' Say 'Abel.'"

"Can she really learn to read that way?" asked Carl.

"I already am learning," said Henriette, feeling special and important.

"OK, what's this?" asked Carl, flipping to the 'B's.'

"You have to teach me first," said Henriette.

" 'B,' said Carl. Here's 'Bach.' Say 'Bach.' And so they continued, learning new letter sounds each day. A few months later, Mother brought home a news sheet from the recently founded Women's International League for Peace and Freedom.

"Here's something for Henriette to read, better than the phone book," said Mother. Henriette pored over it, sounding out words from the letters she'd learned. Though she couldn't make sense of them, she'd felt secure — she was becoming the person Mother wanted her to be.

LEAVING THE HAPPY MEMORY BEHIND with a feeling of apprehension, Henriette raised a hand to the heavy wooden door, and a different picture sprang to life. One afternoon, years later, she'd planned to welcome Father home from a business trip with a gift of chocolate cigarettes. Wearing her pre-teen knickers, she tiptoed into the dining room and fanned a halo of chocolates at Father's place.

Soon after, when the family gathered, Mother said with her critical frown, "Pants are not appropriate for dinner. I've told you that before."

"I know," said Henriette, looking down and putting a hand to her short black curls, as if to remind herself that she was still intact.

"She wants you to call her Tom," said Carl to Mother, and Russell seconded him with a nod.

"Her name is Henriette," said Mother. Henriette envied the twins their closeness and their shared nerve to down squirrels with their catapult, rules be damned, and she intended to remain Tom as long as she could. The front door opened, and Father made his way to the dining room, bending to kiss Henriette.

"You're late," said Mother. "We couldn't wait. Soup's cold." Father backtracked to his own end of the table. Henriette's heart sank as she watched the respected advertising man shrink, bit by bit, into the angry object of Mother's rulings. She held her breath, waiting to see if he would like her surprise. He gathered the chocolate cigarettes in one sweeping gesture and threw them at the wall.

"What's that?" asked Mother. "Who put that there?"

"It was me," said Henriette, sounding like a wind-up toy with a recorded voice. She wouldn't cry. She gave an extra twist to the coiled spring in her belly that held the anger she didn't dare feel.

"I work all day," said Father. "I've worked all my life, so my mother and sisters didn't have to, so you don't have to," and he stood and waved his arm to include the table, the room, the world.

Mother rose and put a hand on his shoulder, saying, "Sears is doing so well now," but he brushed her aside, sputtering. "You don't know what I gave up...what I survived...look at the coal strikes...Sears could be destroyed...I need...I need...more than candy cigarettes... you can't even keep my soup warm," and then his cough took over. He clutched his chest, sank into his chair, and his tantrum escalated into a familiar attack of breathlessness and fury. His temper made his heart go wild, and his weak heart made him angrier. Henriette never knew when to really worry and when to just wait.

"Try breathing slower and deeper," said Carl.

"What good is that going to do?" asked Russell.

"Calm down," said Mother to Father. "You're making yourself sick. Unions are no threat to Sears." Then, to Henriette, "Pick them up." Henriette gathered the cigarettes from the floor, ashamed but wondering what she'd done wrong. Mother passed bowls of bright-green asparagus and mashed potatoes and a platter of sliced beef. Henriette cut her food into pieces, and then used the potatoes as glue to construct miniature houses of beef and asparagus. Soon she had a little village, cut one house in half, and pretended to take a bite.

"You'll always look like a boy if you don't eat more than that," said Mother. See if I care, thought Henriette.

Later that night Father came to Henriette's room, sat in a chair, and said he was sorry he'd thrown her cigarettes at the wall. He hadn't been angry at her, just upset to come home to cold soup.

"None of you can comprehend the landscape of endless winter I knew as a child," he said. "The only warm place was under my mother's layered skirts." He looked down, elbows on knees, and the bald spot shone pink on the top of his head. Henriette tried to imagine him as a sad little boy but could not. He looked up, eyes weary, cheeks sagging. "Before I left school for good, the teacher would beat us, and I told myself I'd always be gentle. I worked every day so my mother and sisters and I could survive. When I met your mother we turned our backs on the past —those sighing accordions and mystic beliefs. We built a castle of reason and sense." His voice deepened to a growl, almost a sob. "So why can't she keep my soup warm?"

Henriette felt overwhelmed by Father's loss and need. She pushed the thrown chocolates to the back of her mind. "Flowers will be coming up soon," she said. "Can we go hunt for Trillium and Dutchman's Breeches?"

"Dutchman's Breeches," repeated Father. "Dutchman's Breeches." He sang the sound and began to smile at the silly name, as he and Henriette often did. She liked searching with him and learning about flowers. Then after slides were made and filed in the trays below the hallway stereopticon, she'd pull them out and stand on a little stool to view the three-dimensional images, surprising guests with all the names she knew and making Father proud. She could not soften Mother's tone or keep his soup warm, much less provide the comfort he needed, but this she'd done many times and would do again.

SHE TOOK A DEEP BREATH and pushed on the heavy wooden door. As she entered the hall, the many layers of the past compressed into a knot that settled just below her ribs. The room engulfed her like the maw of a beast, sucking her in and snapping shut, stripping her of each new-found competence. There was a price, she realized, for the golden-age feeling, and she knew she couldn't afford it.

She entered the living room and found Russell listening to the family's first radio, a floor-model Philco "Baby Grand" whose polished wooden console rivaled the fireplace as the room's center. Folding chairs with arm rests and thick fabric seats made a temporary half moon around it. A couch, coffee table, plants, and magazines crowded into the space remaining, and light from a large window dispersed the furnishings, giving the illusion of space.

Thinner and quicker than Carl, though often mistaken for him, Russell sprang up to embrace Henriette, asked her about the university, then listened briefly to her skeletal answer before launching into his own enthusiasms. In his second year of graduate business school at Purdue, he was studying the psychology of advertising.

"It's all about the spoken word," he said. "People hear this disembodied voice, this 'visitor in the living room' as they call it, and they'll do what it tells them to." Henriette took a seat by the radio, frowning with doubt.

"I've been following the show about the kind country boy in love with the spunky newspaperwoman," she said. "Will love triumph?" Russell laughed and sat across from her.

"Probably," he said. "But not as certainly as the all-important 'word from our sponsors.'"

"You assume everyone is gullible," said Henriette.

"I assume everyone likes to hum a jingle," said Russell. "Then, when you can't get it out of your head, it influences your behavior. That's the new psychology." Henriette walked around her chair and leaned on the back, thinking about Russell and Carl. In spite of their differences — Carl with his problems and theories; Russell the well-adjusted, good-humored, social twin — they were both studying psychology.

But Carl's psychology sought access to the tortured human soul — his own — while Russell's was stuck on the surface. "I wish Father would understand the new thinking about persuasion," said Russell. "Then maybe he'd help me get a job." Henriette ached to give Russell Father's interest and approval — she'd gladly give up a little of the love Father had for her — and her stomach lurched.

"You don't have to confront him head on," she said. "Why don't you bring it up gently?" Russell turned the radio back on, and a symphony filled the room. They listened for a while without talking, ignoring the sounds of Father coming home from work and leaving hat and coat in the hall. He entered the living room, wearing his usual three-piece suit and pocket watch, and Henriette smelled the cool menthol of his Listerine aftershave, an odor she could not help associating with the antiseptic's bitter taste and alcoholic sting. Mother still insisted her children gargle with it daily to prevent sore throats and use it as shampoo to combat dandruff.

A stream of gibberish blasted in a monotone from the speaker. Father winced, then turned it way down, so the final, drawn-out words — so-o-old, American — sounded as though they came from the distant end of a tunnel. Father shook Russell's hand, then wrapped his arms around Henriette and held her tight, kissing her on the cheek. She shrank from the medicinal smell and wriggled out of his embrace, resisting the urge to wipe the cool wet spot on her cheek. "You should listen, Father," said Russell, raising the volume again. "That's a tobacco auctioneer advertising Lucky Strikes, and his voice is coming into more and more homes each month. People will buy what he tells them to." He turned to Henriette. "You've heard those ads, haven't you?" Henriette nodded as Father pulled up a folding chair, and they all sat down around the radio. It dominated the space the way its sound dominated the air, and their seats seemed to radiate from it.

"The mail order catalogue still reaches more people than any other medium," said Russell. "But soon no one will read what they can hear." A young female voice on the radio sang about Sunbrite cleanser, then invited girls to join the Sunbrite Junior Nurse Corps, promising them a pin and a handbook if they sent in a label and pledged themselves to fight dirt. Father's eyes clouded over and he turned away from Russell, curling to one side. Russell got up and walked to the other side of Father's chair, facing him.

"Nothing will replace the catalogue," said Father, refusing to look up at Russell. "It's a fixture in homes all over the country."

"Russell didn't say, 'replace,'" said Henriette, and Father gave her a sharp, startled look.

"I said, 'take advantage of sound,'" said Russell. "You don't understand the primacy of the spoken word. Read *The Psychology of Language*."

"It can't hurt to read it," said Henriette. The muscles in Father's face began to twitch, and Henriette wished she could take back her words.

"Don't tell me what I should read," he snarled, heaving himself to his feet and stamping a shiny shoe. "Or what I do or don't understand. When I come home I expect respect, not some raucous radio assaulting me or some whippersnapper telling me my business." Father's glance took in Henriette as well as Russell, and she shrank, frightened. "I know more about advertising than you'll ever know, so you mind your own business, and I'll mind mine," he shouted.

Oh God, thought Henriette, now I've done it, and waves of regret swept through her. The sounds of Father's raised voice brought Mother from the kitchen.

"You should have a rest before dinner," she said. "I'll call you when it's ready." Father trudged to the stairs, and Mother turned to Russell. "Leave your father alone." Then, to Henriette: "You should know better than to let your brother upset your father."

When Mother had returned to the kitchen, Russell said to Henriette, "I'm the only one in the family who wants to go into his field. But he doesn't seem to care. I try to bring him up to date, and he goes into a temper, then leaves me batting at air, looking like a fool."

"Maybe you should stay away from the catalogue," suggested Henriette. "That's his work and his pride. Do you want me to talk to him?"

"Nah," said Russell. "Nothing's going to change the old codger. I'm going for a walk," and he took his jacket from a hook in the hallway.

"Be back in time for dinner," called Henriette out the door, hoping she would not be left alone with the parents.

"Sure," he called back. Now he was gone, and she stood in the hallway, feeling out of place: no longer belonging at home and not fully a citizen of anywhere else. Russell needed Father's support, and Father needed Russell's approval, but she couldn't make it happen. This week she'd met a fascinating if unattainable man, and she'd failed horribly at therapy. Anxiety, desire, shame, and ambition competed for space inside her like weeds in a garden, and yet the minute she walked in the family door she was slotted right back into old roles.

She glanced around the too-familiar entryway, wondering if panic would pop out from behind the tall wooden stereopticon or swoop down the curving stairway, but her feet stayed firmly on the ground, and the ground remained solid. Where should she go? Not to the kitchen, where Mother was banging pots around and just waiting to give her an order. Wherever her place might be, she knew how it would sound: not raggy but snazzy, with lots of brass. She returned to the living room and turned the radio on, twisting the dial until she heard jazz.

MOTHER'S SILVER BELL ANNOUNCED THAT dinner was served in the formal dining room. Henriette turned off the radio, and Father's bed creaked as he rose and headed downstairs. Russell came in the front door, looking more relaxed. Henriette sighed, resigned to the slow and painful rituals of sipping without slurping, breaking bread before buttering, slicing with the right hand, and shifting the fork to eat. Like a beam of light, a thought suddenly struck her: she didn't have to lie anymore about Carl watching out for her. She could let the light shine on her comings and goings without concealment, because the South side was now her home. Not a smothering home of plush dolls and warm milk, but a burning hearth from which smoke could rise and go out into the world. What a relief to discover the truth about this one thing! Oak Park was merely a place she visited, and tomorrow night she would go home to Foster Hall.

Part II 1931-1932

Chapter 6

On a late afternoon at the start of Winter Quarter, Henriette stopped by the anthropology office to see about future course offerings and ran into Dilly.

"A few of us are going to the Lucky Laundry for a drink. Want to come?" he asked. Henriette raised her eyebrows, trying to stall for more information. "It's a speakeasy," said Dilly. "Don't worry, the door is off the alley, and the coppers are all paid off. Some of them even drink there." Henriette gave a quick thought to her clothes: gray sweater, plaid wool skirt, knee socks and flats. She guessed she looked OK for a speakeasy and said yes.

Professor Henry Hankton joined them and a half dozen or so other students, and they walked to a storefront with a laundry sign, then around the back to the entrance. Inside, the room was dark and plain, with round wooden tables and bent-metal chairs that scraped harshly on the cement floor as people stood or sat. Three bare bulbs hung from the ceiling, and a small crowd occupied a few tables or crowded around the dresser that served as a bar. "Tap your feet and sing bobby-doddy-doo, keep the beat and sing bobby-doddy-doo," sang a vocalist from a Victrola in a corner.

"Get the light stuff," said Hankton. "The White Lightning."

"Before they use it on the clothes," said one of the students, and everyone hooted. Jowly and balding, Hankton's build and manner were imposing, but his eyes crinkled with amusement even when he didn't smile. He wore a three-piece suit and kept the jacket on in the chilly room. Henriette thought his round bald held must be stuffed to bursting with ideas, for he'd published in journals of sociology and anthropology as well as political science, and she hoped he'd notice her. She dipped her tongue in a shot glass of clear liquid and found the taste harsh, not herbal like the bathtub gin she'd tried, but burning and bitter. She would drink it in tiny sips. The others threw back the shots and relaxed in their chairs, looking around to see who else was there.

"Professor H.," said one of the students, leaning forward. "I've been wanting to ask you, how do you square your ideas about democracy with propaganda? You say propaganda is necessary to make democracy work, but propaganda doesn't respect truth, does it?" Hankton took off his heavy black-rimmed glasses and rubbed his eyes.

"The elite are the primary holders of power in society, and their propaganda is necessary to disseminate information," he said, tilting his chair back and tapping his shot glass on the table. "People in a democracy don't often inform themselves, and they need others to understand what's best for them. Psychoanalysis can help us understand who's qualified to belong to that elite — that's where the 'insight interview' comes in." Henriette thought of her parents and their faith in the wisdom of ordinary people, a belief shared by social workers like Jane Addams and sociologists like Dr. Dubois, but she wasn't ready to challenge Hankton on first meeting him. Her head started to go bobby-doddy-doo with the music, and she nodded in time. "Let your voice get hoarse and passionate," went the song. "Up to you to take the tune and fashion it."

Hankton leaned over the table to look directly at Henriette. "You look so young," he said. "Have you had your coming out party?" Some of Henriette's parents' daughters had made debuts, but she found the custom ridiculous.

"I don't see how I can *come* out, when I already *am* out," she said. Everyone laughed.

"How about a debut in a speakeasy?" someone suggested, and all raised glasses. "That'd be the berries," said Henriette, joining in the toast.

"Good-looking boy over there," said another student to Hankton, gesturing behind him. The professor glanced over discreetly, then signaled the bartender for another round.

"Nice," said Hankton. "But brunette." Dilly turned to Henriette, who raised her eyebrows to let him know she'd heard.

"You OK?" he asked.

"Yeah, but this stuff is strong," she said.

"Just take it slow and easy." He leaned across the table toward Hankton. "Do you think social science can ever affect the way people live, improve social conditions?" The other students stopped talking and looked from Dilly to Hankton.

Hankton considered, looking first at the ceiling and then around the table, as though surveying his subjects. "In the hands of the right people," he said. "You have to have political power to produce effects on others, but you have to be careful of the desire for domination. We all have it, but we have to channel it for constructive ends. Psychoanalysis can help us discern motives, but you can't change living conditions without power." Amen to that! — thought Henriette. Look at what happened to Sacco and Vanzetti.

"I understand that," said Dilly. "But how can you depend on some elite to discern motives? In a liberal democracy we have checks and balances to protect everyone's interests."

"Checks and balances can't undo the effect of propaganda in

a democracy, where demagogues can sway voters," said Hankton. "Consider Germany. Hitler got over eighteen percent of the vote a few months ago."

"Is democracy in Germany a lost cause?"

"Probably." Hankton leaned forward to address Dilly directly. The overhead bulb cast a mask of shadow on his cheeks, changing his appearance from lordly to conspiratorial. "Hitler promises power to the powerless. That's what the Germans want after Versailles, the right to arm themselves. Their unemployment rates are as high as ours, and their inflation is more than you can imagine. I'm not saying that might makes right, but social scientists have to engage in politics — who gets what, when and how — if they want to effect change."

"I'll drink to that," said Dilly, and they all raised glasses. "Where I come from, people think the whole world lives the way they do. I want to understand different cultures, maybe improve living conditions."

"I think you're more interested in politics than motives," said Hankton.

Henriette tried to think about what she'd heard. Could her mixed-up feelings be reduced to who got what, when, and how? She drained her glass, and music by the Boswell Sisters joined alcohol to blur the room. "Hear the beat of dancing feet," she sang quietly along with the Sisters, twisting her shoulders in time, feeling saucy. The song slowed to a bluesy, stomping rhythm, and its power gave her courage. She heard the door open and felt a draft, as a slender blond man entered alone and ordered a drink at the bar. She reminded herself that the best way to handle authority figures was direct aggression tinged with girlish love, and an inspiration as sudden as a giggle prompted her to speak.

"Professor Hankton," she said. "I see a good-looking boy that just came in, a blonde." Hankton turned his solid bulk in the chair and looked over at the newcomer, while the others looked back and forth from Henriette to Hankton, a few surprised and smirking, but most admiring, she thought. The professor raised his glass to Henriette, drank and rose. Henriette was tickled with herself. She'd offered something to the professor, who would now remember her, and she'd challenged propriety just enough to garner attention without attracting criticism.

"We should get something to eat," said Dilly to Henriette. Her feet tried to tap a little doody-doo as she rose from her seat, and she stumbled against him, laughing. They said goodbye to the dispersing group.

"There's a Chinese place Carl found," she said. "I think it's just down the street." They ambled down 55th Street, the cool air bracing in the early dark, music still playing in her head. At the restaurant they settled across from each other in a small red-leather booth, bathed in warm, reddish light from Chinese lanterns hanging above. Tinny music interspersed with static came from a small radio.

"Sounds like my old crystal set," said Dilly. "I loved tinkering with that thing, searching and searching for a sound." The owner came to greet them. "What's good tonight?" asked Dilly.

"You like bones?" asked the owner. "Chinese people like bones — Americans, no." Dilly questioned Henriette with his eyes, and she nodded.

"Bones are OK with us," he said.

The owner brought them a platter of chicken in bony chunks, burnished a deep red-brown, with a bowl of fragrant salt for dipping; another of shrimp with lobster sauce, the shrimp in the shell and covered with thick egg and ground pork; and two bowls of rice.

"Lobster sauce," said the owner, pointing to the shrimp. "Pork and egg, no lobster."

They leaned in close over the food, poured the sauce on the rice and scooped it up with chopsticks, talking and slurping, then gnawed chicken 'til nothing was left but naked bone. Dilly peeled a shrimp and held it out in his chopsticks for Henriette. She bit it in half and suddenly became conscious of her mouth and jaw, chewing, and his eyes hungrily watching. How could he desire something so unseemly? "Here," he said. "Eat the rest," and left the chopsticks in her mouth for a second so she could suck the sauce from them. She lowered her eyes and smiled, while her whole body warmed.

"Your professor is quite a guy," said Henriette. They both continued peeling the shrimp, sucking the shells and licking their fingers.

"Yeah, he lectures all over the country," said Dilly. "I think he's brilliant, though sometimes I'm afraid his idea of democracy is closer to Jefferson than Jackson — all that talk about elites and propaganda. Democracies need faith in people.

"Even Henry Ford?" asked Henriette.

"He gets one vote, just like everyone else," said Dilly. "Hankton uses all the important new ideas in the social sciences, but he never forgets you need power to change how people live — who gets what, as he says."

"Is he really a pansy?"

Dilly looked surprised. "I don't know," he said. "He's not married, and he seems to like boys. Maybe girls too."

"Oh," said Henriette, voice flat. "I might be like that." She made a point of saying this to show her modernity, freedom from prejudice and broadmindedness, but in fact she didn't know what she was. She aspired to be an adored girlfriend and eventually, a wife, but her night with Lucky had made her fear that she'd been made wrong somehow. "Everyone is like that on some level," she continued, sounding to herself like a teacher, wiping her fingers on a napkin. Dilly took a sip of his tea. "It just depends on how much you're willing to know about yourself."

"Umm," said Dilly, setting his cup down. She searched for his gray-green eyes, but he avoided hers, and his black brows contracted. She bristled. Her words had been a test, and she wanted approval, or at least acceptance. The man who'd been so forthright when he fed her the shrimp seemed to have retreated into a shell, and she wanted to lead him out, to teach him about what went unmentioned in Kitichara. Her eyes settled on his mouth. No, she said to the warmth that rose, unbidden, from her groin and reddened her cheeks. Not yet. She wouldn't let herself think about the mouth that had gnawed on bones with such unbridled enthusiasm until she was sure he would respect her need to contain emotion with words. Still, his muscular lips pursed and released as he planned words, his symmetrical teeth like sentries guarding a cavern where a pink tongue slithered, then peeked out for a moist prelude to speech.

He looked up, his eyes now probing. "How can you say 'everyone'?" he asked. "Not me. I just go for girls." He paused. "Like you," he said, eyes softening. "I go for you."

A smile flitted across Henriette's face, and she looked down, suddenly shy, then resorted again to words. "Freud thinks we're all bisexual to start," she said. "Most grow out of it."

"Well I've always liked girls, as far back as I can remember," said Dilly, and he asked for the check. "But if Hankton's deviant in that way it's his business, an illness and not a crime. I say live and let live." As he walked her to Foster Hall he took her hand, his dry, substantial one enfolding her own damp, cold one. A flood of hope as she returned the squeeze, and then a shiver. What might he expect? Her hand clutched his involuntarily, and she feared she'd given a wrong signal. No more than a gentle kiss, please, not tonight.

At the door he turned to her. "I meant it," he said, smoothing her hair away from her face. "I like you a lot. You're funny and smart and beautiful, and I love the way you walk, like a long-legged bird." Before she could say anything, he took her in his arms and kissed her, lingering on her mouth, not challenging her closed lips. His hands on her back and faint smell of masculine sweat felt like a beacon of promise that she might become a real woman, lovable at last, but the feeling dissipated. Something had "ripped the life out of her body"— whether Huxley's "Jesus, Newton and Henry Ford," her first lover's vulgarity, or the unbelievable afternoon when she lay with a book and an apple on her living room couch — and it couldn't be restored with a hug and a kiss. She pulled away ever so slightly, and he let her go, clinging to the hand that trailed on his arm as she said goodnight. Relieved that he had demanded no more of her, courting her kindly and at least tolerating her ideas without insisting on full explanations, she let herself in and walked slowly up the stairs.

How different Dilly was from what she had expected to find at the University, a small-town boy in some ways but a boy with a world-sized mind. Would he ever discover the riches of psychoanalysis? She smiled to herself, remembering the proffered shrimp, the lingering chopsticks, his declaration. Apparently Dilly found her attractive, even when she was chewing. His friendship with Professor Hankton appealed to her as well, not just the camaraderie or the intellectual dialogue but the practical realism. Who gets what indeed! If she'd learned to wrench what she needed from her Oak Park family, she might not be struggling now for insight on Dr. Whitson's couch.

For an instant she pictured Dilly's hairy arm raised, his big hand clenched into a fist, and cowering below him, one of those beefy boys with peanut butter breath who'd teased him as a child. Now for sure he'd be the biggest boy on the block. Then she lowered the fist and gave the hand a rifle, raising it to aim not at tomorrow's dinner but at Lucky, the man who'd shamed her, now staring, fixed in the crosshairs, about to be felled. She dismissed the image, so unlike her, but it left a residue of enchantment with the mysterious T.A. She'd never met anyone like him before.

Chapter 7

Henriette found her interest in the Apache growing, nourished by a Winter Quarter class with Professor Isidore Daniels. She remembered his attendance at the Left-Wing Students' and Workers' meeting and the way he'd stood to applaud for Harold Overstreet, the Marxist economist and friend of Carl's. Her friend, too, though he might not remember dancing with her at the Sunset Café the night when she'd first heard Louis Armstrong play. She couldn't forget.

Daniels had collected stories, and Henriette began to read them. She found the adventures of White-Painted Woman even more engaging than those of Jane Eyre and Elizabeth Bennet, as everything about anthropology took on Dilly's charm, though secretly she wondered if the Indians really believed their fantastic myths about Child-of-the-Water flying through the sky on a cloud after his death, or Killer-of-Enemies acquiring cattle for the Indians by stealing them from the crows. She wondered how Daniels had learned all these stories and how you got the confidence to talk to informants or gained their trust.

"Stay away from the Agency," said Daniels, when she asked her question in class. "You have to go through them, but never go to them directly. The Agent is the enemy of the Indian. When they see you have nothing to do with the Agency, they'll open up and start to become your friend." Henriette repeated this advice to Dilly as they walked across the quadrangle between classes. Chicago's wind was roaring between buildings, and Henriette grabbed her scarf to hold it around her head. Dilly's velvet collar was buttoned high around his neck, and traces of snow blew along the sidewalk.

"I don't believe that," said Dilly. "I can get information from the Agency as well as the Indians. Why use just one when I can have both?"

"Because the Indians will see you as an enemy," said Henriette, her words like spades digging hard ground. "You'll be the white man who took away their game and their land." Why couldn't he just agree with her? She couldn't tolerate losing and despaired of winning, and the thought of arguing exhausted her.

"I didn't take anything away. I suppose my ancestors did, at least the Huguenots that came in the seventeenth century, but I'm a scientist, investigating what happened." Dilly frowned and lowered his head.

"You can't avoid the role of the enforcer if you talk to the Agency. You'll be like a copper."

"What's wrong with police?"

Henriette was shocked. Coppers had been the enemy for as long as she could remember. She dropped his hand and turned to face him. "Police close down protests and arrest marchers on picket lines," she began. "They're the hands of the system that executed — murdered! — Sacco and Vanzetti for being immigrants and Anarchists. Even my parents were horrified by that injustice." Now they were sparring, and icy fear rose from Henriette's stomach to her throat.

"Where I come from," said Dilly, "police help lost kids find their way home and keep the big boys from beating up the smaller ones. They saved me from some bruisers when I was a kid. Sacco and Vanzetti died four years ago, right?" His voice was oddly calm and obstinately reasonable, as though he disagreed with friends every day and always knew he was right.

"Welcome to the city," she said. "Welcome to the world. You have a lot to learn. Yes, four years ago, but more comes out about it every day. A Massachusetts lawyer just revealed what that judge said, the one who denied them a new trial: 'Did you see what I did to those Anarchist bastards? That should hold them for a while.'"

"I'll have to learn more about it," said Dilly.

IN THE SPRING, WORD OF a threatened lynching made its way from a small town in Alabama up to the newspapers of Chicago. At first the news was overshadowed by the sentencing of Al Capone to eleven years in jail, and the awarding of the Nobel Peace Prize to Jane Addams. Then Chicago learned that eight or nine Negro teenagers had been discovered on a train with two white women, who accused them of rape. A mob of armed white men stopped the train in a town called Paint Rock, loaded the teenagers into a flatbed truck, drove them to Scottsboro and threw them into jail. Rumor had it that these young men, aged twelve to nineteen, had been faced by a mob intent on murder, armed with battering pole, rope, and guns. Only a brave sheriff had saved them, walking out the jail door and through that crowd, swearing to kill the man who tried to stop him. He'd called the governor, and the governor had sent in the National Guard.

Then the papers began to report the accusations, the speedy trials, and the joyful circus atmosphere in the town of Scottsboro, where a band played "It'll Be a Hot Time in the Old Town Tonight," as all but the youngest of the teen-agers were sentenced to execution within twelve days of their arrest. A crowd of ten thousand cheered. The National Association for the Advancement of Colored People offered to help with the young men's defense. Henriette had grown up admiring the N-double-A, which her parents had supported from its founding. By the fall the case had also attracted the support of the International

Labor Defense League, legal arm of the Communist Party, and the two organizations competed to represent the young men. As the case attracted national and international attention, the parents of the young men chose the ILD.

Henriette thought of the electrified August night four years before when Sacco and Vanzetti had died. Her sticky sheets. Carl's ghostly scream. Vanzetti's offer of forgiveness. At the time a lawyer had said, "It's as hard for an Italian to get a fair trial in Massachusetts as it is for a black man to get a fair trial in the South." It was still possible that justice for the young men might prevail. The Scottsboro Boys had to be saved.

HENRIETTE'S ANTHROPOLOGY CLASSES GREW MORE varied and challenging as she advanced, and she let Alabama slip to the back of her mind, trusting that appeals were in progress. She took a full load of classes in the Summer and Fall Quarters, bored by the detailed kinship diagrams of structure and function studies. Still, she recognized the necessity for a scientific approach to the discipline. Ethnographic novels, like Oliver La Farge's *Laughing Boy,* delighted her. Culture History and Art and Folklore also appealed, and she absorbed the cultural relativist views of Franz Boas, Professor at Columbia, who opposed the social Darwinism of physical anthropologists like Madison Grant. Boaz did not believe there was such a thing as "primitive" societies or more "evolved" cultures. Distancing herself from the social idealism of her parents, she felt realistic, a little cynical, enlightened, and, above all, modern.

Dilly did not ask her out again after the night at the Lucky Laundry, and she feared he was beyond her reach after all. Perhaps she had not responded warmly enough when he kissed her or been too brazen about bisexuality. Perhaps she'd been too quick to criticize the police. Angry, critical thoughts rushed to her defense. He was too conservative, too narrow, and she should look elsewhere. But she couldn't stop thinking about him, and she felt shy whenever she spied him across the quadrangle or passed him in the Social Science building. He always greeted her with a polite smile but didn't seem moved by the sight of her. Damn.

ON A SATURDAY MORNING IN November, Henriette wandered down the dormitory hall to Nadine's room, knocked and entered. Nadine was sitting at her cluttered desk, where flyers for the Wobblies advertised festivals of hobo song and advocated workplace democracy. The room was more Spartan than Henriette's and Effie's, with bare floor and unadorned window, but the shelf over Nadine's bed overflowed with poetry, from collections of Sappho, Homer, and Shakespeare to T.S. Eliot, Ezra Pound, and recently published moderns like Robert Frost and Hart Crane. As Henriette thumbed through a copy of New Masses, a poem jumped out at her: "The men are revolution, who move/ in spreading hosts across the globe." She pictured a wave of men like ants spreading across the round globe that sat in Father's study at home, the tiny creatures multiplying and diverging until they covered the whole surface. The poet Edwin Rolfe was unknown to her, but farther on she found a favorite, Richard Wright, who proclaimed, "I am black, and I have seen black hands, millions and millions of them." Again the small multiplied until it became huge and strong. The agony of Sacco and Vanzetti transformed into the triumph Vanzetti foresaw.

Could she ever play a part in something so big and important? If she could be an ant among ants or a hand among hands, perhaps she could stop looking on and enter the river of action that counted. She pictured herself swimming in that river, buoyed by the water and borne by the current, no longer oppressed by civilization, her body and mind united by shared desire. The thought was intriguing, if scary, and the hope was like really living for the first time.

Back at her desk she mailed $1.50 for her own subscription to the magazine, and an acknowledgement soon arrived on *New Masses* letterhead addressed "Dear Miss Greenberg" and signed by the Business Manager, Sarah Segal. Miss Segal invited Henriette to stop by the office if she were ever in New York and hoped that Henriette would encourage her friends and classmates to subscribe.

Nadine invited Henriette to come to New York for Thanksgiving, and Henriette jumped at the chance to visit the city and to see Nadine's home. Henriette called Mother, sitting up straight in the hallway phone alcove and leaning into the wooden, wall-mounted device, straining to appease and knowing she would disappoint. Mother was blazing, barraging Henriette with questions about Nadine's family, what they did and where they lived. And how did Henriette expect her mother to prepare dinner for all the aunts and cousins by herself? Henriette hunched her shoulders and cowered as the questions rained down guilt, unable to feel the gathering clouds of her anger. Holding the long earpiece away from her ear, she looked at the voice coming out, now tinny. "I'm going to go," she said into the mouthpiece, still holding the earpiece away and sounding firmer than she felt.

"You must at least come home the weekend after," said Mother, and Henriette agreed.

THE ABRAVANELS' APARTMENT WAS A second-floor walk-up in Greenwich Village. Their building pressed up against its neighbors, leaving no room for a yard. Nadine pointed out the mezuzah on the doorpost as they arrived, and Henriette nodded, concealing her ignorance of what it meant. Mrs. Abravanel greeted Nadine with a big hug and Henriette with a pat and a smile, inviting them into a living room with a saggy looking couch and worn carpet. Beyond an archway, eight chairs squeezed tight around a dining table.

"Call me Marjorie," said Nadine's mother, leading the girls past the small, hot kitchen to the room with twin beds where they would sleep. Another bedroom and an enclosed back porch completed the floor-through apartment. Back in the living room, they greeted Nadine's father, just home from work. Henriette had been unsure about meeting him, given her own father's temper and tendency to get too close to her girlfriends, and she shook hands shyly. Heavyset, with dirt under his fingernails, he welcomed Nadine with open arms and Henriette with a firm handshake.

"Eddie," he said, and Henriette tried to picture her father with a nickname. Eddie's construction business had ground to a halt since the Crash, he explained, and he was working as painter and plumber, whatever he could get to keep going. Apparently he'd grown accustomed to hard times and didn't intend to let trouble interfere with his enjoyment of the holiday.

THE FIRST AFTERNOON IN NEW York, the two girls walked through the great marble arch onto Washington Square, then prowled the surrounding side streets. A light mist dampened the fall night and haloed the yellow streetlights, and the narrow streets twisted and turned like alleys, so dark corners suddenly opened onto bright storefronts, their light bouncing off the wet pavement. A window showcased a dress with a huge collar and plunging neckline and a swimsuit that covered arms but left the midriff bare.

"Would anyone ever wear that?" asked Henriette.

"They're one of a kind," said Nadine. "More like paintings, for display." They continued, Nadine elbowing through crowds and pointing out lofts where artists lived and showed their work, past house fronts jammed up against each other with stairs leading to ornately carved front doors and mailboxes perforated in elegant patterns. Old, intricate, and venerable. Impressions and people zoomed by so fast it seemed like the city itself was anxious. Everything too close. Compact and tense in the eyes, like Henriette herself.

When they got cold, they settled in a café on MacDougal Street, knees nearly touching, and drank espresso in little glasses with lemon peel floating on top. The hot, bitter drink tore a veil from Henriette's eyes, ears, and skin, giving her the world in vivid color and taste, almost hurting. Nadine's dark hair fell across one eye, and she leaned her ample arms on the table, nursing the coffee. Rising steam condensed on her skin, giving it a soft sheen.

"You've read my poems," said Nadine. "I think you know how I am." A shudder of apprehension went through Henriette as she realized that Nadine was going to talk about this openly. They'd become good friends, but Henriette relied on limits to intimacy. She attempted a neutral expression. "I'm a woman who loves women, a Lesbian," continued Nadine, her eyes searching Henriette's. Desperate to seem knowledgeable, Henriette was caught between the suspicion she'd gleaned from the poems and this frank confession, which knocked her off balance with its honesty.

"Yes, I did, or I thought…" Henriette tucked her feet back under her chair. Nadine's eyes softened with empathy.

"It's all right," she said. "It can take a while to get used to. And we can be better friends now we've talked about it." Henriette blinked, and the bright room seemed to vibrate with shock. How odd it was to know and not know something at the same time. She'd hoped she could just keep living with the sophistication of knowing and the safety of ignorance, but now Nadine was forcing her to acknowledge the fact, and she was scared.

"I understand. I know all about it," said Henriette, talking her way into a place where she didn't have to think about what loving women really meant. "Like Edna St. Vincent Millay, who used to call herself Vincent. I've read *The Well of Loneliness* too."

"I wasn't talking about a book or a famous poet," said Nadine." I was talking about myself." Henriette was confused again. How did people do this, let their true selves and feelings just blossom on their skin and fill the air around them with whatever their personal effusions might be? The girls walked home in silence, and Henriette thought of the night at the Lucky Laundry and her talk with Dilly at the restaurant. He'd been so loving that night, and she'd spoiled it by her breezy suggestion that she "might be like that" herself, like Henry Hankton. Dilly would never be so frank about Hankton as Nadine was about herself. Henriette wished she could put Nadine and Dilly in a room together, so Nadine could back up Henriette's broad-minded views and tell her if Dilly was too bourgeois. It hardly mattered now.

For Thanksgiving dinner, Mrs. Abravanel accompanied the traditional turkey with Jewish dishes Henriette had never eaten: honeyed carrot tzimmes and savory buckwheat kasha with mushrooms. She relaxed and discovered that she could eat in the atmosphere of the Abravanels' casual, argumentative dining room, where everyone tucked napkins into collars, served themselves food and passed it around, drank homemade wine and talked and smoked, expressing their opinions, free to disagree without rancor.

THE ABRAVANELS HAD LONG TRUSTED Nadine to go about on her own, and the next day Henriette and Nadine rode the bus up 5th Avenue to the office of *New Masses*. By the door a vendor was hawking hot chestnuts, and the girls smelled charcoal as they rang the bell. A thin woman with a black sweater tightly wrapped around her, perhaps fifteen years older than they, answered the door. She wore no make-up and welcomed them with a smile. "Are you Miss Segal?" asked Nadine.

"We're Henriette Greenberg and Nadine Abravanel, students from Chicago."

"Of course," said Miss Segal. "And you're our new subscribers. Come in, take off your coats, and call me Sarah." They all shook hands. The office was dusty and chilly, with three large wooden desks and plain folding chairs. Each desk held a big typewriter, and a man with slicked black hair, parted in the middle, sat at one, smoking a cigarette and typing. One grimy window looked out on the street, and piles of manuscripts and stacks of back issues filled all the corners of the room. "Let me show you around," said Sarah, introducing them to the black-haired man, the editor, who stopped writing just long enough to greet them, unsmiling. In the back, at a long table, a lanky man with sandy hair and a slightly crooked nose was putting labels on stacks of magazines.

"This is the mailing table," said Sarah. "And this is Phil, who helps us out and keeps us peppy, as well as writing plays."

"When I can't get a job," said Phil, pausing in his work and appraising the girls, head tilted to one side. He leaned against the table but held labels in his hands and continued tearing them apart. "Which is most of the time."

"Henriette and Nadine are from Chicago, the University," said Sarah. "We're hoping they can help strengthen the Chicago-*New Masses* connection."

"I can write letters asking friends to subscribe," said Henriette. "I'd be glad to do that."

"Very good," said Sarah. "That's what we need."

"Have you been so kind as to invite them to the party?" asked Phil. Sarah explained that on Saturday the magazine would celebrate its fourth birthday as a monthly at a John Reed Club, with musical groups from the Workers Music League and Mexican dancers, as well as toasts by Theodore Dreiser and Dorothy Parker. Henriette stood frozen, New York overwhelming her. Might she really attend a party at a club named for the man who'd reported the ten days that shook the world? In the presence of writers she'd read in the *New Yorker*?

"If, by any chance, those writers are still sober," added Phil. "I hope you'll indulge us with your presence. You have something important to contribute, namely, the idea that the University of Chicago is not just a bastion of privilege." He kept his eyes on Henriette while talking like a book, and she guessed he was interested in more than her revolutionary fervor. He was polite, but his attention felt wrong — too sudden and too mannered. Suddenly she thought of her parents, surprised that they could come in handy.

"My parents belong to a Unitarian Church and outreach center in Chicago," she said. "A lot of their friends might want to subscribe, and I could write them." The ants were marching two by two.

"Are they interested in Proletarian literature?" asked Sarah.

"Some are. But who doesn't want to read Langston Hughes and Hemingway?"

"Good girl," said Sarah, giving her shoulder a squeeze. "Would you write from Chicago?"

"Sure, I'll do it as soon as I get back."

"See you tomorrow," said Sarah, and the three walked to the door. "It'll be a hell of a party."

Henriette and Nadine took the bus to the Trade Union Unity League on West 17th Street, where the party would be held. The newspapers had reported bomb threats. Feeling deliciously revolutionary and scared enough to make their teeth chatter, the girls checked the street outside for the Radical Squad's riot wagon, reputed to carry tear gas bombs and submachine guns. So far there were no coppers around, but Henriette felt Father's disapproval all the way from Oak Park. She hoped she wouldn't get into trouble.

Inside, colored lights and paper lanterns decorated the cavernous hall, while posters for *The Daily Worker* and *Workers Age* lined the walls. The big crowd was much more varied than they had expected: older people, in three-piece suits for the men and silk blouses and pearls for the women; dancers in bright, long skirts and low-necked blouses, braids falling to their waists; men in blue work shirts and pants; the occasional man with a monocle accompanied by a lady in fur with multiple rings on her fingers. Negro musicians on the bandstand warmed up with dissonant wails and snippets of melody, while the crowd milled and talked in English and other languages, maybe Yiddish, perhaps Spanish. Sarah flew from group to group in the dark blue cotton dress she wore to the office, with puffy caps at the shoulders and a red scarf around her neck.

Henriette and Nadine slipped into the sea of talk and music. A band played "Pack up your troubles in your old kit bag and smile, smile, smile," and smiles abounded, relieving Henriette's anxiety. Soon Phil descended on the girls, wearing a bright red shirt, and put an arm around each of their shoulders.

"Our young visitors from Chicago!" he exclaimed. "Can I fetch you ladies some punch?" He brought them cups of liquid, sweet and fruity with a burn at the end. Sarah swirled past, welcoming them, but Phil stayed, introducing them to passing poets, union organizers, and supporters of the magazine. Nadine found people she knew from the National Student League and drifted off.

"I don't want to impose my presence on you any longer than you wish," said Phil after a while, leaning down so Henriette could hear him over the music and talk. He made her uncomfortable, but she didn't want to be left alone in this crowd.

"I'm glad you can tell me who's who," replied Henriette. The band stopped, and the *New Masses* editor rose to the speaker's platform to thank people for coming and recapitulate the magazine's history and mission, then introduced Theodore Dreiser, a man with heavy jowls and thick white hair.

He spoke slowly, his words falling like grains of sand, only gradually joining to form a solid ground for his message. "I've just returned from the Soviet Union," he began. "They're collectivizing farms from Moscow to Vladivostok, modernizing agriculture and industry. And in that young country, I want you to know, racial discrimination is against the law. Forbidden. Whereas right here, right now, in our very own state of Alabama, nine young Negro teen-agers are languishing in prison, awaiting death, with no evidence against them. Let me tell you the story."

"In March of this year, a group of boys and two white girls hopped a freight gondola. White and Negro boys got in a fight, and the white boys fell or were thrown off. They wired authorities to stop the train. The two girls accused the Negroes of rape. Anyone who understands the psychology of Southern people realizes that the news of Negroes alone with white girls is enough to make rape a fact. " Dreiser raised his arms and voice and slowed still further. "Where is due process? Do we let the mob rule? Stop this legal lynching! Demand justice! Support the defense of the Scottsboro Boys!" The crowd roared its support, Henriette along with them, and goosebumps rose on her arms. Dreiser circulated a letter addressed to the Governor of Alabama and signed by the National Committee for the Defense of Political Prisoners, of which he was chair. Other signers included anthropologist Franz Boaz and writers Malcolm Cowley and John Dos Passos. Henriette's parents were as ashamed of the convictions in Scottsboro as Mr. Dreiser, and she was glad to add her signature.

Then Dorothy Parker, only slightly tipsy, with broad-brimmed hat curved seductively over straight bangs, told of her trip to Boston a few years before to protest the execution of Sacco and Vanzetti. She'd been arrested, along with Edna St. Vincent Millay and Katherine Anne Porter, convicted of "loitering and sauntering," and fined five dollars. Now she charmed the audience with a rhyme about wishing for a limousine and getting just a rose.

Sarah waited for laughter to die away, then took the microphone. From her slight frame came a deep and resonant voice, as she thanked contributors to the evening and to the magazine, pointing out individuals and groups in the house. She spoke of the seven million unemployed, some here in the room and herself soon to be one of them, if the magazine didn't raise the funds to pay her. "Musicians, dancers, and writers have given their time and skill tonight to entertain you, and each of you can and should give as much to the cause of the unemployed," she said, making eye contact with as many individuals as possible. "When you write out your checks, don't think of me or the magazine's paltry production costs, but think of the voice the magazine gives to the seven million starving in Hoovervilles and on breadlines." Her voice rose, and she opened her arms to embrace the whole hall. "*New Masses* speaks for the seven million. If you gave a dollar for each of those unemployed" — she paused, then shouted, arms raised overhead — "we'd raise seven million dollars tonight." Henriette was awed at Sarah's persuasive and courageous speech. It seemed she, like Nadine, held nothing back. And Mr. Dreiser? He'd actually made the trip to the Soviet Union and knew whereof he spoke. New York was the furthest she'd been from home, and she felt a prick of ambition to step out herself, into the abrasive world.

A Negro man in a dark suit mounted the bandstand and began singing in a bass voice, a capella, to the tune of the "Battle Hymn of the Republic":

When the union's inspiration through the workers' blood shall run,

There can be no power greater anywhere beneath the sun;
Yet what force on earth is weaker than the feeble strength of one;
For the union makes us strong.

The band came in behind him, piano and sax swelling the sound and bass drum booming. The crowd joined on the chorus, Henriette pouring a sense of devotion and commitment into her alto singing voice: "Solidarity forever, for the union makes us strong." Verse after verse and chorus after chorus, the song united the singers. Ushers passed baskets. Solidarity — that's what Henriette felt. Solid earth beneath her feet, voice rising to the sky, and the crowd connecting her to all humanity. Here she didn't have to stand apart; here she could disappear into the multitudes and still count, still be part of something that might change the world. Dr. Whitson should see her now, should know how she felt, should understand that this was all she needed — solidarity. The trip would make analysis obsolete, and Henriette couldn't wait to tell the doctor.

Suddenly Nadine was by Henriette's side, black hair flying and cheeks glowing pink. "Wasn't she wonderful?"

"And how," said Henriette, surprised by a break in her voice, so strong a moment before.

Nadine moved on to say a few more goodbyes, and Henriette stood with Phil, who leaned on a wall, long frame all bent angles, and said, "I can't help but admire your utter independence and charming self-assurance." Henriette wondered if it were really she he was talking about. "You are one of those rare females who is both lovable and capable," he continued. His tone unnerved her. Was he angling for intimacy she didn't want? "It's a good thing you're going back to Chicago. I think I could become frightfully unhappy over you."

Frightfully unhappy. She wished she could have that effect on even-tempered Dilly. His long-ago kiss. The squeeze of his arms. The union of brain and body that made him move like a pacing tiger. She'd like to escort him right into this John Reed Club and introduce him to her new friends, but first she'd have to explain who John Reed was, and once he knew, he might walk right out. No matter how much he favored Andrew Jackson's common man over Professor Hankton's elites, he'd never sympathize with revolutionaries. Maybe that was why he'd let her slip away.

THE TWO GIRLS LAY IN their beds late that night, rehashing the party.

"Sarah was so brave," said Henriette. She propped her head on one hand. "I think I have a crush on her." She surprised herself with this admission, but the dark made it easier to let feelings make their way into words.

"Is it more than a crush?" asked Nadine.

"I don't know. I'm glad you talked to me in the coffee shop, and I am crazy about Sarah. Does that make me like you?"

"Not necessarily," said Nadine, putting her hands behind her head. "Well, what do you dream of? Men, women, what?" Henriette closed her eyes and let her mind roam. She was silent for a moment.

"I'm singing with a band," she said. "All the musicians are black, and we sleep on the bus as we travel. Each day we play in a new town, and I'm the white girl who stands up front and sings," and she sang a line, her deep contralto almost tangible in the dark:

Pack up all my cares and woe, here I go, singing low;
Bye, bye, blackbird. There somebody waits for me;
Sugar's sweet; so is he.
Blackbird, bye-bye.

THE SWEETNESS, THE LONGING, AND the sad farewell made her throat ache. Springs creaked as Nadine rolled toward her in the bed just three feet away, and Henriette squinted, trying to see Nadine's face and considering whether this might be an invitation. Henriette did love Nadine's warmth, wisdom, and generosity and almost wished she could slip across the chasm of possibility to snuggle under Nadine's comfy covers, but snuggling was bound to lead to a place she couldn't go. In fact, the thought of sex with anyone but herself was unimaginable unless it had an element — God forbid! — of force: the alien from space, the dark stranger who climbs in a window. Her needs were her own private shame, the shame that had paralyzed her, pinned like a butterfly on her living room couch, eating an apple at a time outside of memory, and she couldn't reveal or share those needs with anyone else.

"I'm hearing music and black men," said Nadine with a smile Henriette could hear. "I don't think you're like me, and it's a good thing too, because Sarah isn't like me either, and you'd be in for a big heartbreak if you were really falling for her. I hope you'll be friends with her for a long time."

"Thanks, Nadine," said Henriette, glad Nadine understood her. Nadine was right that she wasn't Lesbian, but what about all the rest their talk had brought up? Sometimes she wanted to crumple up her badly made self and throw it away. If only she could forget the past she couldn't quite remember and stop it from jumping out of dark rooms, sweet songs, and friendship.

Next morning, Henriette could smell the party's smoke lingering in her sweater and skirt. She had taken a small part in something important, and it had been fun and worthwhile. She'd held her own at the party, been friendly to Phil without encouraging him unduly, and she would help *New Masses* get a few more subscriptions. Who gets what, she thought. How Hankton's motto simplifies things. Against her will her thoughts returned to Dilly, far away and long ago.

Chapter 8

Arriving at the house in Oak Park for her promised visit, Henriette entered the hallway and watched the majestic staircase spiral out of sight, feeling like a character in a melodrama, an unwitting accomplice to the scene about to unfold. Father's stereopticon waited for viewers, stolid, atop wooden drawers of wallflower slides, but no ghosts jumped out from behind it.

"I'm home," she called out. That was her opening line.

Mother emerged from the kitchen, wearing an apron, and gave her a peck on the cheek.

"Your room's all ready. You can go up and change," and she pointed to the small suitcase Henriette had brought. "Russell's already here, upstairs. Carl's on his way. Dinner's at six, of course." Henriette had not intended to change and decided to try out this small rebellion. Upstairs she passed the twins' room, where signs nailed on the door still said "Throw the Rascals Out," "Britannia Rule the Waves," and "From the Prison to the White House." Feeling a twinge of her old envy of her brothers' closeness, she knocked on the door of their inner sanctum.

"Yes?"

"Can I come in?"

"Sure." Russell sat slumped on the edge of a bunk bed, elbows on knees. On the floor rested the catapult he and Carl had built to fire missiles at squirrels from their second story window.

"Give me a hug," she said, and he stood and embraced her lightly, then sat again. "I want to tell you about college. I went to New York for Thanksgiving and a party for *New Masses*…"

"Slow down," said Russell, with a tired laugh. "What's *New Masses*?

"A left-wing paper. I'll give you a copy when I unpack. Then you should subscribe."

"Not me," he said. "Not if it comes by mail to Purdue." He shook his head and spoke with effort. Henriette sat on the bunk beside him.

"You look like you're in the dumps," she said. He picked up the catapult and aimed it at the window, sighting along his arm.

"I don't know," he said, lowering the catapult. "I don't see much future in my studies, and times are hard and getting harder. The house is like a tomb. Father says nothing about getting me into Sears. I'll be done with business school in two years, and jobs are impossible to get these days if you don't have a connection." Henriette thought of Dilly, who might have an even harder time.

"What about friends?" asked Henriette. "Have you met any girls at Purdue?" She had a queasy feeling that this was the wrong thing to ask, but she didn't know how else to put it. Russell smiled apologetically and shook his head, then took a breath.

"I don't think you can imagine Purdue," he said, words emerging slowly from the fog that seemed to surround him. "The way you and Carl talk, you wouldn't survive a day there. No one talks about neuroses or Communism, let alone sex. Purdue is one big lesson in how to fit into the real world. And it's hard to get along there with a name like Greenberg."

"There are lots of Jews at Chicago," said Henriette. "My roommate, Effie — she's Jewish, and so is my friend, Nadine. She's a wonderful poet, and she doesn't care what anyone says. You and Carl didn't use to care either," and she pointed to the nails driven into the door over parental objection.

"Well Purdue's as Protestant as Oak Park, and there aren't any Jews there, or at least any visible ones besides me. I'm thinking of changing my name."

"You are?" Henriette was taken aback. For all her hope of escaping, she'd never thought she could cut that particular family tie. Though in a way Mother already had. When she'd traveled as a girl with her own father, selling Levis door to door in Indian country, he'd tried to gather a *minyan* for Sabbath prayers. He wouldn't count Mother because she was a girl, and she'd decided then and there she'd never be a part of that religion. So perhaps Russell was merely carrying out Mother's intention.

"I'm trying to fit into the world outside this house," he continued, "and Purdue is teaching me that I have to re-design myself entirely." He pushed the catapult away. Now the twins' shared room seemed outmoded, covered in dust, and Henriette thought with nostalgia of the days when the door was closed, and everything inside was mysterious. Thuds and groans from behind the door — collaboration or conflict? Either way, she'd felt excluded. Each of them had always watched so closely what the other thought and did.

Voices from below indicated Carl's arrival, and soon Henriette heard the kitchen door swing open. Probably Carl was with Mother, turning down the oven temperature and telling her the broccoli was boiling too long. Then footsteps on the stairs. A knock on the bedroom door, and Carl entered, gave Russell a rough hug, and turned to Henriette.

"Hi," she said, suddenly awkward, unsure whether she was a college student and friend of Nadine or still Father's favorite and Mother's barely acknowledged girl. Carl gave her a hesitant peck on the cheek, as though he, too, was confused which one she was. "We were talking about Purdue," said Henriette. "Russell said he was thinking about changing his name to something less Jewish."

Carl gave a hoot. "Who are you going to fool?" he asked. "A skunk flower by any other name..."

"Look who's talking," scoffed Russell. "The big psychiatrist who thinks he's going to get rich."

"Married, too."

"Go ahead. Play the part. See where it gets you."

Wait and see," said Carl. Henriette wanted to talk about New York and *New Masses* but realized her interests paled before her brothers' strident competition. Everything they said seemed to carry coded meaning. She went downstairs and asked if she could help. Father was not yet home. Mother frowned briefly at Henriette's outfit.

"You like this sweater, right, Mother?" she asked, the need to please straining her voice.

"Anything so long as you're clean and decent," said Mother, sighing as she began to ladle celery soup from a pot on the iron stove into bowls.

"Won't we wait for Father?" asked Henriette.

"Certainly not," said Mother. The house felt empty without him. Henriette carried a bowl of soup into the formal dining room, where the table was set for five at one end, and the polished wood spread beyond the settings like a dark sea under moonlight. The grassy smell of celery, Henriette's favorite vegetable, wafted from the soup, and she inhaled, comforting herself with this small pleasure. The boys came down, still talking loudly as they took seats. Mother said grace. Here Henriette had no lines. The vacuum of Mother's expectations sucked at her, and the voices around her faded, while words she'd heard during her year at home rose and echoed in her mind.

I DIDN'T KNOW YOU HAD A GIRL. That was Mrs. Witherspoon, a founder of Abraham Lincoln Center, social outreach program of All Souls Church, where Mother served on the Board. "A daughter, imagine!" Mrs. Witherspoon had said on meeting Henriette. "I knew about your sons."

Mother had become more and more involved in the Center's services as Negro migration to Chicago increased, and Henriette went with her one morning, dressed carefully in white cotton blouse and dark skirt. She knew how much Mother respected the Center and how high her standard would be for Henriette's behavior in front of the other volunteers, mostly members of All Souls Church. No low-waisted flapper look today. But nothing Henriette wore or said or did could meet that standard, for All Souls belonged to the halcyon period of Mother's life, the days of her courtship and early marriage, while Henriette belonged to the disappointing present.

Leonard, the family's Negro driver and the only servant they retained, arrived at nine and pulled the car around the front of the house. The two women got into the back seat. After passing a few blocks of stately homes, they drove across muddy prairie to the tenements of Chicago's West side. Brightly colored laundry hung on rickety porches, and children ran in the street, rolling marbles, skipping rope or picking rags. A group of men warmed themselves at a big can filled with fire and smoke, and the bitter smell filtered through the triangular no-draft window.

"Close the no-draft," said Mother, wrinkling her nose, and Leonard pushed it closed. From a storefront, a long line of people stretched to the corner and on around the block. Henriette leaned forward to speak to Leonard, seeking an ally.

"Why are the men in line?" she asked, afraid she knew the answer.

"Soup," he said. "They're waiting for soup. See the bowls in their hands?" His voice was gruff, and Henriette regretted her stupid question. The thought of all those people with nothing to eat was horrible, and she felt powerless to do anything about it. The blue of Lake Michigan appeared out of the window of the car, a dark, white-flecked expanse that met the sky's paler blue at the horizon. She thought of wading into that frigid water, feet growing numb, then knees, then thighs, until all feeling was gone. Suddenly the terror of not being gripped her, and she raised the back of a hand to her mouth, as if to stifle a yawn, but bit down hard on her knuckles. The sudden pain returned her to the reality of the car, and tears threatened. She needed someone. Not Leonard, not Mother, but whom? Maybe her work today at Abraham Lincoln Center could forge a connection between herself and the hungry mob, could at least provide a warm coat for someone shivering, could comfort her own soul with a little human kindness. Mother's high-principled philanthropy was as ironclad as her rules about dinner and her corseted body, and neither would bend to find Henriette adorable or give her a hug. The car turned south and proceeded inland, where occasional vacant lots, overgrown with weeds, appeared among tenements.

"You were born just blocks from here," said Mother, as they pulled up in front of an imposing, red brick building. "At Michael Reese Hospital." Henriette winced to recall the familiar story of the agony her birth had caused Mother, the shrieks and blood that had indentured the infant girl, creating a debt she could never repay. And that baby, now grown, bore the burden of a parallel body, condemned to the same suffering.

Henriette dragged herself out of the car, dreading the hours under Mother's management. Inside, the building bustled with activity. Classrooms were filled with nursery-aged children, and meeting rooms held adults. One large room contained clothing in piles, and Mother assigned Henriette to a big bag, designating locations for shirts, pants, and accessories. Henriette shook out a pair of pants and smoothed it, holding it by the sides of the waistband. "Not like that," said Mother. "Hold it by the front and back, to get the crease in front."

"Yes, Mother," Henriette said, wishing she could be just numb enough to get through these hours without risking utter annihilation. Other volunteers arrived, and Mother chatted with them, introducing Henriette but never slowing in her work. About noon a Negro woman in a broad-brimmed hat entered the room, a fox fur around her neck. She wore a wool suit in a dark red color and looked to be in charge. Mother hurried over to Henriette and tapped her arm.

"That's Mrs. Witherspoon. She's one of the founders. We serve on the Board together. Mother returned to her pile of clothes, but now her smoothing and folding had a new urgency, and she looked up from time to time to follow Mrs. Witherspoon's progress. The founder walked slowly around the room, greeting each of the volunteers. Finally she came to Mother.

"Good morning, Mrs. Greenberg," said Mrs. Witherspoon. "And who is this?"

"My daughter, Henriette," said Mother. "This is Mrs. Witherspoon, a founder of Abraham Lincoln Center." Henriette extended her hand and received a limp shake.

"I didn't know you had a daughter," Mrs. Witherspoon had said. "A daughter, imagine! I knew about your sons." Mrs. Witherspoon's eyes had alighted briefly on Henriette and then slid away like gelatin from a spoon. Unmentioned and unseen, she could just as well have waded into that cold water. Panic had risen in her again, and she'd excused herself and run to the bathroom, trying to get out of her skin. She threw cold water on her face and wondered how much longer she could stand being nothing and no one.

Henriette looked down at her soup bowl, as empty as she, then up at Russell and Carl, with a rueful smile that apologized for her absent-minded eating. She wished she hadn't come home or that Father would arrive. She carried the bowls to the kitchen, and returned with a serving dish of Shepherd's pie, beef stew topped with mashed potatoes in little brown peaks. Mother brought buttered kohlrabi. They took their seats as Father entered and smiled to see his daughter.

'You're home,' he said, and rushed over to kiss her on the cheek, then shook Russell's and Carl's hands and gave Mother a peck.

"You're late," said Mother. "We've had the soup." Father retreated to his end of the table. While Henriette poked her Shepherd's pie apart, arranging bits in a circle around the kohlrabi, her parents discussed the Japanese invasion of Manchuria (bad) and violence on the streets in Germany (worse). Mother blamed them both on the worldwide Depression and attributed that to "the reckless self-indulgence of recent years."

"Self-indulgence?" asked Carl. "Is that a euphemism for the pansy clubs? You should go sometime. They're hotsy-totsy." Russell exchanged glances with Mother. She sniffed and scowled at Carl.

"Self-indulgence!" said Father. "That's nothing compared to what's happening in Germany. Have you heard about Mrs. Sinclair Lewis's book, *I Saw Hitler*? She says he has his own army, men in brown shirts making Jews scrub the streets. Soon it will be the pogroms of the Pale all over again."

"I read her piece in *Cosmopolitan*," said Henriette. "She goes by her maiden name, Dorothy Thompson, and she's not scared. She called Hitler "little, insignificant, almost feminine.""

"She says Hitler has gone legal," said Mother, nodding to Henriette. "Making speeches and campaigning for votes. While here it's all freewheeling speakeasies and so-called fun. Thank God Miss Addams organized Juvenile Protection to look out for the children."

"A newsletter like *Friendship and Freedom* does no harm to children." Father's face began to get red, and Mother put a calming hand on his arm. He jerked it away and stood halfway up from his chair. "You listen to me. The Human Rights Society sent out one edition of their newsletter, and the next thing you knew, the founders were in jail, and the post office was helping the police identify everyone who received a copy. It's more like Germany than America. I wouldn't call that freewheeling."

"Those — let's say, eccentrics — can control themselves, and so can you," said Mother. Father's cough took over, and he sputtered and clutched his chest, his tantrum escalating into a familiar attack of breathlessness and fury, but this time he began to stagger, and his eyes rolled upward.

"Get his pills!" commanded Mother, and Henriette raced up the stairs, returning with the bottle of tiny glycerin capsules. Father was slumped in his chair, face pale and sweaty, and Mother slipped a pill into his mouth and under his tongue. Everyone watched anxiously as his breathing slowly returned to normal and his color came back.

"I'll call Dr. Patches," said Mother. "We'll see him tomorrow."

"Solidarity" notwithstanding, Henriette continued her sessions with Dr. Whitson. At her next appointment, she thought of the day she helped Mother at Abraham Lincoln Center. She began again to imagine the frigid lake and the way it could numb your toes, your ankles, your whole self. She described the feeling, skipping over the panic that had followed, and said, "I wouldn't mind giving up at all."

"Say more about that," said Dr. Whitson.

With a flash of anger, Henriette was tempted to mimic the doctor's oft-repeated phrase in a nasty tone, but stifled the impulse. "Everything is just too much," she said. "What a relief it would be if it were over!"

"Do you ever wish you were dead?" asked Dr. Whitson, surprising Henriette with the direct question. Dead, dead, thought Henriette. She'd seen herself as though dead two years ago — in fact, that was how she'd ended up on this couch — but she wasn't about to open that embarrassing can of worms. Once you started on a subject in the charged and anxious space of this little office, you couldn't get away from it. "What are you thinking about?" asked Dr. Whitson.

Henriette sighed and wondered how long she'd been lying there without saying anything. "I'd like for everything to just go away. But I don't really care."

"I think you do care," said Dr. Whitson, using more words than she had all fall. "I think you're afraid that anything or anyone you really care about will abandon you. You fear that you are worthless. Do you remember anything else about the day you went to Lincoln Center?"

"No, just that I didn't want to go, and Mother kept correcting the way I folded the clothes. I can't do anything right, not there or at home. She keeps needing me and needling me, complaining she's tired or in pain —'I grated my finger, and I shrieked with pain,' she says, or 'I have terrible cramps, both gastric and colonic'— and whatever I do makes it worse." A long silence followed.

"What about your father? asked Dr. Whitson, finally.

"She orders him around too, and she makes the rules. He's sweet when he's in a good mood, photographing wildflowers, but you never know..." her voice faded off. Silence grew and filled the small office until Henriette imagined she could hear the plants growing and herself shedding cells and manufacturing new ones. Maybe it was time to really answer Dr. Whitson's question.

"One afternoon, when I was in high school, I borrowed a book by Margaret Sanger. Mother admired Sanger and read her newsletter,

The Woman Rebel — 'No Gods, No Masters' was its slogan. But this book, *What Every Girl Should Know*, came out of Sanger's work on birth control. I came home and lay down on the living room couch with the book and an apple. Father came home early, sat down by me, and started…talking and touching my leg."

"And then what?" Henriette said nothing. Dr. Whitson persisted, "What exactly did he do?"

"I'm not sure I remember it right," said Henriette, though the memory was etched in her brain and body, sharp and vivid. Sanger's book was contraband, passed around high school in a plain brown wrapper, while its author had been arrested and her clinic closed down long before. Returning from school, Henriette had begun to eat and read about sex, birth control, and venereal disease, and she was still reading when Father returned early from work and sat on the couch beside her. She set the pamphlet upside down on her stomach and put her hands behind her head. Father began talking about spring, while his hand, which seemed to belong to someone else, caressed her stockinged calf, her bare knee, and then her thigh. This could not be happening, she told herself. Some demon had risen from the book to inhabit her father, her erratic but usually conventional, always hard-working father. Paralyzed by disbelief and wondering what she had done wrong, ashamed and unable to look at him, she lay pinned like a butterfly as his hand approach her private center of feeling.

"All I know is I couldn't move," said Henriette. "Father was doing something he would never do, and he was just looking off into space and talking about flowers."

"Tell me what he did," said Dr. Whitson. Paralyzed by this demand, Henriette tried to hold back tears, but they threatened to leak out anyway. "Did it happen more than once?" Silence. "Your shame is caused by your own feelings. They were aroused first by the book you were reading and then by whatever happened with your father." Now Henriette was furious. She'd been disgusted, not aroused. How could the doctor expect her to spell out things she herself could barely believe? And saying it once wasn't enough?

The doctor continued her questions. "Why did you lie down to read on the living room couch? Couldn't you have gone to your room?" Henriette wished she'd never broached the subject. How could she not be ashamed? Silence reigned for minutes, and soundless tears spilled onto her cheeks. The feeling of being helpless, trapped by unwanted feeling, was real. Her father and his hand could not be. She must be crazy, she thought, and hurried to change the subject.

"Remember the boy I met?" she asked. "He's hasn't asked me out since that first time."

"Why do you think that is?"

"Well, he comes from a failing farm, hunts to survive, and has never been analyzed. Maybe we're just too different." Henriette detected Dr. Whitson's little smile sound. "I can't stop thinking about him."

"Maybe you were too quick to reveal yourself," said Dr. Whitson. "Get to know him on a casual basis, little by little, and entrust your demons to me." I just tried to, thought Henriette, and you only made it worse. "Time to go. See you next week." Henriette left, head swimming. In fifty minutes Dr. Whitson had changed from a blank canvas into a vivid and opinionated person who misinterpreted her dangerous memory and then, for the first time, gave her advice.

Chapter 9

Lucky had not attempted to see Henriette after the night they'd spent together, and she thought he'd forgotten her entirely, but now he began to write to her at the dorm, telling her that she was with him in spirit all the time. "You aren't much trouble," he wrote. "You fit in nicely. In fact you're necessary." The idea of being Lucky's mental companion appealed to her. She wrote him back and began to carry him along with her as well. But when he began to address her as "darlink" and sign off, "all of my love," she shrank. She couldn't help but admire his contempt for propriety, and she even felt kinship with his freedom to say what he wanted, when he wanted, but her words about sex floated at a distance, detached from feelings, while his words riled her up, exciting and disgusting. She was appalled when he wrote of his lewd wish for "a widow who would offer room and board in exchange for three to eight orgasms a day." Probably her fault. If she were properly made, Father's hand would never have shamed her, and Mother would have boasted about her as freely as she must have done about the boys. If Henriette were made right, she could grow up and accept Lucky's language.

One day, after Thanksgiving, she recognized his handwriting on an envelope in her mailbox. With a mixture of private pleasure and dread, she took the letter to her room to read. Effie was out, and she closed the door, then unfolded the yellow paper and focused on the uneven, typed characters.

"I'm remembering the lovely rise of your breast," she read. The intersection of their bodies rose vividly in her mind, and she screwed up her face as if to scream, but all that came out was a squeak and a tear. It was unbearable that her body should be in that letter, next to his widows and prostitutes. She didn't get it. Even though she'd felt reduced to a thing by their intimacy, she thought it must signify some kind of serious intent on his part. How could he know her body so completely and not care at all about her self? Apparently he intended to see her again. "I dream of you and wake up all wet," he wrote, and she shuddered at the thought of meeting him again in the flesh. Unable to throw either him or his letter away, she tore it into halves and quarters and then tucked the fragments into her diary.

HENRIETTE WAS DRINKING COFFEE AT Carl's on a snowy Sunday morning when Russell turned up carrying a black suitcase. "Wait 'til you see this," he said, breathless and exuding cold air. He whipped off a scarf and jacket and knelt by the suitcase. "I borrowed it from school to show to Father. He wasn't very interested, but you will be."

He unlatched the clasps and removed an oblong shaped brown box with two small dials, a face with numbers, and a square opening covered with cloth. "It's a portable radio," he said, lifting it with care. "It's like discovering you have wings. All you need is air, and you can hear sounds from all over the world. I saw this ad for it with a girl who was literally blown right off her feet, and I had to try it. You can take it anywhere, and you won't believe what you'll hear."

Henriette remembered Dilly's interest in crystal radios. "I know someone who would love this," she said. The departmental secretary was glad to give her his number, and she called him up. He sounded happy to hear her and said he'd soon be over. Russell plugged in the radio and began fiddling with the dials. Loud static attacked their ears, and he turned down the volume.

"Don't think you're going to get anything," said Carl, and offered coffee.

Soon Dilly arrived and looked from one brother to the other. "Which is which?" he asked.

"My brother Russell," said Carl. "Russell, this is Dilly. Anthropology student. Henriette's friend." Dilly and Russell shook hands.

"You'll learn to tell them apart," said Henriette, taking Dilly's coat. "Carl's face is a little broader, right here, through the cheekbones," and she threw the coat on a chair and reached up to measure Carl's face, one hand on each side. Dilly joined Russell on the living room floor, adjusting the antenna and trying different positions for the box.

"I used to spend hours fooling with my crystal set, searching for a voice or a tune."

"Just wait," said Russell. "This will be corking." Suddenly music came through loud and clear, and a man's voice began to sing, "I've said skidoo to the hard-time blues, and from here on in, I'm smilin' through." Henriette cheered, and all crowded closer to listen. A doctor came on, promoting goat gland transplants for impotence, and promising permanent cures in a Cadillac version for the rich, and a poor folks' version for everyone else. The suggestive "Organ Grinder's Blues" began to play, but instead of "Take your organ, grinder, and grind some more for me," the doctor sang, "Gonna get me some monkey glands, be like I use to wuz." Russell and Dilly hooted with laughter and delight, and Henriette and Russell danced around the room. Carl was silent.

"We got it," crowed Russell. "That signal's coming all the way from Mexico. You're listening to a border blaster, a monster so powerful you can hear it anywhere, and they broadcast whatever they want. The U.S. can't stop them. Isn't it amazing?"

"Amazing yes, but what he's saying is a bunch of jive, pure malarkey," said Carl. "Someone should stop that guy from selling glands."

"It's wonderful that the signal travels so far," said Dilly. "How do they do it?"

"Seventy-five thousand watts in the transmitter they tell me," said Russell. "And there's some kind of sky wave. The radio waves bounce off the atmosphere, like skipping rocks across a pond, and travel all over the globe." The four settled around the radio again and listened as an announcer introduced Sarah, Maybelle, Jeanette, Helen, June and Anita Carter, who sang, "Keep on the sunny side, always on the sunny side, keep on the sunny side of life." Talks on graphology and temperance followed, each speaker asking listeners to send in a dollar.

"What a crazy galoot!" said Carl. "As bad as those Listerine rumors Mother falls for, claiming it can clean your floor or cure the clap."

"Carl," admonished Henriette, nudging him with her elbow and trying to transmit some of the room's high spirits. Russell looked like he'd like to heave some pudding across the room and watch it settle into his brother's thick curls.

"They try to shut those stations down," said Russell, as he packed up the radio. "But they can't reach over the border. Sounds have wings — all they need is air, and air doesn't know borders. The radio waves are free as the breeze and go wherever it blows."

In December Carl invited Dilly to join his Wednesday poker group, where students, reporters, and political activists played for pennies in a smoky apartment. The two men became closer, found a place and moved in together. The living room looked out on an airshaft, always dark, but the white stucco walls and ceiling of the small kitchen reflected sunlight from a back porch, and bedrooms in front and back of the apartment gave them room to sleep and study. Now Henriette got to see more of Dilly and found herself reigning at the apex of a triangle. Perhaps this was what Dr. Whitson had meant by "a casual basis."

A small pressure cooker came on the market, adapted for preparing meals — a new toy for the men. One Saturday they found some plums still for sale and took them home to experiment, stopping by Foster to pick up Henriette on the way. On the apartment's radio, Louis Armstrong sang, "I'm a ding-dong Daddy from Dumas, and you oughta see me do my stuff. I'm a ping pong Papa," and he segued into scat. Dilly joined in, improvising syllables the way Satchmo did, holding up the cooker's lid and dancing with it. Henriette sang along, grabbing another lid and making it dance with Dilly's. The lids made a syncopated percussion accompaniment to the scat, and Henriette added her own syllables, feeling her hips loosen and soften her awkward angles. Carl checked a recipe. They filled the pot with fruit, sugar, and water; closed and locked the lid; put on the pressure regulator; and turned on the heat. Carl pulled out his watch with a second hand, and they waited, staring at the pot. Soon the regulator began to jiggle a little and then to rock.

"How long do we cook it?" asked Dilly.

"Try five minutes," said Carl.

"Time it exactly. It says not to overcook." Dilly read the instructions, and Carl followed them. After five minutes, Carl tipped the regulator, and reddish steam hissed out. Carl jumped back, tipping it still further. The steam hissed louder. The valve flew off, and Henriette yelped, ducking into the living room.

"What the hell!" yelled Carl.

"Sonovabitch!" said Dilly. They both pulled back to the doorway as steam spurted from the cooker in a great fountain, red deepening to violet as it rose, thinned, and spread to settle on the white stucco walls and ceiling, coating the room with a sticky, purple layer. When at last they opened the cooker, there was nothing inside but a few bits of blackish peel.

Henriette fled to the living room, and the men joined her. All collapsed on the couch, gasping and laughing, Henriette's shoulder bumping into Dilly's and pressing close as the laughter dissipated. A few minutes later they took rags and tried wiping the walls, but it was hopeless.

"What will the landlord say?" asked Dilly. "Looks like expensive damage."

"The landlord's not your father," said Carl, dropping his rag in the sink. Dilly continued wiping, and Henriette took Carl's rag and began helping, knowing Dilly had to worry about money and hoping Carl hadn't offended him.

"Isn't your mother looking over your shoulder?" asked Dilly.

"I've got Mother under control," said Carl. "I've already taught her how to cook properly. But she's a big hater, and that's no way to live. I intend to change the world by changing people, freeing their creativity and ability to love. And believe me, a purple kitchen is more creative and works just as well as a white one." Henriette saw Dilly wince at "hater" and then shrug before dismantling and washing the pressure cooker. They all returned to the living room, where Carl sprawled on the couch. Gray light filtered in from the airshaft and cars honked outside.

"Things are getting worse all over," said Dilly. "No jobs anywhere, so many hungry here and back home in Kitachara." Henriette thought of the people living in boxes on Lower Wacker Drive, huddled under blankets or over cans of Sterno, desperate for warmth. In the year since the Crash things had only gotten worse. "We have to work harder for change in the system," she said. "Subscribe to *New Masses* and sell the paper." Her suggestion sounded hollow, and she realized she'd heard no news of the Alabama Supreme Court's ruling on the appeal of the

Scottsboro Boys. The young men had been languishing in rat-infested Kilby Prison for nine months now, waiting for news, and the Court was taking its time.

"Nothing wrong with the system," said Dilly. "It's worked before, and it will work again." Then, to Carl: "What do you think about left-wing politics? Do you think they've got answers to bread lines and unemployment?"

"No, and I don't think any kind of politics has answers to war or common unhappiness or any other human ills," said Carl, sitting up and leaning forward, elbows on knees. "Economic disaster is a sign of something wrong with people. We need a whole new theory of human nature that fosters development, and I'm determined to find it."

"That sounds grandly ambitious," said Dilly. "Big theories tend to lead their followers astray."

Henriette returned to scrubbing the rough, resistant stucco, as though her efforts could bring her closer to Dilly. His presence flooded her with both warmth and doubts. What if he was too knowledge-able, too competent, too sane? And what if she was too young, too timid, too neurotic? She needed both Carl and Dilly, and she needed them together. Her whole body strained to make them see each other's points of view. "What about Freud?" she asked. "He's got a theory of human nature."

"I'm studying Freud, and soon I'll be starting a training analysis at the new Institute. You have to get started on your own analysis before you're admitted to the program. It can take years," said Carl with a sigh. "But I question the importance of the father, of the Oedipus complex." Now his voice slowed and grew direct. "And I hate and despise the idea of achieving manhood. I've no intention of becoming my father."

"I don't want to be like my father either," said Dilly, standing and turning on a floor lamp. "The old duffer's a penny pinching Republican.

But I damn well want to be a man, even more of a man than Father. I want to be like my grandfather, a Democrat who went to Washington to work for Grover Cleveland in the Post Office. I want to be Grandpa in the photo where my father and uncles are little boys, and Grandpa sits in the middle all regal with his foot on this square pillow." Dilly sat up straight and pulled a crate over, put his foot on it, and surveyed an imaginary brood. "That's manhood to me. Nothing wrong with that!"

"Manhood means being finished, perfected, caged in a box defined by conventional society," said Carl. "That word echoes in my head like a death knell, tolling doom. Ma-a-an-ho-o-d." As he drew out the dirge and drowned out the radio, the color left his face and his eyes squinted like a trapped animal. He put his head in his hands and shook it, then ran his fingers through his hair. "Are you going out?" he asked Dilly. "Cause I'm going to sleep, and you could get some milk and coffee. We need both." He stood and headed for the back bedroom. Dilly and Henriette were left alone.

"He's been sleeping days when he's not on call and studying all night," said Dilly. "He often asks me to bring him things. I don't mind. I mean he can't very well go shopping at night."

"You know, it's that — well, he doesn't like open spaces," said Henriette, warning herself not to say too much. "Sometimes he's afraid to go out. I know it's strange."

"He seems OK to me," said Dilly, "and he goes out to class and the hospital. What's his problem?"

"He's had questions and theories about human nature all his life," said Henriette, "and intense fears too. He had St. Vitus dance as a child, twitches and jerks. But I never heard him talk before about the death knell that echoes in his head." Was Dilly blind or more accepting than she'd thought? He'd said, "Live and let live," when they'd discussed whether Hankton was a pansy. This day had brought them closer, even if they were still just pals. Something massive was shifting inside her, like magma restless below a crust of earth, and she waited to see what might break through.

CARL CALLED HENRIETTE THE NEXT weekend and suggested they both take Dilly to see Bughouse Square, where a crowd would listen to poets, cranks, and left-wing soap boxers exercise their right to free speech. The three strolled around the edge of the park among hobos and well-dressed couples, the women in cloches pulled down close to the eyes or elaborate hats with flowers or feathers. Furs warmed the necks of some of the women while others wore only babushkas. Hatless, Henriette walked securely between the two men, close to Dilly, and thrilling whenever she brushed against him in the street. She thought she caught him looking at her with soft, admiring eyes, but she couldn't be sure. Ahead of the three walked a very tall woman in spike heels with an upswept hairdo, topped by a hat with two small birds. A full-skirted coat covered her body, and her hips swayed as she walked.

"Elegant," said Henriette, pointing.

"Some hat," said Dilly. Carl smirked and picked up the pace, so the group divided and walked past the lady. As they rejoined, Carl spoke under his breath.

"Take a look when you can." Henriette walked on and then looked over her shoulder. The woman's cheeks and lips were rosy, and her eyes were outlined in black. With a disorienting jolt, Henriette noticed the gray of a five o'clock shadow on her chin. Her eyes searched for breasts, but the coat concealed the body. She turned to Carl and Dilly.

"Is she...?" Carl nodded yes, smiling and suppressing laughter, and Dilly looked confused.

"Sneak a peek," said Carl as he pulled them aside to find places for listening in the square. Dilly's eyes followed the hat as its wearer walked on.

"You're seeing the Pansy Craze," said Carl. "They're all over the clubs." He sang a few bars:

Masculine women and feminine men;

Which is the rooster and which is the hen?

"Do they get into trouble?" asked Dilly.

"Yeah," said Carl. "The Vice Squad is closing down the clubs, but new ones keep popping up." Henriette glanced around at the crowd with curiosity and suspicion, trying to spot another person of confusing sex.

"Look," she said, noticing Russell on the other side of the square with a group of friends, dressed fashionably in plus eights. "I thought he was at Purdue." The three walked over to greet him, and he seemed both surprised and embarrassed to see them. He excused himself and stepped away from his companions.

"I came in for the weekend," said Russell, speaking quickly, eyes down.

"Where are you staying?" asked Henriette.

"Don't ask him that," said Carl. "He's staying up here, goofing around with a bunch of sissies at the Bally Hoo Café." He punched Russell's arm.

"Lower your voice," said Russell. "You don't know anything. You read all that psychiatry and don't know a thing about people, least of all yourself."

"That's your opinion. Wait 'til you meet the girl I'm dating, Dorothy," said Carl. "I'm grooming myself for success. You want a job and a good life, you need a girl. I'm gonna get married, become a psychiatrist, and make $100 a day."

"Just forget you saw me here," said Russell. Carl laughed and said "Sure," in a tone that sounded like "Not on your life." Speakers began haranguing the crowd, speaking through a bullhorn. First an atheist declaimed about the evils of religion, and then a religionist preached faith. A Chinese student spoke against foreign aggression in China, and Wobblies spoke up for workers' right to strike. Why did no one speak for the rights of people who loved their own kind, Henriette wondered. In such a free-for-all of opinion, could that be the one subject forbidden? She shivered at the thought that serious support for homos might provoke severe retaliation, like the response to *The Well of Loneliness* or the Society for Human Rights. Finally the three got cold sitting and listening, and headed for home.

SOON AFTER, DILLY INVITED HENRIETTE to take a break from studying and join him for coffee. A second chance, she thought, and warned herself not to be too critical, to be prepared for difference. She put on her favorite corduroy slacks, green sweater, and warm wool coat, and met him downstairs at Foster Hall. Walking west on 59th Street, they watched the sun turn bright red behind the leafless trees, then turned toward 57th. He took her hand.

"Some grad students are having a party next week," he said. "They asked me to play my violin."

"Have you played long?" she asked.

"Since I was a kid. My mother taught me. We play duets, violin and piano. Playing piano is the one thing she most loves to do." Henriette winced at the thought of those intimate duets — envying the closeness but also suspicious of the bond between mother and son.

"Do you still play?"

"Once in a while, if someone asks. But anthropology is what I'm doing now." They arrived at a corner coffee shop and took seats on one side of a booth. Dilly ordered coffee and doughnuts for both of them, and the waitress brought coffee in thick mugs and shiny, puffy rings of dough. "Have you ever played?" asked Dilly.

"No," she said. "No one played in our house. Father's the only artist in our family — he photographs wildflowers."

Dilly broke off a chunk of doughnut and ate it. "Not bad," he said. "But not like Mother's. When we had the fat to fry them, she used to make them at home. I loved them fresh from the boiling pot, powdered sugar melting on top." Nostalgia, thought Henriette. Another bad sign. She couldn't stifle critical thoughts. "Does your mother cook?" asked Dilly.

"Yes, but nothing like that. Three-course dinners, and you'd better be on time. In our family Mother wields a hatchet and Father obeys — when he's not having an attack, which could be his heart or his temper." The thought of Father's temper reminded her of what Dilly had said about shooting deer, another difference. "But no guns, thank God," she continued. "No guns in the house." Dilly raised his eyebrows.

"Everyone has guns in Kitichara," he said. "We have a gun rack on a wall in the garage, full of rifles and shotguns." Henriette pictured the bullet's work she'd heard of: an entrance wound like a dime, and an exit wound like a basketball, flesh exploded. Her mouth twisted and a shudder rose from her gut to her shoulders, a vibration that started in abhorrence but betrayed her with shivers of admiration. Dilly trafficked in real things, like life and death, the depths she skated over with words.

"Those guns lie between us and starvation," said Dilly. "Father surveyed lumber in the north woods before he started farming, and he always carried a gun." He put a soothing hand on her arm. "People have to eat. We all kill to eat. Even if you don't see it." The bottom fell out of Henriette's stomach at the mention of killing. Dilly moved over closer to her, so their thighs touched. "I worked on a dig last summer," he continued. "We found arrowheads and the sharpened stones the Indians used to scrape hides — all that was left of their skills and culture. I'd rather see animals killed than Indians." Part of Henriette wanted to surrender to him entirely, to say "yes" to him, guns and all, but the more she wanted to fling herself at his feet, the more she needed to hold her own.

"No one kills Indians any more," she said.

"I didn't know anything about Indians until I started studying them," said Dilly. "Indians used to work on our farm at harvest time, and I thought they were sort of like Negroes, uneducated people who helped with the heavy work."

Henriette sat up straight and her voice squeaked upwards, "Negroes uneducated?" How could a graduate student in anthropology be ignorant of the Harlem Renaissance, of Negro history? She turned towards him, and a little air space opened between them. "How about Booker T. Washington and Frederick Douglass? How about all the new Negro poets?"

"I guess I need to do some reading," he said. "And you might have something to learn about Indians. We didn't just fight them, you know. We infected them — smallpox."

"Not deliberately!" she said.

"Deliberately or not, they died just the same. By the thousands. Digging is hard. But after a while the shards and stones begin to add up. At the end of a summer on the dig, I began to realize that the Winnebago who worked on the farm, poor as they were, were the bearers of the complex culture that we're now trying to reconstruct." Dilly's eyes grew shiny. "From cooking tools to housing to kinship systems to myths, Indian cultures are right under our noses if we pay attention. I want to study the native people we've been overlooking for so long. A culture decimated, but beautiful. As beautiful as music." He turned to her and touched the side of her face, as though she, too, were beautiful as music. How extraordinary, thought Henriette, to sit in this cracked leather booth and discover guns, music, ignorance, and tears — almost — in this person who apparently found her lovely. He cleared his throat. "I'm sorry," he said, "My job is not to get carried away but to understand the past in ways that might apply to improving the present. Who gets what, as Hankton says."

"What about your music? Did you hope for a musical career?"

"At one time, but I didn't make it." As they walked back to Foster, streetlights casting tall shadows beside them, Dilly told how his family had scrimped and saved for him to go to Eastman School of Music. His mother had gone with him to Rochester and stayed while he took extra lessons, but he'd failed the entrance exam and come home to attend the state university instead.

Henriette was impressed with the way his family had support-ed him, while hers was still locked in their habitual tugs of war. Dilly might be ignorant of Negro culture and perhaps blind to the psyche, but he was so sensible, accepting failure without being destroyed by it and then choosing another path. Dilly's life made the histrionics of her home seem like a bunch of overgrown, intertwined vines sealed off from the real world and its concerns. Was it because they were trying so hard to escape the past: the shtetl's dirt floors, smells of schmaltz and cabbage, the *minyan* that wouldn't count a girl? Hell, Henriette didn't want the past either, but Dilly and his parents seemed satisfied with who they were, no matter how much they might regret loss or failure. Dilly took Henriette's hand, and her spirits rose.

"See this hand," he said, raising his and hers together. Little tufts of black hair sprouted from the muscled fingers. He opened them wide, and hers opened too. "It can play a 10th on the piano. It's not the hand of a violinist. After a concert once, I shook the hand of the first violin of the Rochester symphony, and it felt like squeezing a soft sponge." He closed their fingers together, and his touch encouraged her to question the past ten months.

"I thought you'd given up on me, and we would just be friends."

"I never gave up. I thought about you too much. You seemed scared, and I was afraid to push." She felt her face redden and squeezed his hand, not wanting to talk about her demons. "Some of your ideas scared me too," he continued. "I thought you might have dangerous friends." She felt her eyebrows arch, suppressed a comment — scaredy cat! — and hoped a kiss would end the need for speech.

She stood with her back to the door of Foster and he kissed her, first lightly, on her cheeks and lips and forehead, and then more deeply, taking her head in his hands and lifting it away from the door, and she felt a great wave of desire rise from deep within her to meet his mouth. Maybe Dilly really was the one she'd been waiting for, her access to freedom, to shedding the ills of civilization, to silencing her talky part and bringing the rest of her to life.

He pulled back, lowering his hands to take hers again, breathing a little faster. "I hope you'll come with me to the party next week."

"I will," she said.

BEFORE THE END OF FALL Quarter, Henriette went to the office of Professor Isidor Daniels, with whom she'd studied Apache myth and language. Short and wiry, with thinning hair, he stood to greet her with a big smile and handshake, then sat back in his chair and put his feet up on an open drawer.

"I've decided on an anthropology major," she said, feeling as though an accidental but lucky ocean current had swept her in this direction. "What do I need to take?" He cleared a space on his cluttered desk, got out a notepad, and reviewed the classes she'd taken up to now. As he listed them, she imagined herself by Dilly's side, the two of them digging and brushing off shards, talking to people who knew the traditional tales. Entering mythical worlds. Rescuing ancient cultures from the crush of civilization. Side by side on a mission and living as one, they'd share food and bed and forge a new path to the future. But this was a fantasy and her major would soon be a fact.

"Will you minor in English literature then?" asked Daniels, cocking his head.

"No, I need to make up for lost time," said Henriette, desire for Dilly adding impetus to the current. "I'll take classes in the summer as well."

"You'll need more linguistics if you're going to work with me and Ivar Ingebritsen," said Daniels, pleasing Henriette with the assumption that she might "work with" them. Ingebritsen and Daniels had published together on the Apache language. Maybe she could become a research assistant. Daniels' eyebrows gathered. "Physical anthropology and archeology are also required, as well as ethnography and field work practices."

"I like linguistics and ethnography. Psychology too."

"There's a good class in psychological anthropology you can take — they read Sapir, Roheim, Benedict, and Mead. Why don't you take my intensive class on the Apache? After graduation…well, we'll see how you do." Henriette knew that Daniels did field work every summer among the Mescalero Apache, and she was thrilled by this hint that she might qualify for a field placement.

Chapter 10

The Christmas-New Year vacation brought Henriette back to Oak Park, and she hadn't been there a day when Lucky called. Intending to keep her distance, she agreed to meet him downtown at a coffee shop near his work. They took seats in a booth, where harsh light revealed Lucky's red eyes and washed-out face. A waitress set down two thick mugs of coffee and a pitcher of cream on the greasy table.

"How's tricks?" asked Henriette, attempting a neutral tone.

"Why wouldn't you come to my place?" he asked, and his unabashed presence reminded her, with a shock, not of herself as a stone but of Lucky's transformation from a verbal, satiric newspaperman to a wolf going after a bone. She explained that she'd decided not to sleep with anyone unless she was in love.

"I adore you," he said. "I worship you. I may be a philandering rake, but my love for you is deeply serious, beautifully concealed."

"Your love for me is hypocritical," she said. "You boast about sleeping with all kinds of girls, even prostitutes."

"But you're the one I want," he said. "Let's get married." Startled, she raised her eyebrows and tried to think of a smart answer.

"The nights would be fun, but what would we do with the days?"

"Come home with me now, and we'll figure that out tomorrow." She shook her head. "What am I supposed to do without you?" Part of her was offended, but another part felt oddly guilty, inadequate and responsible for disappointing him. For all his bluster, he seemed like a hot-air balloon that she might puncture with a glance.

"Haven't you heard of sublimation?" she asked. "That's what you have to do — sublimate. Or come out to Oak Park, and I'll introduce you to my roommate, Effie. She's home for Christmas vacation too."

"Goddam, little girl," said Lucky. "I'm no way looking for introductions. I'm righteously indignant when you fear for my nights. What you won't give me, I'll get for myself."

She slammed her mug down on the table. "You've got to be the damned lousiest man this side of the Rockies. God, I hate hypocrites." Before he could see her tears, she was gone.

Winter Quarter: snow blanketed the campus and deep cold settled into bricks and bones. The cardboard dwellings that had dotted the Midway in the fall disappeared, then reappeared in the maze of tunnels and passageways that underlay the city, the system sometimes used by Carl to avoid open spaces as he made his way around town. In flimsy encampments of cardboard and cloth, men and women wrapped in layered rags crouched over cans of Sterno, heating beans or soup. It was scarcely warmer here than outdoors, though somewhat protected from the wind. What would these people use for a toilet, wondered Henriette, and how could they escape the accumulating grime? Her troubles shrank to the size of a pin, and she was glad the party would be simple and inexpensive, with music by students and punch most likely spiked with homemade spirits.

Henriette was ready when Dilly arrived at Foster, carrying his violin. Little pleats on her green satin dress ran from each shoulder to a high waistband, and lily-of-the-valley cologne gave her an aura of spring. A trace of rouge sweetened her lips. Shrugging into a dark woolen coat and wrapping her head in a scarf, she caught Dilly's admiring glance.

"You're togged to the bricks," he said, eyes scanning along the pleats and down to her hemline. "Ever have one of those flasks that slips into your garter?"

"No." She backed away and smoothed her dress. "I'd rather not get caught carrying booze."

"Coppers wouldn't bother with a bit on your body. They're too busy emptying barrels of beer down the drain. Makes a man weep."

"What a waste of time and hooch," said Henriette. It was already dark, and Dilly took her arm as they hurried to an apartment several blocks away. Bright light and chatter. Strangers and friends milling around, drinking and smoking. Orange crates full of books lined the walls, and others served as wobbly coffee tables, holding ashtrays and glasses.

"Come in cats and check your hats; I mean the joint is jumpin'," sang Fats Waller from a Victrola, and couples danced the Lindy in the living room, the girls' skirts rising as they twirled. The movement and music assaulted Henriette, and Dilly guided her out to the kitchen, where a big bowl held yellow-orange liquid and chunks of ice.

"Hi," said Dilly to a young woman who stood by the punch bowl, ladling out glasses and handing them around. "Katya, my friend Henriette." Henriette extended her hand and felt a decisive shake, then raised her eyes to see breasts that strained against the buttons of an embroidered blouse, a rosy face and two long, blonde braids. "Katya is from Germany," said Dilly. "She's in anthropology, already studying for prelims in her first year." Katya's stocky body and blue eyes looked plain and healthy, and her gaze was direct. Henriette hadn't anticipated meeting Dilly's other women friends, and she stiffened.

"I interest myself in American Indians," said Katya, in heavily accented English. "Real ones," she added with a rueful smile. "Not like 'Winnetou.'" She described the romantic, stereotyped character of

German storybooks and his blood brother, Old Shatterhand. "I never believed in those so-called Indians myself, any more than I believed in Bambi." Henriette had read *Bambi: a Life in the Woods* as soon as it came out in translation, and now she smiled vaguely, her mind racing to compare herself to Dilly's friend and see how she measured up. "I suppose Heidi is just as much of a stereotype," said Dilly.

"You're right," said Katya. Then, speaking as though to a child, "We don't sleep on straw, even in the mountains, where I grew up." Henriette took a big swallow of the sweet, stinging drink and thought: If Katya's a tree, then I'm a vine, slender and elusive. Dilly's got to prefer the vine — but how can I be sure?

"Was it difficult to come here?" asked Henriette, setting down her empty glass.

"Nearly impossible," said Katya, moving away from the punch bowl. Others crowded in to help themselves. "Impossible to stay and survive — impossible to leave. By the time I get out, you have to take a wheelbarrow full of money to buy a loaf of bread or a quart of milk. Six million unemployed, including me." A survivor, thought Henriette. Like Dilly.

"Tell us how you got by," said Dilly. Henriette moved closer to Dilly and watched his face as Katya talked. He put an arm around Henriette, and she snuggled into it, but he kept looking at Katya.

"You should see the bright lights of Berlin, where I was in school," said Katya. "And the cabarets. I go to the Tingeltangel and laugh until I almost choke when they make fun of our pompous leaders," and she puffed up her chest and lifted her chin. "Their convenient marriages or inconvenient affairs," she went on, face alight with subversion. "Everyone was corrupt."

"But what about bread and milk?" asked Dilly.

"For that: work hard, win a scholarship, come to America," she said with a harsh laugh. "Then discover things aren't much better here."

"You're right," said Dilly. "Our unemployment is just about as high."

Katya leaned in closer to both of them. "Is very bad in Germany now. People are desperate, and more and more are turning to the Nazis, to Hitler. Did you know his party won eighteen percent of the vote in the last election? Seems like no one in America notices or cares."

Henriette spoke up. "People here are struggling. Many lost family in the Great War. They don't even want to think about Europe." She wondered if Dilly's father could have fought against Katya's dad.

"Think about our losses," said Katya. "And huge reparations we have to pay."

"My father says Hitler blames your troubles on Jews and Communists," said Henriette.

"Or 'degenerates,' anyone not part of the 'master race.'" Katya's smirk put the terms in quotes. "The *Sturmabteilung*, the SA — Nazi paramilitaries — they're everywhere in their brown shirts, going after Jews, Slavs, gypsies. "

"Does anyone oppose them?" asked Dilly.

"Communists and Social Democrats," said Katya. "But they're too busy fighting each other to form a united front against Hitler."

"Trotsky's always advocated a united front," said Henriette.

"Why unite with Communists?" asked Dilly, dropping his arm and turning to Henriette. "You don't get liberty and equality that way."

"Unite and fight," said Henriette, addressing Katya. "Don't you think that's the way to defeat Hitler?"

Katya shrugged. "I hope I can stay here," she said. "I love your music. I first hear Duke Ellington when the Chocolate Kiddies come to Berlin. So primitive," and she shuddered. "Such earthy joy."

Dilly winced. "I wouldn't exactly call it primitive," he said, then met Henriette's eyes.

"Hardly," said Henriette, smiling just enough to acknowledge Dilly's glance and proud to have learned there was no such thing as a "primitive" culture. Now they would be "we" and Katya the outsider.

"You know what I mean," said Katya. "More barbaric, not so stiff and civilized like we are in Germany." Henriette and Dilly locked eyes just as a man tapped Katya on the shoulder and asked her to dance. Dilly refilled glasses, then moved with Henriette to the living room.

The apartment's close atmosphere heated up as more people arrived, and the air thickened with smoke. Dancers ricocheted together and apart as though connected by rubber bands, and sweat sprayed, dampening the air. Everyone absorbed punch, the noise level rose, and Henriette grew more and more quiet, her mind checking constantly on who noticed her and whether they smiled or frowned. Moving from group to group, Dilly kept her by his side, but he failed to focus on her and seemed to find others more interesting. What good was a kiss if she couldn't have all of him?

Across the room she spotted Nadine's square shoulders and long, black hair. Her friend, someone she could offer Dilly. Together they angled their bodies through the crowd. Introductions, handshakes firm on both sides. Nadine pulled back, and Henriette could see her sizing up the boyfriend.

"I've heard about you," said Nadine. "The anthropologist. Have you been to the pueblos, seen the tribes dance to make the rain fall?"

"Yes," said Dilly. "And they do. They dance and sing all day, with absolute conviction. None of this polite 'greet the neighbors,' like in church. Ritual's a matter of survival in the pueblo, and it pulls you in, mesmerizing. You should go some time."

"We should all go," said Henriette.

"Is life on the reservations as hard as they say — everyone poor and sick?" asked Nadine.

"It's a harsh life," said Dilly. "They've lost so much land and resources, but they're rich in stories and skills." Henriette looked from one to the other. "So you're a poet — Henriette's told me," said Dilly.

"Yes, and a journalist — for a living. My father's construction business is collapsing, and I have to work. I'd like to report the truth about Indian living conditions."

"Nothing will change unless people know about it," said Dilly. "We'd make a good team."

Strange how two such different people, the radical Lesbian poet and the liberal social scientist, could hit if off so well.

The host called for quiet and announced the evening's live performance: solos on saxophone, penny whistle, and violin. Everyone found perches on the floor, on radiators, and the arms of chairs. Dilly took his violin from its case and crossed the room, tuning it, while Henriette found a seat on a window ledge and held a half-full glass.

A man with a sax played a chorus of "Somebody Stole My Gal," and Henriette wondered what Dilly would play for this group of cool cats. Then the fellow with the tin whistle played an Irish jig, and everyone clapped along. As soon as Dilly played the first notes of "She'll Be Coming 'Round the Mountain," people joined in and sang. Henriette sang too, glad he'd found something everyone liked. He put the violin away and went over to Henriette, as sounds of applause, chatter, and Fats Waller singing "Lulu's Back in Town" rushed in to fill the silence. She jerked when he touched her arm and almost dropped her empty glass.

"You did well," she said, with a faint smile.

"Want another drink?" he asked.

"Sure." He brought it back and she took a sip. Thoughts began to bump up against each other. Jazzy dancing and music. Dilly, what she wanted, his eyes skidding away. Too many people. Each image and idea appeared bright and interesting before it was shoved out of the way by a new one. The crowd diminished as the evening grew late, and Dilly began talking to the two other musicians, whom he introduced to Henriette, smiling down at her and touching her shoulder. Everything blended and swirled, tigers into butter or something, and Henriette watched at a slight remove as they got out instruments again.

The small crowd took seats, Katya among them. The musicians played a few familiar requests, and then someone called out, "Play Sam Hall."

"No violin for this one," said Dilly. "You two play and I'll sing." He began, slow and deliberate.

Oh my name is Samuel Hall, Samuel Hall.
Oh my name is Samuel Hall, Samuel Hall.
Oh my name is Samuel Hall, and I hate you one and all.
You're a bunch of muckers all, god damn your eyes.

The virulence of the words and the conviction with which Dilly delivered them sobered Henriette like a blast of cold air. This was the infant violinist, the scholarly T.A.? Yes, but it was also the farmer and hunter after he'd had a few, no doubt as many as she. He began another verse, telling the story of a man condemned to hang, and his voice grew louder and stronger, seeming to gush directly from an unseen source. The saxophone joined in, low and strong, supporting Dilly's bass voice, while the penny whistle danced around, a bird perched on the gibbet. Sam Hall was going up the rope to hang until he died, and Henriette watched him, mouth open. Dilly's hands began to tremble as he sang, not the violinist's practiced vibrato but a spontaneous shaking. He grasped his hands together, but the trembling increased as he sang:

Let this be my parting knell, parting knell.
Let this be my parting knell, parting knell.
Let this be my parting knell, hope to see you all in hell,
Hope to hell you sizzle well, god damn your eyes.

"Bravo!" cried Katya, and everyone joined in applause. Dilly nodded acknowledgement but looked taken aback by something — his vehemence? His daring? Henriette had no idea what could have made him angry enough to sing that song from the heart or the gut or wherever the seat of anger was. His audible rage connected with something deep inside her, something frightening. She could never, would never sing a song like that. But anyone who could condemn his foes to hell, even if it made his hands tremble — that person could break the ties that bound her to her family and get her out.

Dilly's daring curse; his strong brows; and the lure of his compact, co-coordinated body all swam together in Henriette's head as they walked back to Foster, and she leaned in to get closer to his smell of sweat and smoke, to breathe him in. He put an arm around her. Dilly's feelings had blasted out in that song, but hers were still locked inside, and she despaired of getting at them. She wanted Dilly's body and brain and eyes and knowledge of hardship, but she couldn't risk revealing that want until she knew she could get it. He hadn't asked her how she felt all evening, and she had to find a way to let him know how impossible life was inside the prison of her skin. "Do you know Robinson Jeffers' 'Medea?'" she asked, her words slightly slurred.

"I haven't read it yet, but I will."

"I am Cassandra in 'Medea,'" said Henriette, addressing Dilly but also declaiming to the night air. Her voice took on an elevated manner, almost singing. "Cassandra says, 'I am a counter of sunrises, permitted to live because I am crying to die.'"

"That's you?" asked Dilly.

Now her voice turned flat and determined. "Yes, that's me. Crying to die."

"Why would you want to die?"

"Because everything and everybody in my life is bad. Mother needs me more and more at home to deal with Father, and that means hundreds of errands and chores, while Father gets mad over every little thing, and you can't tell whether he's fussing or really sick. I'm a prisoner, and I'll never be able to leave." Her usually low voice edged upward. "If I'm going to live," she continued, "I have to be god, in charge of who stays and who goes." She turned and walked backward, facing Dilly, eyes fierce. Clouds chased each other across a full moon, and she raised her face to shout at the sky. "I am god." Then, voice lowering, "At least for the moment." Roaring again like a sea breaching dikes: "I, being god, have decided to abolish everything but music and myself. No more human beings, no more drama, no more dark and light stuff, no more sanitary lingerie, no more nickel slot machines or dog races or amusement parks. Nothing but me being god, and music." Henriette knew with one part of her that this was just what Dr. Whitson had warned her against, exposing her demons to Dilly all at once, but another part wanted to let Dilly see all the unsprung springs and odd-shaped pieces that popped out of her and find out if he could help her put them all back inside. He stopped, looking frightened, then folded her into himself, arms, scarf and all, as though he were literally compressing the pieces back into one whole. Her shoulders shook. Hiccups threw her against him, then slowed and disappeared. After a while, she turned to walk by his side, and he kept an arm around her shoulder as they continued in silence, breath steaming into the cold.

"I don't understand why you're crying to die," said Dilly. "Do you really mean it?" He paused, but she was silent. "Dying is forever," he said. "My brother Finn — the one whose coat I wear — he died." Henriette looked up.

"That's awful," she said, shocked out of her self-absorption. "Oh Dilly," and she took both his hands. "What happened?"

"I was in Madison when I got the telegram. Finn had finished college and expected to work on the farm, but there wasn't enough money for another hand, so he got a job teaching flying. Barely knowing how himself.

"How could that be?" asked Henriette.

"Flying was mostly barnstorming, and pilots got hired to do stunts or sell rides," Dilly said. "Licensing and registration were just coming in." He kicked at the ground. "Mother was furious when he proposed taking that job, and we all counted on Father to stop him. Father had taught us to hunt and fish and chop wood, and it was his job to talk sense into Finn, but no." Dilly's hands began to shake with anger, and he clasped them together in front of him. "God damn *his* eyes." Henriette raised her hand to his arm and felt the tremor of his hands spread to his whole body. "Finn was bound to crash, and his student died as well."

"Dilly, I am sorry," said Henriette, as she turned and slipped easily into his arms. He rubbed his head on the side of hers and kissed her ear. How could she wish for everything to be over when Dilly was holding her and death was his enemy?

"We've had to carry on," said Dilly, as they continued to walk, not touching. "My mother suffers the most, and I try to look out for her. No one should choose to die. You wouldn't, would you?" Both were silent for a while, walking in the dark. The wind picked up and whistled around their heads, and Dilly returned his arm to Henriette's shoulder, shielding her from the breeze. She leaned her head against him. "My father volunteered to fight in the Great War when he was over forty," said Dilly, "because he'd gotten skin cancer and thought he'd die anyway. So he left Mother alone with three kids — was that right?" Henriette shook her head no. "I was only five and didn't understand anything, except Mother crying and Father leaving."

"How is he now?" asked Henriette.

"He looks peculiar," said Dilly. "One ear is missing, and his mouth drags down on that side, but he's fine. Same old tightwad." Henriette smiled, enjoying her solidarity with Dilly against parents, but her stomach turned at the thought of serious illness. When she had said "crying to die," she'd meant an end to everything, not lingering and suffering. "You can see a lot of people who really chose to die if you visit the Kitichara cemetery some time," Dilly continued. "It's full of suicides and murder victims, many killed by husbands or wives."

"Murder in Kitichara?" asked Henriette, pulling away. "I thought small towns were a refuge from gangsters and rum runners and all the evils of the city."

"They are now. But forty years ago, during another terrible depression, so many people up north gave up or went berserk, like it was shameful to keep plugging away, day after day. The old-time ministers preached nothing but purity, and they drove people to despair. Wisconsin's small towns were death traps."

Henriette thought about what her parents had been doing forty years before, celebrating bright lights and cultural achievement amid the splendors of the Columbian Exposition, the 1893 World's Fair. Frolicking, while Dilly's forebears stood on the brink of disaster. Those were the good times in Mother's memory, the subjects of countless bedtime stories. Henriette had often pictured her young parents visiting that fairyland of white, pillared buildings surrounding a blue lagoon, all brilliant in the sun, Mother in a long, bustled dress with a fichu at the neck and Father in polished shoes with spats and a bowler hat, admiring inventions like the long-distance telephone and the moving pictures of Edison's Kinetoscope. When night fell, electric bulbs and searchlights lit up the whole White City with a brilliance they'd never seen or dreamed of. Suddenly the rough-and-tumble world of Chicago acquired a European patina, and her parents felt newly at home in a world as cultured as their ambitions, confident that Father would continue to thrive and rise in his new job with Sears Roebuck, writing the catalogue.

Henriette wished she had been there, an unborn homunculus, taking in the lagoon, the lights, the Ferris wheel, and the risqué dance of "Little Egypt" on the Midway, which her parents had avoided. Of course they'd been ignorant of the fire that would destroy those sturdy looking buildings, actually made of inflammable gypsum and jute, or the rancor that would infect their marriage, as children deprived Mother of the education a man would surely have gotten, leaving her chronically furious and cheating Father of her affection. Maybe Henriette's parents had fallen into their own death trap.

"I have no regard for people who choose death in a pinch," continued Dilly. "I don't believe you really want to give up." Henriette knew she hadn't thought fully about what she was saying. Sometimes it seemed like the words took over, and she'd rather liked her list of things she was condemning to the gallows while she was being god. Now Dilly was encouraging her to think more than twice. His sense was beyond common, a kind of deep knowledge of what was important, things on which you could base a life, as solid as rocks or high as stars. That knowledge was embedded in his graceful body, taking shape from his mouth every time it formed an ordinary word, springing from the wildly cavorting dark hair that sprouted from collar, cuffs, and the backs of his fingers, as he embraced her with his long arms.

"Look," he said. "You can be Cassandra, and I'll be your gatekeeper. Not everyone can have access to the prophetess. Cassandra and her gatekeeper." She saw his head turn, knowing the moonlight silhouetted her long, straight nose and high forehead. His proposal gave her a role and a script. "Cassandra and her gatekeeper," he repeated, and she nodded. She could live with that for a long time. They walked in silence to the door of Foster Hall, where they kissed and murmured together until they agreed she was no longer crying to die. Monitors came to lock the dormitory door, and she went upstairs.

Chapter 11

Early the next day, Dilly called Henriette and asked if she was feeling better.

"I'm OK," she said, in a voice he could barely hear. They arranged to meet in Foster's dark, wood-paneled lobby, where they sat on scratchy, overstuffed chairs. After last night's revelations she felt freer with Dilly and had thrown on an old flannel shirt of Carl's. But Dilly's clean-shaven face and white, open-collared shirt made her feel unwashed, and she hoped she didn't smell of yesterday's smoke or last night's restless sleep.

"I was afraid my music would bore the swanky guys and gals at that party," said Dilly. "I didn't decide what to play until I heard the jig."

"Your song was a bit corny. Not dopey. Maybe derpy."

"I'll settle for that. I'll be a derp. Your derp." He moved over to sit on the arm of her chair, and she leaned her head against him, then sat up straight.

"You make me a bit uneasy when you play the violin," she said. "I see you at your mother's knee, *embraced by love and poverty.*" Her tone put the phrase in caustic italics that she regretted but couldn't stop. "The kind of thing you might hate at the time but yearn for all the rest of your life. Your playing reminded me of my father when he wants us to look at his photos of wildflowers through the stereopticon. He's trying to preserve the past in pictures. Isn't that what you were trying to do with that violin? Turn back into the little boy whose mother accompanied him on the piano? Reliving the past with all its hopes and disappointments? I say to hell with the past. Cut it off and throw it away. The present is tough enough without all those old attachments."

Dilly stood up and started to pace. "Wait a minute," he said. "I don't want to throw away the past. I admire and respect it, sometimes more than the present. Think about my Grandpa, the guy with his foot on a pillow." He echoed the pose, sitting straight and raising one foot. "I always carry his watch with me." He withdrew a pocket watch with chain and held it to his ear for a moment. "And my mother's father was a poet, as well as a Congregational Minister. They give me hope, like dances for the Indians, hope of climbing out of this cesspool of failure."

What had happened to the moment of closeness when he'd said, "I'll be your derp?" She'd messed it up, and now he was deflating the moment further with family facts. "My father's been wallowing in that swamp since way before the Crash. Counting every penny and still getting poorer and more conservative by the day. The fool's bound to vote again for Hoover." Henriette wanted to side with Dilly against his father, but it was too late. "Mother's been sinking in his shipwrecks for ages," Dilly went on. "Meeting with her clubs and giving teas when she really wants city life, music, and culture. Father thinks I'm too big for my britches, and I hope I *am* too big for *his* britches. My grandfathers were successful, and I hope to follow in their footsteps."

He returned to the arm of her chair and stroked the back of her neck. "I like you in that shirt," he said. "Do you wear it in bed?"

"Sometimes," she said, suddenly embarrassed. She'd intended the shirt to be informal, even familiar, but not exactly reminiscent of bed wear.

"Look," he said. "You wouldn't want me headed for failure, would you?" It wasn't a question but a reminder of good sense, and he leaned down and kissed her, once, twice, three times, urging her out of her acerbic mood. "Let's go over to my place and make some breakfast." Carl left for the hospital as they arrived, on call for twenty-four hours.

"I'm going to fry eggs," said Dilly. "But I'm not used to doing it without Carl."

"Whose eggs are these?" asked Henriette, taking some from the fridge.

"Carl and I share everything," said Dilly. So that was how Dilly rebelled, with a big heart. Generous, like his wide-roving mind, his sensual mouth.

"I'll help," said Henriette, putting butter into a cast iron pan and turning on the flame.

"Let it get almost brown, right?" asked Dilly, peering into the pan.

"Yes," said Henriette, smiling at his concern. "I'll break the eggs in."

"Be careful of the yolks," said Dilly.

"Silly Dilly," said Henriette. "What are you so worried about?"

"I don't want to waste any of the yolk." They let the eggs cook until the edges were crisp and brown and the whites just firm. Henriette picked up a spatula. "If you take them out now, the yolks might break," said Dilly.

"What is it with you and the yolks?" asked Henriette. "Something about eggs, the ovum, the mother-lode…hmmm."

"I just don't like to see it go all over the place," said Dilly, reaching for the spatula.

"Yes, spread out, running free, its innocence forever lost. Like when you discover your mother loves your father more than you," she said, and waved the spatula just out of his reach.

"Hey, let me take them out of the pan," said Dilly, ignoring her words and trying to grab the spatula, which danced back and forth between their hands until he snatched it away from her. He scooped up the eggs with skill and put them on plates with buttered toast, and they sat down to eat in the dining alcove, Henriette humming and acting pleased with her interpretation, Dilly silent. He broke bits off his toast and dipped them in the egg yolk, then ate them one by one.

"Do you remember that loss of innocence?" asked Henriette. "Discovering that your mother loves your father more than you?"

"Certainly not," said Dilly, his face pale against the heavy brows. "I never believed or even hoped she loved me more."

"Think back." Henriette dipped her chin as though looking over glasses. "You might learn something."

"You don't know anything about my mother," Dilly began, but Henriette was slicing down the middle of her yolk, releasing a yellow flood, and Dilly stopped talking and winced.

"See that? I can do whatever I want," Henriette said. "If I want to slice an egg down the middle, I just slice. Have you noticed? It's because nothing matters. If something's a problem, I step aside and let it happen. Nothing bothers me."

"That's one way to solve problems, I guess. Might not be very effective."

"You know Huxley's *Point Counterpoint*?"

"No, who's Huxley?"

"Aldous Huxley," she said. "You'd like his book, *Brave New World*, just out. But I'm talking about an earlier one." He reached for her foot under the table. She responded to his play for a bit, then tucked the foot back under her. Dilly finished dipping the yolks and moved on to cut and eat the white.

After a few forkfuls, Henriette pushed her plate away. "Huxley thinks progress is dehumanizing us," she said. "*Point Counterpoint* has this character, a writer named Philip Quarles. He's an intellectual who can be whatever he wants: kind, mean, skeptic, humanitarian. I'm like him: I can be anyone, do anything, but there's no real me. Psychopathic as hell, I know." She wondered if she'd said too much.

Even Dr. Whitson didn't know she was Philip Quarles, with no self at home inside her skin.

"Is that why you talk so frankly about sex but keep avoiding it?" he asked. Henriette felt herself turn red and hot and then began to shiver, as tremors rose from the base of her spine to her hands, her sweat now clammy. She wrapped the flannel shirt more tightly around her. She couldn't look up, couldn't speak. Pounding in her ears. Rasp of Dilly's breath. Herself revealed, naked as the emperor in new clothes. Give me back the doltish guy who doesn't notice much, the blind farm boy! Now she would have to prove herself in bed, as she'd tried to do with Lucky, and sex would never be spontaneous or free.

After a minute or an hour, Dilly said, "You don't have to answer that. I just wondered why you keep bringing it up."

"I never will, ever again," she said, arms tightly crossed.

"Maybe that feeling, that there's no real you, is a symptom, not a reality," said Dilly, reaching for her hand and uncrossing her arms. "Maybe the real you is a lot of different things."

"No," she said, pushing his hand away, tears filling her eyes but not spilling. If she let him know her body before he understood her soul she might come apart, as she had with Lucky, and find herself staring down at her numb and abandoned shell. "You don't understand. I can't make up a self where there isn't one. I have to find the real one underneath. My life's been a mess from the start, but I won't let myself be trapped by the past."

"I won't trap you," said Dilly. "I'll help you get out."

"It's not that simple," she said. "I've been trying to escape ever since the year after high school, but each time I go a little farther they pull me back, like a yo-yo. I have to keep checking on them, with Father sick and furious, and Mother overburdened, ordering him around and demanding my help."

"It's natural to be concerned about your parents," said Dilly. Henriette's tears welled up again, then subsided. A solitary drop rolled down one cheek, and Dilly reached up and caught it on the back of his hand.

"What exactly do you need to escape?" he asked.

"I'll invite you home to meet my parents and have Dinner, with a capital 'D.' Then you'll see."

"I'd love to come. Now what are we going to do about your egg?"

"I can't eat it, will you?" she asked, blowing her nose. With a chivalrous gesture, he scooped up the egg yolk with her toast and continued eating and mopping until the plate was clean. As they got up from the table, he began to sing and dance a bouncy fox trot with an imaginary partner: "Potatoes are cheaper; tomatoes are cheaper. Now's the time to fall in love." His raised arms invited her to join him and she stepped in closer. "The butcher, the baker, the old candlestick maker, gave their price a downward shove. Love may not be nutritious, but boy, it's delicious; now's the time to fall in love." Round and round the apartment they circled, skirting the chairs and bumping into the couch, Dilly looking right into her eyes, until the apartment seemed to spin.

"You're spunky today," she said.

"I'm all boy and a yard wide." He gave her a final twirl. "And we're a regular pair of Castles. All singing, all dancing." They collapsed onto the couch, laughing and holding hands. He reached to embrace her, and she kissed him briefly, then pulled away. He pulled her back.

"Carl's on call. Stay a while." She hesitated and he clung to her hand as she pulled away, looking at her with a mix of longing and irritation. Of course he expected to cash in on her words, but she wasn't ready — not yet, not now. She had to find some way to gather up and bag the smell of apple and the choke of its juice, the sight of herself inert on a slab, the jolting charge of intimate touch and the access it gave to her private feelings — she had to fill that bag with stones and throw it from a bridge before she could give all of herself to Dilly.

"I've got to go," she said and caught a trace of impatience, even anger, in the squint of his eyes. She thought of the round glob of chocolate pudding long ago, the courage it took to heave it across the table, the confidence the boy with the throwing arm must have felt that it would remain connected, hand in hand like cut-out paper dolls, to all the others at the table, no matter what mess the pudding made when it landed, and she marveled at the possibility that a person could unleash an impulse as furious as an attacking dog and not lose all relationship. Rupture was always possible. She'd held herself aloof from that dinner scene, but now she wondered: who was the bystander whose memory kept that angry arc alive, and what did she see in it?

Chapter 12

The Alabama Supreme Court confirmed the Scottsboro convictions in late March. Dilly and Henriette walked across campus, trudging through mud-colored slush. "They'll appeal to the U.S. Supreme Court, won't they?" asked Dilly.

"Of course, but not every claim gets a hearing," said Henriette.

"The rushed trials, the ineffective lawyers, the all-white juries," said Dilly. "You'd think they'd have a case."

"Yes, but the men are still sitting in jail." Newspapers had reported the narrow spaces in which the young men were held, right next to the execution chamber. The electric chair, known as "Yellow Mama," had replaced hanging in Alabama in 1927, and the young men could hear every sizzle and spark and groan of one like themselves expiring.

"Let's wait and see," said Dilly.

"I'm afraid it will be Sacco and Vanzetti all over again," said Henriette. "Even when the judge's bias in that case was exposed — referring to them as anarchistic bastards — it didn't help. And international protest couldn't save them either. I doubt attitudes in Alabama are any better."

"But the Supreme Court is far from the South," said Dilly.

Henriette hunched her shoulders with abhorrence, and then changed the subject. "You know, May Day's coming up. There's going to be a big benefit on Haymarket Square for the Free Tom Mooney campaign. Want to come?"

Dilly looked dubious. "Who's putting it on?"

"The International Labor Defense League. It'll commemorate the Haymarket martyrs." Dilly looked blank, and Henriette perked up, eager to teach him. "The Haymarket Massacre took place right here in Chicago — the origin of the worldwide workers' day, May Day."

"Oh," said Dilly. To him, May Day was probably for children and baskets of flowers. "What do they defend? The International...whatever it was?"

"They defend leftists who get into trouble." She knew he'd never come if she told the truth, that the ILD was the legal defense arm of the Communist Party.

"Prelims are getting close, and I'll have to study," he said.

"I guess you don't care if you miss my recitation," she said and spun around, making her skirt fly up. "I've been working on it for days. I'll be playing the Spirit of Haymarket." Her voice quivered, but he seemed not to notice. She knew he believed in justice and equality for everyone and cared so much about Indians — so why couldn't he see the need to defend the unfairly accused?

"You can say it for me later," he said, and took off, leaving her standing there, her hands and feet and voice frozen as they strained for words and gestures that would pull him back. She walked slowly backwards, words of apology stuck in her throat, shoulders hunching forward with the urge to touch him. Apparently he hadn't noticed the unraveling threads lying limp between them. Anger festered below her ribs, and she tossed her head, trying to talk herself out of disappointment. She'd been spending too much time with him anyway. After all, she was on her way to overcoming the restrictions of capitalist civilization — damn Henry Ford! — and discovering her own brave new world. So why did she feel so depleted? Without him she was empty, and she felt desire rise and spread from her depths out to the tips of her fingers, making them stretch and curl as though to interlock with his. The seed pods swirled, thick, sticking in her hair and gathering around her feet, coating trees, benches and everything she passed, dimming colors and blurring edges. The world retreated, and she wandered, blank, among gray ghosts.

MAY DAY DAWNED UNSEASONABLY HOT. The League had asked Carl to cook for the cause, and he and Henriette took over Mother's kitchen, laying out loaves of rye bread, slicing them thin and cutting out rounds for canapés. Following one of Mrs. Moody's recipes, he laid thin slices of smoked salmon on the bread and covered them with mayonnaise sharpened with mustard and black pepper. Just below the surface of Henriette's mind, Dilly's absence rankled, and she compared his caution unfavorably with Carl's willing participation. She wanted so badly for Dilly to see her perform. Deep inside she also felt his presence would protect her when she risked exposure to an audience — Carl would be useless for that. She shrugged and told herself to forget Dilly, while his absence kept reminding her of loss, like a missing purse with everything she needed inside.

Mother hovered near the door, criticizing Carl's technique and asking him when he would be through. She needed to fix Father's lunch. Father fumed, objecting that his house was being used for some Socialist cause. Henriette helped Carl with delight, shielded from the parents by her brother and seeing his star rise at least briefly in the contested kitchen.

Over the salmon on each slice went two very small sardines, placed head to tail, like siblings sharing a bed. Over that went grated cucumber, the cucumber salted and squeezed to remove excess water. Sardine tins littered the kitchen. Drips of fish oil. Dirty bowls. Carl chopped ice from a big block with a pick and layered the canapés on wax paper over ice, while Henriette ran upstairs to change into her costume. She smoothed the dress over her hips with a pang that Dilly wouldn't see whoever she might become in that dress.

They packed everything in the car and took off, Henriette proud of Carl's triumph and exhilarated by the morning spent with her expert brother. At the corner of Randolph and Des Plaines, Carl placed his trays on a table and began to sell the canapés for the inflated price of fifty cents apiece, proceeds to benefit the international Free Tom Mooney campaign.

A temporary platform had been erected on the Square in an effort to mimic the wagon from which famous speakers had once declaimed, and signs posted around the platform promoted the ILD and Wobblies. Henriette made her way through the crowd to the platform and climbed up to greet the MC, dressed neatly in a three-piece suit, hair parted in the middle. He stepped to the microphone and introduced Henriette: "The Spirit of Haymarket." The stage cleared to reveal her, proud to embody that spirit. With a rush like wind blowing through her, she saw herself in the vanguard with the MC, spearheading the revolution with poetry. Rumor had it that William Patterson, head of the ILD, would make an appearance, and Henriette thought she spotted the serious-looking Negro with steel-rimmed glasses and round, fleshy cheeks among other brown and white men in the crowd. She thrilled to think this defender of Sacco and Vanzetti might hear her recital. Men in three-piece suits and ladies with wide-brimmed sun hats filled the chairs in front of her, while younger men in plus eights and girls in fringed flapper dresses and cloches stood on the sides. Children scampered all around, and birds sang in the silence that greeted Henriette's appearance.

"Sleep softly…eagle forgotten…under the stone," she began, reciting Vachel Lindsay's poem about John Altgeld, confident that the crowd knew the story of the Illinois governor who'd pardoned the convicted Haymarket martyrs. Henriette looked out at the audience, meeting eyes. "The mocked and the scorned and the wounded, the lame and the poor," she continued. Dilly should see her now. Words like that could prickle skin, topple monarchs, raise the dead. What had happened to her study of poetry? When had she given it up for anthropology? She didn't know, and there wasn't time to think. "A hundred white eagles have risen, the sons of your sons." Her white dress blew around her knees, as though agitated by the hundreds of eyes all focused on her. Like long ago, when her brothers had taught her to read, she was seen and heard. Then the eyes began to prickle, an annoying, challenging sort of sting, as though questioning her right to hold their gaze. She thought she spotted Lucky in the audience, cigarette in his hand and a cynical look on his face. People shifted in their seats, and programs rustled. She concentrated on the poem. "Time has its way with you there, and the clay has its own." The eyes were becoming buzzing gadflies, swarming in a sea of funereal suits, dotted with harsh reflections from pomaded hair. Where were the nods of approval, the smiles of encouragement that she needed to keep going? What if the real spirits of those who condemned the Haymarket martyrs rose up to hate her? Sure, Governor Altgeld had pardoned the men, but too late to save more than one. Maybe Dilly was right to avoid the radical left. Tom Mooney had been framed and sent to jail — the same might happen to her. She needed Dilly now, and she scanned the crowd as though her eyes and her fervor could make him appear. The morning's exuberance and sense of conquest drained out of her, and she looked at the MC for help. He looked back in a neutral way and waited for her to continue.

She had to get out of here, to find a safe place from which to watch if the compressed lips and stares turned into curses or rotten tomatoes. She went on speaking, but she could hear her voice flatten, absenting itself from Lindsay's firm cadences and convictions. How did people take center stage without risking attack? She needed to stop occupying space, but there was no place to go. Breathing and speaking too fast, she read the last lines. "Sleep on, O brave-hearted, O wise man that kindled the flame. To live in mankind is far more than to live in a name. To live in mankind is far, far"— a sharp, deafening explosion sounded close by. Screams, scrambling. Hot, metallic smell. She crouched and hugged her knees, breath coming in spasms. Gunshot, now what? Body frozen, eyes darting, yearning for Dilly. Where were his warmth, competence, knowledge of guns?

A gang of young, Negro men, apparently actors, stormed the stage. Harold Overstreet followed, tucking a gun into his belt, playing a liberator who'd broken the Scottsboro Boys out of jail. Harold had fired into the air, of course, but Henriette still struggled for breath, and fear exuded from her skin, drops of moisture crawling along. The danger of eyes was past, but this new threat had sharp edges like rock or metal and killing speed. Dilly — she longed for him, for Sam Hall's damnation of eyes. All the quick-firing nerves of the last few minutes joined forces and funneled into one strong blaze of ardor, a flame that consumed disagreement and difference and left nothing to separate their skins but thin bits of cotton falling to the floor. The actors ran and crouched, hiding beside and behind the stage, and the audience applauded.

"It's OK boys," said Overstreet. "You're safe here. Come on out." Slowly the actors took places around the stage in various positions, some standing and facing the audience, some in frozen running positions, some sitting. "There's no tar boiling here in a barrel for you, no feathers waiting to pierce your burned skin, no mob gathering for the pleasure of torturing you and then watching… you…get… lynched," said Overstreet, his voice getting deeper, louder and slower as he continued, until Henriette could almost smell the tar heating and hear the screams of a man about to be burned alive, the screams of a man who actually had been lynched the previous year not two hundred miles from where she was standing right now. She doubted Dilly knew about that. He would surely hate lynching as much as any man alive, even if he wouldn't join with Communists to fight it. Her terror onstage a few moments before and her fright at the gunshot left her trembling, cold and damp on the hot day, standing in the wings and imagining the horrific scene of Overstreet's words. The actors began to speak in a formal style, each taking a line.

"Times were bad.

We searched for work.

From town to town.

No place to stay.

We were on a train.

We rode with freight." The actors pitched their lines on different tones, creating harmony with a sort of speech-song, as they moved together to form a massed sculpture of bodies.

"A fight broke out.

The white folks left.

Two stayed behind.

When we got off,

Those two cried 'rape.'

Rape! Lynch! Lynch! Rape!" they cried all at once in jagged and syncopated rhythms. Then the single lines resumed.

"Now we're in jail

Condemned to die

All innocent

Unless you fight." Then, in unison:

"The whole world sees America's shame

So save our skins, and save your name." The young men formed a phalanx, arms over each other's shoulders and began a tonal chant: "Unite and fight, unite and fight." Over their carpet of sound, Harold spoke.

"These men may have escaped the barrel of tar, the feathers, the mutilating mob waiting to string them up, but they await their legal lynching with equal dread, and the whole world is watching with disgust and horror as their date of execution draws near." Now the boys' chanting rose in volume, joined by Harold, as he added his bulk to their wall of bodies, and they all marched forward, off the stage and through the crowd, which chanted along with them, "Unite and fight, unite and fight, unite and fight."

Henriette chanted and applauded with the rest, and her heart pounded in her throat at the sound of this powerful resistance. The enactment made Scottsboro real, dragging her over the line from gadfly eyes to facts like shackles. But this was just a play. No one would really break the boys out of jail, and if they did, an appalling burning and hanging would surely follow, the very kind of illegal lynching the governor of Mississippi had recently vowed to allow. No way out.

Suddenly she thought of Nadine, forced to leave school and go to work. She was in Alabama now, investigating the truth about the Scottsboro case. Such work would take so much more bravery than attending rallies in Chicago or parties in New York. Nadine had entered the minotaur's lair, where white was always right and questioning that system always wrong — and punishable.

Like a tiny geyser of fiery water the thought erupted: she should go herself. She should get on a train and go and find Nadine, help her seek the truth. You? she asked herself. The girl who was terrified to stand before a friendly crowd and recite a well-loved poem? But that was different. In Alabama she wouldn't be performing or demanding attention. She'd be a cog in a wheel, an ant among ants or a hand among hands, as she'd often wanted to be. And what about the girl who had been prepared to throw herself into Dilly's arms a moment ago, yet just the other day had been afraid to sleep with him? Don't be a fool, she told herself. Do it.

Out of nowhere Lucky appeared at her side. "What are you doing here? With the ILD?" he asked, not waiting for answers. "You're asking for trouble, and I'm pretty sure you'll get some."

"What's it to you?" she asked.

"You forgot, I'm the guy who wants to marry you — and, I'm sure you remember, your uh. . . first. . ." his expression between a leer and a sneer, lewd as before but newly angry. Henriette trembled. She hadn't wanted to make him mad. "Please leave me alone," she said. Turning away, she went to help Carl empty ice water from washtubs and load them up in the car, and when she looked back, Lucky was gone. As she worked she felt the fading pain of the thought that had flashed into her mind as she recited: whatever happened to her love of words like Vachel Lindsay's? Had she lost track of what she'd loved first and most? Dilly's anthropology had rolled right over her love of poetry. A good thing, she thought. Anthropology made clean science out of the murky human relations over which she'd agonized for so long, just as Dilly cut through her mixed feelings with straightforward admiration and desire. For a moment the mean look in Lucky's eyes troubled her thoughts, and she pushed it away. He was acting ridiculous and should best be forgotten.

Fortunately there was still a month of school for her to decide whether, how, and when she would actually go to Alabama. Now she had to find Dilly. She and Carl piled into the car to drive back to Oak Park.

"The time will come when our silence will be," began Carl, reciting the words of the Haymarket martyrs. Henriette joined him to finish, "more powerful than the voices you strangle today." Then, like the martyrs on their way to the gallows, they began to sing their favorite anthem of true-blue revolution, the one that came before Solidarity, before the Internationale: the Marseillaise.

Henriette's alto joined Carl's bass, and their voices rose, summoning the children of the fatherland to greet the day of glory. Like Lindsay's, these were words that became acts and leveled mountains. What if all her quirky words joined forces with Dilly's knowledge of act and fact? Together they could be more than either one alone. She stuffed the soft dangers of eyes, hands, and words in a bag and let it sink, weighted, to a place out of sight, determining to live in the rocky land of practical reality.

Voices of brother and sister grew stronger and louder as the song raised the bloody flag of tyranny and resolved to stand fast against it, Henriette envisioning freedom from parents and capitalism and everything in the bag all at once. Throwing back their heads, they sang the call to arms at the top of their lungs: "*Aux armes citoyens. Marchons! Marchons!*" Their voices faded to silence, but the song's ecstatic sound continued to reverberate down through the ages and in the car, while scents of fish and lemon rose from the empty tub to enliven the air with possibility.

As soon as she got back to Foster, Henriette stood in line for the hall phone, called Dilly, and told him she had to see him. They met the next day in the central quadrangle, and he greeted her with a quick kiss on the lips, as though he'd forgotten his recent abrupt departure. The hot spell had passed, and the day was chilly and wet. Blooming pansies drooped under the weight of drops of rain.

"So — how was the rally?" asked Dilly.

"It's a long story," said Henriette, feeling like she'd been away from him for months. How could she tell about her panic, the Scottsboro play and her new feelings about him all at once?

He glanced at the leaden sky. "Let's get out of the rain," he said. He put an arm around her shoulder. They hurried into Swift Hall and down to the basement coffee shop, ordered coffee and took seats next to each other in a dark corner. The place was half empty, and others read or talked quietly.

"The rally was tremendously exciting," said Henriette, and then stopped, afraid of revealing too much about the gadfly eyes that had threatened her.

"Did they like the poem?" asked Dilly.

"Probably. Maybe." Then, eyes down: "Actually I got scared. I was afraid they might hate me." He took her hand, and her cool fingers embraced his warm ones. "I just felt so naked and alone up there on the stage."

"I should have come," said Dilly. "You could have looked out and seen my friendly face." She nodded.

"I wished you were there," she said. "And I wished it even more when they had this play about Scottsboro." Her voice rose, agitated, as she described the gunshot and the performance.

"I'm sure those fellas will eventually get a fair trial," said Dilly. "Our legal system guarantees it."

"How can they?" asked Henriette. "There was no real evidence, no friendly witnesses. The ILD calls the process 'legal lynching.' Don't you want to stop that?" Her fingers tightened on his, as though she could squeeze her sense of injustice into his flesh.

"Of course I do," he said, covering their joined hands with his free one. "Any kind of lynching is a terrible crime. It's a question of what's most effective. Remember Hankton's dictum? Who gets what, when and how? You need power for justice, and power lies with the legal system. And now the Supreme Court has agreed to hear the case."

"That's such good news," she said. "I don't think methods matter as long as we both want the same thing." Their eyes met above their joined hands, and she could almost see thoughts intersecting like cogwheels in his mind, choosing remedies that work over hopes and dreams. Real solutions and real danger could chase away chimeras and give new meaning to the fragile life of the body. She searched for words for the ravishment she'd felt when the actors had stormed the stage and she'd flashed on Dilly singing "Sam Hall." "When I was at the rally and all that chaos exploded around me, I knew I wanted you more than anything. We belong together." His eyes softened, and he took her face in his hands and kissed her long and hard. She smiled and sighed before speaking, wondering if she were blushing. A percolator bubbled behind the counter, and she looked around to see if anyone had seen them kiss. No one was staring, and she squeezed closer to him.

"Did you know Nadine is in Scottsboro right now, reporting?" she asked.

"I didn't, but I'm not surprised," he said. "I hope she doesn't get hurt. She's taking a risk hanging out with those labor defense fellas. Think about lost opportunities, jobs — trouble, sooner or later." Henriette resolved to say nothing about her brief thought of going to Scottsboro herself and turned the talk to the Apache stories she'd been reading, stories they could share.

Chapter 13

As Henriette's study of Apache linguistics deepened, she became fascinated with the ways that words could mean, suggest or deceive, weaken or strengthen a person, transmit a curse or a blessing. Apparently the words that she tossed in the air like ping-pong balls carried weight for others, like sticks and stones. Her professor, Ivar Ingebritsen, a colleague of Isidor Daniels, had studied and transcribed the Chiricahua Apache warpath language, a special language learned by adolescent novices as part of their training for raids and battles. The language empowered and protected the speaker, the way singing "Solidarity" had strengthened her in New York.

The next Friday Dilly called Henriette. "Want to join me at Ingebritsen's tonight?" he asked. "He's having some students over."

"If it's for graduate students, I'd be crashing the party."

"No you wouldn't. You'd be my date." She smiled, suddenly shy. Back at Foster she debated what to wear. Students in this department didn't dress up much, so she decided against silk and chose a gray, percale frock with the hem well below the knee and livened it up with a red scarf. Dilly picked her up, and they walked to Ingebritsen's, where dark green walls reflected firelight, warming the room. Ten or twelve graduate students wandered around or talked in small groups, nibbling on nuts, olives, cheese, and crackers arranged on low tables. Dilly introduced Henriette to his friends, guiding her from group to group by the elbow. Names and faces blurred. Professor Ingebritsen sat at a low coffee table in the center of the room, and soon everyone gathered to hear him explain a drink preparation. He bent over his project, sparse strands of brown hair combed across a bald, shiny head, and then held up a bottle of clear liquid.

"This is kirsch, an *eau de vie* made from cherries and pits, the French version of my native aquavit — water of life," he said, lecturing on language as though in the classroom. "It's nothing you'd find in a speakeasy." He poured several ounces into a pitcher with ice and added a cloudy syrup he identified as orgeat, almond flavored. "I brought both bottles back from France," he added, squeezing in a couple of lemons and stirring. "This," he said, "is a Silver Shadow," and he poured the potion into glasses. "Think of the shadows cast by the midnight sun on snow-capped mountains above the Arctic Circle in Norway." The students accepted glasses and toasted the professor and each other.

"Is there another way to make it if you can't get that stuff?" asked Dilly, pointing to the clear bottle.

"Try bathtub gin," said one of the students, and everyone laughed.

"You're scientists," said Ingebritsen. "Experiment!" Henriette took a sip. At first it tasted like the hated Listerine, but then almond sweetness and clean-scented cherry subdued the bitter alcohol. Soon things got fuzzy, like walking along the edge of a fjord and dropping painlessly into the dark sea below. As she sank, she wondered if she faded away in others' eyes as well. It was comfortable to disappear around Dilly, but the comfort collided with her desire to turn heads, leaving her stranded on a rough sandbar between the anesthetic depths and the sea of applause she always craved. She heard Dilly talking as though from a distance.

"How do they make *eau de vie*?" he asked, picking up the bottle and checking the name. Henriette took another sip and let her eyes drift across the room. Three women stood talking, perhaps a few years older than she. They all wore pants — pants at a party! — and one wore a man's flannel shirt in bold plaid. Another had her hair in braids. Female linguists. They looked utterly at ease with each other, gassing in their work clothes, and Henriette feared she would never be competent to join their ranks. But she was going to sleep with Dilly. Sleep with, shack up with — she played with the language of pairing and imagined a place for herself at Dilly's side, admired and beloved more than any female scientist. Female work is bound to stink, anyway, she told herself. Only the males do anything worthwhile. Dilly turned back to her, hand kneading her shoulder.

"How do you like it?" he asked.

"It's OK," she said. She saw her opportunity to speak to the professor. "How do you find out what a word means when you don't know the language?"

"You have to learn some of it first, some vocabulary and grammar. Isidor Daniels and I have been working on the Chiricahua language for years. And the informants speak English," Ingebritsen said. "There's always gesture. But warpath language is harder, since it's made up of circumlocutions, like the word for house. Literally, a house is 'a mass of mud lies,' when you're on the warpath. The word for fire is even more obscure — it's 'that which tells a story.'"

"That's wonderful," said Henriette. "As if each word were a little poem." She snuggled against Dilly. Then she relegated the most successful and well-known women in anthropology to an unattractive category with a name that made her smile: post-menopausal baboons.

"Maybe we should go," said Dilly.

"Yeah," she said. He polished off her drink, got his coat, said his goodbyes, and steered her out into the cold.

"We can go back to my place," he said. "Carl's on call tonight. He'll be at the hospital 'til morning." She inhaled sharply. If only Dilly's forthright declaration would steam right over the dangers of frowns, reminiscent smells, and unwanted touches, leaving a clean slate. She still hoped to overcome civilization's discontents and undo the damage wrought by...who were Huxley's trio? Jesus, Newton, Henry Ford. All those guys who destroyed the life of the body. Huxley's summation was quotable and cute, but no way equal to the mix of lust and terror that had overcome her at the Haymarket rally when her body had been threatened. She huddled closer to Dilly as they walked the few blocks to the apartment. Once in the door he kissed her hard, tongue snaking through her lips, his whole body clinging until she pulled away.

"I need to breathe," she said, throwing her coat on the sofa. He went to the kitchen and ran a glass of water, then offered her some. She took a sip.

"How about it?" he asked, with a sort of leer that embarrassed her. Her nerves fired haphazardly. Now was the moment — and now, and now — that would seal or destroy their alliance. If she were ever going to stand up to real opposition, she would need to have all of him behind and within her: curly body hair, octave-spanning hands, radiant warmth and passion. She would need his calm confidence in the face of argument, his rare but potent fury, and his knowledge of what happened when steel met explosive powder. And she needed to give him all of herself, to unite with him body and soul.

Wordless, she let herself be led to the bedroom. Each removed clothes in the dark and slipped under the covers.

"What about safety?" asked Henriette.

"Don't worry," said Dilly. "I have rubbers." Embarrassed by the word, she waited. He turned toward her on one elbow and touched her face, sliding his hand to her breast and her belly. As it moved into her thick pubic hair, she pushed it away, frightened by her explosion of feeling and his access to its source. He circled her with both arms and embraced her, sliding a leg between hers, and that felt good. Her hands on his back detected all-over fuzz, and she thought of the plush dolls of childhood, but when he began to move against her, a gorge choked her throat, and a smell like old fruit leaked out of the bag she'd determined to sink, a smell of apple cores left to turn brown on a window sill. When he rolled on top of her, she realized with an inner smile that his penis was like an oyster swallowed — once inside, it was gone. She embraced him, feeling just a trace of pleasure. The warmth rose and filled her with a feeling like hope, like maybe the world could be healed, the unnamable damage undone. Then she realized she might not be doing enough to deserve this good fortune. She should reward his virility, and she would do her part. She began to move with him and moan, pacing her breathing to his and letting him think they were side by side on the same roller coaster, cresting and plunging to earth in perfect unison.

RELIEVED TO HAVE PASSED THIS landmark with Dilly and unwilling for Carl to find her there in the morning, she dressed and hurried back to Foster through deserted, foggy streets, after assuring Dilly that she walked home alone all the time. It was only ten, and she carried a lit cigarette as defensive weapon, ready to push it at anyone who might assault her. A light rain was falling, and gray mud sucked at her flats. Trudging down the street to avoid the shadows, she imagined the watery muck entering at her feet and spreading pollution up her legs, filling the cavity of her torso, until it joined the filthy fullness at the back of her throat.

There must exist somewhere, she thought, a beautiful, oceanic sexuality that could carry her away on wings of ecstasy and love. That's how sex should be, ecstatic, like in the movies. She would leave her body with its itches and needs and be transported into clouds of bliss, like Hedy Lamarr, with no annoying snaps or zippers or anatomical parts. Her chest might heave (close-up here) or her forearms rise to cover her face, a mere twitch of her eyebrows hinting at climax, but the rest of her body would cease to exist, blended in perfect harmony with that of her lover.

She remembered Dilly's smirk — soft, desirous, and a little greedy when he'd said, "How about it?" Sex certainly hadn't been the experience of perfect unity for which she'd hoped, each inside the other, sharing arms and legs. They were inarguably different in more ways than one. Her throat ached. She walked faster and began to run, but the smirk and the question continued to sit at the upper left corner of her mind and hold her captive, suggestive and disgusting. She ran faster, shaking her head, but the look just sat there, perched in its corner. Tears mixed with sobs as she ran. Then the heavy wooden door of Foster stared her in the face, slamming the look away. She paused, stamped her cigarette on the ground, opened the door, and went up to her room.

HENRIETTE AND DILLY CONTINUED TO sleep together as May warmed into June, thrilled by subterfuge when they sneaked into her room at Foster or took advantage of Carl's nights on call at the hospital, but soon Henriette's bad feelings percolated through her fakery. Some days her reluctance wore him out, and he came before she'd even opened her legs, making them both feel like failures. One night he rolled off her, exasperated.

"What do you want?" he asked. "Seems you don't want sex, just snuggly-wuggly cuddling."

"Hell no," she said. "If I acted like a teddy bear, you'd probably chase me like a six-year-old, prick in hand."

"Sounds like fun," he said. "Maybe what you want is a knight in shining armor, someone to sweep you off your feet and into rainbow-colored clouds."

"I do want a knight, the palely loitering kind."

"Well, my idea of knights is old, bold and not so particular. You know that one?" She refused to acknowledge the well-worn joke about "screwing them perpendicular" and turned away. "I'm sorry," he said. "I just want to be your dope, your derp, your dallying dildo." He turned toward her and put an arm around her waist.

"Don't be juvenile," she said. "You're idiotic, despotic, quixotic." She laughed at the words but curled up into a ball, shrinking from the hard insistence that now approached her from behind, searching between her folds for feelings.

DESPITE THESE DIFFICULTIES, THEY BEGAN to regard themselves as a couple. Henriette liked her new status but felt confined. There was something blunt and stubborn about Dilly with his big head and hands, something knobby and rough like the potatoes that filled his family's fields. He'd rebelled against his father's ungenerous and conservative politics, but she could tell his rebellion only went so far. His feet were still rooted deep in agricultural soil, and his manners in small-town propriety. She had never thought she would be with anyone who hadn't been analyzed, and Dilly wasn't interested. She doubted he ever would be. But he was reliable and single-minded, an upcoming academic, and she was proud to be sleeping with him.

Chapter 14

Henriette greeted Dilly formally at the screened-in porch when he arrived for dinner in Oak Park. He paused at the curving staircase, looking up, and Henriette wished she could infuse him with knowledge of everything that stamped or sneaked or scurried up or down those stairs. She took his hand and led him to the living room, angling her steps to show off the stylish, asymmetrical drape of her flowered dress over her right shoulder. She hoped he'd be unnerved by the house, like she was, to start. Then she wanted to see him pit his professorial intellect and farmer's knowledge of acts of God against whatever subtle confusions the family could offer. Carl and Russell rose from the couch to greet him.

"No one will give you a drink around here," said Carl. "Have some giggle water." He pulled out a flask, got glasses from the dining room, and poured whisky neat for himself and Dilly. Russell declined.

Mother marched from the kitchen, tall and stocky with apron, gray woolen skirt and sensible shoes. She planted her feet and appraised Dilly, looking askance at the glasses in their hands, while Carl introduced them. "Diller," she repeated. "Unusual name," and she offered a brusque, firm handshake.

"We call him Dilly," said Henriette, talking fast. "No one ever says Diller. It's his mother's family name: originally d'Ailly, French. So Dilly's really closer to the original. You should call him Dilly too."

"Dilly," said Mother.

Henriette felt a sudden urge to explode the conventional deceits of the family dinner. She pressed her lips together and just avoided saying, "He's an early hominid, Mother, and I'm sleeping with him." She pictured two naked, upright apelike people, covered with hair, opposable thumbs on their feet, walking arm in arm. A strangled laugh escaped her throat, and Mother glanced at her sharply before returning to the kitchen. Henriette settled with the men in the living room.

"How are things at Purdue?" Dilly asked Russell. "Will you go back?"

"Probably," said Russell. "I need the degree, and the school is a necessary lesson in conformity. The worst part is finding a job afterward."

"It's no better in anthropology," said Dilly. "You're lucky if you can make two thousand bones a year. Please don't tell your parents. Still, it's better than you can do farming."

"Who's farming?" asked Russell.

"That's what my family does," said Dilly. Silence.

"It's easy to get an internship in medicine," said Carl. "And they pay you nothing at all. So drink up!" He refilled their glasses, and the turn of a doorknob announced Father's arrival. As he entered the living room, soft brown eyes hesitant, Henriette rose to greet him. He put an arm around her waist, and she turned away, winding herself neatly out of the embrace, then introduced him to Dilly.

"How are you feeling?" Henriette asked.

Father shrugged. "Dr. Patches says I have to slow down," he said. "But that's not an option. You know how it is in advertising. If you don't go forward, you go back." He addressed Dilly. "Young man," he began, and Henriette winced, thinking how little Father knew or would ever know about Dilly: Fuzzy animal in bed, potato farmer, respected academic, singer of "Sam Hall." Soon Father would have to refer to him as Doctor Brannigan. "Would you like to see my three-dimensional photos of wildflowers?"

"Father," said Russell. "Let the man sit down. Carl just poured him a drink."

Soon Mother appeared, apron gone, a beaded choker at her neck, to announce that dinner was served. Dilly unfolded his napkin with care and began to tuck it into his collar, then glanced around the table and spread it in his lap instead. Henriette nodded approval.

"The greengrocer always saves me the freshest spinach," said Mother, as Father carved the well-done shoulder of lamb. Mother spooned out the creamy green.

"We grow our own vegetables," said Dilly. "That means we have all we can eat in the summer, then live from the root cellar in winter — mostly potatoes."

"Farming..." said Father. "That must be really difficult these days."

"Nearly impossible," said Dilly. "That's why I'm planning to teach."

"You can't make much teaching, I don't think."

"No, but people will always need to learn," said Dilly. "And anthropology can help different cultures understand each other." Carl and Henriette exchanged glances. "Governor Roosevelt has done a lot for education in New York," continued Dilly. "If he gets elected it could improve my chances."

"And show those noisy Reds that capitalist democracy can work," said Father.

"I'm sure it can," said Dilly, warming to the subject. "Combined with social programs, like the Governor advocates. Then we'll have more jobs, and the Reds won't have so much to talk about."

"That's what Julius Rosenwald, my first boss, wanted. Education and better jobs for everyone. But Sears has changed. Now it's staunch against the unions."

"What do you think Roosevelt would do about the Nazi surge in Germany?" asked Dilly. "In the two years since the last election Hitler's upped his percentage from 18% to 37%. That's scary."

"Roosevelt would stay out of it, I'm sure. Conditions here are way too terrible for us to get involved in foreign affairs. No one wants that." Henriette felt torn between dislike of Dilly's agreement with Father and relief that the two were getting along. She retreated to her private reflections. Why should eating be public and social, while sex was private — well, semi-private — and personal? And what about defecation? Each of the complex people at this table was really a tube, food in at one end and waste out at the other. How it would simplify things if everyone shared her vision. Suddenly her chewing felt noisy. A loud glunk as she swallowed.

Dilly took a deep breath. "I think a great deal of your daughter," he said to Father.

"I hope you treat her like the lady that she is," said Father, stern. Dilly nodded compliance. "And the brilliant, beautiful woman she is becoming. Ever since she was a little girl…." His voice edged upwards and began to squeak. Little girl, lady, thought Henriette. Does he picture me in a chastity belt? Apparently Dilly wasn't the only one Father knew nothing about.

"I'm not an outlaw on horseback, sir," said Dilly, apparent unfazed by Father's sudden emotion. "I'm not going to swoop her up and carry her away."

"No," said Father with a sigh, glancing at Henriette and then down at his plate. How could Father not rejoice at her good fortune, to be admired by this smart, ambitious man, on his way to the Ph.D.? Apparently Dilly had cut a wire supporting the family portrait, and it hung at an awkward angle.

Mother moved stiffly, serving little wedges of white cake with a yellow sauce, while Carl and Russell whispered. Henriette stood by, not touching dessert, then burst into the scene to show Dilly how to eat the cake. "This," she said, in a theatrical, singsong voice, "is the spoon with which you cut the cake." She stood, hands raised, then lowered one hand on the dessert spoon lined up above the plate. "And this," and her other hand fluttered down, "is the fork with which you eat the piece you cut. Be careful." Her voice turned witchy. "That sharp little fork could make some nice holes in flesh." Mother and Father were silenced. Carl and Russell laughed in the satisfied way they always did when lines of force in the family portrait were exposed. Dilly patted Henriette's hand as she sat down, saying, "It's OK. I'll be careful." Everyone pushed back from the table, as though agreeing to retreat from the threat of Dilly's hint of serious courtship.

AFTER THANKS AND FAREWELLS, HENRIETTE walked Dilly to the train. The minute they were out of the house she threw her arms around him, and he picked her up and whirled her, both laughing, as they reviewed the evening and imagined what the parents would think if they only knew what Henriette and Dilly did at night.

"You handle them so easily," said Henriette, as they walked arm in arm.

"They seem normal to me," said Dilly. Normal! But she was relieved that Dilly didn't look too closely. "Except your father," continued Dilly. "When I said I really like you. Ha! That blew his wig." She wanted to respond in the same light vein, but her throat thickened .

"Don't worry about him," she said, her throat still lumpy. She tightened her grip on his arm. "Remember when you said you'd be Cassandra's gatekeeper? Will you stand between the parents and me?" Her voice caught and came out high and reedy. He frowned.

"They'll need to trust me if we're going to stay together," he said, putting his free hand over hers on his arm. "That's what I'm hoping for."

"Stay together," she said. "That sounds good." She laid her head on his shoulder and sighed. "But I don't know about trust."

DILLY PLANNED TO VISIT KITACHARA before heading to Oregon for the summer, and he invited Henriette to come and meet his family. On a Saturday morning they packed up some bread and cheese and a thermos of coffee and took off.

"How's the old flivver holding up?" asked Henriette.

"It'll get us there," said Dilly. The first commercial car radio had recently come on the market, but radios cost a quarter the price of a car, so the couple made their own music, singing Governor Roosevelt's campaign song. "Happy days are here again/The skies above are clear again/So let's sing a song of cheer again/Happy days are here again." It was fun to sing but impossible to convince themselves that things were getting better. Seventeen thousand veterans of the Great War, most unemployed, had descended on Washington to march for their unpaid bonuses, and Hoover had authorized General MacArthur to rout them. Convinced that the march was a Communist conspiracy, MacArthur sent in Cavalry backed by six tanks, pursued the men to their main camp across the Anacostia River, and finally burned it down. Two dead, over a hundred arrested, many injured. The image of fire in a camp of homeless veterans, along with their wives and children, was as terrible anything the Depression had yet produced. No president could be worse than Hoover, and the couple placed some hope in the upcoming election.

As they drove out of the city, they amused themselves by reading rhyming signs posted along the side of the road: "Golfers/If fewer strokes/Are what you crave/You're out of the rough/With Burma Shave." Further north, spring regressed. Leafing trees turned to barren twigs; green fields gave way to frosty ones, and patches of snow replaced mud. They pulled off the side of the road just after crossing a one-lane bridge and sniffed the air, then walked back. Below the railing ice was breaking up, and water flowed under and around it. "That creek is full of fish," said Dilly. "Right about now deer are giving birth and keeping their fawns hidden in the woods while they forage for food. We probably won't see any."

"How do you know?" asked Henriette.

"You spend enough time in the wild, you get to know its rhythms, its sounds and silences. It's like learning a tune by heart. Listen." He led her a little ways into the woods, parting branches, and they listened to sounds of scampering feet and birdsong.

"Would you really shoot a deer?" asked Henriette.

"Not now — it's illegal. But in the fall, of course." Henriette hoped she'd never have to witness a deer, such a delicate creature, with a hole in its heart. Back in the car, they ate, tearing chunks from the loaf and warming their hands with the hot cups.

"Peaceful," said Henriette.

"Yes," said Dilly, patting her thigh. "Peaceful and beautiful." They drove past the Brannigans' potato fields and arrived at their house in town. Dilly took Henriette's hand as they walked across the lawn to the wide, wraparound porch with its suspended porch swing. Rose, Dilly's mother, came hurrying through the dining room to the front hall, wearing an apron.

"Delighted to meet you, my dear," said Rose with a warm smile. "Make yourself at home. You can have the guest room, and Dilly will sleep on the sun porch." Henriette glanced up the stairway that turned abruptly away from the small entryway. Clay, Dilly's father, was coming down, and she couldn't help looking at his face, a series of mountains and valleys, the cheek hollow and the mouth running downhill toward his chin on the side of the missing ear, making his expression dour.

"How do you do?" said Clay, and he and Henriette shook hands.

"Why don't you show Henriette her room?" asked Rose. Dilly picked up Henriette's small bag, and they climbed the stairs.

"You knew we couldn't sleep together, didn't you?" asked Dilly, once they were out of earshot.

"Of course," said Henriette. "Your parents seem friendly and direct. That's what matters." He kissed her, pressing her close for a moment, and she nuzzled his cheek. Then he led her to the back stairs, telling her how he and his brother, Finn, used to scamper down them on cold winter mornings in search of the kitchen's warmth. Dilly hadn't mentioned his brother since the night of the musical party, and now the past seemed to swirl, enfolding Dilly in a homecoming bitter with absence, but even that absence was clear and comprehensible. They walked downstairs.

"Can I do anything? asked Henriette.

"No," said Rose, moving with familiar ease from stovetop to oven to check on a roast, releasing delicious smells. A few hairs escaped from her pure white bun and curled around her face. "Just have a seat in the dining room." Dilly and Henriette sat in the formal room on ladder-backed chairs. Curved armrests distinguished the chairs at the head and foot of the table, and plants on a trellised rack occupied a corner by the window. Through an open door Henriette could just see a gun rack on the wall of the garage, and she blanched at the array of weapons, wooden parts burnished and metal parts blue-black, looking cold. She put her foot on a small bump in the rug under the table and caught Dilly's eye with a question.

"Bell to summon the maid we've never had," said Dilly. "That's your napkin," he continued, pointing out a blue cloth rolled up and held by a wooden ring. "It'll be yours all weekend." Henriette removed it from the ring and spread it in her lap.

Soon Clay joined them at the head of the table, and Rose served chicken noodle soup. Clay asked about Dilly's work, and he answered with enthusiasm, describing the inventories he expected to make of food, clothing and other aspects of material culture at Klamath Indian Reservation but saying nothing about his hope of learning more about myth and ritual.

"I hope you'll be careful with money," said Clay. "I remember your accounts never balanced in college."

"They balanced more or less," said Dilly, glancing at Henriette and looking irritated. "I've got a small grant from the Social Science Research Council. The expedition is giving me a place to stay and food, and the money's just enough for gas and booze." What nerve, thought Henriette, remembering the tiny, detailed rows of figures Clay had written out for Dilly, a budget for his first years in college. Dilly had showed it to her with a bitter laugh, then touched it with a match and watched it burn.

Clay frowned. "Have you thought of getting a better job?" he asked.

"I'm getting a Ph.D., Father," said Dilly.

"We'll see where that gets you," said Clay. Dilly and Rose exchanged glances, then looked down and ate soup, while distant voices of children playing filtered through a barely open window.

"Looks like that rich New York Governor might defeat President Hoover," Clay said. "I'm sure he'll know how to waste money."

"Maybe he'll put the economy back on its feet," said Dilly.

"Spending money never made money," said Clay. "Abandoning the gold standard was like pushing off in a boat without a compass." Rose started collecting soup bowls, and Henriette got up to help her. From the kitchen Rose brought a roast of venison and set it on the table before Clay, who sharpened a knife on a steel and began cutting thin, rosy-centered slices.

"Have you ever eaten venison?" Rose asked Henriette.

"No," said Henriette. "But I'd like to try it." She thought of their pause in the woods, and Bambi edged into her consciousness like a deer peeking into a clearing. Henriette shooed her, and she bounded away.

"It's like beef," said Rose, "but leaner."

"And tougher," added Dilly. "Henriette likes to chew." Henriette set a bowl of mashed potatoes on the table and Rose brought gravy in a boat-shaped dish and a molded salad: shards of cabbage and carrot embedded in green gelatin.

"The new lime Jell-O is all the rage," said Rose. "Have some," and she spooned a shaky mass onto Henriette's plate.

"Thank you," said Henritte, and her stomach fluttered.

"What about you?" asked Rose. "What are you studying?"

"I'm in anthropology too," said Henriette. "I hope to go to graduate school after college and maybe do field work in New Mexico." She spoke up willingly, proud to have a plan that dovetailed with Dilly's and faintly aware that she was outdoing Rose in education and ambition. You had to watch out for mothers if you were going to love their sons.

"Aren't you afraid of the drought and the dust storms?" asked Rose.

"It *has* been dry," said Henriette. "But I'm looking forward to the desert. It's stark but beautiful. My professor does field work there." The gamy flavor of venison woke up her taste buds, like her favorite, stinky Limburger cheese. She found she could relish small pieces, but if she ate too much the deer that died crowded into her consciousness, and she turned to the safer potatoes.

"I envy you young people, all that traveling," said Rose, and a shadow passed over her face, turning her mouth down at the corners. Finn, perhaps. The death trap of which Dilly had spoken. Henriette swirled mashed potatoes with her fork so the gravy found a channel and ran down to the plate. Then she sampled the molded salad's mix of crunch, spurt and slither, discovering a hint of invisible pineapple. Not bad. She wondered if she would ever be able to cook like this. Rose brightened.

"I'm going to be making my own little trip," she said. "Aunt Flora's in the hospital with pneumonia, and I'm going to go down to Milwaukee to help with the children."

"You'll like Milwaukee," said Dilly. "They've opened four new theatres in the last few years. You'll have something to tell about at Travel Club."

"Milwaukee doesn't mean travel to the Wilsons, the Tates, or anyone else in the Club," said Rose. "Travel is Paris, the Dolomites, skiing in Kitzbühel, for those who can afford it. Still, I'm looking forward to Milwaukee."

"We're glad to help Aunt Flora out," said Clay, his tone a flat betrayal of his words.

"Don't ever let yourself get trapped in this town," said Rose to Henriette. "It saps the hope right out of you." Startled by Rose's frank warning, Henriette got up to help clear plates. Rose brought out a pan of ball-shaped, brown envelopes of dough, sitting in a sea of thick, brown syrup. "Apple dumplings," said Rose and served them up with agile pride, spooning a little of the syrup over each crisp dome. Henriette poked at the construction, shattering the tender crust to reveal a whole baked apple, the core removed and stuffed with nuts. She collected fruit, crust and syrup in one spoonful, and a panoply of sensations flooded her mouth. The apple still tart, crunch of nuts. She closed her eyes. How could crust be so crisp after baking in a swamp? And over all, brown sugar's memory of molasses mixed with butter leached from the dough. Rose may have lost hope, but her hand was still liberal, con-signing all these good things to one night's dessert. Henriette opened her eyes and, glancing at Rose, saw not just acceptance but possibly affection in the making.

After dinner Clay and Rose went out on the porch, leaving Henriette and Dilly alone.

"Let me show you our guns," said Dilly. "When you get to know them they're not so frightening." Henriette hesitated. "They're useful, like knives in the kitchen." He led her out to the garage. "You could learn with a shot gun," he said. "They're lighter and easier to handle." He took down a long gun with smooth, wooden stock and placed it in her hands. "Feel the weight," he said. Heavier than she expected, it felt electric, as though quivering with its potential for violence. She gave it back quickly. "It's not loaded," he said, smiling. "Look," and he removed the magazine to show her. "Now you put it back," he said. He held out the gun and she tried to do as he said, but her stomach threatened to reject the deer she'd just eaten. There was no turning back from the harm guns could do, and she didn't want to know how they worked or even think about them.

"Let me show you how to hold it," said Dilly, and he placed the gun against her shoulder, showed her the trigger and how to aim. Now she felt silly, like a character in a Western movie.

"Lesson's over," she said. "This is not for me."

"I thought maybe we could hunt some pheasant tomorrow," he said, wistful.

"You go," said Henriette. "Not me. At least you don't have guns like coppers carry around in their belts and use to intimidate people."

"No one keeps those on this kind of rack," said Dilly.

Alone in her bed that night, Henriette relaxed, at peace with the family she'd just met. Love for Dilly poured out of her into the darkness, and she hugged a pillow to her chest. How unreachable he'd seemed when she'd first met him, a T.A. and a respected graduate student. Now she knew his muscular body as well as her own, and she saw in Rose the source of his animal grace and white hair. She'd thought his family might be a hurdle, but they seemed to like her. Normal, that's what they were. She wouldn't let herself think about what her parents would say if they knew about his guns and hunting. And they didn't need to know.

ON DILLY'S LAST DAY IN Chicago, he and Henriette met for lunch on campus, carrying sandwiches from the C-shop out into Hutchinson Court, where they ate in warm sunshine.

"It seemed to go well with your parents," said Henriette. "Did they say anything about me being Jewish?"

"I told them you were Unitarian," said Dilly, "and they asked me if that was anything like Anarchist." Laughter. "They don't know anything but Protestant," he continued, pronouncing it Pro*test*ant. "Except for Grandpa Brannigan, the man with his foot on the pillow. Of course he was Catholic, coming from Ireland, but he married a Pro*test*ant. After his priest castigated him from the pulpit, he left the church and never went back." Dilly took her hand. "I'll miss you. Will you be sure to write?"

"Of course. Don't worry."

"I do worry. About you. Will you be OK?" He watched her nibble and stare into space, then turn to him with a faint smile.

"Moving back to Oak Park will be hard. But I'll be fine, silly Dilly. Everything will be all right."

"Don't get in trouble while I'm gone. Steer clear of those Communist parades," he said. She wondered if he were really more worried that she would plunge into a downward spiral of upset or act on her desire to escape civilization's constraints. Probably, but none of these were as challenging or frightening as what she was really thinking of doing.

"Are you kidding?" she asked. "I go to those things all the time.

"All the same," he said, "I hope you'll be careful."

Settling into the comforting zone of his concern, she hugged and kissed him good-bye. She hoped her talk had not outrun her competence. "Don't take any wooden nickels," she said, seeking a tone lighter than she felt.

"Abyssinia," he said, waving as he walked away.

"Be seeing you too," she said. She trusted him to write and to keep her in mind, and she'd do the same, but how would she cope if living at home left her weepy and hopeless? And if she escaped to make her daring trip, she'd face hatred that made home look like a parlor game.

Chapter 15

Summer heated up, and lawns grew thick and lush in Oak Park, masking tons of dirt beneath. Henriette hadn't fully anticipated how Dilly's absence would leave her: stranded in Oak Park, embracing space. Beyond the window Mother's perky flowers invited Henriette to their cool undersurface where roots sought water and worms tunneled. She'd have a place there, sooner or later. Sooner. Feeling itself was a burden she needed to shed, and she envied the earth. Grains of loam infiltrated and clogged her veins, then came to settle in the empty pit of her stomach, where they seethed and bubbled in digestive juice, restless. She longed for a current to catch or a tail to latch onto. *Vaporize, volatilize, amortize*: she collected ways that she might disperse or do away with her parents or herself.

She began to sleep longer, sometimes fourteen hours a day. Dilly wrote, but mail took over a week, airmail was prohibitively expensive, and long distance phone calls were out of the question. She pictured her words wandering across the vast plains, stumbling over the Rockies and searching the coast for Dilly. "At the moment the health is bad," she wrote, "and I need lots of sleep and milk or sun or something. I guess I'm really on the skids, but it doesn't matter much to me."

Two weeks later she received a reply. Dilly expressed concern for what he took to be physical illness, and it made her furious. She would have given him her diagnosis if she'd had one. But two weeks was much too long for a quick retort, and her irritation multiplied as she read his breezy report. He'd gone out on the town with other graduate students and Professor Hankton in Berkeley, where the professor was teaching for the summer. They'd gone "sightdrinking," as Dilly wrote, staggering from a ferry ride across the bay to one open-air seafood stand after another, while brightly colored kites flew overhead in San Francisco's brilliant sunshine. Then it was a bar or two, a striptease joint, and back to the ferry, now under a sky filled with stars. How could Dilly be having so much fun when her life was turning more unbearable by the minute? Soon he would be heading up the coast toward Klamath with a stop at his Uncle Rob's near Mendocino. Life in Rob's cabin would be spare and constrained, Henriette guessed, and she welcomed the limit on Dilly's freedom to carouse.

A FEW DAYS LATER, HOPING to run into a friend, she took the train to Hyde Park. A slight young man approached her as she walked across campus.

"I'm Patrick Harding," he said. With wavy, brown hair, high cheek bones and an ingratiating smile, he was almost too pretty for a boy. "I saw you on May Day," he said. "You were wonderful, a true Spirit of the Haymarket. The way you just turned as the eagles rose in the poem and then brought your hands up. It was beautiful." He lifted long-fingered hands to illustrate, turned them over and let them fall. "What's your connection to the ILD?"

Surprised and flattered at the compliment, Henriette told him how she'd met Harold Overstreet years ago at the Sunset Café and later heard him speak at the Left Wing Alliance. She'd volunteered to help out whenever she could, and they'd asked her to recite the poem. Patrick was in the same year as she, also fond of English literature, and they slipped easily into talk about Aldous Huxley, F. Scott Fitzgerald and poets from Keats to Pound. He seemed young to her, and she felt in charge, relieved to talk to someone who didn't require translation from farm to city or anthro to psych. He invited her to go to the movies that weekend, and she felt a moment of doubt, wondering how that would sit with Dilly. But Dilly could hardly expect her to stay sequestered for four months. She accepted.

Friday evening they took the train downtown and saw "Grand Hotel," with John and Lionel Barrymore and Greta Garbo, and Henriette was ravished by the self-centered and stunning star, Grusinkaya, played by Garbo. In the darkened theatre Patrick's hand sought hers, and it fit easily, the fingers flexible, like hers. Grusinskaya swept across the room, low-cut gown flowing, every eyelash expressing demands for attention and love, and Henriette wished she had the nerve to discover that character in herself, to try on that imperious voice and glance. Yet when she had demanded attention, like on May Day, it had turned dangerous. If you asserted your right to the center knowing you lacked something, knowing you were damaged, well — you'd be under the spotlight with no place to hide. And Lucky had somehow sensed her vulnerability, turning up to criticize her working with the ILD, reminding her of the night they'd spent together, acting like she owed him something. Henriette was careful never to give offense, and Lucky's anger felt newly dangerous. How could she even think of going to Alabama when she was afraid to stand on a stage or face a resentful, disappointed boyfriend?

A few days after the movie Henriette ran into Patrick on campus and stopped to chat, leaning against a tree. Slight sweat under her arms, on her forehead. Self-conscious charm in the tilt of her body as she talked. Rough texture of bark delicious on her back. He invited her for coffee, and they walked across the main quadrangle and down

University Avenue to the C-shop. At first she felt like a kid playing hooky, but soon she began to feel lightheaded, then anxious. There was too much air in the summery day and not enough ground.

Something insinuated itself between herself and the world, an awful sort of veil that crept between her and the gusty day, souring her mouth and fogging her eyesight. She squinted, trying to peer through, but she was stuck, unable to touch the outside world, which retreated like a train disappearing into a tunnel. Apparently Patrick noticed nothing amiss. After a brief talk, they went their separate ways, but the veil remained, gray and sticky, filming her eyes and ears and tangling around her feet.

HENRIETTE'S LATE-JUNE BIRTHDAY DAWNED CLOUDY and hot. She tossed off the covers, dreading a day she would spend inside her own skin, put some bus tokens in her purse and left the house with no idea where she would go. She expected nothing and would get nothing from the day, but everyone should know she needed all the everything she'd never get. Where were bunches of yellow roses and garlanded cakes, ribbons and gifts and accolades? Where in hell was Dilly? He'd written her in pencil on lined yellow paper, but apparently he'd forgotten her birthday. If the parents insisted on the "happy birthday" farce, they could do it tonight. She was nobody, and she didn't care.

She got on a bus going anywhere and sat down. The driver ignored her birthday too, and she stuck her chin in the air, thinking, "I'll never tell." She rode the bus to the end of the line in a distant suburb, angry words boxing each other in her head. Dilly should know; how could he not know? He knows I like roses; he wrote me on yellow, but no yellow roses. That bastard did nothing; he never sent roses; just wrote me on yellow; it shows that he knows. The words circled into rhymes in her head, driving her crazy, as though they were making fun of her righteous anger, making her sound like a fool. *Write me, you bastard!* She scrawled on a piece of paper, and then tucked it into her purse to mail later. She crossed the street, got on the bus going the other way and went on riding to nowhere all day, speaking to no one, sitting through the bad tea party in her head. If she couldn't get through the day, how was she going to get through the summer?

SHORTLY THEREAFTER PATRICK CALLED HER, and she met him at I-House, where they ate meatloaf and mashed potatoes in the cafeteria. He looked at her with big eyes that shined with adoration and suggested she come with him to his dorm room. She hadn't expected this invitation and hesitated, remembering Dr. Whitson's total silence when she'd talked about the life of the body and her goal of liberation. But the doctor was on vacation for all of August, and sex might propel her through the veil, she thought, jerk her feet from the gravel and release her to the life other people seemed to live all the time. Dilly was gone. He'd left her to rot and she needed something, someone. She would not be using Patrick. She was just trying to survive. She knew she was sick; she knew she was crazy, but the talky part of herself went on telling her she was free and could do whatever she wanted, so why not?

Girls weren't allowed in the men's dorm, but she had girlfriends who'd been in there. You just dashed through the hall and disappeared. In the morning, you waited until most people had left for early classes, then sneaked out. She pictured herself flitting in and out of the dorm, as ghostly as the Spirit of Haymarket, and she told herself it would be a fine escapade.

Patrick entered the dorm first, checked the hallway and signaled "all clear." Laughing, she scampered up a few steps and into his room, where he closed and locked the door. Now what? she thought. He kissed her, and they played a little tongue-tag, but he didn't seem to know what to do next. Already her stomach felt jumpy, and she wondered what she would do if she needed a toilet. She scanned the room for exits and found only solid walls, a firmly closed window and the locked door. They sat on the edge of the bed.

"I think you're wonderful," he said, touching her hair with hesitant fingers. A sensation like moths flapping inside her head distracted her, and she tried to brush them away, plucking roughly at her hair and ears. Was the next move hers? The men she'd been with so far took care of things themselves.

"Are you OK?" asked Patrick.

"Yes," she said, but now the moths had filled her whole body, batting their wings against the wall of her stomach and inside her legs and arms, making her skin unpleasantly sensitive. Patrick got up and turned out the light. She heard him shed his pants in the dark, and he sat by her, ran his hand up her thigh and reached for the elastic on her panties, pressing her down on the bed as he pulled them off. This time, she thought, she wouldn't just lie there like a corpse; she'd take control. He moaned approval when she touched him, then raised on one elbow and buried his fingers between her legs. She jerked back, body and soul repulsed, letting go of him and pushing his hand away. Something choked her like fruit juice that runs down your throat on the sly. His hand kept seeking her, and every time it got close her body threatened to fly apart.

"Turn on the light!" she cried, jumping out of bed.

"What's wrong?" he asked, his face alarmed in the sudden light. She smoothed his thick, tousled hair.

"Let's undress and get properly into bed," she said. "Then I'll be OK." His eyes squinted, and his erection peeked out from between his shirttails, making her laugh. Now the initiative was hers, and she was at the helm. Back in bed, she opened her legs, willing the moths to settle and her body not to feel too much, holding both the dark and his hands at bay. In the morning, desperate for a toilet, she escaped through the empty hallway and the front door, but the fluttering moths and the choking sensation returned at odd moments during the days that followed, making clear thought impossible.

She couldn't decide if she'd taken a step toward liberation or betrayed her love for Dilly, but either way she felt worse each day. Maybe she was just punishing Dilly for his bars and striptease joints, for his freedom to roam while she was stuck here. But revenge didn't count for much if he wasn't even worrying about her. He seemed to be drifting away, and the vision of herself cut off, alone in a rocky moonscape, made her tear her hair and dig fingernails into her skin, anything to replace bad feeling with simple pain. She tried to throw up, but there was no way to get out of her skin. She would stop eating. Nothing sweet or rich. No tearing meat from bone. Not even crunchy celery, her favorite. Eating was one thing she could control.

TWO WEEKS LATER, ANOTHER LETTER from Dilly arrived, and Henriette sat on the bed in her room staring at the envelope. Even the paper seemed to reprimand her for spending the night with Patrick. She tried to remember Dilly's friendliness, the weight of his body on hers, his fecund smell and his fuzzy back, but he remained a flat and brittle critic, telling her she was bad. He was right. She pulled out the letter and read:

"Boiling hot in the Central valley, and no trees around Uncle Rob's bungalow. He's got a young wife, Polly — well they're not exactly married — and Rob says it would cost him his job if anyone found out. And they've got a beautiful new baby. He claims his separated wife has been driving around in disguise, threatening to kidnap the baby while he's in Sacramento. Feels like I'm in a movie."

Henriette imagined his square-nailed fingers typing out the letters, hunting and pecking, and she typed out her response in her mind.

"If I were there I could help you understand the complex tensions in that sun-baked bungalow. Looks like you're going to have to manage by yourself." She stopped typing to blurt, "Who cares about all those people? Why don't you ask about me?" But she was not Grusinskaya and could never say that aloud or on paper.

"Two guys from the Indian Service came to dinner last night, looking like they'd never been closer to the reservation than the Agency office," continued Dilly's letter. "Then they told this stupid story about an old Indian at Zuni who sold chickens, and no one knew where he got them. Turned out the Indian kept a fox on a leash, took the fox out nights and turned him loose in the neighboring henhouse. Then he collected the dead chickens, fed one to the fox and sold the rest. That story's pure hogwash, typical of stories designed to make Indians seem clever primitives." Told you so, thought Henriette. Stay away from the Agency.

"And why couldn't these guys relax and enjoy the evening? Maybe they belong to a bourgeois subculture where formal hospitality, with its clear rules, is easier to accept than informal friendliness. Call it a bourgeoicracy." The new term made Henriette smile, and his parsing of hospitality released a flood of longing for the man so generous with his eggs and whiskey and whatever he had. But even as he came back to her, round and real, she despaired at the deaf ear he turned to his own silence. She wrote that she'd given up eating.

Two weeks later, Henriette received a letter written just before Dilly left Uncle Rob's. She closed her door and opened it. "Did your guts go haywire?" he wrote. "I didn't know you'd given up eating altogether. What's the dope?" A white space on the page felt like a breath. "Uncle Rob had to go to Sacramento," continued the letter, "and I agreed to stay with Polly and the baby, protect them from potential kidnappers. Polly went out to the truck to say goodbye and discovered a gun on the seat.

She was furious, afraid Rob would get hurt. She wanted him to leave it at home, and they fought and fought. I went inside and looked at the baby asleep in her crib and felt as helpless as she. Finally I marched out to the car, stepped between them and picked up the gun from the seat, saying I'd keep it until Rob got back." Henriette tried to imagine Dilly grabbing the gun. Did he leap to the car, snatch the gun and hold it overhead, like a swaggering Wild West hero, or did he approach with cool, calm authority? Probably the latter, with a slight tremor of uncertainty, but the cold weight in his hand would have convinced him he'd done the right thing, and then he would have walked straight into the house, putting the gun in a safe place and leaving Rob and Polly with nothing to fight over. There was something final and deathly attractive about a gun on your side, like getting the last word. And you'd better mean it, because you couldn't take it back.

She wondered if people carried guns in Scottsboro. The coppers would, of course, but people on the street? Reading Dilly's letter about a real confrontation made her Scottsboro plan feel like fantasy — foolish and risky fantasy. She imagined Dilly warning her in no uncertain terms about the dangers of the trip he knew nothing about, but would he even care? She sat with his letter in her hand, wondering why he bothered to write if she had disappeared from his life.

"Then I took the baby for a walk," the letter concluded. "She looks at me as though I were the whole world, and I wish I could spirit her away from this quarreling family and surround her with love and care. I want one of those." Dilly had never said anything about children before, and Henriette herself had no particular interest in babies. Everyone had them, of course. Babies were one of many milestones you had to pass before the world would let you go, but Dilly's outpouring of love? She needed it too much for herself to think of giving it away. Dilly would soon be at Klamath, and maybe Henriette would be in Alabama after all.

PATRICK CALLED DAILY, AND SHE told him she couldn't see him or even talk to him. He pressed her, calling her "darling" and saying he was desperately in love, and she told him he could send her a letter. "I had the most awful feeling when you said you were ill," he wrote. "It frightens me, because it makes you so inaccessible." She still refused to see him, knowing the last thing she needed was someone frightened of her mental state and looking to her for strength. She wrote back:

"Perhaps because I am expert at this compulsive-obsessive verbalization I see a little more clearly than you seem to just how abysmally I have failed. All I am doing in this relationship with you is attempting to annex you, body and soul, to the already large structure that I am to myself. I shall not die — perhaps I shall never die, but I shall sleep forever in my effort to escape the waking world. The loan of your penis was much appreciated. Perhaps it was the most important annexation."

HENRIETTE NEEDED TO TALK TO Nadine, knowing her friend would reproach her lightly for her night with Patrick — not another lamebrain! she'd say — and nudge Henriette out of her black mood with energy and direction. Nadine would be fired up about the election in November and waiting impatiently for the Supreme Court's ruling on Scottsboro. Henriette wrote to the Abarvanels asking what news they had of their daughter. If she was alive, well and still reporting, Henriette could join her, and together they would demonstrate against the Scottsboro convictions and sentences, in support of the pending appeal. Nothing could be worse than stewing through the summer. She would tell her parents she was going to visit Nadine in New York, and her daring would make a silly mud puddle of the swamp in which she'd been wallowing. No one need know where she'd gone. Not even Dilly.

Chapter 16

A terse note arrived from the Abravanels expressing regret and disapproval of their daughter's trip to Alabama. They'd lost contact with Nadine, and they had no address or phone number. Henriette remembered meeting the family in New York. Big hugs. Turkey, tzimmes, homemade wine. Now, nothing. Either Scottsboro's chaos had cut communication or worse: Nadine's parents had broken with her. A landscape of rock and sand, populated by scorpions, unrolled in Henriette's imagination. No human connection. Nobody. No bodies. The axe had fallen for Nadine, and the least Henriette could do was go and find her abandoned friend.

They'll never miss me, she lied to herself as she tucked toothbrush and comb into a small necessaire. She folded cotton clothes into a satchel, hoping she'd be brave enough to shed the good little girl she'd been all her life, to actually do some good. At the station she purchased a round trip ticket on the Illinois Central Railroad for $15 and pulled out the scrap of paper saying, "Write me, you bastard." She penciled a caret between "write" and "me" and wrote "about" just above, tucked the scrap into an envelope, and wished it safe travels on its journey to Klamath. Her stomach settled, and her gaze pierced the veil that had separated her from the world. She would need quick perception and thought for this trip, and she felt ready, better than she had in a long time.

As the train pulled out of the station, light shone late on tenements, then suburban houses and finally broad fields of corn not yet
knee high. Farther on, spring became summer, foliage growing fuller
and greener, vines reaching out as if to strangle anything in their way.
The land stretched out flat to the horizon, baking under the setting
sun, and cows whizzed by. Cocooned by the container of the train,
Henriette faced gray plush seatbacks with dainty white anti-macassars
to protect the headrests from greasy hair. To her right the empty seat
and narrow aisle provided an exit, while to her left the window allowed
her to peer into people's backyards, her speed rendering her invisible.

"Are you traveling alone?" The conductor intruded, big jowls too
close. He took her ticket. "How far?" When she said she was going to
Scottsboro, the conductor drew back.

"You don't look like one a them agitators," he said. Was that what
she was? No, she was going to find Nadine. She pictured her friend as
a journalist, asking questions of people on the street and jotting down
notes. Then she tried to conjure peaceful demonstrations, women in
long dresses and big hats, carrying signs and singing, while men in
white, linen suits shook hands and agreed to disagree.

But the National Guard was still there. Not to deal with signs and
singing. They were needed to save the young men from lynching. She
screwed up her eyes and tried not to see the night riders' ritual of boiling tar, burning, piercing, and hanging Negroes, common in the South
and even, not too long ago, in Indiana. Fear invaded her cocoon and
dried her mouth. "I'm going to visit a friend."

"Well you and your friend better be careful," said the conductor.
"No telling what all's going on down there. Lotsa people going there,
lots getting inta trouble."

"I'll be careful," she said, opening a book and pretending to read
until he moved on. Mother had given her this copy of Jane Addams'

Peace and Bread in Time of War when she was nine. "Read it and you'll make a difference one day," she'd said. Henriette had been too young for the book at first and later, resistant, but now that she was defying her parents, it interested her, a justification for her trip. Perhaps she could make Mother proud, could compel Mother to mention her daughter along with her sons. She read one paragraph three times over, unable to concentrate, then left the book open on her lap. The train jerked over a trestle bridge, and Henriette peered through the window into dark water below. At this moment, Nadine might be in handcuffs. Or worse, surrounded by short-haired, sweaty white boys who grabbed her flesh, undoing their belts. Could Nadine be in jail? The Sedition Act had been repealed twelve years earlier, and no one could be imprisoned for speaking her mind. Henriette's stomach lurched upward as though she were falling off the trestle into the dark, suffocating void.

Light faded, and soon she grew drowsy. Memories of a protester she'd met as a child surfaced in a waking dream, and she wrapped herself in that happy moment. W. E. B. Dubois had come to speak at her parents' Unitarian church, and they had invited the visitor to a reception in their Oak Park home. Henriette was seven and thrilled to meet the soft-spoken hero of black folk. She and her brothers stood on display at the foot of the stairs while Mother presented them to Dr. Dubois. Henriette wriggled in the scratchy collar of her velvet dress and wondered what she could do to win the admiration her parents lavished on Dr. Dubois. He was smaller than Henriette expected, with a well-trimmed beard and mustache, tan skin and fiery eyes. He shook each of their hands with his fingertips and made a slight bow from the waist. The children took seats on the floor as everyone settled, seated or standing, to listen to the speaker.

"Dr. W.E.B. Dubois needs no introduction," said Father. "My wife and I want to welcome him to our home." Dr. Dubois spoke in a low, controlled voice.

"It does honor to the Greenbergs," he said, "That they have me here, regardless of whatever threat my presence may impose." The crowd applauded lightly, and Father bowed acknowledgement. The voice continued, meandering up and down as though walking over gentle hills, while occasional applause showered down like rain. He welcomed the mostly white audience to join the struggle. "Now let's sing," he concluded and taught them a verse of his version of "My Country 'Tis of Thee," intoning the lines so the crowd could learn the words. They joined in, quietly at first, then raising their voices to fill the room and shake the dining room's chandelier.

My native country thee
Land of the slave set free
Thy fame I love.
I love thy rocks and rills
And o'er thy hate which chills
My heart with purpose thrills
To rise above.

DAYLIGHT WOKE HENRIETTE. SHE MADE her way to the bathroom at the end of the car, freshened up, and began to read. Jane Addams had opposed the Great War when that was unpopular as well as illegal, and Henriette felt concurrence — she would make herself unpopular, even if legal, in Alabama, and Jane Addams would be company. As she read, she began to understand what Mother admired. Miss Addams debunked the myth of the noble soldier, expressing compassion for the young recruit forced to disembowel a fellow human with a bayonet. Henriette tried not to imagine what these words meant: the thrust into resistant flesh, the agony, the leaking gut, the pervasive stench. And patriotic bastards had passed the Sedition Act and forced Miss Addams to shut up. Henriette would stand up for peace and justice both. The moths, the veil, the birthday bus, the solace she'd sought from Patrick — all these she shed like the outgrown tomboy clothes of her childhood. But Dilly was very much with her. She looked at her hands and wiped a bit of sweat from her forehead, then ran her eyes down from her breasts to her feet. Same body, same person. His mother might go as far as Milwaukee on her own, but never Alabama. Dilly would surely write *about* Henriette if he knew. He'd try to stop her. "Trouble, sooner or later." She didn't intend that he should find out.

THE AIR IN THE TRAIN heated up, and the conductor opened windows from the top, letting in the acrid smell of coal smoke and the occasional cloud of soot. The corn in the fields of southern Illinois was at least thigh-high. They crossed into western Tennessee, and towards noon they stopped. Henriette got out in search of a breeze, but the air here seemed full of warm water. She walked around the small station, listening to the drawn-out vowels of southern speech. The words in her head took on this fluid sound, one word dripping into the next, like molasses accumulating around her feet and slowing her down.

In Memphis Henriette changed to a train headed East, and a woman flopped into the seat next to her. In a cotton dress printed with white and yellow daisies and a straw hat, she pulled out a fan and fluttered it in front of her face.

"Hot in Memphis," she said. "Ah was visiting mah sister. Who you visiting?"

"A college friend," said Henriette.

"Oh, yawl're college girls," said the woman.

"In Scottsboro," added Henriette.

"They say there's ten thousand visitors there, mobbing the place.

What they see, ah don't know," said the woman. "They're all a bunch of hoboes, you know, the white girls and the Negro boys. If they'd bought their seats on the train, none a this woulda happened."

"But if they're only guilty of riding the rails, should they pay the price for rape?" asked Henriette.

The wiry woman leaned in so close her sharp chin almost poked Henriette's shoulder. She spoke sotto voce. "Nine black boys and two white girls together in a car?" she asked. "You got another name for it?" Henriette flattened herself against her seat and then shrugged, shivering inside, suspecting this was just a taste of what she'd get in Scottsboro. The woman sniffed and settled back into her seat, straightening the skirt beneath her. "A body dasn't talk like that in Alabama," she said. "It's yawl they'll be stringin' up next."

Henriette lined up her allies: Theodore Dreiser with his plea for the future of the accused. Mother with her abhorrence of violence. Dilly with his faith in democracy, advocating for Indians and anyone weak or oppressed. Even Father. Though he, like Dilly, wouldn't ally himself with the Communist ILD, he would never stand for Scottsboro's travesty of due process. But Henriette was heading into the woman's country, where she would be vastly outnumbered. The defense had won a stay of execution pending appeal to the U.S. Supreme Court, and in May they'd won a hearing. The crowds in Scottsboro would be angrier than ever.

As the train crossed the state line the soil turned redder, until the rolling green hills stood out like bright jewels against the tilled ground, split open like a wound in the fierce sunlight. Farms and fences and men working fields grew denser, and Henriette wondered if the people in those fields or behind those barn doors would consider her an "outside agitator."

And the locals weren't the only ones who might resent her presence.

She'd heard rumors that the N-double-A was trying to win the boys' defense away from the ILD, hoping the legal system would free them. Lots of luck, thought Henriette. No matter what Dilly thought, that system had already failed them. Only a bigger, stronger crowd could defeat Scottsboro's threat of mob rule, and the ILD was rallying people to demonstrate. Henriette thought of Dilly and the virulent conviction with which he'd sung Sam Hall's condemnation of the gawkers watching him go up the rope to hang: "You're a bunch of muckers all, god damn your eyes." That sort of audible rage, multiplied by hundreds and thousands, might be able to do what Alabama's legal system could not. She remembered the smoldering spirit just below the surface of Dr. Dubois's polite demeanor, bleeding through his satirical song. He must have known that he would have to fight the most dastardly of white folks. Henriette thought of adding her voice to the powerful songs of people all over the world, and tiny bubbles of hope rose. They coalesced and speeded upward until her best tunes — the Internationale, Solidarity, the Marseillaise, even Bye-bye Blackbird — joined forces to lift her spirits and stand beside her like friends. There was nothing more she could do to prepare, and Dr. Dubois would surely support her choice.

The train slowed as fields gave way to small farmhouses, cars dismantled in the yards, and brown-skinned children playing among rusted debris. The Negro side of town. Then white frame houses, well-kept lawns and quiet streets led towards the station. Henriette began to shiver despite the heat, knowing that life would soon confirm or refute all she'd imagined, and no anticipation could save her from the harsh reality of what might happen. She hummed "My Country 'Tis of Thee" to herself, mentally singing Dr. Dubois's words, as the train came to a stop. Then she closed her eyes for a moment and stepped into Scottsboro, picturing her action in reverse, going home.

"Waiting Room FOR WHITES ONLY by Order of Police Department" read a metal sign mounted on the wall of the train station. Henriette had heard of Jim Crow laws, of course, but the raw disrespect of the harsh sign chilled her. So much for Dilly's idea of police showing small boys the way home. Shoulders, elbows, and hips bumped and shoved her and feet trod on hers, obliterating her thoughts, while everyone talked at once and faces shone with sweat. She let the human current carry her toward the town center, a big square surrounded by armed officers, who held the crowd back. Facing the square was the Courthouse, a massive red brick building with four pillars and two cannons in front, more officers guarding the doors. Signs saying "colored enter in the back" the only evidence that Negro people lived here.

The crowd roiled and roared, carrying Henriette along. Big, fluffy trees lined the streets around the square where people milled, ducking their heads to avoid low branches. Many who tired of standing sat on curbs or the square fenders of parked cars, careless of keeping clean or offending owners. Smells of unwashed flesh. Orange peels and food wrappers accumulating. Shade as sticky as the sun. Benches for "whites only."

The National Guardsmen, attentive and neat in pressed khaki, stood alert but eerily calm, as though their heavy-looking guns and fixed bayonets could erupt into action without causing a wrinkle or a sweat. The civilization Henriette had so recently disparaged now seemed the only thing between her and carnage, and she wished she could walk back through time. Not knowing what else to do, she kept walking, whole body alert to Dilly's warning, ready to duck into a doorway or run for cover at any sign of conflict.

A Negro man in overalls and a floppy, cloth hat approached. Just as she opened her mouth to speak to him, he stepped off the sidewalk into the street.

"Excuse me," she said and asked for the ILD office. The man looked startled and removed his hat. "Don't know miss," he said, smiling, with a little bow. "Sorry miss. Don't know. Never heard of it. No way miss." He bowed again, replaced his hat and continued a few feet before returning to the sidewalk. Henriette turned and watched him walk away. She had expected to encounter unrest on the part of Negroes and whites, but not this deference. What might the person inside be thinking or feeling? Anger stronger than thrown pudding or shouting parents or revolutionary music, she guessed. She had to find the ILD office, her only link to a bed and the hope of finding Nadine. Ahead she saw a white woman wearing opaque lisle stockings despite the heat, supportive shoes and a baggy housedress. The woman was walking slowly, and Henriette tapped her shoulder.

"Could you help me?" she asked, feeling the weight of her suitcase and the exhaustion of her night on the train.

"Whatcha want?" asked the woman, moving something around in her mouth. Henriette asked for the ILD office, spelling out the name. "Where yawl from, anyway?" asked the woman, suspicion in her gaze and voice.

"From Chicago," said Henriette. "I just got here."

"We don't want you here," said the woman, tucking something into her cheek. "Can't you see we got too many visitors already? Cluttering up the town, trying to tell us how to live our lives. Stirring up the darkies, uppity one minute and sulky the next. Yawl oughta stay home and mind your own beeswax." Henriette tried to move past, but the woman grabbed her arm. "Listen to me," she said, fingers digging in. "Trouble's coming. You stay out of it."

"OK, OK," muttered Henriette, under her breath. She hurried away, a sob escaping from her throat. The clerk in a general store directed her to a second floor office a few doors down.

International Labor Defense League said black letters in a glass panel on the door. Inside, a gaunt, middle-aged man looked up from a desk covered with mimeographed sheets and folded leaflets, a huge typewriter, a full ashtray, and a package of Listerine cigarettes. A fan from the window blew through his sandy hair, which stuck in damp wisps to his pale forehead, and his short-sleeved shirt had stains of damp under the armpits.

"Yes?" he asked, in a hurry. His voice, Midwestern.

"I'm Henriette Greenberg. I came from Chicago." She heard a tremor in her voice and raised it, seeking control. "By any chance... do you know... Nadine Abravanel?"

"There's more than you can count come down here," said the man. "Can't help you." Henriette looked for a place to sit, moved a stack of papers and sank. The typewriter came between her and the man.

"The ILD in Chicago said you'd find me a place to stay," said Henriette, "The town doesn't seem friendly."

The man barked a humorless laugh. "You came by yourself?" He peered over the typewriter. "How old are you anyway?" She added two years and said, "Twenty-one." He shook his head and frowned. "What you gonna do here?"

"I came to work. To help." The man scribbled on a note pad.

"Here's a woman who can give you a bed," he said. "Be down at the Courthouse square tonight at six. Pass out these leaflets and talk to as many people as you can." She stood and reached over the typewriter to take a stack of leaflets. "Smash the Scottsboro Lynch Verdict" read the legend, illustrated by a man swinging a big stick at a noose. She flinched at the image and the slogan, but of course, that's exactly what the sentence was, a legal lynching. She saw herself trespassing on Alabama's most deeply valued customs, a way of life that allowed professing Christians to commit murder without guilt. Henriette hesitated, unwilling to return to the street. "You're here to protest injustice, right? Then protest! Whatever it takes to be heard!" The man's left hand dismissed her while his eyes and his right returned to the typewriter.

"Is there anything more I should know?" she asked, unfolding the paper with the address. "To be safe?"

"You're in the wrong place for safe, lady," he said. She blinked and looked at the note.

As SHE WALKED AWAY FROM Main Street, the streets grew small and dusty, shaded with some kind of big oaks. A young mother pushing a carriage pointed the way to Henriette, staring after her with curiosity but asking nothing. Soon she arrived at a white frame, two-story house with a garden full of purple coneflowers. She climbed the front steps to a small porch and rang the bell. An older woman answered the door. Her round cheeks and belly and her white hair, swept into a soft bun, reminded Henriette of Dilly's mother. Henriette introduced herself and showed the note.

"Goodness gracious, come in," said the woman. "I'm Delores. All the way from Chicago! Don't tell me you came alone!" Tension flowed from Henriette like water. She dropped her suitcase, and her legs seemed to melt as sweat poured down her ribs. Delores led her out to the bright kitchen, offered her a chair, and poured her a glass of sweet tea. Henriette drank it down, then caught her breath. As Delores re-filled her glass, Henriette asked if she knew Nadine.

"So many been coming in and out, getting arrested, going to jail, getting out of jail, there's no way to keep track of all of them. But no, I haven't seen your friend."

"Jail?" asked Henriette. How could this pleasant woman talk so lightly about jail? "What sends people to jail?"

"Ask too many questions. Cross the tracks and talk to Negroes.

Look too close at the defense, ask how the defense lawyers were chosen and what kind of job they did."

"I'm supposed to pass out leaflets around the Courthouse tonight. What should I do?"

Delores' voice sharpened and dropped a register. "Don't talk to Negroes. Don't raise questions about the defense. Dress proper: knees and shoulders covered. This is a lynching town — that's why the National Guard is here, but sometimes even they can't save you. Jail might be the safest place to be." Henriette pictured the midnight mob assembling, as they had two years before in Marion, Indiana. They'd scout out their pray and hunt down a man to be burned alive, then hung from a tree as warning to his fellows, while the mob re-tired to coffee and camaraderie. The pang for Dilly she'd felt on May Day surged inside her now. Oh Dilly, please be here. You were more than right. Not distant consequences. Trouble, sooner. Henriette took a deep breath and listened to it come out in little shuddering gasps.

Chapter 17

After a bath and an early supper of greens with ham, red beans, and rice, shared with Delores, Henriette tucked leaflets into her bag and set out. Arriving near the Courthouse, she found the square empty except for the National Guard, who stood at attention, bayonets fixed, ties neatly tucked into khaki shirts.

The air stilled in the early evening, as though the square were holding its breath. Crows flapped and cawed from the tops of the trees, swooping down for a bug or a dropped bit of garbage fermenting in the heat, while a group of boys played marbles on a curb, laughing.

"Whites only," said the square's one water fountain.

Men in vests, jackets and fedora hats began to gather on the streets around the square, loosening their ties in the still-warm evening. A few women strolled in pairs, wearing sleeveless, calf-length dresses with dropped waists and soft draping at the collar. Boys and girls in casual pants and skirts, some perhaps from out of town like Henriette, stood in small knots talking and joking. As more shops closed for the day, workers joined the all-white crowd, some with hands dark from grease, some with garters that might hold sleeves out of ink. Men who looked like farmers wore plaid work shirts and overalls, necks burned red from sun. It seemed that everyone had a place to go or a friend to talk to, and Henriette felt utterly alone, her concealed leaflets marking her. License plates on cars parked around the square read Georgia, Tennessee and South Carolina as well as Alabama, but Henriette doubted these visitors were here to protest. They'd come for the show. This is it, thought Henriette, removing her leaflets from her bag. Do it, now. Hands frozen, she wandered among people, meeting no eyes, and listened.

"Why's the Guard still here?" A group of men in overalls smoked and speculated.

"Prisoners might get moved."

"No one wants to wait — kill them now."

"You think the Guard can save them from the mob?"

"They saved them once."

"Waste of time and money. Why keep them safe so they can fry?" Guffaws. The sound of band music drifted through the air, and Henriette recognized "Dixie." Land of cotton. Old times not forgotten. The sound put a festive veneer over the self-righteous conversations and made the evening amble feel like a nightmare amusement park, where a hall of mirrors turned murderous wishes into pleasantries. Goosebumps rose on Henriette's skin despite the warmth. She gathered her courage and offered a leaflet to a pair of well-dressed women, but they brushed it away like a mosquito, looking right through her. She walked more quickly through the thickening crowd, offering leaflets right and left. People began to coalesce around speakers competing for attention, and voices swirled and swelled, becoming a single low-pitched growl. Across the square, Henriette thought she saw the sandy-haired man from the ILD office, now wearing a work shirt and overalls. She made her way around the square to the other side and tapped the shoulder of a red-haired woman waiting for the man to speak.

"What's his name?" she asked. "I met him, but he's changed clothes. He never told me his name."

"That's George Maurer," said the woman, "from International Labor. We're demanding a new trial. " Henriette offered the woman a leaflet, and she accepted. Now Henriette had a place to be and a colleague, if not a friend, and she observed her fellow listeners: a man with a walrus mustache and a pot belly bursting through suspenders, jacket over his arm, and the woman who'd said "we," middle-aged and slim in a straight black skirt and tailored white shirt.

"People here would rather kill a northerner then listen to him," whispered the woman, her curly hair just touching Henriette's cheek. "Those clothes are camouflage."

"We are witnesses," Maurer began, speaking through a big megaphone, "to a frame-up. Not a hundred feet from where we stand nine young Negroes are languishing in the bullpen, without adequate food or clean beds. If they rebel against their death sentence or complain about conditions, the state declares a riot and calls in the infantry to put them in irons." The hair on Henriette's neck stood up to think she was actually here, playing her small part in this demand for justice.

Maurer pulled a folded newspaper out of his jacket pocket and waved it. "The *Jackson County Daily Sentinel* calls them 'Burly brutes. Fiends,' it says. 'Savor of the jungle. Meanest African corruption,'" Maurer's voice grew louder and slower. "The boys's parents scraped together sixty dollars and hired a real estate lawyer to defend them. He talked to them for twenty minutes and told them to plead guilty. No witnesses but the boys themselves were called to testify in their defense. You call that a fair trial?" The crowd quiet now. "The jury took only three days to convict and forty-eight hours to sentence these men to the chair. The state asked for life imprisonment for the youngest, thirteen-year-old Andrew, but the jury held out for death. What faith can we put in the legal system when the jury demands more punishment than the state?" A sound of disgust swept through the crowd

like an ill wind with cries of "Go back home" and "Leave us alone."
Henriette looked behind her and saw a sea of hats and caps, hundreds
of men who would surely oppose the few ILD supporters.

"Time is running out," continued Maurer, speaking faster. "The
U.S. Supreme Court is hearing the case. We demand a new trial.
Join all who protest injustice in New York and abroad. Organize!
Demonstrate! Raise your fists! Stop! Stop legal lynching! Stop legal
lynching! Henriette joined a few others around her in the chant, just
mouthing the words at first, then giving voice, and finally filling her
lungs and shouting. Smack. Wet on her cheek. Smoky smell. A crawling sensation, something dripping onto her shoulder. She looked left
and saw the pot-bellied man viewing her with contempt, wiping his
mouth. She cried out, and her stomach revolted. Unthinkable, that he
had spat on her. The red-haired woman pulled out a tissue and wiped
Henriette's cheek, acknowledging with a slight nod and raise of eyebrows that this could be expected. Henriette gagged at the sight of the
brown, viscous stain on the tissue. Perhaps she was risking more than
she'd intended. Her gut took another turn, and nausea joined itself to
fear: maybe she should have been satisfied to be Mother and Father's
obedient daughter or allied herself more closely to Dilly, who knew
how to take charge of a gun. She might never be able to go home.

MAURER HAD FINISHED HIS SPEECH and moved on, and Henriette
introduced herself to the woman who had helped her. "Mary Landau,"
the woman said in a voice like a hammer on nails. "I'm from New York.
Was that your first taste of Scottsboro?"

"I just got here," said Henriette.

"Scared?" asked Mary.

"Yes," said Henriette, glad someone had asked.

"That's good," said Mary. "It's best to know the enemy. Maurer's gotten death threats, and organizers from the ILD have to dress like farmers to get access to the prisoners and their families."

"Death threats?" asked Henriette. Mary seemed to know her way around, but each bit of information she shared was another rock of fear in Henriette's gut.

"We all get them," said Mary, pulling out a letter from her purse. "If we get a new trial, I'll be part of the defense team." She showed the letter to Henriette with a sort of grim relish. "This one is from the Klan. 'Ask some white man,' she read, 'to account to you why a rapist is under conviction to be electrocuted, and see the accounting you'll get. A necktie of hemp and your rotten carcass decorating a telephone pole or a tree.'"

Henriette shuddered. "Has anyone from the ILD been killed?" She didn't want to hear the answer.

"Not yet," said Mary, The band struck up "Hail, Hail the Gang's All Here."

"Have you run into a young woman named Nadine Abravanel?"

"No, sorry," said Mary. "Come on, let's move those leaflets. We're after more than a trial." She pulled out leaflets like Henriette's from a shoulder bag, and the two set off, offering leaflets to kids in shorts, ladies in pink, light blue, and violet dresses and men in blue overalls. They reached out to hands calloused or nails painted red, glimpsed faces tight with anger or frowning, glanced at mouths shouting or lips pursed, shoulders hunched or arms raised, the hand clutching a stone or tomato. The light turned the courthouse a vibrant orange and then waned, leaving the sky a watery blue up high, fading to indigo and then black at the horizon. Gaslights came on, and faces flitted by.

HENRIETTE HAD CIRCLED THE WHOLE square, losing track of Mary, and was back on the opposite side when she heard chanting coming from a group around Maurer.

Unite and fight. See the light.

Now's the time to do what's right.

A LOW RUMBLE, LIKE DISTANT thunder, as the people around Henriette started muttering, accosting each other.

"How long they expect us to wait?" A wizened farmer with a cane pressed his lips into a grim line, his eyes popping out like a frog's.

"We've been patient. We waited for the law, the jury, the judge, the trial." A thin man with mustache yellow from tobacco juice hawked and spit, and Henriette turned away.

"No more waiting!" People around them took up the cry. "Enough waiting! No more!" They began to stamp their feet. Then, in time, chanting:

We've been patient. We won't wait.

Death to the brutes whose crime we hate.

Bystanders joined the crowd, and all began to march around the square towards the group near Maurer, chants competing. Stuck among hostile people, Henriette tried to worm and wiggle her way through the crowd, sure she would be safer close to Maurer. Voices yelled "Go home! Go back! Get out!" growing louder, and the dense crowd pressed forward, until she could barely stay on her feet. Pinned, she heard shouts and screams just ahead. She ducked down and squirmed between flailing limbs until she was among sympathizers, where a heavy woman with a smell like orange put an arm around her. "Here, honey," said the woman. "You stay with me," and they joined in the ILD chant.

The crowd surged back and forth like a monster with a will of its own, and Henriette was caught within it, forced to stagger and clutch at strangers. Grasping at shoulders, belts and skirt hems, she and the woman went down and hit the ground, hard, the woman on top.

Cement and grit. Wedged between street and heavy, pounding flesh, Henriette's head banged on the ground, and dust filled her mouth. She gasped, coughed, sputtered and spit. Unable to rise, she tried to curl and cover her head as people trod on her and fell over her. Curses. Cement cold on her cheek despite the hot day. A mewling infant cried — it was she. Someone yanked Henriette's hands behind her back, locking them together, then hoisted her to her feet. Blood ran down her forehead, but she couldn't reach up to wipe it away. Rough fingers dug into the tendons of her neck.

"You're under arrest," said a big, unshaven man in T-shirt and work pants. Badge on his belt, next to a holstered gun. He marched her over to a van and shoved her into the back with several others. Rumble and bump. Tears running down her face. Fear that her bowels would let go. Pounding in her head, ache in her shoulders. The woman who'd protected her had disappeared. Where were parents, friends, the ordinary people she'd always thought were good at heart? The scrapes on her knees and the cut on her forehead burned, and blood dripped into her left eye. She twisted her head to try to wipe it off but couldn't even reach a shoulder. Dropping her head to her knee, she managed to smear a bloody stain on her skirt, but her shoulders screamed at the motion. Raising her head, she looked around.

Five or six white men were sitting with her on the benches that lined the van, lit by a bare bulb overhead. Probably not protesters. More likely, men who rode with the Klan by night. Anyone of them could be a hate-filled Lucky, thinking of her as meat and ready to jump on her. If they realized why she was here…Thank God, they were as cuffed as she. They might have gotten rough and rowdy in the square, but the law would likely slap their hands and let them go. Maybe the coppers were the real criminals, as she'd often thought, and now she was at their mercy. Her teeth began to chatter, and the trembling spread to her whole body. If she were ever to get out of here she'd have to think fast, minute by minute. Reality stared her hard in the face. No moths, no veil.

White men in plain clothes unloaded the van and marched the prisoners into a small office, where a man in a green-visored hat sat behind a wooden desk. A sign read "Jackson County Sheriff." The Sheriff cleared his throat and spat in a cuspidor by his desk, and Henriette wished for the neatly dressed National Guard with their clean, tan uniforms.

"What's this rag-tag crew?" asked the Sheriff.

"Loitering," said the cop who'd brought them in. "Disorderly conduct. Actually brawling." The Sheriff proceeded to book each of them, holding up the pen for those who couldn't write. They touched it, and he noted their names in a big book, then made their big X mark beside it. When he came to Henriette, he paused, then gave her the pen to sign her name.

"You're too young to be in this kind of trouble," he said. "In future stay home."

"All I did was pass out leaflets," said Henriette, trying to keep the chatter out of her voice. "Asking for a new trial."

"Let's see one a them leaflets," said the Sheriff. She pulled one out and gave it to him, fearing this was a mistake. He looked at the image and laughed, loud and long, showing it around to his deputies. "How's a little girl like you gonna smash any noose? he asked, miming a rope around her neck and pretending to yank on it. His face grew serious, and he leaned in, smells of his lunch in her face. "You interfere with the way we do things and you'll be in trouble like you cannot conceive. I saved the prisoners from the mob one time, but I'm not gonna save you and your pals from the people of this town. You'll get what's coming to you."

Henriette wanted to say something noble and brave, but all her words had been trampled out of her and then stifled by the Sheriff's hands, circling her neck and yanking, grin on his face. A vicious clown. "And if you thought you were going to cozy up to the colored and spread your ideas here in jail, you got another thought coming. My jail is well segregated."

Her wrists finally freed, she was dumped in a cement cell with a single bulb. She put a hand up and felt a big lump where her head had hit the street, then looked around for a place to sit. Some dozen women in torn and streaked clothes sat or lay wherever they could find a spot and looked up at the newcomer without sympathy or interest. Dirty mattresses lay here and there on the floor, and Henriette squeezed in, sitting next to a sullen-looking girl about her own age. The girl stared straight ahead as Henriette tried to slow her breathing and stop her chattering teeth.

"Is there a bathroom?" asked Henriette. The girl pointed to a curtain at the back of the room. Henriette picked her way over feet to a bucket behind the curtain, overcome with shame that her smells and sounds should fill this crowded space. The girl watched her return.

"You got beat up," she said, her face streaked with dirt. "I look bad, but I ain't hurt none. You from here?"

"No," said Henriette, guarded.

"Protesters was out there I heard." The girl touched the dried blood on Henriette's forehead. "Don't want them boys to hang. They get you?" Henriette shook her head no. "Colored will get theirselves killed." The girl shrugged. "Can't be helped. What you come here for? Ain't nothing here. No jobs, no work."

"What do you do?" asked Henriette.

"Starve. Steal. Had a job in the cotton mill, worked fourteen hours a day for four-five dollars a week, then lost it when the Nigras come along and work for less." Henriette had expected to protest in collaboration with Negroes as she had in Chicago, and she yearned for that spirit of unity, marching and singing.

Workers, farmers, Negro and white
With lynching bosses we must fight.
Scottsboro boys shall not die.
Scottsboro boys shall not die.
Workers led by ILD
Will set them free. Set them free!

The song had soared with its promise of victory while black and white marched together for the first time since 1876, when segregation was legalized. But such a march could never happen here. Delores was right. It was risky even to talk to Negroes.

"Nigras getting all the jobs now, what they is, and that ain't much." A heavy, middle aged woman sitting across the bull pen chimed in, moving a stick around in her mouth as she spoke. Henriette pointed to her mouth, raising her eyebrows.

"Snuff stick," said the woman. Henriette wondered whether Mary and George had been arrested, and she listened for Mary's Northern voice. Could Nadine be in this jail, caught in the brawl or in another one on another day?

"No Nigras after your job," said a skinny woman with thin hair tied back, addressing the one with the snuff stick. "You'd walk the streets to put a piece of bread in your mouth."

"Who you calling a chippy?" The heavy one raised her voice. "Ain't a one of us here hasn't gone hungry for days at a time, turned a trick once or twice." Whack. The thin-haired woman slapped the first one's face, knocking the stick out of her mouth, and jumped on her, shouting. Cries rose around the bullpen: "Lay off! "Cut it out!" "Leave her alone." The tumult subsided to rumbling, grumbling and restless turning as some tried to sleep and others complained of hunger and thirst.

Henriette was hungry too, her appetite aroused by the threat of real deprivation. She wondered how long she'd been here. "Do we get food in the morning?" she asked.

"If you can call it that," said the heavy woman. "Durn thin porridge." She held out a small jar. Here. Have some snuff. Helps with the ache." Henriette thanked her, refusing. Apparently there was more than one shadow world here in Scottsboro. Negroes lived across the tracks, but somewhere else these poor white people lived on the edge of starvation. They would never join forces with Negroes to work for change.

No Mary, no Nadine. Much as Henriette wanted this night to end, she dreaded morning. Inevitably her cellmates would be curious, and she couldn't conceal her story forever. They were a tough and angry lot, might even be acquainted with the white women who'd been with the accused on the train. Obviously they shared the accusers's background of poverty, unemployment, vagrancy, maybe prostitution.

The air grew thick and fetid with toilet smells, and the walls seemed to be closing in, squeezing Henriette closer to these strangers. Panic started like a spark inside her and she cast her eyes about, searching for a glimpse of daylight, evidence of a world outside. The spark flared as she realized she might be stuck here for hours or days, even weeks. Weeks without bath or decent food or friendship, and soon they would know all about her. Locked up, she'd never find Nadine. She stood, clenching her fists, cold sweat breaking out all over her. No sensible plan. No way out. Unable to stay still, she began to measure the bullpen with her feet, walking along one edge, then between mattresses to the other side, until she was all the way at the back by the smelly curtain. If she kept moving, she could get through these seconds, and then the next and the next. Back and forth and around. Against the back wall, near the toilet, a woman sat on a mattress with her head on her knees, long black hair hanging forward in greasy hanks. Slowly, she raised her head, revealing a bright flush and red spots all over her face. It was Nadine.

"Nadine!" Henriette's voice a shouted whisper. "Nadine!" she crouched and took Nadine's hot hands, but her friend's eyes remained blank, and Henriette wondered if her own bumps and bruises had made her unrecognizable.

"Nadine?" she asked. "It's me, it's Henriette." Joy at finding Nadine quickly turned to horror at her confused condition.

"But you can't be here," said Nadine. "Are we somewhere else?"

"I came here," said Henriette. "I came to Scottsboro. I came to find you." Henriette put an arm around her, bursting into tears. Nadine radiated heat from every part of her body.

"You're burning up," said Henriette.

Nadine hung her head again. "I'm sick," she said.

"How long have you been like this?" asked Henriette. Nadine shrugged, fell over sideways on the mattress and closed her eyes. Henriette had to do something, but what? In the movies prisoners had a right to one phone call, but she was worlds away from movies, rights or phones. She touched Nadine's shoulder.

"Do you know where you are?" she asked. Nadine nodded, "yes," without opening her eyes. "Where are you?" asked Henriette. Nadine shrugged. Henriette felt the blazing forehead, then looked up.

"She's really sick," she said. "Anyone know how long she's been here?"

A young woman next to Nadine woke up and sat, brushing short brown hair from her forehead, looking sleepy. "Bout a week, I reckon. She'd been over to the Nigra side of town, she said, talking to the families, getting their stories. Said she'd put them in the papers up North.

Folks here don't like that — we neither. Sheriff's deputies rounded her up along with some a them she talked to, probably over in the Nigra jail right now. We stuck her back here by the bucket, she too sick to mind."

"Do you know when she got sick?" asked Henriette.

"Two-three days ago, I think. She was talking sense until yesterday," said the woman. Do something, thought Henriette. Right now. No time for ants or hands. Her friend was sick and sinking, and she had to get her out of here. She rose, crossed the room to the door and pounded on the bars. "Hey!" she called out. "Someone in here is sick."

"They don't care none." The woman next to Nadine lay down and covered herself again. Henriette walked back to them.

"My friend is sick," she raised her voice enough to be heard by those nearby. "Very sick. You can't stand by and let her die." She repeated these words three times, passing from woman to woman and nudging their shoulders.

"Let us sleep," they muttered, turning faces away.

Henriette stood in the middle of the cell and called as loud as she could. "Wake up!" My friend is sick! Get her help! Help me get her help! Don't stand by and let her die!"

"What she got?" A woman rubbed sleep out of her eyes.

"I seen her when she came in." The woman who'd been sleeping by Nadine spoke up. "I seen her get them spots. It's jail fever."

Now Henriette had a name, though she didn't know what it meant, and she shouted, "Jail fever, jail fever," calling the other prisoners to join. "Get a doctor! Get a doctor! Get this baby outa here!" She marched to the cell door and rattled the gate, her panic released into action, spirits lifting as the women began to respond. They might be poor, hungry and prejudiced, but they could still rally to help a fellow human being. "All together now," and most of the women joined Henriette rattling the door and stamping on the floor. "Jail fever! Call a doctor! Get this baby out here!"

A sleepy guard ambled over. "If y'all don't shut up, y'all be here anoth-er week. Now what's this about fever?" He unlocked the cell door, and the inmates opened a path to Nadine. He nudged her shoulder, and she rolled on her back, mouth open, eyes partly closed, eyeballs rolled up. "She looks pretty bad," said the guard. "Yeah, jail fever, I'd say. You her friend?" Henriette nodded. The guard wandered out, leaving Henriette to wonder if he was going to call an ambulance or just go have a smoke.

ONE MORE DAY, AND NADINE might have died. That's what they told Henriette at the hospital, after they'd started IV fluids and given her aspirin. Typhus was common from the lice in the jail, they said, and more than half who got it didn't make it out.

"We'll keep you hydrated and fed," said a nurse. "Improves your chances. They used to starve patients, made them sicker than ever."

"What about new drugs?" asked Henriette. "Can penicillin help?"

"Here in Alabama?" asked the nurse. "We'd never get it. Might not help anyway." They cleaned and bandaged Henriette's scrapes, and she sat by Nadine for two days and nights, her own eye turning black, as Nadine's delirium and rash slowly faded, and she sat up in bed.

"We are going home now, aren't we?" asked Henriette.

"Hell, I wouldn't stay here if they paid me," said Nadine. "But I'll report everything I saw and heard." Henriette marveled at Nadine's re-silience, while she herself felt the ground beneath her feet shifting and slipping in ways she couldn't name. While Nadine awaited discharge, Henriette returned to Delores' to tell her what had happened, pack, and thank her. The two sat in the quiet kitchen, drinking sweet tea.

Delores shrugged. "You were lucky you paid with nothing more than bruises."

"I wonder if the demonstrations do any good," said Henriette.

"Do you think the boys' parents are right, to choose the ILD over the N-double-A to defend them? I think Dr. Dubois would approve."

"Actually he doesn't," said Delores. "He thinks the N-double-A's reliance on the legal system is a better strategy." Henriette frowned. "Dubois wants to save the boys' skins before he saves the world," continued Delores. "The ILD cares more about pointing out the failure of capitalist justice than keeping the boys alive." Henriette had always thought of the evils of capitalism as personal affronts, limitations on her own growth and development, interferences with the life of the body. Life of the body! She'd certainly experienced that here in Scottsboro, and she flashed on the crowd, the cruel cement, the jail's confinement. The body had lessons to teach, and they weren't all pleasant.

She remembered Theodore Dreiser's heartfelt and reasoned speech in New York. He'd viewed the injustice of Scottsboro as a blot on the U.S, but he was equally concerned about nine young men, strangers, maybe, but individuals, as real as the women in prison, as real as she. It hadn't occurred to Henriette that principles of justice and the fates of individuals could be at odds. Dilly would understand that. But not before he'd chastised her for taking risks and maybe rejecting her for allying herself with the ILD. She wondered if she would ever tell him about the trip.

She'd found and saved Nadine, but accomplished nothing for the convicted men. The women in the jail cell had rallied to help her, yet despised those she sought to help. No way could she stand up against mouths that spit, hands that wrote death threats or marauding mobs. On the ground, mouth filled with grit, she'd cared only about saving her own skin.

The sinking sun suddenly showed orange on Delores, making her round face smooth out and shine like a fat, wise, Buddha. That face might be the last sign of real goodness on this earth. Henriette got up and gave her a big hug. The next day Henriette and Nadine walked to

Scottsboro's train station with its little peaked roof, glad that neither citizens of Scottsboro nor visitors from other states could distinguish them from the gawking crowd. The band played its macabre tune, and the train chugged out of the station and carried them back to Chicago. By the time they arrived, the lump on Henriette's head was small, and her black eye was almost gone.

Chapter 18

Henriette slept badly her first night back in Oak Park. Exhausted from her experience and the long train ride, she'd expected to rest at home, but the bed remained alien, a reminder to her skin to stay on guard. Intermittently, she dreamed she was still in Scottsboro, and in the morning, her limbs were heavy and her eyelids wouldn't stay open. It was Saturday, and she sat in the kitchen drinking black coffee and wondering why it no longer uplifted her morning. The kitchen's familiar flowered curtains and big black stove seemed like realistic touches on a stage set, while Scottsboro's screams and blows hammered in her head. Sun streamed through the window. The garden beyond offended with its orderly staked tomatoes, not yet ripe, and its cheerful petunias, oblivious of their dirty roots. The chair that used to mold comfortably to her contours now chafed her bruised limbs and refused to acknowledge their experience of boots. It seemed the ordinary world had jerked sideways a few feet while she was shouting and falling and finding Nadine, and now she was sitting just outside it, more of a bystander than ever, wondering why no one else could see the violence that lurked just below the placid surface. Coffee sloshed around inside her, acidic and bitter.

Mother sliced bread and cracked eggs, her broad back as unaware as the garden. "How was New York?" she asked.

"You look thinner," said Father, not waiting for her answer. "Did you forget to eat?"

"I was busy," said Henriette. "But New York was hunky dory."

"I lived for months on cabbage and potatoes as a boy," said Father. "It's a crime not to eat when you can." Scottsboro had obliterated Henriette's determination not to eat, and the melting butter smelled delicious. She turned to Mother, feeling indebted. "I read the book you gave me on the train — *Peace and Bread*. It's wonderful. Miss Addams understands how brutal force can be." Mother stopped working, face relaxed and receptive.

"If we could live the way Jane Addams proposes, there'd be no more hunger and no more war." Henriette nodded, but the book's vision clashed with the thump of her head on cement, the shout of "death to the brutes."

"Yes," said Henriette. "But some people can be mean and vicious. Think of how Miss Addams was silenced and nearly ruined during the big Red Scare."

"Silenced, yes — for a while. But she didn't give up. She worked for peace her whole life." Mother turned to cut oranges and squeeze juice. Words struggled to escape from Henriette's throat. Not now. Someday for sure she and Mother would talk about peace, protest, and principle, even about Henriette's trip to Alabama, but not today. If Mother and Father knew where she'd gone, they'd lock her up in the house. No need. She was grateful to be safe and had no intention of going anywhere soon.

Butter sizzled, browning and Henriette inhaled deeply. Tears welled in her eyes at the odor of comfort, and she stood up and threw her arms around Mother from the back, saying, "Thank you." Mother cocked her head like a startled bird, a puzzled smile on her face, while her practiced hand poured eggs in the pan.

FIRE BURNED WITHIN HENRIETTE EQUALING the July heat outside as she tried to make sense of all she'd seen and heard. Needing to talk, she called Nadine, who was working as a stringer for the *Chicago Daily News*. Nadine invited Henriette to join her for lunch. Henriette found Nadine at a desk in a busy, noisy room, people rushing and typewriters clattering with importance. They met with a warm hug, Nadine's bulk making Henriette feel like a bundle of twigs. Seated at Toffenetti's nearby, they ordered pineapple and cheese sandwiches, jellyroll, and coffee for thirty cents apiece.

"I feel like I left part of me in Alabama," said Henriette. "The part that took comfort for granted and worried about nothing so much as exploring myself and pleasing my difficult parents. What about you?"

"I left that part of me behind a while ago," said Nadine. "But I know what you mean. All this hoopdedoo," and she swept her hand through the air, indicating the white-topped tables, shiny soda fountain and leather stools. "All this can seem like window dressing when you've seen people treat each other like things."

"Yeah," said Henriette. "But you can cross from there to here, and I can't."

"But you did," said Nadine. "Right in the middle of all that danger and despair, you stepped across and saved my life." Henriette closed her eyes and saw herself locked up with women who'd gladly pull her hair and punch her gut if they found out who she was. Nadine leaning back on the filthy prison couch, giving up. The electric charge that had surged from her heart to her fingertips, legs, and voice, propelling her to the cell door.

"I won't, can't, put myself back there," said Henriette. "There is too dreadful, and here seems totally false."

"Give yourself time." Nadine sounded like Dr. Whitson.

Henriette paused. "How did you go on? After what we saw in Scottsboro?"

"I jumped back into the struggle," said Nadine. "But everyone's experience is different. I got very sick and almost died in Alabama. I could have been silenced forever. That made me want to get the word out. So I write about it. What's it like for you?"

"I bounce back and forth from hugging to hitting, almost. I hate my parents' smug confidence in human perfection, shouting at each other all the while. Then I hate myself for needing their house, warmth and food, for keeping me safe from my enemies." She frowned and looked down at the sound of that word. "I never thought that anyone would hate me, but now I know that some do." She paused, then met Nadine's eyes. "I just saw too much. It shook a faith I didn't know I had."

"Faith?" asked Nadine.

"In people. In the way things are. In the way they're supposed to be. I'm so confused. I'm ashamed to say that I'd never go back to Alabama." Her voice threatened to break and she cleared her throat. "I need the 'window dressing'— the civilization I've always despised — as much as anyone, and I'm disgusted with myself. And my parents — so damned high-minded! They skate on the surface of napkins on laps and spooned-away soup and never suspect that people are bad." She paused, face flushed, shocked by all she'd blurted. "I mean me," she said. "I'm no better than any. Now I can't just go back to pretending I'm a good-little-girl at school."

"You don't have to be any one thing," said Nadine, touching Henriette's arm. "Anything you do to help a person increases the good in the world. Look what you did for me."

THE CONVERSATION STAYED WITH HENRIETTE after they left. She wasn't sure what she'd meant when she'd said her faith had been shaken. It felt like all her troubles with Mother and Father and all her bad feelings about herself and her sex had existed in a sort of cocoon where the rule of law combined with customs and schedules to keep bloodlust under control. Now the cocoon had been slashed, and what flew out had been transformed. Not butterflies but strange birds with sharp beaks and talons. Some lashed out, eager to destroy the false world in which they'd been protected, others mourned their loss, while still others laughed, like crazy loons, at their former naiveté.

Henriette's mood ricocheted. She'd clench her fists and squeeze out a scream of exasperation at her own sheltered existence and then tremble at the memory of her feet, marking off the panic-inducing perimeter of the bullpen, surrounded by women who'd soon want to tear her to pieces. Whenever she had enough inner peace to think, a darker insight threatened, a fear that people were really bad. If that were true, then her habitual sense of rot at her core would not be neurotic and curable, as she'd liked to think, but an intimation of truth. And if people were evil, how was she to live?

Chapter 19

Alarmed, Henriette reached out to Dilly, as when she had been frightened by the gunshot on May Day. Her arms lengthened and thinned as they wound across the plains and over the mountains, weaving through Oregon's dense forests to grasp him and bring him back. But what did he know about Scottsboro? In some ways, more than she. He killed to eat and knew cold and hunger. In other ways, maybe nothing. He had such faith in the democratic system. He might not even believe that people in Scottsboro had called for "death to the brutes."

But Henriette had to get through the minutes, hours and days that lay ahead, with or without Dilly. Casting about for a plan, she remembered Nadine's words about helping one person. Whom could she help? Delores had opened her house to all comers, gladly receiving anyone who came to protest the convictions. Henriette thought of her face, round and Buddha-like, glowing orange in the setting sun, when they'd said good-bye.

That was it! That was how she'd help. The sofas and beds (spare rooms, too, with brothers away) of Oak Park could be put to good use. Bring me your tired, your poor! She'd call up the Chicago ILD and offer the house. She could make up their beds and cook her guests breakfast and talk as they ate, sprawled over the living room, porch and kitchen, the Harolds and Marys and Guses and workers from cities and towns in the North and the South. She laughed with triumph as bourgeois furnishings turned into instruments of the struggle. Even Dilly would approve of her generosity — though not, she knew well, of the ILD's link to the Communist Party.

She remembered how her doubts had dissolved into joy when she'd sung along at the *New Masses* celebration in New York. She'd even thought she was through with analysis. Now she sang the Internationale to herself, "Arise, ye prisoners of starvation, arise, ye wretched of the earth," as she developed her plan. While Mother was out, she called the ILD office downtown, told them she was newly returned form Alabama, and asked if they needed beds for people coming to town. Doubtful at first, the person who answered the phone questioned transportation from Oak Park to the loop, and Henriette explained the convenient "El." A demonstration in support of a new Scottsboro trial was planned for the following week, and people were already arriving from around the Midwest, from East coast and West, a few from the Soviet Union. How many beds? Henriette did a quick count. Carl's and Russell's, two sofas, that's four. The floor? Sure, the floor. Six will be fine. Tell me when. She hung up the phone, audacity tingling her skin, and listed her tasks: sheets and blankets, coffee, bread, oatmeal and eggs.

"I'M HAVING A FEW FRIENDS over," she told Mother later that day.

"Tell me who and when, and we'll plan dinner," said Mother, setting down bags and removing her hat.

"It's not like that." Henriette's face turned grim. "No dinner. People coming from out of town to demonstrate for a new trial — in Scottsboro, you know."

"OK," said Mother, doubtful. "I'm glad we can help. Do they mean to stay here?" Henriette nodded.

"I guess two's all right," said Mother. "With Carl and Russell away."

"Leave it to me," said Henriette. "I'll take care of everything." Mother looked worried but said no more. Henriette counted blankets and checked her supplies. A week later, Father at work and Mother putting in her usual time at the Abraham Lincoln Center, people began to arrive. First Mark, clean-shaven, soft-spoken. He'd been organizing the steel mills in Indiana, planned to march in the demonstration and then return home. Easy guest. She showed him to her brothers's sanctum, and he left for the day. Then came two New Yorkers in open-collared, sweat-stained shirts, mumbling names. Long-time workers with the ILD, they were used to making do and gladly took the second bed in her brothers's room. One would sleep on the floor — they'd be here for a week. A week in the same house with Father? Henriette swallowed her doubt. A couple next, he Russian, speaking no English, and she, French. Grateful for her high school language study, Henriette pointed to the living room sofa. "C'est tout," she said. "Rien de plus," hoping her meaning was clear. The woman and man spoke Russian together, pointing to the sofa and the stairs, then settled two small suitcases in the living room and left. Mother came home in the late afternoon and questioned the cases.

"You'll like them," said Henriette. Surely Mother would thrill that her sofa could serve as a bed for a Soviet Russian. "He speaks only Russian. She translates to French."

"I only speak Spanish," said Mother. "And why not upstairs?"

"Some others are up there," said Henriette. "Don't worry. They'll all be out late. Remember, no dinner. I'll take care of everything."

"Keep the place clean," said Mother. "And quiet. No waking Father at night."

At nine her parents went to bed, and Henriette awaited her guests, pacing from sofa past fireplace. The family had recently bought the new automatic Victrola, and Henriette loaded records on the spindle. Around ten her guests drifted in and introduced themselves to each other, full of excitement from travels and news about the next day. The New Yorkers turned out to be bald-headed Gerhardt with small, round paunch and taller, beak-nosed Jerry. No one had a last name. "Spin the platters," called someone, and Rudy Vale sang, "Once I built a railroad, made it run/Made it race against time/Once I built a railroad, now it's done/Brother can you spare a dime." Bottles of hooch came out of back pockets, and smoke filled the air, while Henriette scrambled for ashtrays and tried to fit in. She'd thought she would tell of her journey, but found her tongue tied, partly from fear that her parents would learn where she'd been, but mainly because too many were talking too fast. This wasn't sweet tea and red beans with Delores.

Soon Gerhardt and Jerry were out in the kitchen, checking the fridge and finding some stew, which they ate, while laughter grew louder. Henriette's energy flagged, and she went up to bed. Alone in the dark, she soon slept, then heard new voices arriving below. Drifting in dream, she refused to get up. Steps on the stairs. In the hall. A door handle turning. Good God, Mother's room! She jumped out of bed and turned on the light. In the hall a new guest with a beard was just closing that door. Finger to lips, he mouthed an apology, said he'd sleep on her floor and walked in. Heavens no. She shook her head and pointed downstairs, miming "sleep" with her head on both hands and "the floor" with her foot. He went down.

The next morning Mother barged into Henriette's room in a loosely tied robe. "What is this?" she demanded, face livid, still puffy, hair standing on end. "What have you done? I said two could stay for a night, and that's all. Your father will be apoplectic."

"We're helping the cause." Henriette, oddly calm. "These people have come from all over to help save eight men from the chair. Don't you want to help?"

"Of course," said Mother, pulling her robe tight around her and tying the sash. "But not if some louts will run rampant all over our house. Our home is a refuge — it's sacred."

"What religion is that?" Henriette scoffed and looked past her mother to see if Father was leaving their room.

"Strangers were tramping all night," said Mother. "The knob of our door..." Father had come up behind her and now put a hand on her shoulder.

"Whatever this is," he addressed Henriette. "Get them out." She repeated her explanation.

"I risked my job once, to have Dr. Dubois, and once was enough." Father continued to stand behind Mother, and Henriette knew with the tiniest twinge of regret that he wouldn't march down on his own, discover more bodies all over the floor and make the guests leave. He'd stand behind Mother, let her swing the ax, and she could be made to delay for the cause.

"They won't be here long." Henriette addressed Father. "They'll stay out of the kitchen until you have breakfast. They won't come back here until you're in bed. See? It won't bother. Now let me get dressed." The parents withdrew to their room, where Henriette hoped a gentle persuasion was calming the waters. Had she dared to do this, to storm their homeowner's citadel?

But no time for doubts. The guests would be waking, in need of a bathroom, and that was upstairs. She dressed quickly and went down, saying no bath or breakfast 'til parents were gone. The Franco-Russian couple regarded her quizzically while the rest lit cigarettes and went outside, where she feared they were watering Mother's nice garden with pee. God forbid the neighbors should see.

Henriette made breakfast, and that broke the ice. Pouring coffee, she discovered that Russians like, "Thé, s'il vous plaît," and everyone laughed at the way she loved butter and salt in her oatmeal. They asked about her, and she told them her story, short version, so glad to have people who knew where she'd been, though they couldn't imagine the trial or jail. They asked how Jim Crow worked and what the law did, unable to fathom the horror of lynching or picture the sheriff's brave walk though the mob, calling the governor to bring in the Guard. The Russian asked for translation of "spare a dime" and began practicing, addressing the others, "Brother, spare a dime? Tony, the man with the beard, said, "Sorry" for opening doors in the night. It turned out he spoke French and could help with translation. The French girl, Denise, told about "manifestations à Paris," where the Négritude movement had the support of Rimbaud and Baudelaire, and Langston Hughes could be seen in the crowds. An actor by trade, Tony would speak at the protest. Henriette planned to accompany the group to the march, and Gerhardt, German by origin, promised to bring meat and cheese from a delicatessen that night. They'd all have a party.

As they rallied with signs, chants and speeches all day, Henriette found herself greeted quite often and wondered how people knew who she was. "See you later," they said. Several hundred took part in the protest, both Negro and white, and many who didn't speak English. It was late when Henriette rode home with Gerhardt and helped him carry the food, which they set up in the kitchen: sliced bread and mustard, butter and cheese, smoked meat and salami. Henriette made herself a generous sandwich, surprised to find how hungry she was.

Many more people arrived after ten, old and young, black and white, and Henriette soon forgot names. "It don't mean a thing if it ain't got that swing," sang Duke Ellington, and many sang along. The food ran out, but booze continued to flow, and the kitchen floor grew sticky with spills. A hand pinched her buttock, and she turned to see Lucky, a hostile tease on his face. She slapped his hand away.

"If it isn't little sister," he said. "Throwing a party."

"You're a fine disease. What are you doing here?"

"Word of your racket lit up the whole march," he said, words slurred, sounding gleeful. "You're going to be in so much trouble. Toodle-oo." He disappeared into the crowd. So many had come that she hadn't invited, and none seemed to notice her gift of the house. She wished for Nadine to bolster her confidence and regretted that Nadine had not gotten word of the party. Ashtrays overflowed and feet ground butts into rugs. Occasional thoughts of the parents upstairs made Henriette queasy, but talking and smoking and eating and joking kept her mind on the crowd. Towards midnight Tony stood up on a stool and proposed a theatre game. Each person should choose an animal and become that creature, showing only by movement and sound what sort he or she was. Be specific. An eagle or parakeet, not just a bird. Try to get someone to guess what you are. Only humans can hate, as we know, so tonight we'll be birds, beasts and fish. We might kill to eat, but never for pleasure, for custom or profit.

Applause followed, then murmurs arose. "Don't tell or discuss," said Tony. Soon one person crouched, squawked and flapped arms while another loped round the room on all fours, a growl in his throat. One on the floor on his stomach was swimming, while another stood on the dining room table, eating leaves from the chandelier.

Henriette had never seen such a thing and stood on the sidelines, watching as more and more people joined in. Her body would never succumb to this game, but she watched fascinated as living and dining rooms turned into jungle. Macaques trilled and hooted, snakes hissed, lions sprang on their prey. Some humans, thought Henriette, will be doing some serious hating around here very soon. She looked at the carpet covered with footprints, shoes on the furniture, air thick with smoke, smells of sweat and spilled drinks and wondered what on earth, air or sea she had wrought. This was helping?

Two figures appeared at the top of the stairs and came down, step by step, eyes aghast, unbelieving, as though they'd awakened to fire. Henriette saw them first and then the giraffe, who glanced from his perch and jumped down. A macaque stopped hooting mid-flight among chairs and dropped to the floor. Finally the undersea creatures looked up and calmed down.

Mother gasped, wordless, as she took in dirt and the damage, over-turned chairs, and spills on the rug. She burst into tears. Henriette rushed to her, appalled at what she had caused, while Father clutched the banister and slowly turned red.

"Get out!" he shouted. "Get out of my house!" He waved his free arm and came down a few steps. "I'll call the police." Then a cough stopped his words, and he bent over double as Mother and Henriette huddled around him. He sank to the stairs, gagged, and struggled for air, his face slowly paling and then turning blue. The crowd grew silent and still. Henriette had never seen him this sick. Filled with fear, she ran for water, while Mother pounded his back. Slowly his breathing and color returned, and the women helped him up and back to his room.

Henriette came downstairs and faced the crowd. "It's his heart," she said. "He's been ill a long time. Not your fault, and I'm sorry. I made a mistake, and my project got out of hand. Now you all must clean up and go to sleep or go home."

Embarrassed and shamed, both by parents and friends, she knew she'd done wrong and regretted it. But the weighty chandelier now hinted at light forest canopy, the rug suggested the relief of cool blue. The challenge of being a creature had frozen her body, but maybe alone in her room she would try, and if there were a next time… wild pony, perhaps, or orangutan. Time to clean up. Many had left, but the houseguests remained, sobered and helpful.

"How are your parents?" asked Gerhardt, putting a hand on her shoulder.

"They'll be OK," said Henriette. "Father has a weak heart, but I hope he'll be better tomorrow. The blame is on me." She pointed to the rug, where a hole had been burned, and her voice trembled. "I was trying to help."

"You did help," said Jerry. "You gave us a bed. And this was one hell of a party."

Tony put his arm around her. "Maybe I shouldn't have started the animals." Their eyes met, twinkled, and set off a laugh. "It was funny," he said. "A whole room of serious leftists turned into birds, beasts and fish."

Mark deputized dishwashers, sweepers and wipers. Denise tied her hair back with a scarf, took up her mop in the hall, and began to hum, while Henriette, crouched over the hole in the living room carpet, gently lifted and mourned the charred strands. What was that tune? French class, of course, and her voice joined Denise while her hands continued to care for the wound.

Sur le pont d'Avignon,

On y danse, on y danse,

Sur le pont d' Avignon,

On y danse tout en rond.

The song spread to the dining room, where Gerhardt picked up the tune, perhaps singing German. In the kitchen the Russian washed dishes, sleeves to his elbows, singing Red Army songs in a deep-throated bass. Amused by the competition of songs, Henriette rose and considered moving the sofa to cover the hole. Two years earlier she'd decided that Hyde Park was really her home. Now she'd transformed Oak Park by breaking the rules and making it home to good cheer, fellowship, and fun. She would have plenty of talking to do in the morning. But she had some new friends, and, like Delores as well as the animals, they were good.

Chapter 20

"I am truly sorry," said Henriette the next day. It was Sunday, and she had slept late, then found her parents in the kitchen, reading the paper, looking disgruntled.

"What were you thinking?" Mother looked up. "Letting that rabble run over our house?"

"Or couldn't you stop them?" Father leaned forward and took Henriette's wrist.

"Don't make excuses," said Mother to Father. "She did what she did." Henriette squirmed. She'd messed up the house and now started a fight. Father would always defend her if he wasn't erupting with anger, and she couldn't help but be grateful. But deep down she wished that just once he'd be brave, stop sneaking around, march down the front stairs and demand the white bread that he'd craved ever since he'd said he liked rye, and Mother forbade him white. Henriette had challenged the household system — why couldn't he do the same? She withdrew her hand, glad at least that Mother was no longer weepy but back to her normal self.

"We cleaned up last night before everyone left," said Henriette. "The carpet — I know. Can we move the sofa to cover the spot?"

"Of course not," said Mother. Father sighed.

"Tell me," Henriette said. "I'll do whatever you say." And she did

Mother's bidding as much as she could for the days that followed. Somehow it was easier now she knew the most harm she could do was to make a big mess. Father still lived, went to work and came home, though the pallor she'd noticed the night of the party seemed to endure. Mother was once again sturdy and firm. Henriette had thought herself central to this shouting house, that if she stepped sideways the whole would collapse in a tangle of passion where no one survived. Not true. So she polished the tarnish and moved a floor lamp to cover the hole. She called up Nadine, eager to tell of the crowd and the game, but the paper said she'd been out a few days, perhaps sick. Henriette waited for Dilly. What would he think about eat or be eaten, bloodlust before breakfast, the bodies that hung from the trees in the South?

LATE IN AUGUST SHE HEARD from him. He asked how she was and if she'd started eating again, and she sputtered at that, remembering the savory sandwich she'd devoured at the party. He still failed to realize he'd forgotten her birthday. He'd begun work as part of a field party under Leslie Snyder, a wiry, middle-aged anthropologist with a handshake that held you at a distance and a gaze that wouldn't let you go. Sleeping in double bunks with five others in a log cabin on the Sprague River, Dilly learned that Snyder was intent on demonstrating the existence of an apocalyptic Prophet Dance among the Indians, dating from sometime in the eighteenth century, before contact with Europeans. How could you prove such a thing without written records? It seemed to Dilly that broken pottery and tools could hardly be evidence of story, belief, or ritual. In any case, he was interested in the living. And Snyder hoarded notes and forbade sharing of information, grating against Dilly's nature.

Over the long summer, while Dilly catalogued items of material culture, he'd nourished himself on a competing hypothesis: that the nineteenth-century Ghost Dances, with their promise of new life, had arisen precisely in response to the destruction of animals, land, and people wrought by European invasion. "Many of the tribes I've gotten to know out here in the West," wrote Dilly, "were forced from their Southeastern homes by President Jackson, the man of the people I've always admired. How can a leader be so good and so cruel at one time? My own French ancestors may have been no better, cheating the Indians and making them sick." So out in Oregon Dilly was finding that even good people were bad. But he didn't despair. "The Ghost Dances fought bitter facts with fortitude, endurance, and hope, the hope of the hopeless," his letter went on. "I'll find some survivors and study that dance if I ever get out of this dismal woods."

Henriette was intrigued by Dilly's enthusiasm but jealous of an interest she did not share. Her desire for Dilly and her fury at his self-preoccupation churned inside her, mixed with an urge for revenge and guilt about Patrick, almost paralyzing her pen. Finally she settled on a cryptic note. "When the analyst's away, the libido *will* get around." Even this Dilly ignored, and the next time he wrote, the tensions in the camp had brought his spirits to a low point. "My hands are freezing," he wrote, "and damp leaves are clumped with mud around the cabin. Imagine a field party led by a sonovabitch, miles from anywhere with a fairy, two bulldykes, one roustabout, sun, wind, and rain, and all so goddammed repressed nothing ever happens except internally. All that love and hate, and it never gets beyond the small intestine. My God, why have you forsaken me?"

Dilly's new awareness of repression cheered Henriette. He was learning to speak her language. She even smiled at his discontent, hoping it would turn his focus to her, and she liked his humorous description of the people with whom he was stranded. It was good to know he could be miserable too — often he was too damn OK. She didn't know where he got the line about God or why he was bringing God into it. She supposed those words had entered his brain in childhood when he sat in the musty basement of that Congregational Church enduring Sunday school. If he could use her talk, she could use his. "Cawdor' is one of God's swellest poems," she wrote back. "You have to read it."

She wondered again if Dilly would still find her attractive, now that she'd gone so far on her own. *Write* ^*about* *me, you bastard!* She'd sent that note from her dreadful birthday on the bus, and now she regretted its helpless tone. She wanted more than ever to confront Dilly, talk to him, hold him, see if he could love the person she'd become, see if she could still love him. In the flesh, though, many things might get in the way. Secrets, yes, but more than that, her despair about people in general.

CLASSES HAD NOT YET STARTED, and the day was warm when Dilly and Henriette met in Hutchinson Court, just outside the C-shop. The sun shone from a bright blue sky, and yellow leaves, clinging to trees, stood out against it. Suddenly shy, as though feeling observed, though no one paused to look at them, they gave each other a peck on the cheek. She settled on a stone bench facing the central fountain, swung her legs back and forth, and watched the show of the ordinary. He stood in front of her, hands in pockets, regarding her with an appraising, maybe mocking smile. The Court filled with students and faculty coming and going from the C-shop.

She searched his appearance for the familiar and noted differences: his white hair was longer, standing up on top and shaggy over the ears, and he'd grown a thick black beard and mustache. Though he still dressed formally for the university in shirt, tie, vest, and jacket, he'd added a floppy brimmed hat, and his straight posture had acquired a sort of loose zigzag, almost as though his body had discovered syncopation. Less neat. More interesting. A land to be discovered.

"It was a hard summer," said Dilly.

"Yes, hard," she said. How much harder it had been for her. Her mouth refused to smile, and her desire for his new, jazzy self gave way to a fury that lurked somewhere inside her muscles, struggling to get out.

"Summer's over," said Dilly, rocking on his heels. "You'll be a junior. What are your plans?" She looked up at the sky.

"Parents 301. Analysis 402. Liberation from the constraints of civilization," she said, hearing herself echoing last year's flippancy.

"I think you've already passed that one," said Dilly. "Is your analyst back?"

"September first," she said. "And not a minute too soon."

"I hope you didn't mean what you said, about the libido getting around."

"Of course I did." Patrick was the furthest thing from her mind at the moment, but she'd stood up for herself in jail and at home, and she wouldn't lie. Dilly would have to pay for a summer's worth of treating her like nothing.

"Are you kidding?" he asked, looking her straight in the face. She shook her head slowly "no," back and forth, the motion regular and mechanical like the tick-tock of a clock. She was silent. "What in the hell does that mean?" he asked. "'The libido *will* get around?'" His voice like a knife poised to dissect. Her head kept saying "no," but her eyes stayed on him. He leaned over and put a hand on each side of her head, holding it still. "What is the matter with you anyway? Just what kind of trouble did you get into? Answer me, dammit!" She couldn't answer. She felt herself slipping back into a frightened, frozen place where any movement she made could shatter fragile ties. All she could see was the face that would soon look away and the back that would turn on her, swelling until it was as big and blank as a movie screen with no film. Somehow it was easier to stand up to hostile strangers than to face abandonment by a friend and lover. A man who hated her enough to spit was her clear enemy, but a lover who'd acquired an ironic smile and joints that seemed unglued could undermine all her resolve. She had planned to make demands on Dilly, but she felt herself begging. Silently she pleaded and promised until a solitary tear escaped from one eye and made a lonely journey down her cheek.

"You went weeks without writing, and then you never even asked about me," she said. "My nineteenth birthday. You never sent roses," she said. "You wrote me on yellow, you bastard. It showed that you knew." Her voice broke, and she put her face in her hands. He grabbed her arm.

"You're nuts. I was out in the woods, miles from anywhere, trying to get by. Roses, good God! Is that why you stopped eating?" She shrugged. "Answer me!" he said again, shaking her arm. Then, more gently, "Look. You can talk all you want about the evils of civilization and the need to be free. You can talk and talk to your analyst. But there's got to be a stone wall between talk and action. You can't be with me and fool around with anyone else, ever. Understand?" Her eyes widened as she loosened his fingers from her arm and rubbed it where he'd left red marks.

"I thought," she said, leaving stretches of silence between the words, "that was the whole idea, to be free...everyone else, you know, everyone else is...oh, sleeping around, or shacked up or something." Her voice faded as the sentence limped to a halt. Don't sleep with other men — that's what he's saying, she told herself. OK, I won't, she said without speaking, then leaned back on the hard stone bench and stared at the fountain, rushing and bubbling and bubbling and rushing like a goddam idiot.

"It doesn't matter what other people do," he said, sitting beside her. "This is just about you and me. We can be free together, as free and modern as you like, but you can't be with other men."

She kept her gaze averted. "It wasn't fun," she said. "I was just trying to survive. I got mired. Couldn't move. Couldn't see out." She passed a hand in front of her face as though clearing something away.

"And sleeping around is how you got free?" He slid away from her and faced her head on.

"I didn't say 'around.' It was just one person, and it didn't help. I'm sorry." Silence.

"I thought about you all the time," said Dilly.

"You're so goddamned reasonable. But the psyche doesn't work that way. If you don't write for weeks, it's because part of you doesn't want to. And if you're thinking about me, you write about me."

"Don't think you can psychoanalyze me." He leaned in and lowered his voice. "You can't second guess everything I do. You're the one who's whacko, anyway." The lunchtime crowd had grown, and a few heads turned to look at them, then quickly turned away.

"Me? Just because I have the guts to understand myself. You need to get your own analyst and find out where you get your tidy bourgeois attitudes."

"My people are not bourgeois," he said, now louder, and she noticed his hands had started to tremble. He crossed his arms and tucked them into his armpits. "They're hardworking and thrifty, people who hang on and survive. What would you know about that?"

She knew a lot, she suddenly realized, and suppressed an urge to tell him about her trip. Not yet. Her chin began to tremble and her mouth to crinkle. She looked away, and Dilly put a hand on her arm. They both sat again.

His voice softened. "Maybe I am more conservative than you. Saner too. I want to work and succeed and care for a family. Take care of them — of you. Remember when I said I'd be Cassandra's gatekeeper?" She nodded and slid closer to him. "When you talk about being 'mired'— is that like 'crying to die'?" Dilly reached a hand to the side of her face, turning it toward him. "Most problems can be solved," he said. He took her hand, and her fingers opened to its warmth, then intertwined with his and squeezed.

"I'm working on it," she said. "And I *am* eating again."

"Good," he said. "Maybe I can help. But forget about how 'everyone' lives. If we're going to be together, it's got to be just you and me." All she'd not told groaned to life inside her, and her fingers relaxed, then slipped out of his hand. They sat silent a while. Dilly rose, and Henriette wished that her voice could say "Stay," could promise loyalty, but paralysis filled all her muscles and bones.

"Think about it," said Dilly, turning away and speaking over his shoulder. "Fish or cut bait." He walked toward the fountain, head down, kicking at fallen leaves. The space between them lengthened, stretched, and thinned. He speeded up and the breeze eddied leaves back over the path. Light faded and the temperature began to fall. The sound of Dilly's footsteps disappeared into the fountain's rush. Soon a building came between them, and he vanished.

Henriette was scared, but she knew she'd survived worse, and she wasn't confused. She had her instructions. It wouldn't be hard to follow them — she'd never actually enjoyed sleeping with men. But the girl who'd been to Scottsboro was not the same as the one who'd slept with Patrick. Dilly didn't know her any more than she knew him. She'd wait. She'd wait as long as it took for Dilly to come back and discover the person the summer had made of her.

She needed to find out who he'd become as well. The summer had certainly challenged his assumptions. Snyder had turned out to be a bastard, hoarding data and spreading distrust among the group. Dilly had seized a gun — with cool aplomb or with swagger? — making peace in Uncle Rob's quarreling household, and the trusting eyes of Rob's baby had grabbed Dilly's heart.

She pictured his back, retreating past the fountain, and every fiber of her being reached out to pull him back. Come know me newly, Dilly, and see if you can love me still. Did Snyder turn you cynical or merely help you see two sides to everything, informing that derisive smile, that looseness in your stride? I bet you'd make a better animal than I. With those long arms you'd swing from trees, though you might hesitate to let your friends pee on your mom's petunias. Let's see if I can still love you.

BEFORE HER NEXT VISIT TO Dr.Whitson, Henriette considered whether she should tell the doctor about Scottsboro. She imagined Whitson's attempt to remain neutral while concealing shock and disapproval of Henriette's run-in with the law, not to mention exposure to typhus. No, she was proud of what she had done and did not want her courage and suffering to be interpreted as foolish adolescent rebellion or female pleasure in pain.

The analyst listened silently as Henriette told about her affair with Patrick and fight with Dilly and then asked, "Do you consider your relationship with Dilly worth preserving?"

"Yes, I do and I'll work on it." There it was again, her need to please. She couldn't help it. *I'll be good; I'm a good girl* — the words ran right along beside the ones she spoke, like a person jogging next to a bicycle.

"How will you work on it?" asked Dr. Whitson.

"Give up my freedom. That's what he wants." She enjoyed her sarcasm, though she knew she was being unfair.

"Is that what you want?"

"How do I know?" asked Henriette. She tried to think about what she wanted. Smiles, yes, she couldn't stand frowns. But really she wanted the courage to run again through a crowd, passing out leaflets to smiles *and* frowns. "I want my parents out of my life," she said.

"We all have desires to get away from our parents," said Dr. Whitson. "But we never fully escape them. I think Dilly wants you to control your sexual desires." I thought we were talking about what *I* want, thought Henriette. I don't want sex — it's way too complicated. I want to be at home in the world. I *was* at home in the world, she suddenly thought, in Scottsboro. Scared, endangered, unrewarded, but I belonged there.

"I took over my parents' house last weekend," she said, and described the party. "I discovered I was at home there in a way I never had been before, even though my new friends were wrecking the place." The leafy chandelier. The foaming rug. "I was doing wrong, and I wouldn't do it again, but damn it, I belonged."

"You are finding ways to live with your parents, to understand them. Psychoanalysis is becoming more aware of the influence social conditions can have on the psyche. I'm thinking of your father and his childhood. Have your studies led you to the work of Geza Roheim?"

"Yes, the man who stood up to Malinowski. He claims there's no Oedipus complex in matriarchal societies." Henriette had been fascinated by Roheim because he brought her two worlds together: anthro and psych. "Have you read the Marxist analysts, like Fenichel and Fromm?"

"Of course," replied Whitson. "Fenichel supports a balance among the biological, the cultural, and the psychological. The whole development makes me see your father as twice deprived, first of childhood succor and second of married love. He was probably driven to seek solace from you, and you may remember only part of what happened. Other parts could be repressed. Your problem comes from your response to his touch, your guilt about sexual arousal." What? thought Henriette, incredulous and sickened. Dr. Whitson was finally admitting the truth of Henriette's memory only to sympathize with Father and accuse her of taking perverted pleasure in something horrible. She refused to believe she had been aroused. It was almost better to believe that her own memory was false.

She was sure of one thing, her symptoms: the nauseating smell of apple that always swelled her throat when anyone touched the central place between her legs. She felt only disgust for whatever had happened that afternoon, and she yearned to escape the smell of apple and the shame. She'd have to rethink what might be real, what repressed, and what imagined.

HENRIETTE AND DILLY WERE NOT speaking in October when the U.S. Supreme Court heard the Scottsboro case and voted seven to two to overturn the convictions. Henriette rejoiced that the men had been spared, at least for now, but was of two minds about the decision itself. The defense had made three claims: that the trial had not been impartial; that the defendants had been denied the right of counsel; and that Negros had been systematically excluded from the jury. The court did not consider the first and third claims but sustained the second, reversed the judgment of the Alabama Supreme court, and ordered a new trial. This narrow ruling said nothing about the guilt or innocence of the defendants, and they were still in jail.

Felix Frankfurter, professor of law at Harvard, wrote in the *New York Times* that the rush to trial in Scottsboro had violated the due process clause of the Fourteenth Amendment. Only once before had this clause been invoked to overturn the conviction of a Negro tried in an atmosphere of racial hysteria. Thus "judicial murder," in the words of the Court, had been avoided. Dilly would surely have liked Frankfurter's careful argument and interpretation of the Constitution.

But Communist commentators, reacting to the Court's statement that the first and third claims were "utterly without merit," saw Frankfurter's response as an admission by a legal scholar that the

Court's decision was nothing more than instructions for legal lynchings, for the men would be tried again in Alabama. Henriette's relief fizzled to think that the men would be tried all over again in the same prejudiced state where she'd been imprisoned and lost her faith.

IT WAS TIME FOR HENRIETTE to tell Dilly about her trip to Scottsboro for better or worse, though her heart pounded at the thought of letting her story take on three dimensions in the space between them. Once out it couldn't be stuffed back inside. But he'd never know who she was if he had no idea where she'd been. And how could she know who he was if she didn't know how he'd react? At a level far deeper than words, she felt she could trust him. She'd choose the right time, and she'd talk.

Even thinking of telling Dilly about Scottsboro turned her heart to his field. For her, Dilly *was* anthropology, and all her desire for him now funneled into the urge to learn. She would immerse herself in the complex drumbeats of native ritual; the earth-beating feet of pueblo dance; the whirling, leaping footwork and the feather headdresses of the Plains; rugs woven from plant-dyed fibers; sand sprinkled into intricate Navajo images grain by grain. All these things were Dilly, and she would get to him through his work.

ON NOVEMBER 8, ROOSEVELT WAS elected President, but happy days did not immediately ensue. Thousands of banks closed, and the economy fell to an all-time low, with over twenty percent unemployment. Nonetheless, the election was one thing both liberals and radicals could celebrate together. A few months later, when 3.2 beer was legalized, students and professors thronged the Lucky Laundry, and Henriette often saw Dilly in the crowd. They greeted each other, cool and casual.

Part III 1933-1934

Chapter 21

In January Hitler was appointed Chancellor of Germany, and in March the Reichstag passed the Enabling Act, giving him dictatorial powers. On a frigid Saturday, the Greenberg children gathered in Oak Park to assess the situation and Father's reaction. The family took seats around the formal table. Hitler's *Gleichschaltung*, the coordination of all aspects of life with Nazi ideology, had already forced the closing of theatres and cabarets and cost many Jews their jobs. An enthusiastic population supported this policy with *Selbstgleichschaltung*, self-coordination. With so many in the U.S. unemployed and going hungry, all agreed with Mother's desire to economize and praised her navy bean soup.

"Mrs. Sinclair Lewis isn't worried," said Mother, recalling the reassuring and flippant tone of Dorothy Thompson's book, *I Saw Hitler*. "And neither is our ambassador. He says the left is more of a threat than the right."

"Who's going to limit Hitler if not the left?" asked Carl. Mother brought plates from the kitchen with squares of toast covered in white sauce, dotted by curls of chipped beef.

"The new ambassador's daughter was in class with Carl my first year," said Henriette.

"She was quite a flirt," said Carl. "She's in Germany with her family now, and writes that the young people are wonderful, with "inspiring faith in Hitler." She actually met him briefly and wrote that he was more like a shy teenager than an iron dictator, a man with quiet charm.'"

"That's the tragedy," said Father. "People are duped. No good can possibly come of Hitler, and we should stay as far away from Germany as we can."

"Of course," said Mother. "We have to stay out of it. The people that support Hitler in Germany are the same as those that try to crush the New Deal here. They think they're being 'patriotic.' Let them be hoist by their own petard."

"I read in the paper that Germans married to American women are mostly pro-Hitler, their wives even more so," said Russell. Mother served lettuce with homemade boiled dressing from a bowl on the table. On the plates, one white sauce bled into the other.

"That's what I meant, about the ambassador's daughter," said Henriette. "It's terrifying, that so many support the new Germany." Then, to Father, "Are you scared?"

"Yes, and that's why I hope we have nothing to do with them." Henriette satisfied herself that Father was not in a panic, but to her the current events seemed like a conspiratorial compounding of evil forces: hatred of Italians in Massachusetts, hatred of Negroes in the South, hatred of Jews in Germany.

MISSING DILLY AND PREOCCUPIED BY thoughts of him, Henriette let Nadine slip from her mind over the winter. The first crocuses were peeking through mud-colored snow when she ran into him on the central quadrangle, looking more scruffy than usual, as though hibernation had mussed up his hair and beard and hardship had frayed his shirt cuffs.

"Can we go somewhere and talk?" she asked. His eyes searched the open and icy expanse and the gray buildings that surrounded it.

"Off campus?" he asked.

"Off campus is good." In silence they walked to a Greek coffee shop where she ordered black coffee, he coffee with cream. She began: "After you left, last summer..."

"Don't mention..."

"I won't." A pause. "After that, I was stuck at home and depressed, afraid I'd go crazy. So I left."

"You left where?"

"I got on a train by myself and rode down to Scottsboro, hoping to find and join up with Nadine. You knew she'd gone down there, right?" She had his attention now. Alarm set his mouth in a line. Afraid of his critical look, she made her voice harsh and forced facts down his throat: the laws of Jim Crow, conditions in prison, her own time in jail, the practice of lynching.

He frowned, dubious. "Wait a minute," he said. "There are laws against that. You can't just kill someone and stroll into town."

"There's a lot you don't know. And more I found out. You should know who I am," she said with defiance. "Nadine got jail fever — that's typhus — and I saved her life."

"You found her in jail?" He sat back, his eyebrows dark millipedes on a pale face.

"Yes. I was arrested as part of a crowd outside the Courthouse, some for, some against the convictions. It turned into a brawl." Her voice hard as his face, she knew she was closing him out by the story she told. She said nothing of hitting her head on cement or of learning survival came first. Nothing of joy at finding Nadine or alarm at her fever. Nothing of triumph at getting her out, nor did she mention her new doubt that people knew how to be human, that the civilization she'd held in contempt and blamed for her failings was really a vital veneer over evils she shrank to imagine. If she said it she might make it true. Worse, if she talked about what she'd barely endured, she'd have to feel it in depth and with sorrow, without danger's fright and hormone-fueled flight to keep her from flying apart.

He took a deep breath, digesting her words. "OK. You were upset before you left home. That's happened before. But surely you were insane to get on that train, a white girl, alone, intending to take on the South."

"Not the South, just the trial. Not alone, with the ILD, and behind them the strength of the Communist Party."

"Henriette!" He took a sharp breath and then lowered his voice. "Don't say that. Some unemployed people have turned to the left, but the tide's turning now, and next thing you know they'll put you in jail in Chicago. Red scares come and go, but they're always in sight. Remember Jane Addams — arrested in one of the Palmer raids and held without trial. And think of your future. No study. No job." He crossed his arms and sat back.

I knew it, she thought. You think me a fool. And I think you're narrow. You don't believe what I saw with my eyes. You still think of people as small-town friendly and fear to give them offense. "I didn't join any party," she said with a pout. "All I did was hand out leaflets. I got into trouble, but jail's where I found and rescued Nadine." She suddenly realized she hadn't talked to Nadine since the day of the march, when she'd failed to show up at the party. If Nadine had been sick, she'd be better by now, and Henriette resolved to call her at home.

"Nadine's a dear friend, and I love her," said Dilly, arms on the table between them. "We don't always agree, but she can take care of herself. You're a smart girl but stupid, yes stupid, to put your life on the line."

"I learned a whole lot on my trip," said Henriette, determined to tell her story without breaking down. "Some laws aren't enforced by police in the South. That's why they called in the National Guard. Lynching is real. Think about it — a ritual. They break a man out of jail, gather a crowd, prepare a site." She slowed her voice to force Dilly to take in the awful words. "Then mutilation…torture…slow burning…hanging. Then meet up for coffee and show off souvenirs."

"That can't go unpunished," said Dilly. "Courts work in this country, and voting makes change. Our candidate won. Roosevelt's been elected."

"Swell. We're sitting in the catbird seat. But Governor Bilbo's proclaimed that he won't prevent lynching in Mississippi at all," said Henriette.

"That's hard to believe, but if so, all the more reason for you to stay home. Imagine if I went to Germany, determined to stand up to Hitler's new secret police, the Ge-sta-po. He gave each syllable the weight of blows.

"You wouldn't do that," she said, then raced on. "Now listen to this. When I came home, I opened the doors of my parents' house for people to stay, people who came from all over to march in the ILD's demonstration against the convictions." A smile flitted over her face. "People camped out on the beds and the floor. With hooch and a picnic, we all had a party. We messed up the house, I'm sorry to say, but cleaned it up after."

"Your parents?" his voice squeaked up. "They must have been outraged." She searched his face for a smile, but it remained harsh.

"Precisely. But everyone lived."

"I think you'd better start making more sense. The party is one thing, small 'p.' Capital 'P, C.P.' is quite something else."

"I know," she said. "They're my friends, nothing more." She sat back, vaguely wondering why she'd told her story so harshly, her version a slammed door as much as his face. Slowly it dawned on her that she'd barely begun to know what she'd felt at that time, in that place. Somewhere inside her each fact that she'd told had an aura, an odor, a key to her feelings, if she would but pause and find out what they were. Walls closing in. Nausea rising. As though fleeing before a great wall of water, her mind ran away from those threats and took refuge in school.

"I've changed my major to anthropology," she said. "Professor Daniels approved."

He leaned forward, spoke sternly, instructive. "A social scientist has to be careful, meticulous, thoughtful, and dispassionate. You observe and don't get involved. Hang around Communists? You'd never get hired." His disgust and contempt spread from her trip to her plan like a smothering blanket. She'd known what he'd say, but some shred of hope had remained that he'd open his arms and admire her courage, help her to sort through the feelings she didn't know how to express.

"I'm glad you're alive," he said, softer, and she warmed at the shift in his tone. "We can rely on the law and the courts to free the unfairly accused. The law makes mistakes, but mistakes can be fixed. Tell me you won't put yourself into danger again." His look of care and concern roused her hope, though she knew he was wrong about law in the South and sometimes the North. Deep down, she wanted his curly-haired body, its flexible strength that could shift like a tree with the wind, its roots firmly fixed in a time and a place. So normal and stable, unlike her, unlike Carl. Too damn OK? She needed OK. He'd been to the wilderness, made friends with Indians, knew how to cope with life good and bad. She thought of his mom's apple dumplings: generous, friendly, bound by the rules of the table, of course, but by rules understandable, simple, and clear. Unlike her own home, where hands made their own rules while eyes looked away, and arguments drowned out her voice.

She gathered her hopes and her doubts along with her things, determined to leave while she still felt intact. Maybe not careful, meticulous, thoughtful. Nonetheless she had entered a culture more alien than any pueblo and walked out unharmed. She could be a good social scientist — school had always been her strength. And Dilly had said he was glad she'd survived and wanted to save her from danger.

Maybe next time they met she'd be able to talk about fear in Scottsboro and what it might mean. For all of Dilly's trust in police and suspicion of her leftist alliances, despite his ignorance of psychoanalysis and love of hunting, she was sure they could find common ground. Their time as lovers took on a golden patina. His newly ambling gait attracted her more than ever with its suggestion of a beat and made her hope they might share a jazzy revelation of life's underside, where a saxophone could question a traditional violin. She determined to work as hard as she could.

ROOSEVELT'S INAUGURAL WAS CAUSE FOR celebration all over the city, and people from Hoovervilles to high rises gathered downtown. Warner Brothers Pictures had been big supporters of the President, and he'd invited the cast of a new musical, *42nd Street*, to attend the event. A gold and silver train, emblazoned with the name "The 42nd Street Special," was transporting the actors from Los Angeles to Washington, with stops all across the country. Dilly called Henriette at her dorm. "Want to go see the 42nd Street train? " he asked. "All our friends are going. Then we could go see the movie. It's the first decent musical anyone's made for years." Henriette welcomed the chance to be with him, though this would be hardly a date.

"Tell me about it," she said.

"It's a story about putting on a show with no money, all the chorus girls depending on the job, and the director himself sick and depressed."

"Doesn't sound happy," said Henriette.

"But it is," said Dilly. "Mostly. And they're calling the train a 'Better times trip, Hollywood on wheels.'"

"I'd like to go," said Henriette, remembering that movies often unlocked her feelings. She hoped for better times for herself and Dilly as well.

On a cold spring night they took the "El" downtown and joined the crowd greeting the train, covered with lights provided by General Electric. Strangers became instant friends with enthusiasm for the inaugural as well as the movie and its stars. A band played the movie's theme song: ""Naughty, gaudy, bawdy, sporty, 42nd Street," and Henriette's spirits rose with the music.

In the theatre, Dilly put his arm around the back of Henriette's chair but did not touch her as the movie's newlywed couple cuddled on the caboose of a train, headed for Niagara, singing, "You go home and get your panties/I'll go home and get my scanties." Busby Berkeley's choreography then jackknifed the train to reveal a row of sleeping compartments, where various couples prepared for bed, singing "Shuffle Off to Buffalo." Verses honored and made fun of marriage until the couples retreated behind drawn curtains. Maybe not as frank as Hedy Lamarr's *Ecstasy*, thought Henriette, but a gasp and a raised arm from behind a curtain, followed by a slow drift to rest, were delightfully suggestive.

Berkeley thrilled Henriette and Dilly again with the big closing number. First a soloist in a theatre sang, "Where the underworld can meet the elite/42nd Street." Then the singer took the viewer to the street itself, where that meeting was enacted in one vignette after another: a nurse spanked a doll, a policeman twirled a stick, and a woman walked a dog, all to "the beat of dancing feet." The camera peeked into a second-floor apartment to reveal a man attacking a woman, who escaped through a window and did a swan dive into the arms of the crowd on the street below. She danced with a man for two beats and then was stabbed by her attacker. At the end the entire crowd became cardboard buildings. Henriette and Dilly exchanged glances of amazement, watching as the city of New York danced before their eyes.

They walked out of the theatre with their friends, blinking. Henriette had been overwhelmed by Berkeley's enthusiastic rhythms; his kaleidoscopic overhead shots of multiple chorus girls; and his bawdy routines. "How can a movie about the Depression be so gorgeous and upbeat?" she asked.

"The dancing buildings were corking," said Dilly. "But no one credited the show's director at the end. His career was over, and the prediction we heard at the beginning — that he would collapse and fail — was fulfilled."

"Somehow that makes the movie realistic, a true story of the Depression, in contrast to the glamorous girls. Both tragic and triumphant. It was beautiful," said Henriette, with the ready emotion she always felt at the movies.

"I'll be humming the tunes," said Dilly, "while I wait to see if Roosevelt can dig us out of this catastrophic pit." As they walked to the train, he whistled the teasing notes of "Shuffle Off to Buffalo."

Chapter 22

The next evening Henriette tried calling Nadine at home, but no answer. No surprise, either, for Nadine often went out in the evening. The following day Henriette tried the paper where Nadine was a stringer and worked on assignment. They said she hadn't been in for a while. Concerned, Henriette wondered if she'd had a relapse of typhus. Perhaps she'd returned to Scottsboro or some other center of conflict, traveled to Russia or buried her head in a notebook of poems. The Abravanels? Nadine might or might not be in touch with her parents. Preoccupied with her studies, Henriette reminded herself to try calling Nadine's mother.

Soon after she met Carl for lunch at the C-shop, hoping she might run into Dilly. She unwound her scarf and put down her books, while surreptitiously scanning the tables. Dilly hadn't asked to see her again after the movie, and she hoped his enthusiasm had not been only for the music and the new administration. The long, high-ceilinged room was full of students and noisy with lunchtime clatter.

"Spill!" said Carl, as they settled at a table with sandwiches and coffee.

"Saw an A-1 movie," said Henriette.

"Don't get behind the grind," said Carl. "Who's got time or moolah for movies?"

"This one's worth it," she said. "It's got music and dancing and even one 'forgotten man,' the one at the 'bottom of the economic pyramid' that Roosevelt promised to help."

"I'll try to see it," said Carl. "So tell me what you're studying."

Henriette described Apache stories and warpath language, then took a bite of a peanut butter and bacon sandwich with chopped sweet pickles. "I want to understand culture, the way things were before civilization corrupted it with cars and factories. That's the source of our problems." She listened to herself mouth old words. Yes, corruption abounded, but civilization was indispensable. Discontents and all. Carl smiled a tired smile, then raised his voice over the surrounding conversations.

"There's a lot more wrong with us than that," he said. "Even Freud didn't know what really goes on, what freezes us in so-called maturity, so that growing up means death to the psyche. Dorothy and I are going to write a book about it after we get married."

"Married?" Henriette jerked to attention. She hadn't even met Dorothy. She remembered the day she'd learned that Carl was dating her, the day they ran into Russell at Bughouse Square. Carl had announced he intended to marry and make a hundred dollars a day, but Henriette hadn't believed him. She'd thought he sounded like a machine, hardly in love.

"I haven't told the parents," said Carl. "Or anyone but Russell, but she and I have decided." In silence Henriette felt Carl slip away from her. "Consider Russell. He's never going to realize his potential. He's virtually disappeared into queersville on the North side — doesn't even want to see me any more."

"That's too bad," said Henriette. Something big must have divided the two brothers, once so close, always competing. Their funny, clever slogans and private jokes. Closed door. Laughing and pounding. The glob of pudding that had arced over the table long ago, the wrist, bony beyond the cuff, the newly muscled arm that heaved it. Perhaps Carl's sudden engagement had upset Russell — it certainly had her. Why the hurry? She'd been suspicious of Carl's plan from the start, but she wasn't clear about what she suspected.

Every aspect of this question was in its own, separate box. The pansy craze with its songs and clubs, fancy clothes and make-up was in one box, now being crushed by the Vice Squad. The yearning to grow and love in her own way, like Stephen in *The Well of Loneliness*, was in an entirely different box, a poignant box where Henriette too belonged, though her desire was for a man. Another box held words, light as air and delightful to play with: queersville, homosexual, intercourse, sleeping with men. A fourth box held anatomical facts about sex, which she did not apply to parents or brothers. A fifth box, firmly locked and pitch dark inside, held evasions and lies about what people did out of sight and mind.

So Henriette accepted that Russell was different and had his own friends, but she did not pluck from the word box to name him or look in the fact box to see what he might do with a man. She couldn't miss Carl's fears and ambitions, and she knew he said they required a wife, but all she felt when she thought of his marriage was loss to herself and, vaguely, to him.

"Isidor Daniels has been encouraging me," she said, eager to change the subject. "He's hinted he might have some research for me after graduation."

"Congratulations," said Carl, looking skeptical. "You'll finish college when I finish med school and maybe be off to Indian country when I get married. "

"So that's your plan?" she asked.

"Of course," said Carl, as though she were a fool to doubt it

A FEW DAYS LATER, HENRIETTE stepped out of the Social Science building and saw Carl and a woman, nearly as tall as he, trudging across the central quadrangle. As they approached, she saw with a tightening in her throat that they were holding hands. Soon the woman's long, curly hair came into focus, but nothing about her looked right for Carl's fiancée. She wore silk stockings, and her heels clicked against the rough stones. Was she older than Carl?

"This is Dorothy," Carl said as they met. "My sister, Henriette." They shook hands, then stood, unsure what to do next. Dorothy suggested coffee, and they settled into one of the C-shop's maroon leather booths, shrugging out of coats. Dorothy's full figure was dressed for work in a navy blue twin set and straight dark skirt. A voice from a radio sang, "You make time and you make love dandy/You make swell molasses candy," and Henriette tapped her foot in time under the table. "But honey are you making any money/That's all I want to know," went the song.

"Carl's told me something about you," said Dorothy, in the tone of an interviewer. Henriette wondered if she'd sounded so documentarian when she'd blurted facts about Scottsboro to Dilly. "You're a student here, right?"

"Yes, I'm studying anthropology," said Henriette. "What about you?" Carl went up to the counter to order.

"I'm through with school," said Dorothy, sitting back and crossing her arms. "I got a master's degree in clinical social work, and now I work with disturbed children." So she *was* older.

"Dorothy can support me through my internship and residencies," said Carl, returning with three cups of coffee and a pitcher of cream and sounding pleased with himself. Henriette winced at his plan, marriage and money paired up again.

"You'll be able to support me when a baby comes along," said Dorothy, adding cream to her coffee and then offering it to Carl. A baby? Surely they weren't planning children already. When Henriette imagined herself sharing bed and board with Dilly, the picture never included a squalling infant.

"Where did you meet?" asked Henriette, avoiding silence.

"At a seminar on play therapy for children," said Carl. "We found ourselves agreeing on everything."

"We plan to develop all sides of ourselves, not freeze into society's roles," said Dorothy. "We'll have an open marriage, with both men and women, as a way to realize…"

"She's just talking," interrupted Carl, addressing Henriette. It seemed that the three of them were in a play, and not a very good one at that, with actors ready to explode out of their roles at any minute.

"Well you know what I mean," said Dorothy. "We don't intend to suffer from civilization's discontents."

"We'll settle for common unhappiness," said Carl. "The stunted development of the so-called mature." Now it seemed like Carl was teaming up with Dorothy to make fun of Henriette. Neither of them sounded like they meant what they said, but Henriette couldn't be sure. Their clever, modern talk made her wish for Dilly's warmth and grounded body, and she thought of the wave of feeling from which she'd recently fled. Maybe Carl was also pursued by what he couldn't say, just pulling words from the word box. Apparently Dorothy was glad to partner Carl in pretense, sparring, and play-acting. At one time Henriette would have struggled to join in, but not today.

"Tell me about your work with children," she said to Dorothy, stirring her coffee into a black maelstrom, then reaching for the cream. Usually she drank it black and bracing, but today she wanted the sweet solace of sugar and cream.

"The parents bring them in because they're acting out, misbehaving at school or at home, sometimes hitting other kids or worse, like setting fires." Alerting the world, thought Henriette. Why didn't I ever try that? "We play games or draw pictures," continued Dorothy, "and pretty soon they're telling me that Mommy doesn't love them or Uncle Jake hits them when they talk too much." Henriette took a sip of her sweet coffee, imagining that scene of trust, playing games with someone maternal who wanted to help her, but she couldn't let herself long for what she'd never get. Dorothy had come to take Carl away, joining in his ironic, coded talk of sex and psyche that left Henriette alone and in the cold.

"Or worse," Dorothy went on, "that Uncle Jake is staying over and Daddy is moving out." Dorothy and Carl laughed at the familiar saga, but Henriette couldn't and wouldn't join in — each moment she liked Dorothy less. "Carl told me you're in analysis," continued Dorothy.

"Yes," said Henriette, chin in air, trying not to show she was hurt. "I've been really lucky to get Dr. Whitson."

"I'm impressed," said Dorothy. "She's at the top of her field."

"Analysis goes on and on, though," said Henriette. "On and on," she repeated, her voice fading into the music and chatter and feeling as though she herself were fading away. "I think I'm interminable."

"Nothing lasts forever," said Dorothy, linking her arm through Carl's, chilling Henriette.

"Does that include marriage?" she asked.

"Henriette," said Carl, frowning like a disapproving parent.

Dorothy leaned forward and touched Henriette's arm with her free hand. "Though you might not like to think it," she said in a tight voice, "the answer is no — marriage lasts." They gathered their coats in another burst of static crackle. Henriette knew she should have kept the banter light, but losing Carl compounded Dilly's distance and left her staring at a vacuum.

On her own, inside the analytic bubble, she'd begun to accept Dilly's standards of faithfulness. Maybe she could be forceful *and* faithful, leaving Carl to that dressed-up, play-acting woman with whom he'd chosen to experiment, if that's what it was. He and Dorothy didn't act like a couple in love. They didn't belong in the poignant box, where she waited and longed for Dilly.

Chapter 23

Henriette was sound asleep on a Friday night in May when the phone began ringing in Foster Hall's little phone alcove. It rang through her dreams until someone finally woke up and went out to answer it. A knock sounded on Henriette's door. "Phone for you." Henriette woke with a start and glanced at the clock. Two in the morning. Frightened, she hurried down the hall.

"I've been arrested," said Russell, voice low and tense.

"What?" asked Henriette. "What on earth for?"

"Nothing," said Russell. "Being on the street."

"Where are you?" asked Henriette, teeth beginning to chatter.

"Twenty-sixth and California. I can't talk long. Someone's got to come down and bail me out — it's a hundred dollars."

"I've got to think. I'll call someone — do something," said Henriette, and Russell hung up. She ached to think how the phone must have jangled and vibrated, nearly falling off the hook, while Russell on the other end yearned to reach through the wire and shake someone awake. She counted her few bills and change, five dollars in all. Calling the parents was out of the question. Father would fume and Mother would shout, and together they would fabricate some lie about why Russell had been arrested, anything to keep from speaking the truth. No, she wouldn't light that fuse. She'd call Carl. She wrapped herself in a robe and slippers and returned to the alcove. Carl was up studying and answered right away.

"Damn him!" said Carl. "I told him he'd get into trouble, hanging around those clubs. No, I will not go down there in the middle of the night, and neither should you."

"You can't just let him sit in jail," said Henriette.

"Watch me," said Carl. "Let him learn a lesson." Henriette replaced the receiver and walked back to her room. Who would help her? Henriette winced to think she still hadn't called Nadine or the Abravanels and wondered if she, too, might have gotten arrested. In any case, Nadine had no money. Henriette wouldn't contact Patrick again. Lucky would know his way around the jail and the courts, but would surely exact a price for any help he offered. Could she ask Carl to wake Dilly at this time of night? A fresh tremor of apprehension flowed through her as she thought of approaching Dilly with real need. Offending him. A warm wisp of hope arose: they might ride together in his car, side by side, into the night. She returned to the phone. Dilly's voice was sleepy and thick, but alerted as soon as he recognized hers. He explained to her that she wouldn't need the full amount of bail but would pay a percentage to a bondsman.

"How much do you have?" he asked.

"About five dollars," she said.

"I'll need some time to raise the rest," he said. "I'll call a few friends and borrow it. As soon as I've got the money I'll call you, and we'll go down together." Relief and gratitude flooded through Henriette. Dilly had never even questioned whether he would help. He just grasped the problem and went to work to fix it. What difference did it make whether you understood your psyche when your natural response was so good?

She attended her classes the next day, but her mind was occupied with Russell: Russell behind bars; Russell sitting on a cement bench, surrounded by disorderly drunks; Russell disgusted by his surroundings, himself, and his life. Poor Russell. Then she hurried back to Foster to await Dilly's call. It came just after supper.

"Hankton loaned me some money and some friends the rest," said Dilly. "We shouldn't have to pay more than a sawbuck on a hundred dollar bond. Where is Russell being held?"

"He said twenty-sixth and California. You know it?"

"Yes, the new jail, next to the Criminal Courthouse. I'll pick you up." They drove silently in the long twilight, and Henriette's skin prickled with heightened awareness at Dilly's close presence, even more vivid than she'd imagined. At the jail, an official told them that a judge in evening court would rule on Russell's case that night, so he needn't post bail. They waited on hard chairs in a green-walled waiting room for what felt like hours, while a few others snoozed, smoked, or read newspapers.

Dilly leaned towards Henriette and spoke quietly. "You know Carl's moving out," he said. Henriette nodded. "Russell came by our place when Carl was packing. He accused Carl of trying to twist himself into a new shape."

"I met Dorothy. I don't know what Carl sees in her," said Henriette, thrilled to be talking with Dilly alone.

"Carl told Russell he needs a marriage to get ahead as a psychiatrist. He has to appear mature and normal, even though he thinks those qualities are straitjackets. And so are social roles like 'masculine' and 'feminine'" A man snored, awoke with a start, and cleared his throat. Dilly leaned closer. "They were spoiling for a fight, and the whole conversation made me nervous. Then Russell asked how Dorothy felt about Carl's ideas. Carl said something about her welcoming some immature variety. He called it 'the polymorphous perverse.'" Dilly colored slightly, whispering the phrase.

"That's Freud," said Henriette.

"Sounds like perversion to me," said Dilly, puzzled. "Funny thing is, in the end they agreed, like they shared some special knowledge. I thought maybe you could help me out."

"They've always been close," said Henriette, knowing she couldn't explain her brothers, happy to share their peculiarity with Dilly, happier still that Dilly was willing to come down here and help out whether he understood or not.

About ten at night, they were escorted into a courtroom where a few others sat. A guard entered from a door behind the judge and led Russell, shuffling, to the stand. His black hair stood out at angles, his shirt collar was open, and his tie hung loose, as though he'd been up all night. The beard that always grew quickly shadowed his jaw, and he kept his eyes down. His body looked caged, as though the smallest flamboyant step or gesture might condemn him. Henriette pressed her lips together and looked at Dilly. He took her hand. The charge of their time as lovers flowed from his fingers to hers and lit up her whole body, bringing a shy smile to her lips. A policemen rose, and the judge nodded to him.

"I picked up the defendant on Rush and Chestnut," he said. "All these inverts were loitering on the street around there. I posed as one of them and offered him money. He accepted, and I arrested him." The judge looked severely at Russell.

"I had no idea why the guy was holding out money," said Russell. "I was just walking with my friends."

"That's what they all say," said the policeman.

The judge addressed Russell. "The behavior of you and your kind is subverting the morals of our city, leading to an increase in vice and crime," he said. "The Juvenile Protective Association has opened our eyes to the rise of sexual inversion, and we need to protect our youth.

Any future occurrence will be treated as a felony. For now you're guilty as charged of a misdemeanor. Released with a fine of ten dollars." He pounded his gavel. "Do you understand?"

"Yes, your Honor," said Russell, and the guard led him out. The three met in the hall outside the courtroom and hugged, Henriette and Dilly relieved to see Russell free and unharmed, Russell almost in tears from his ordeal. Dilly paid the fine with the money he had borrowed, and Russell promised to pay it back. By now it was eleven, and the streets around the jail were dark and deserted. They headed out into the warm night.

Apparently they had left the huge building by a door different from the one where they'd entered, and they stood looking around, trying to orient themselves. Darkened bungalows lined one side of the small street and the Cook County Jail, the other. Tall fences around the jail were topped with rolls of concertina wire that sparked with light reflected from their deadly little knives, and lookout towers at each corner of the fence glared with menace down at the street. The recent crackdown on pansy clubs had led to a rash of arrests for "disorderly," and a ragged procession of those released from night court filtered onto the street: bulldaggers dressed like men in tuxedoes, some with top hats; men in high heels with long, blond wigs; and other men and women who just looked disheveled like Russell, ordinary clothes in disarray. They were only a few blocks from the gateway to Little Village, where Czech and Bohemian bars and restaurants would keep the street lively until late, but here all was quiet and dark. The newly released scurried quickly away, observed by a group of three or four young men standing under a streetlight.

"Here come the fags," said one in a loud voice. "Creeping out of jail," and they all laughed.

"I think it's this way," said Dilly, pointing down Twenty-Sixth Street.

"Let's go." He took Henriette's arm, and the three walked close together.

Slow footsteps sounded behind the three as the men began sauntering after them, following at a distance. We're in Chicago, thought Henriette. We're in sight of the law. Nothing can happen.

"Time for a party," said a mocking voice.

"Yeah, party with the Ethels," said another.

"Here come the scum," said another voice.

"I don't like this," said Russell under his breath. Henriette glanced back. How could trouble have found her so soon again?

"There's five or six of them now," she said, and grabbed Dilly's hand on her arm, heart pounding.

"Don't look," said Dilly. "Just ignore them."

"Just ignore them," said Henriette to Russell. Sweat ran down her sides. Hate-filled voices were following her and those she loved, and tramping feet came closer. Coppers, they needed some coppers. Dilly's good ones could save them. They walked faster.

"We're two blocks away from the car," said Dilly. "If I remember right."

"These sissies think they can disappear," said a voice in the crowd behind them.

"We'll get them."

"We've got them." Laughter. A mock effeminate voice said, "I am so scared." Jeers and echoes, "Ooh, scary."

"I've got to get out of here," said Russell, darting glances right and left. The South had come North, it seemed. The three walked faster.

"If you run," said Dilly, "they'll be on top of you in a minute. Keep your head and walk."

"Get the fag, get the daisy, get the fag," the men started chanting in unison.

"They're gonna get me," said Russell, "They wanna lynch me. I gotta run."

"They can't," said Henriette, her voice a high whine, but she'd heard "lynch" and saw the noose, fire, and knives. She suppressed a scream and hurried on.

"They can. They will," said Russell, his voice desperate. Feet pounded behind them, and Russell bolted, heading down an alley. Henriette howled with a low, grating sound and ran to a fence at the side of the alley, crouching beside a garbage can, and covered her head with her arms.

"No, no, no," she said to herself as shouts and fleshy sounds of struggle filled the night air. A shot rang out, silencing everything with its harsh report. Henriette looked up, peering into the dark, afraid that the worst had happened. Saliva tasting of metal filled her mouth, and she thought she might throw up. Rising slowly, she just made out Dilly standing down the alley, holding a pistol at arm's length in both hands, swinging the gun in a slow arc back and forth across a dark mass of men. Like ice melting, tension flowed out of every muscle in her body as she realized the shot had come from him. Protected by a garbage can, she watched Dilly wait until all the men had stopped moving and had turned to face him, hands in front of their chests, palms reflecting white from the pale light of a single streetlamp, as if to say, "Hey, only joking."

"That was a warning," said Dilly. "Now turn around and go home and leave the man alone." Dilly stood where he was, the gun like a beacon pointing out each man in turn, as they muttered retractions, shook their heads, and slunk off down the alley. Henriette got up, shaking and numb, and came to stand behind Dilly.

"Where's Russell?" she asked, barely able to form words.

"I don't know," said Dilly. "Wait 'til all these bimbos are gone, and we'll find him." Dilly stood with his gun aimed until the alley was empty. Footsteps sounded from porch stairs, and Russell emerged from behind a fence. Henriette ran to him and hugged him.

"Are you OK?" asked Dilly. When Henriette looked back at him, the weapon was gone.

"That was close," said Russell. "Those goons mean business." Then, looking down at a spreading stain, "I need to change my pants."

"We'll drive you home," said Dilly, and they went to the car. Henriette's heart clamored and then slowed as they drove in silence. How could they have been so near to the Courthouse, in a major northern city, yet so far from the rule of law? This wasn't Germany, where the law would do nothing to protect Jews or gypsies or dissidents. And homos? Homosexual organizations had been banned and their members were getting arrested. Anyone deemed "unworthy of life"— the sick or disabled — was sterilized by force. Henriette's despair had lifted with the night's excitement, but now it settled like fog around her. A smell of urine spread throughout the car, and Henriette wondered whether she too might stink. Mingled with the meaty smell of sweat and urine's sharp ammonia was a faint, crisp odor of gunpowder, reminding Henriette that the gun was still somewhere near, and she wished she could tell Nadine about Dilly's triumph.

What was Dilly doing with a pistol, anyway? How did he carry it, and where was it now? This was no hunting gun. Did Dilly have contact with the city's infamous gangs of rum runners? She'd treated them as a joke, but there was nothing funny about any of the night's events. She hoped Dilly wouldn't interrogate Russell about just how he'd gotten arrested and why he'd been chased. Naming it could only add shame and embarrassment to what Russell had already suffered. She needn't have worried. Dilly was even more discrete than she. Henriette looked at his profile and saw no difference from the man she'd known before, but when she thought of him aiming his pistol down the alley, his big head became the turret of a tank, scanning right to left, ready to fire volleys and mow down a crowd. Apparently a layer of force lurked inside some people, deeper than fighting words, raised voices, or thrown food, more powerful than hypocrisy or creeping fingers, strong enough to take on the lynching South. It seemed the sense of irony Dilly had acquired in Klamath had done nothing to dilute the force and rage of his Sam Hall —— "God damn your eyes" — and Henriette was glad. She needed that. Dilly had turned strange again and still more interesting. She wondered where to start, getting to know this new person.

Chapter 24

It was too late at night for Russell to return to Purdue, and Henriette decided to stay with him in Oak Park to help him explain to the parents what had happened and ask for the money he would need to pay Dilly back. Dilly dropped them off, and they let themselves in silently and went to bed.

"What a nice surprise," said Father on Saturday morning, drinking coffee in the kitchen as Russell and Henriette came down the back stairs, tousled and sleepy. "You're looking good," he said to Henriette. "Have you put on weight?"

"Maybe a little," said Henriette. The smell of frying filled the air as Mother made French toast on the stove. She turned to give each of the children a peck on the cheek, and Henriette pulled back.

"We have to tell you something," she said.

"Oh?" said Father.

"I was out with friends night before last," said Russell, sitting uncomfortably on the edge of his chair. "Just hanging around up North. We weren't doing anything." He paused, looking down. "I got arrested," he said.

"What?" said Father, setting his coffee cup down hard. "What for? How is that possible?" Mother turned off the stove and faced them.

"How on earth...?" she began.

"You have to understand..." began Russell.

"I don't have to do anything," said Father, lips pursed.

"Listen," said Henriette. "People get picked up every day for loitering in the city." She tried to calibrate the precise amount of information that would satisfy them without pushing them over an edge they couldn't tolerate. "They get arrested," she said, "just for being on the street, having fun with their friends. Russell was in the wrong place at the wrong time. It's a misdemeanor, nothing more." She laughed inside. If they knew *she'd* been arrested herself! They must never find out.

"Loitering?" asked Mother. "Why were you loitering? Why didn't you just go wherever you were going? Law-abiding people don't get arrested."

"Actually they do," said Russell, voice harsh. "Arrested and then hunted down by thugs."

"What are you talking about? This makes no sense," said Father, not waiting for an answer. "You don't get arrested for nothing."

"Did you run into thugs?" asked Mother, now worried.

"We did," said Henriette. She hadn't planned to tell this part of the story, but now that Russell had started she had no choice. "We left the jail after eleven and a gang of goons chased us down a few streets, thinking we had money.

"Did anyone get hurt?" asked Father.

"No," said Henriette. "But they surely intended to steal whatever we had and might have done if Dilly hadn't scared them off with his gun."

"Gun!" said Mother. "What was he doing with a gun?"

"He hunts, Mother," said Henriette. Then slow and deliberate, as though speaking to a child: "He knows how to use a gun." Mother's abhorrence of guns would surely prevent her from registering the difference between taking a rifle or shotgun into the woods to hunt and carrying a pistol under your clothes in the city.

"That Diller? The one who came to dinner? You don't mean to tell me he carried a weapon into this house?" Henriette shrugged.

"He saved us," said Russell, voice tremulous. "If you care two cents about us, be glad he was armed."

"I can't be glad about anyone with a gun keeping company with my daughter," said Father.

"We're not together anymore," said Henriette.

"The Women's League for Peace is trying to get guns outlawed," said Mother. "Frederick Douglass fought for education and equality, not guns." She drew herself up and raised her spatula as though it were a finger to shake in Henriette's face. "Dr. Dubois stood here in our living room talking about the need for protest, but he didn't carry a gun."

"Russell had to pay a fine," said Henriette. "I paid half, and Dilly raised the rest. We need to pay him back, and I need my five. Ten bucks altogether."

"I expect my children to stay out of trouble," said Father, already surrendering. He reached into his pocket and pulled out a ten-dollar bill. "Remember, that's almost two weeks worth of groceries for our family." Then, to Henriette, "Stay away from that Diller." He turned to Russell. "You, young man, watch your step."

"Thanks," said Henriette, and pocketed the money.

Mother turned the stove back on, using the spatula to turn the French toast. "He did look rather primitive, sort of Neanderthal."

"He's a sweet boy and smart too," said Henriette. "You have to get to know him."

"I don't have to do anything," said Father. "Have nothing to do with him, now or ever. He's a man of violence and unworthy of you."

Henriette was shocked. Father's sudden temper was familiar, but now he sounded cold, detached. With a queasy certainty she knew that meant he cared too much, that he might not survive if she ever really grew up, married or moved away. Suddenly she thought of Dr. Whitson's view of Father as conditioned by his upbringing, and she wondered if she could ever confront him. Dread began to accumulate like rain filling a bucket. Was it possible the parents, who fought over her so endlessly, might never let her go? They could bind her to them by cutting off support, and she'd be trapped, her voice smothered as it always had been. Maybe she didn't deserve the escape for which she'd hoped and planned so long. An old hollow fear sidled up, reminding her that she was essentially lacking, her insides numb and silent like the bottom of the sea or the bedrock underneath a world of dirt. *I didn't know you had a girl.*

"She won't see him," said Mother, patting Father's arm. "Not that barbaric boy. Don't worry." Then turning back to Henriette, "You won't ever use a gun, will you? Tell me you won't."

"Of course she won't," said Father. Henriette remembered the alien weight of the shotgun on her shoulder when she'd visited Dilly and the far more distasteful look of the cold, metal pistol, and she knew she would never touch the thing except to push it away, but she would not give the parents the satisfaction of voicing her antipathy. How could they continue preparing breakfast in complete incomprehension of what she'd been through: the devastating phone call, the tense wait on hard chairs, the punitive judge, the hate and violence that could only be stopped by greater force, the closeness of death. Death was everywhere: North and South, in small towns and cities, in jail and on the streets, in Germany and here, and the parents seemed oblivious. Maybe the only thing stronger than death was a gun. Mother served the toast, and Henriette ate a few bites.

"Enough," she said. And to Russell, "Let's go." They headed for the train, walking in silence. Russell was her brother, and Dilly had saved him. In mind and heart she agreed with her parents about guns, yet where would she and Russell be right now without Dilly's weapon?

From time to time in the hours and days that followed, she found herself returning to the mystery of the gun: its sudden, alarming blast of sound; the hot, burned smell; the small working parts she'd never seen; the way those parts collaborated to explode; and the incisive way they changed hate to feigned apology. And Dilly had held that mystery in his hand, then made it disappear, hidden somewhere close to his skin.

THE NEXT DAY HENRIETTE FOUND Dilly in Harper Library studying for prelims. He motioned her out to the hall where they could talk.

"How did it go for you and Russell in Oak Park?" he asked, arm above her head against the wall, speaking in a low, intimate voice. Henriette stood with her back to the wooden wainscoting, looking straight ahead. She shrugged and reached into her purse, removing a wallet and taking out a bill.

"Here's what we owe you," she said, handing it over and meeting his eyes.

"They gave it to you just like that?"

"Actually they were more upset about you carrying a gun than us being chased. I told Father we weren't keeping company any more, and he was relieved."

"Hey, wait a minute," said Dilly, standing up straight. "I saved their son, and now they think I'm some kind of bruno, packing heat?"

"I didn't tell them the men were after Russell. They wouldn't understand. I just said they were yeggs hoping to rob us."

"Oh," said Dilly and waited, as though debating whether to ask a question.

"They're not important," said Henriette, and brushed them away with her hand. Tears overtook her with a choking rush. She hid her face, embarrassed to stand crying in the library hall. "What?" asked Dilly, but she couldn't answer. Russell was safe, Scottsboro was far away. Something about the angles of their bodies as they leaned against the wall, his hovering concern. She couldn't stop, and he led her away from the reading room, looking for privacy. Outside was cold, and doors were locked or held toilets. Trying door handles, he found one that led to the stacks and guided her down, still sobbing. At the end of a corridor, they wedged themselves in a webby corner, surrounded by books, and sat on the floor.

"I was so scared," she said, the words streaming with water.

"On the street?" he asked.

"In the South." She told about spit and falling and yanking, the van. Her panic in jail. "And then last night. It's too much." Fresh tears came and she cried on his chest, while he soothed her back.

"I've messed up your shirt." Her crying subsided to hiccups. He offered a handkerchief, fresh from his pocket. She blew her nose.

"Have you ever told anyone what really happened in Scottsboro?"

"Not even myself. I'm afraid and confused about what I found out. It's like I woke up to a world without a foundation. Bottomless. I think I'm still falling."

"You're not falling," said Dilly. "I've caught you," and he tightened his arm around her.

Shoulder to shoulder and hip to hip they sat, enfolded in silence. Sun shone from a small window near the ceiling. Dust settled on books.

"How do you live when you find out what people can do?" she asked, feeling the foolish simplicity of her despair.

"We've all done bad things, or our ancestors have. My French forebears traded with Indians, taking their furs for a song," said Dilly. "Most of the tribes in the West were force-marched from the East."

"I went to Scottsboro to help save nine men, but soon I discovered I had to save me." She shivered and threatened to cry again.

"Everyone deserves a fair trial," said Dilly. "It's good that you wanted to do your part, but why would you team up with Communists? We've already got a great system: elections and juries, lawyers and courts."

Henriette sighed, her breath still uneven with tears. "I doubt the young men will ever get a fair trial. Only whites serve on the juries down South, and the Supreme Court refused to consider that claim."

"Maybe you hoped to accomplish too much, too fast. Legal processes take time. I don't trust master plans or grand ideologies, right wing or left. You can make a good life by helping where needed, like what you did for Nadine." Nadine, she thought, with a gulp of guilt. She must call the Abravanels. Dilly's words echoed Nadine's, though Henriette knew they'd never agree about just what the system could do or not do. Wedged between wooden shelves, watched over by books, she felt safe in a nest. Dilly's world seemed a good place, and perhaps he'd invite her to join him and stay. She'd surely say yes.

He called her the next day to see how she was, and they met in the C-shop. Suddenly shy, she thought of their intimate time in the stacks, their confessions a deeper connection than sex. "Do you carry a gun all the time?" she asked, thinking of her parents' objection.

"No-o-o," he drawled, looking unfairly accused. "I carry it when I might be in danger, like hanging around a jail at night. My A1 .45 is the gun my father was issued in the army, and he gave it to me. Aside from your trip to the South, you've led a protected life."

"I'm beginning to realize that." She would not tell him her parents had forbidden their meeting. That was her problem, and she'd find a way.

"Now what about Russell?" asked Dilly. "He's not effeminate. Is he really a sissy?"

"Not all homosexuals are alike," said Henriette.

"Hankton's not at all effeminate," said Dilly. "I doubt he's even a pansy."

"I don't doubt it," said Henriette. "But you go ahead and think of Russell like Henry the omnipotent if you like," and she raised her chin and smiled. Dilly seemed willing to leave the question in a gray zone, and Henriette heard a nice clink as she dropped it into her word box. Her tears and his comfort had opened up parts of herself she'd thought bricked up for good, and desire streamed from her pores.

"Let's go for a walk," said Dilly.

"I'm hungry," said Henriette, remembering how attractive Dilly had found her appetite. "Let's get something to eat."

"The Chinese place?" asked Dilly, and Henriette agreed. Dusk was cooling a late spring day, and tangential light made leafing trees glow bright green. They greeted the restaurant's owner, took seats, and asked for the economical meal they'd eaten so often as friends and then lovers: wonton soup, pork with bean curd, extra rice.

A pot of tea and two cups arrived, and Henriette cradled the round cup, blowing on it.

"I have troubles to tell as well," said Dilly. "There's something amiss in Kitachara." He curled the edge of his napkin, looking down.

"There's trouble all over," said Henriette. "Unemployment and hunger here, burning books in Germany. How is it going for your parents?"

"The price of potatoes keeps dropping, and the family makes do with less and less. They don't know which side their bread is buttered on — they wish Hoover were still President. I don't know how to help." Soup arrived, steaming, and they ladled portions into bowls for each.

"We're lucky," said Henriette, and Dilly nodded.

"There's more to it, though," he said, eating spoonfuls of soup. He put down his spoon and leaned in, lowering his voice and glancing right and left. "Last time I was there my parents weren't speaking, and Mother had moved out to the sun porch. All they said to me was, 'You picked a bad time to come home,' and 'There's nothing you can do.'"

"What do you think?" asked Henriette.

"I don't know. Maybe something happened when she went to stay in Milwaukee. She stayed longer than planned, and she had a good time. I'll be damned if I'll ask. If it's a secret, there's a good reason. I'll let it stay that way." He sat back, jaw clamping down. Henriette picked up her spoon and turned her attention to the soup, biting on a wonton and feeling the spurt of juice, watching Dilly do the same. Maybe she should have kept her night with Patrick a secret. But perhaps if Dilly suspected his mother of unfaithfulness, it would soften his attitude toward her own misstep.

The food arrived, and they sucked in slippery bean curd and chewed on reddish barbecued pork, mixing the juice with rice and seasoning it with soy, using chopsticks with expertise. The long silence filled with sounds of slurping and sipping, and then Dilly spoke. "What happened to us?" he asked, reaching across the table for her hand. "Let's talk about it. Why couldn't we get along?"

"You thought I was sleeping around," said Henriette, pulling her hand back. "You wanted me to be more like your people." Dilly winced.

"Well, now you know my family has its own troubles." Dilly's voice thickened with feeling, then cleared to sound more objective. "Like all families do, after all."

"Not like mine," said Henriette.

"You thought I was provincial and conservative, always supporting the status quo, too tame for your revolutionary friends," said Dilly.

"And too nit-picking in your research, and blind to what goes on inside you," she added. Henriette waited a moment, then blurted, "I think you made me out to be sleeping around so I could be your floozy while your mother remained on a pedestal, inviolate." Dilly frowned and looked like he wanted to protest, then finished off his tea and asked for the check. Henriette felt guilty about letting him pay, knowing she had her allowance and he had only the little he earned. But she knew he would be demeaned if she offered to help.

"Let's walk," said Dilly, and they left. A few blocks later they arrived at the Midway's broad expanse, where grass was covered with leaves. "I miss you," he said. "In fact I've been missing you for ages."

"I don't think you ever loved me," said Henriette, looking down.

"That's not true." She could feel Dilly's eyes watching her closely. "I did, and I still do."

"Do you really mean that?" Henriette turned to face him in the twilight. His slight frame seemed to blend into the background of the craggy, pseudo-Gothic chapel behind him, and his figure took on its rocky stability and promise of refuge.

"Yes," he said, and took her in his arms, then pulled back. "Let's just say we were stupid to give up what we had."

"I believe that." Red rose in Henriette's cheeks, and the muscles of her face came to life. She turned to face him and skipped a few steps backward down the sidewalk. "Stupid, when we should have been smart."

"Yes, stupid to be angry and resentful and hurt, when we could have comforted each other," said Dilly. Henriette waited for him to catch up with her. "When we fought, I felt awful, sick and confused."

"I didn't like it any better than you," said Dilly, taking her hand. "I think we should stick together." They continued walking.

"What about your girlfriends?" asked Henriette. "I see that Katya flirting with you every time I turn around."

"I had fun with her, but she's not important. Don't worry about her. What about you?"

"I've been alone for a year, ever since the horrible summer."

"I bet men clamor at your door, Cassandra," said Dilly, turning towards her and smoothing hair away from her face. "I think you need your gatekeeper. Cassandra and Delicio." Someone to stand by her

— that was what she needed. If Professor Daniels gave her the field placement she hoped for, she'd be heading out into the desert this summer. Mother would nag her to come home and threaten her with Father's failing health.

She turned to Dilly and smiled. "Delicio, my derp."

"Let's go home," he said, and they headed towards the apartment on Maryland Avenue. The air stilled as dusk came, and their shoes scuffled in the silence. His hand tugged slightly on hers.

"You'll be leaving so soon," she said, holding him back.

"I have to go to Klamath to work on my thesis. I'll visit you. It's a promise." He lifted her hand and kissed it, then rubbed it on his cheek. She threw her arms around him. Holding each other tight, they hurried to his apartment.

She wondered if this time would be different, if she'd finally surmount the divide between the self that yearned for union of body and soul and the self that despised the beggar she became if she let herself be aroused. She intended to do her part, giving herself to the experience and coming in what Freud had taught her was the right, mature way. But Dilly had learned some things about women since they'd last been together. In bed he embraced her with one arm while the other hand crept up her inner thigh. She pushed him away. He stroked her back for a while, then slipped a hand around and under the curve of her buttock. She stiffened.

"What's wrong with a little finger fucking?" he asked.

"You bastard!" she said, springing up. "You make it into a dirty joke. You make it vulgar, and I can't do it." She grabbed a sheet and held it in front of her, looking down at him.

"Vulgar!" said Dilly. "Did you think Cassandra and Delicio were going to have a fairy-tale romance with a chastity belt? Sex isn't chaste; it *is* vulgar." She drew her knees up to her chest and tucked the sheet around her. A minute passed. "Are we still going to be together, after you leave?" she asked in a small voice.

"Of course we are," he said, reaching up to stroke the back of her neck and her hair, until she snuggled down next to him. He performed as she had first expected, then, and afterwards they slept.

Chapter 25

One time ended and another began when Henriette called the Abravanels.

"We heard from her when she got back from Alabama," said Marjorie, her usual deep and cheerful voice now high and thin. "She had a cold that got worse. Walking pneumonia, but then she got better. After that we didn't hear from her for months." Henriette grasped these details to avoid the assault to her heart that rushed along the line from New York. "We know you found her there in jail and helped her get free. We didn't approve, you know." Marjorie's words tumbled out, garbled with sobs. "But that means nothing now. She's gone, impossibly gone."

"Gone? Gone where?" Henriette's teeth were already chattering. "Gone" slammed work and love and jazz and falling and finding entirely out of her mind. Her belly threatened to turn inside out, revolting at information that could not be stopped from slithering through her ear to her unbelieving brain. Death was not just everywhere, it was right here, displacing life, jerking her into the no time of forever. Nadine had been found on the floor of her apartment, and Henriette would never see her again. "That can't be," said Henriette, already crying herself. "I had lunch with her after we got back, and she was fine. Recovered from typhus and healthy."

"Not any more," said Marjorie, voice flattening. She informed Henriette of details: there were no signs of foul play. The medical examiner had determined the cause of death: a cerebral aneurysm. "Lurking inside her ever since she was born," said Marjorie, beginning to cry again.

The dormitory's phone alcove felt like an ice house, and Henriette knew she would never forget this chilly station at the edge of absence, cigarette burns on its wooden desk, the grimy receiver she held in a clammy hand and the phone cord she wrapped tight around her other wrist. And she would never be able to remember what she was supposed to be doing, what classes or chores or appointments were lined up, waiting for her to re-enter the time of her life. From now on, everything would be after.

"What can I do?" asked Henriette, cursing herself for the preoccupations that had kept her from contacting Nadine for so many months.

"There's nothing anyone can do," said Marjorie, and Henriette hung up the phone. She walked slowly back to her room, got into bed, and curled into a ball, continuing to cry. She rocked back and forth, saying to herself, "It should have been me. It should have been me. My life is worthless. Hers was important. It should have been me."

In the morning she called Dilly, and he came right over. In his arms, she cried out the little she knew about what had happened. "It should have been me," she repeated.

He held her and rocked her. "You were a wonderful friend to Nadine," he said. "Her poems have outlived her, and you'll always have those. Life isn't fair — I learned that when Finn died. But you can't substitute one death for another. There's no way you can make it be you."

Chapter 26

Needing to share her sense of loss with those who had been wounded most deeply, Henriette called the Abravanel's home a few days later. A stranger answered.

"Nadine was my best friend." Henriette's voice broke, and she imagined the once-joyful room on the other end of the line with curtains now drawn and voices hushed.

"Are you the one who found her in Alabama?" The stranger did not sound friendly, and Henriette knew she might be unwelcome for her support of Nadine's work in Scottsboro.

"Yes." Henriette paused, not knowing what else to say. She ached to reach through the line, as though she could still find Nadine on the other end, but the stranger's voice was cool and objective, explaining that the funeral was over and family and friends were gathered for the Jewish week of mourning, sitting Shiva.

"Please tell her parents I loved Nadine and I'm thinking about them." Henriette realized there was nothing more she could do, so she stayed in Chicago and shared her grief with Effie, Dilly, and a few other classmates.

Henriette had always carried Nadine in her hip pocket, a source of spunk and courage, even when they didn't meet regularly. Now, since her death, Nadine sometimes seemed as present to Henriette as though she were still working at the newspaper downtown, a train ride away, and the memory of her solid flesh, thick black hair, and cheerful contempt for pretense would bring tears of disbelief. Emptiness would take over, and she'd cry herself to sleep. A young person could be snatched away as quickly as a leaf could fall. She and Dilly shared this knowledge, and it created a new connection between them. Henriette tried to keep Nadine with her as she moved forward with her studies, but when she thought of all the poems Nadine might have written and all the marches she might have led, a regret deeper than any personal malaise purpled all her days.

ON A MONDAY MORNING SHE went to see Professor Daniels. Pages of precise, handwritten notes covered his desk, and earth-toned Indian pots, decorated with geometric designs, held pipes and pens.

"I'll graduate in June," said Henriette. "I'd like to apply to graduate school. I wondered if you might have some work for me in the summer."

"Can you type up notes?"

She gulped, seeing herself as a secretary. "Is that the best way to start?"

"See these?" He pointed to a pile of papers filled with tiny, penciled handwriting. "There are three times that many in my files in Tularosa, on the Mescalero Reservation. My wife, Betty, and I will be heading out there in June to do fieldwork, and we stay the summer. You could come along to type up my notes and eventually learn to work with informants. You'd get room, board, and a small stipend." The idea of informants sounded good to Henriette. "I suppose your parents are prepared to pay your graduate school tuition," Professor Daniels said. She gave a slight nod, hoping it would turn out to be true.

AFTER GRADUATION SHE RODE THE train thirty-six hours to Tularosa, New Mexico, rocked to sleep in a narrow Pullman birth and drinking coffee in the wood-paneled dining car in the morning. The train tore through fields of grass that stretched to the horizon, rippling in the wind, then clung to the sides of mountains above cascading streams. The grandeur of the landscape made her feel small and lonely, and she wondered if she would be equal to the task: transcribing field notes and later gathering information from Apache Indians, reputed to be silent and stoic, the ancient warrior seething below the mask of adaptation. The bookwork part would be easy for her, but silence was another story. There would be no Nadine to cheer her on from a distance or give her courage. She hoped that the Daniels would become her friends.

The professor met the train with a car and drove through the sage-covered desert, rock formations rising like ships from the sea and turning pink in the setting sun. Evergreens furred the mountain to the tree line, and a white peak glistened above.

"That's the Sierra Blanca," said the professor in his teaching voice. "It's the Apache's holy mountain, sacred to all three tribes: Mescalero, Jicarilla, Chiricahua. You can see why — it's cool and fresh up there compared to the desert below."

"I know," she said. "I did my homework." By the time they arrived at the one-story adobe house where the Daniels lived, stars had filled the sky with myriad points of light and a shimmery streak of Milky Way. Henriette tightened a sweater around her as she gaped at the heavens. "The desert turns cold at night," said the professor. "Let's go in."

Mrs. Daniels greeted Henriette, wearing shorts, sandals, and a man's shirt tied in front, revealing a strip of midriff below. Her dark blond hair bounced in a ponytail, and silver earrings dangled from her pierced ears. Like a gypsy, thought Henriette, or some sort of artist. Not at all like a faculty wife.

"Call me Betty," she said, and led Henriette into a central room with an all-purpose wooden table, tall filing cabinet, gas stove, and sink, as well as a sagging wicker couch with red and blue flowered pillows on top and two overstuffed chairs. "Power goes off when it storms." Betty edged past a chair to open a cabinet with candles and matches. "We eat breakfast here and take our other meals with Mrs. Pepper, a quarter mile down the road." Off the main room was Henriette's small bedroom with narrow iron bed and one little window high in the tan wall. The room felt oppressive and smelled of earth.

"Are the walls really made of mud?" asked Henriette.

"Mud and straw," said Betty with a laugh, patting Henriette's arm. "Adobe bricks dry in the sun and get hard as rocks." Henriette ran her hand over the wall, detecting bristly bits of straw and wondering if rain could turn bricks back to mud. "We're a little cramped but cozy," continued Betty. "You'll get used to it." Henriette felt glad to be living simply when so many back home were huddled under cardboard, hungry.

"You should call me Izzy," said the professor, bringing Henriette's luggage to her room. Right, thought Henriette. First names are good. She carried her big black typewriter into the central room and put it on the table.

That night Henriette lay awake. The cold night air crept through the window, and the cry of a coyote made her shiver. So much depended on how she met this summer's challenges, but right now, more than anything, she needed a friend. The swish of Betty's hair and muted jingle of her earrings (Navajo silver?) made her appealing, and she seemed kind and lighthearted, still attractive after years of marriage.

THE NEXT MORNING HENRIETTE PUT on shorts and tied her shirt in front like Betty, midriff bare. After breakfast she sat down to start typing Izzy's thick sheaf of field notes on the social organization of the Chiricahua, while he left for the reservation, seventeen miles away, to talk to informants. The tiny handwritten notes were detailed:

interviews about tribe, clan, and local group membership; difficult to read; obsessive and irritating. Henriette thought back to the poetic warpath language she'd learned about briefly from Ingebritsen and wished she were studying something so interesting.

While Henriette typed, Betty made more coffee, swept up the ever-accumulating dust, and did laundry in a big tub where she had collected rainwater. Betty sang as she worked, "I can't give you anything but love, baby," and threw in a little dance step as she sashayed around the room, hips swiveling. Even the thick walls couldn't keep the room cool, and Henriette's fingers began to stick to the keys and the paper. At noon she went outside. Light danced off every rock and seemed to lodge in her brain, and the sky overhead was so dark blue it verged on black. How could you think in a place that bombarded your senses like that? A few hours later, Izzy came home from the reservation, bearing mail.

"Anything for me?" asked Henriette, getting up.

"Dilly wrote you airmail," said Izzy. "He must think money grows on trees." Fussy Izzy. "When can I see the reservation?" she asked, sinking into the chair at her worktable.

"Take it easy," said Izzy. "First learn how to take field notes and interview informants. Later you'll meet the Agent and get one of your own."

"Didn't you say the Agent was the enemy?" She'd fought with Dilly over that, he defending the Agent, coppers, the whole damn system.

"He is," said Izzy, straightening. "But he provides the informants as well as a car. We need him." The thought of typing up notes day after day in this small house without music or movies or any place to go made Henriette feel claustrophobic. Wasn't all academic work like this, listing things no one really needed to know? Or counting beans that could sprout and grow on their own without anyone ever knowing how many of them there were? Bean counters. She didn't want to be one.

In her room that night she opened Dilly's letter. "Now that we are apart you are just as constant in my life as when we were together," he wrote. Thank God for that. He would be her companion and connection to the wider world while she buried herself in Izzy's painstaking observations. She hadn't told her parents that she and Dilly were together again, and she hadn't told Dilly that her parents had forbidden her to see him. He favored secrets anyway, and it was easier to skip over things at a distance. At least she was now earning her own room and board and might someday not need her parents. The desert kept her hidden and safe — no parents, no Patrick, no Lucky. Only Dilly did she miss.

Two days later Izzy drove Henriette partway up the mountain, where they could see the reservation as a whole. They got out of the car and walked. Brown, dry-as-dust hills dotted with sage surrounded them, and green patches of cottonwood below signaled the locations of water. A group of tents downhill made up a small settlement, and Henriette watched as women fed wood to cooking fires and men moved back and forth among the tents. A hide was hung up for tanning, and children played with a barking dog. It seemed unreal, as though figures in an exhibit had just been wound up and set in motion. Slowly the word "encampment," familiar from Izzy's notes, came to life, and Henriette sensed there might be something here beyond observations of custom, something crucial for her life. She looked up at the white peaks of the Sierra Blanca.

"Gorgeous," she said. "But useless to the Indians, this land that no one else wants."

"You've only begun to see the hardship of Apache life," said Izzy. "The poverty and illness."

"Is unemployment as bad here as in the city?"

"Worse. But the Indian Division of the Civilian Conservation Corps is putting some of the young men to work — on digs, building schools, and such." Henriette felt a rush of admiration for this man who came here every summer and told the Apache story to the world. News arrived in Tularosa by mail, some days late, and papers reported the bold programs of Roosevelt's first hundred days, but Apache deprivation still dwarfed the city's Hoovervilles.

On a Saturday afternoon, Betty and Henriette planted zinnias and nasturtiums in their front yard, Henriette feeling domestic and getting more and more fond of Betty. She'd noticed that Betty helped Izzy with the work but got no credit on any of his publications. Izzy was clearly crazy about her, touching and kissing her whenever he could. Henriette wanted that for herself, but she wanted recognition as well.

That night they drove to Alamogordo to eat steak in a restaurant. Izzy and Betty didn't drink, so Henriette made do with "happywine, a kola drink," a local specialty. They stopped at White sands on their way home. Brilliant white gypsum dunes rippled and rose, stretching for miles and miles under a moon "as big as God's stomach," as Henriette later wrote to Dilly. She hoped he would visit soon and see all these wonders for himself. If something so pure and beautiful could go on and on like that, maybe the light could flood her own life, even the darkest places, and she could live without fear of being revealed.

News of the Scottsboro trials traveled faster now that the case was becoming well known, and it made its way to the desert. Some of the young men's parents were currently touring Europe, raising funds and spreading the word, and protests had spread to Switzerland, France, Germany, and Spain. Black and white demonstrated together for the first time since the abolition movement. Forty thousand people signed a petition for a protest March on Washington.

"I feel like we should be there," said Izzy, eating green chile at Mrs. Pepper's.

"At least sign the petition," said Betty, explaining the case briefly to Mrs. Pepper.

"I'd like to march," said Henriette. "But you couldn't pay me to go to Alabama." The steamy South seemed so far away from the desert, suddenly cold at night. The spicy chile prickled her tongue, and she glanced out the window at stars dotting the sky.

"We're doing our part in another way," said Izzy. "Anthropologists can show the world that no human is better or worse than any other, and neither are cultures, despite all their differences. Franz Boas set us straight."

"But look out for those physical anthropologists," said Betty. "The ones like Galton that try to prove racial superiority. Hitler's making use of their theories right now, with his sterilization program, and they've written some of our marriage laws here at home." The idea that any anthropologists could consider some people "unfit" for marriage or children was enough to kill Henriette's appetite, and she left her chile unfinished.

THAT SUMMER THE SCOTTSBORO BOYS were tried a second time with a change of venue to Decatur, Alabama. The defense hired Samuel Leibowitz, a lawyer and mainstream Democrat from New York, reputed to be the best in the country after Clarence Darrow. No leftist, he claimed to have faith in the fairness of all, North and South. He presented a rational, legal defense, but took care to bring two New York homicide detectives with him as bodyguards. Three hundred people crowded the overheated courtroom.

Leibowitz insisted that the prosecutor address Negro witnesses as "Mister." The prosecutor refused, and angry crowds gathered outside the courtroom threatening to lynch both defendants and defense. Again the National Guard was called, and five members were assigned to Leibowitz. One of the alleged victims of rape testified that it never occurred, and the Morgan County solicitor claimed that this witness couldn't understand Leibowitz's "Jew language." The solicitor asked, "Is justice in this case going to be bought and sold in Alabama with Jew money from New York?" The judge ordered the Guard to shoot to kill.

One of the accused was convicted and sentenced to death, but the sentence was suspended and all the remaining trials postponed, pending a motion for a new trial. The judge reviewed seventeen pages of evidence, set aside the verdict, and ordered the trial. The prosecuting attorney removed this judge and replaced him with one without a law degree or even a college education. The jury deliberated for one day, convicted, and sentenced the men to death once again, then returned them to the filth of the Kilby death house. Henriette was outraged but distant from the events and glad she was safe, suspended in the purity of desert sun and moon, wrapped in the kindness of the Daniels.

As the summer grew hotter, Henriette pulled her hair off her neck with a red ribbon and dressed her slim body in halter-tops and shorts. She dug into the notes and began to find them more interesting. Chiricahua marriages were arranged, she discovered, and the couple lived in the woman's house, where the new husband had responsibility for the wife's whole family. Matrilocal, they called it. The husband almost the slave of his in-laws. At the same time, the husband couldn't see his mother-in-law's face, and the two had to practice avoidance, never speaking to each other. Apache were bound to each family member by demanding obligations for food, pelts, and attendance at ceremonies, and penalties for failing to meet them were severe. To Henriette it sounded like a parody of her parents' home, where Father earned the living but Mother made the rules. And Izzy's objective notes disguised the fury of Apache hostilities in much the same way that her parents' neat façade of high-minded rationality masked their late-night rages.

In the evenings Henriette wrote regularly to Dilly and to her parents, keeping their letters in separate files and not allowing them to touch one another. Delays in mail and the limited hours of the telegraph office made communications as static-filled and intermittent as a crystal radio. Dilly's letters arrived weeks after he wrote them, full of departmental gossip, fears about his doctoral research, and descriptions of the parties where he got oiled as an owl. His life seemed cluttered with multiple people and problems, while hers was distilled into the desert, the small house, and her deepening friendship with Izzy and Betty. When she looked inside, Nadine seemed smaller and farther away, but the retreat of grief was also sad.

AFTER HENRIETTE HAD SPENT THREE weeks transcribing notes, Izzy took her aside. "Tomorrow you'll start working with an informant. He's going to take us to a funeral. Man shot by a Mexican sheriff. Apache bury their dead immediately, right where they lie. It's one of the most important and unusual Apache rituals." A funeral, thought Henriette, drawing back, both glad and sorry that she'd missed Nadine's. The grief of bereaved parents would have been unbearable. "Sounds interesting," said Henriette, trying to express academic curiosity. "Do they have graveyards?"

"No, they avoid the dead in every way possible," said Izzy. "After they bury someone, they move the camp away, so no one can ever find their dead relatives. The dead ones and anything connected with them can cause sickness, even death, and Apache avoid their clothes, their houses, their names. Sometimes the dead return as owls and speak to the living in their own language." Henriette's breath caught at these words. Apparently Izzy knew about something she'd never even imagined.

If she could converse with the dead, she'd have some words to say to her family's matriarch, Father's mother, the grandma she'd never met. She'd grab Grandma Bertha by the shoulders and show her how she'd raised a man whose sudden tempers made him dangerous and pitifully weak, whose love was prone to trespass. If she could converse with the dead, maybe Nadine would come to live in her hip pocket again.

"You mustn't say anything about the ghost sickness or owl sickness," continued Izzy. They call it 'darkness sickness.' So observe as much as you can, and be careful what you ask." I'm always careful, thought Henriette.

SHE PUT ON SHIRT AND jeans, and Izzy drove her to the reservation. He introduced her to the agent, who called the informant, Charlie Kenasy, into his office.

"You know Professor Daniels," said the agent. "And this is Henriette Greenberg, his assistant. You'll be working with her." Charlie shook her hand without smiling. He looked to be middle-aged, maybe thirty years older than Henriette, beardless, with shiny black hair gathered into a leather band at the nape of his neck. He wore blue jeans and boots and glanced down at Henriette's feet.

"Good," he said. "You're wearing boots. There's deep brush where we're going. Welcome to Liberty Country." Henriette scanned his face for irony and saw no emotion, but how could the name not mean its opposite? She imagined the powerful warrior his grandfather must have been, kicked out of his ancestral home and imprisoned twenty years in Florida, then plunked down on a few desert acres, "reserved" for Apache. Liberty Country! A dark unrest could inhabit a thing called by its opposite. She remembered the coyote's howl and shivered. Henriette and Izzy climbed into Charlie's car, and they drove over rutted roads.

"Got to get him in the ground quick," said Charlie.

"Who was the man?" asked Henriette. Izzy shook his head and

frowned, and Charlie clapped his hand over his own mouth. Henriette gulped and resolved to hold her tongue. She flashed on Nadine's once-familiar face and body and wondered if she had been buried quickly. Of course her name was remembered and would be repeated for years to come. How unthinkable to eradicate a name!

At the burial ground they tramped through brush, and burrs stuck to Henriette's Levi's. A small group of Indians stood at a distance on the barren plain, late afternoon sun beating down and reflecting like exploding asterisks off silver buckles. Why so few people there? Sounds of weeping and wailing blew toward them, carried on the desert wind. Beyond the burial cluster, red mesas rose against a merciless blue sky, and the dry air allowed no mist to soften the outlines of the mourners. They began to tear their shirts and rip off necklaces in what looked like an orgy of grief, and Henriette felt wrong to intrude on such deep emotion. What business did she have to be standing here making mental notes while these people were in the thick of living and dying?

Charlie steered them towards the coffin. There in a wooden box lay the dead man. Henriette had never seen a dead body before, and she averted her eyes, but not before she'd glimpsed a buckskin shirt and, just above, the cyanotic, rigid features of a face with pennies on the eyes. So that's what Nadine had looked like on the floor of her apartment, what Henriette herself would look like when dirt won out. A wet drop ran from her armpits down her ribs.

Just beyond the coffin, four men with spades sweated heavily, digging in the hard ground. They grinned, their frightened faces like masks of death, as the mourners brought clothing, tools, and photos of the dead one up to the grave and left them to be buried with the body. Each aspect of this ritual seemed like a useless protest against the inevitabilities of dust storm and sun and baked earth, all that this country had seen fit to give to the Indians who'd once had it all. A woman knelt near the box, holding a crying, sniffling baby with a bad cold.

"His child," said Charlie, pointing. He'd been young, then, like Finn, like Nadine, and Henriette wondered how he'd gotten into the fatal fight and whether anyone would prosecute the crime. The widow rose and stepped back, and the crowd began to move away from the coffin, Henriette and her companions with them. A white minister stood near the box and intoned, "I am the resurrection and the life." The wailing grew louder, drowning him out, and a man came forward in a fringed shirt and feathered headdress, a zigzag of white paint across the bridge of his nose. He carried sage branches.

"The shaman," said Izzy. The shaman placed the branches at the head of the coffin and spoke to the dead man. Charlie translated: "Don't you ever turn your face to us. Don't look back. Keep on going. Don't bother your wife or child." The gravediggers resumed their task with a fury, rushing to accomplish the burial, while the mourners hurried away from the coffin, forming a distant half-circle. The sun dipped behind the mesa, and a cool breeze chilled sweat. A wave of terror passed through Henriette, and she found herself standing on an edge she'd never known before.

The shaman, the dead man, and the mourners seemed to move back and forth in a passage between two worlds: the living and the dead. The mourners and the gravediggers were clearly terrified of the dead man, while the shaman confronted the dead one's power. She glanced around quickly, wanting to leave before it got darker and starlight alone would show the way. Her throat thickened, and she inhaled sharply. Feeling faint, she grabbed Izzy's arm, and he steadied her, apparently untroubled, then stepped away. Suddenly she felt conspicuous and wondered if she were being watched. Perhaps her alien white-girl skin made her stand out in the dark, like phosphorescence. She glanced at her hands and saw only shadows, but the sense of being seen persisted. Night surrounded them, velvet thick, and the desert itself seemed to come alive. Henriette listened for sounds of activity, checking the ground around her feet. Something touched her cheek, an insect or a bat, and she brushed it away. An owl hooted, and the mourners' wailing rose to screams of fear, competing with the grunts of the gravediggers as they lowered the coffin into the grave and covered it with rocks.

"Against marauding animals," said Charlie, as the stones clattered in the dark. "Step back. Be careful." So he, too, was scared of the open passage, of the owl, of whatever or whoever might be watching the scene. Only Izzy appeared calm. The members of the burial party picked up the boughs the shaman had prepared and brushed off their arms and legs, taking care to brush off the baby as well, but did not offer the branches to the visitors. Henriette brushed her face and arms with her hands and hoped no one noticed. Then they threw the branches toward the grave and hurried away.

Henriette was silent as the three drove home, eager to talk but not wanting to reveal her feelings or fence in her experience with words. She'd been frightened but also awestruck. Something entirely new was opening to her in this borderland, somewhere between ponderosa and sagebrush, on the fine line between mesa and sky. She replayed the moment when the shaman had urged the dead man to leave the living in peace. His focused attention had shone a beam of light on a passage of which she'd never conceived. And though she was an alien observer, a little white girl out of place, something or someone had noted her presence, considered her part of this complex and mysterious world. They dropped Charlie off and drove home.

"Everyone was scared, and I was too," said Henriette, sitting on the edge of a chair. Betty sprawled on the wicker couch, flowered pillow under her head, while Izzy relaxed in the overstuffed chair.

"It takes time to understand it," he said. "It's the power of the dead I told you about. Close relatives and the newly dead are the most dangerous. If you owe anything to the person that died, he may seek revenge. Anything connected with the dead one can make a person sick. It goes 'from the head to the heart,' as they say. They get palpitations, choke, and faint."

"Can they avoid that darkness sickness?" asked Henriette in a small voice, careful to use the right term and fearing even her questions could cause her harm.

"Get rid of all evidence of the dead one's life," said Izzy.

"Never mention his name again," said Betty, her tone lighter than her words.

"Destroy his home and build a new one in a new place. Change the baby's name, because the dead man used it," said Izzy.

Henriette could hardly believe what she heard. How could these people do without monuments, memorials, all the things that helped one remember? "Will anyone be punished for the crime?" she asked.

"Crimes on the reservation are up to the feds," said Betty. "The FBI. But they don't care about Indian country." Crimes unpunished added to Henriette's fear, but the opening she'd sensed lured as well as threatened, and she would not renounce or deny it.

A vague hope had long lurked in the recesses of her mind that she could journey to the shtetl where her father had been raised and undo the deprivation that he'd suffered. She saw herself travel back in time, unweaving tangles, until she found herself in a tiny hut beyond the Pale where Bertha still struggles, her husband ill and dying. Bertha has three baby girls, five mouths to feed, and only one pair of hands, her son's, to feed them. She tells him, "Go! Black shoes, chop wood, sell candles, anything to help us live." Henriette sits her down and says, "We'll find another way. I'll bring potatoes, cabbage, bread — you keep your son in school. He'll learn to read, go on to university." Then Henriette would travel down the years, the passage now illumined by the learning Father had always craved, to see him standing tall and confident at the family table, calmly making his demand: white bread. Then home would be a nurturing hearth and she, the smoke ascending. Apple smells would disappear, and she'd be free to love a man.

"I've got to see another funeral," said Henriette.

"Be careful what you wish for," said Izzy, but her thoughts raced ahead. Whether the risk was genuine or merely superstition, she had stood on a precipice, and the limits of her world receded, her horizon widening to include a new vision of what was real. She couldn't help but hope for the impossible: once again to find Nadine.

"I never thought that Apache really believed in Child-of-the-Water or White-Painted Woman, but they seem to have no doubts about the power of the dead or of the shaman."

"I think they believe it all," said Betty. "Sometimes I start to believe it too." She rose and sat on the arm of Izzy's chair and tousled his hair. He rested his hand on her thigh, and Henriette envied the couple their freely expressed affection, then blushed to think what they would be doing later in bed. "Apache live and sometimes even die by their convictions, " continued Betty, admiration in her tone.

"My parents have convictions," said Henriette. "About non-violence and equality. But those abstract ideas are nothing like belief in powers that can heal or kill you."

"I think the Apache know some things we don't," said Betty, breezy, rising to fetch glasses of water.

"They know a life of the spirit, beyond the material," said Izzy. "I observe their belief, but I stay aloof. Anthropologists are participant-observers. Don't go native on me! We have to keep the science in social science. And remember, an informant is not a friend." Henriette hoped she hadn't disqualified herself as objective, but she resisted Izzy's skepticism. The life of the spirit she'd sensed was clearly dangerous, but also powerful and desirable. She'd felt its beckoning, and she vowed to search for it in every rock and crevice, cave and outcropping of this rich and barren land. The world she'd sensed had a place in it for her, maybe even an anchor for her life, and she vowed to face the danger and find the opening again.

Liberty Country, she thought, mulling over Charlie's term. She wanted to write this new experience and tell it to the world, but not yet. That wisp of an urge, to tell a true story, felt vaguely familiar, and she wondered for a moment what had happened to her old desire. Poems and stories had once been the center of her life. Then Mother's grasp and Father's needy rage, her own desire for Dilly, and opportunities with Izzy had rushed in, and poetry's portrayal of seen and unseen worlds had given way to counting upright apes. Maybe now would be different.

OVER THE NEXT FEW WEEKS Henriette visited Charlie regularly, and his unsmiling face became familiar. She learned from him to recognize bird and animal sounds, moving silently among the living, knowing the dead were just out of sight. One afternoon they walked around the summer tents clustered near the Agency, watching women roast hearts of agave plants in shared pits or line wicker water jugs with caulk. Leaving the encampment, they hiked through sagebrush, and soon they were among trees. Little blue flowers appeared on the forest floor.

"Were you related to the man who was shot?" asked Henriette, hoping it was better to say "shot" than "died." Charlie looked at her sharply, then up toward the trees, pointing out a bright red bird with black wings and tail, perched on a limb. He crouched and remained still as the bird flew away. Henriette had grown accustomed to Charlie's communication by gesture and act, and she also sat. The sun warmed the pines, releasing the odor of sap, and Henriette felt her black hair absorbing the rays. After a while the bird returned and perched on the same limb, then left and returned a few times. Charlie rose, and they continued walking.

"Vermilion flycatcher," he said. Henriette nodded acknowledgment. The path grew steeper, and Henriette began to sweat, while occasional breezes refreshed her like tiny, welcome icicles. They walked in silence for several minutes, and Henriette began to doubt he would ever answer her question.

"Same clan," he said, pointing towards and then away from himself with an open-handed gesture that seemed to indicate emptiness. Henriette stopped walking and faced him.

"You," she said, pointing. "And he," and she gestured similarly to the empty space. "Same clan?" He nodded yes and then resumed walking, head down. Henriette's head buzzed with questions she didn't dare ask, about whether the two had been friendly or hostile and what obligations, met or unmet, had existed between them. If Charlie's clan was anywhere near as complicated as her family there'd be a hornet's nest of possibilities, and she feared violating taboo. Yet he'd already given her a lot. She'd sat still for the bird and waited while it forayed for bugs, and she'd been amply rewarded. She resolved to be patient and wait for more.

HENRIETTE'S TIME IN TULAROSA WAS getting short. She met Charlie at the Agency and asked him to come outside.

"Can we visit the place where the man was buried?" she asked, knowing she shouldn't.

"No," he said, frowning and touching a finger to her mouth. "The People stay away from there." They walked as usual, and midday sun released the smell of pine. She let "The People" sink into in her mind. Apache were not one among peoples but the only one. Narrow focus could create a depth of vision that rendered opaque surfaces transparent, like the way the shaman's words and branches had penetrated to the murdered man's intent. She couldn't leave Tularosa without exploring that place of exchange once more. Her need to know what Charlie knew gaped like a hungry mouth, and she yearned to suck his secrets out of him, to find herself again in vivid air, on palpitating earth. That night she questioned Izzy and Betty about the identity of the man who'd been shot.

"They probably keep names at the County Courthouse in Alamogordo," said Betty. "But be careful what you're getting into. Native taboos are serious."

"Maybe you've become too involved," said Izzy. "Respecting informants means keeping your distance. There are some things it's better not to know." Henriette knew she should heed their warnings, but her need was too great. Her only hope was to reawaken Charlie's memory and knowledge of the night the man was buried. The following Saturday, while Izzy and Betty shopped in Alamogordo, Henriette slipped away to the County Courthouse, looked up the coroner's records. Checking that no one observed her, she found the name of the murdered man, at least his English name, Harrison Biminiak.

It was time to say goodbye, and Henriette met Charlie for a final talk. They drove to Ruidoso to hike.

"I was scared the day I met you," she said. "The day of the funeral. I felt something come alive all around me that day." Charlie said nothing but smoothed back his long hair and kept his hands there, covering his ears. "Did you owe him anything — your clansman?" asked Henriette. Charlie frowned and shook his head. Don't do this, Henriette told herself. You will endanger yourself, Izzy, Betty, and Charlie, poison the well of the summer. But against the sensible words clamored a desire stronger than needs for air, water, or sex, a need to discover and know and travel the truth of the open passage, the real world of which she was a part and always would be, alive or dead. "Did you ever fail — the one who used to be called — Harrison Biminiak?" she asked. Charlie stopped and faced her, hand on her mouth, look of horror in his eyes. Immediately she tried to suck the name back inside, but it was out, batting its wings in the space between them. "I'm so sorry," said Henriette, but apology was useless. Like an angry owl the name flapped, its black eyes accusing, and Henriette wondered how she could have been so arrogant as to think she could use it to satisfy herself. Nadine would not have done that, nor would Dilly. Charlie turned abruptly and headed down, leaving her to catch up behind him.

She hurried along, nauseated by regret and fear, trying to understand what she had done. Her mistake was much worse than violating a religious taboo. It had nothing to do with religion. Religion was rules for behavior, the Judaism of which she knew nothing or a high school girlfriend's Catholic Mass where she'd once seen robes, hocus pocus, and candles. The power of the dead man's name came not from religion but life, a life previously unknown to her. Apache, The People, lived in The World, a place crammed with more and more potent reality than she'd ever experienced before. As she stumbled downhill, scrub grass, cactus, and insects grabbed her attention, each life full to overflowing with its own being. She squatted down and observed a beetle as big as her thumb ambling along. Its six articulated legs co-coordinated perfectly, and two long antennae swept the path ahead. Protective spikes covered a collar just below its head, while its back shone with shifting iridescence, green to blue to black. A wood-eating beetle, a type studied by Izzy and Betty. These beetles could smell smoke from miles away, and it guided them to forest-fire feasting. The beetle's perfectly designed senses, its hungers and angers, its beginning and end made up a unique life, like Henriette's own, and its transparent form revealed The World, the true substrate behind or below the shifting scenery of her days.

Reason told her that no name or ghost could really harm Charlie or herself, but she wasn't sure, and shame for her mistake haunted her. She wondered if The World might turn against her or worse, if she had violated The World. Could the dead, like the living, wish her ill? She scrambled down to the car, and Charlie drove back to the Agency in silence. She doubted Izzy and Betty would find out what she'd done, because any mention of it would repeat the name and thus compound the danger. Apache mouths would remain closed.

Chapter 27

That night in her room Henriette opened a letter from Dilly. "To hell with digging," he wrote, "in the County Courthouse or in the ground. To hell with history and documentary evidence, a la Snyder. I have to find someone who was around in the late 1800s, who experienced the Ghost Dance revival first hand and knew how it felt and what it meant. Surely more than who got what, when, and how, for it didn't get the Indians much. There's a special power in those pounding feet and all-night-singing voices." So he'd sensed it too, something that suddenly came to life and chiseled a chink in the wall that divided the ancestors from his informants. She thrilled at this connection between the two of them, and then shuddered with regret at her violation. Dilly's letter continued: "I'll be in Tularosa soon. Should I fetch our supplies from the apartment and send them to you?"

"No," she wrote back, smiling to herself at her intimate conspiracy. "It's against the law to send those things through the mail. Just bring them."

"God is having a hard time keeping the sun in the sky without you and me to make good weather for him," Dilly wrote. "Love, love, love from Cassandra's Delicio." How disappointed he would be if he learned what she'd done.

DILLY ARRIVED IN TULAROSA HOT and tired after two days driving. He took her in his arms, and she hugged him long and hard. "You're tan — you look great," he said. "But so thin." He ran his hands down her arms, pausing at the elbows and again at the wrists.

"I've been working hard, I guess," she said, pulling away, not mentioning her worries about him and her parents. "And I am eating. My research is a problem. I suppose you brought our supplies?"

"In there," he said, indicating his suitcase. She led him to the garage where Izzy had made a place for two to sleep. From under layers of underwear, he extracted a red rubber douche assembly and a small cotton bag containing jelly and pessary.

"Good," she said, stuffing them back under the underwear. "Now Izzy wants to show you his little empire."

After dinner that night they went for a walk, the moon big and bright over the desert, each clump of sagebrush and thick leaf of century plant casting a quivering shadow.

"Let's get married," said Dilly.

"I do want to get married," she said. It felt more urgent since Nadine's death. Now was the time to do what you intended. "Do you think we could manage — I mean, without my parents?" They walked on a bit, not touching, and a breeze came up, caressing hair and skin. He wanted her — that was keen — but how could she ever tell Mother?

"They wouldn't want to help us?" asked Dilly.

"I'm not sure. Maybe not after we were married," said Henriette, unable to speak the complete truth.

"We might be able to live all right at Klamath. My research grant provides the cabin. Wood for the stove is free, and the forest is full of game, fish, and berries. All we'd have to buy are potatoes, and I make enough for that and more, if we're careful." Dilly began to hum,

"Potatoes are cheaper, tomatoes are cheaper, now's the time to fall in love." To Henriette, marriage sounded like a wild and wonderful adventure. Dilly would hunt and fish to feed them, and she would wear boots and a lumberjack shirt, keeping house in the woods, as brave as she'd been in Alabama. But none of this would be real unless she could tell.

She took his arm again and resumed their walk. "I went to a funeral with Charlie," she said, and tried to describe the ubiquitous fear, the shaman's conversation with the dead, the screams of the mourners and the owl's shriek. She took a deep breath and exhaled slowly. "Have you ever experienced anything like that?"

"Sort of — in the groups I study. The Ghost Dancers believed they could bring back the dead. Nadine was tuned into that — remember her poem about them? But I'm a social scientist and committed to the observable."

"Like Izzy," said Henriette, missing Nadine with a pang, heart and voice hardening to conceal her regret. "But how can you describe belief and ritual without experiencing its power?"

"The participant-observer walks a tightrope," said Dilly. "You've got to keep your balance."

A laugh trickled out of Henriette. "I think I fell off."

"Maybe you got too close to your informant."

"Never a friend, so Izzy said. But no, I'm not exactly friends with Charlie. He's more than that, a sort of guide. He led me to places I didn't know existed, terrifying but awe-filled places where the living somehow traffic with the dead. I had a glimpse and wanted more. I still do."

"Just don't tell the Dean," said Dilly. "You know how he is about emotion. If you hit him with an emotional onslaught he'll just say it's not science. Am I horning in too much, categorizing your poetry?"

"It's not poetry," she said, a pout in her voice. "And you know I'm not interested in bean counting." She retreated behind her blank surface.

"There's no rush about making a proposal."

"OK, no rush," she said, detaching her hand from his and crossing her arms. The moon passed behind a cloud, and the night darkened.

"You shouldn't feel pressure," he said, putting his arm around her shoulder. "You could read for exams at Klamath and take them in Chicago the following summer. We could be married by then."

"We could get married," she said. "But don't let's ever publish on the same thing at the same time." Inside Henriette, Mother rejoiced in her boy babies and forgot the one that, sadly, was made the same as she. "The female work is always so bad."

"Some of it's terrific," said Dilly. "Look at Mead and Benedict. We can be married and be anthropologists both. What do you say?"

"First I'd have to TELL MOTHER," she said. She typed the capital letters in her head, and they jumped around as she imagined the consequences of speaking her decision. "T" and "L" and "M" fell against each other like dominos, clashing and clattering, until Father was broken in pieces and Mother dissolved into tears.

HENRIETTE SHOWED DILLY AROUND THE agency and the reservation, introducing him to Charlie, but she knew he didn't see what she saw or feel what she felt. She hadn't realized how much the desert's mysterious beauty and the Apache way of life had infiltrated her heart and mind. The funeral, her talks with Charlie, life refreshed by distance from civilization — all these had put her in touch with life's elementals, like rain, sun, and packed earth, flash-flooded arroyos that washed houses away and spring warmth that nurtured the tiniest seedpods. Dilly's down-to-earth pragmatism began to seem crude. His voice echoed in her head like a tease: "No emotional onslaught...

categorizing your poetry." She'd come through this desert transformation, survived the dust and the isolation — for what? — to be put down by university science? As her desert time approached its end, Henriette grew more determined to find some way back to the living, crawling earth and the inhabited air she'd first sensed at the funeral.

DILLY AND HENRIETTE CLUNG TO each other on his last day in Tularosa, standing beside his car.

"I want to stay here," she said. "And get closer to what I've just touched. But face it: I have no measurable results, no excuse for spending the Research Council's money."

"It's better you leave with what you have," said Dilly. "All ethnographers stay too long. All work looks worthless after a while." A gulf opened between them as she thought of the inestimable value of her Apache experience.

"I doubt I can turn the summer into a thesis proposal," she said, tailoring her words.

"We'll be married by then anyway," he said, but she couldn't say "yes" until she'd dealt with the telling. She watched Dilly drive away, headed for Berkeley where he would spend the rest of the summer doing research with Professor Hankton. The car vanished in a plume of dust.

SHAME FOR HENRIETTE'S MISTAKE HAUNTED her. Unlike the concrete dangers of Scottsboro, these threats floated, uncertain. The thought of marriage without material for a thesis felt like a trap, closing. She didn't know how she could ever study for exams in the wilds of the Klamath Indian Reservation, with no libraries or professors to help her, or how she would find a master's thesis topic, now that she'd poisoned the source of her data. The one inspiring thing she'd found was inaccessible.

She pictured Dilly in Berkeley, on the town with Hankton, inventing spectacular drinks in bars, feasting and carousing, maybe even taking in a strip club. She should have gone with him to Berkeley or said she would definitely marry him, but then the specter of parents had loomed, and she hadn't known where to turn.

Soon Henriette received a letter from Mother. She planned a three-week trip to Bermuda by boat at the end of August. Henriette was to accompany her and Father. Henriette dreaded the thought of three weeks confined with her parents in a stateroom and hotel, as well as continued separation from Dilly, but the secret knowledge of her hope of marrying disarmed any resistance she might have had to Mother's plan. Her rebellious party in Oak Park had been child's play compared to the permanent separation of marriage. Telling was bad enough, but marriage with no plan for research was almost as sickening as the waves that would rock the boat to Bermuda.

MORNING DAWNED HOT AND DRY on the first day of Henriette's last week in Tularosa, and Betty wiped sweat from her forehead as she made coffee and fried eggs. "Harold Overstreet's coming for a visit," said Izzy, sitting down to eat. "Did you know him in Chicago? Marxist economist?"

"Vaguely," said Henriette, joining him at the table. "I met him before I started college. He was a friend of my brother, Carl. And I think I heard him speak once at a Left Wing Students rally."

"That's him," said Betty. "The old economic determinist." Henriette slipped back in memory to the night five years earlier when she'd gone with Carl to the Sunset Café and Harold had asked her to dance. She hadn't even known how, but the music and Harold had carried her along, and her spirits had been raised right up out of the pit of home. The sounds of jazz had charged the air that night, and Satchmo had sung a song about death, her friend on sad days. She'd noticed that he greeted it without fear, with a bouncy welcome. "Bye and bye," he'd sung. "When the morning comes. All the saints, the Lord is gathering home." Maybe Charlie was not in danger after all.

Harold arrived that evening with a bottle of contraband whisky, wearing shirt and tie, and Betty introduced Henriette. "Do you remember meeting me a long time ago?" she asked, shaking his hand. She'd forgotten how big he was, taller than Izzy or Betty, with a slight paunch and the fresh smell of roll-your-own tobacco. "I'm Carl Greenberg's little sister. You danced with me once at the Sunset Café."

"Well sure enough," he said. "I remember that. You've grown up." His eyes ran from her head to her feet and back up. She lowered hers. Betty took Harold's bottle and set it down by the sink, and Izzy showed him a sleeping bag and tarpaulin he'd rigged for cover by the side of the house. They all went to dinner at Mrs. Pepper's and ate stacked enchiladas topped with fried eggs, while Harold interrogated Izzy about reservation economy and labor practices. After dinner, back at the house, Harold poured himself and Henriette some whisky and filled the glasses with water. Izzy and Betty declined. Henriette took a sip of the drink and winced at the aged, brown taste and the burn. Nothing could undo the mistake she'd made, but alcohol could numb the pain and ease the fear.

"Times are hard all over," said Harold. "But it's worst in the city. Can't pay the rent, they put you out on the street." He told them that the "indignation marches" were still going on, where people rallied to put the furniture back in the house. "Then the coppers come and start in with the clubs. Only the churches stand up for the people." He began to sing, and Henriette joined him:

Give me that old time religion
Give me that old time religion
Give me that old time religion
It's good enough for me.

With a twinkle in his eye, he started a new verse, and Izzy joined in this time:

Give me that new Communist party
It's good enough for me.
It was good for Brother Lenin and
It's good enough for me.

Henriette felt a twinge of nostalgia for the carefree person she'd been when she'd sung with the ILD marchers in downtown Chicago. Harold took a big swig of his drink. "The CP helped the Negroes but never understood the importance of the Church," he said. "That's why I never joined. The Church has always been first and foremost in the black community, even when slavery destroyed the family. But anyone wants to help us, we take it." He turned to Henriette.

"What about you? I thought you might go into political science, you were such a determined young radical back at the University."

"I *was* determined," she said. "Right after that May Day show you put on about Scottsboro, I went with the ILD to Alabama. I passed out leaflets and got caught up in a demonstration that turned into a brawl." She spoke blithely, the events made distant by the power of her recent experience.

"What?" Betty and Izzy asked at once.

"Good for you," said Harold. "I hope you didn't get hurt."

She told the rest of the story. "My parents don't know. Please don't spread it around. They'd try to lock me up, and Dilly still fears I'll smear him red."

Betty and Izzy nodded agreement. "You were so daring," said Betty.

"You actually did what we just talk about," said Izzy.

"I think the demonstrations helped," said Harold. "The governor of Alabama got fifty thousand telegrams about the case. And when Leibowitz insisted the prosecutor call the black witnesses "Mister," that turned attention to the all-white juries. The Supreme Court refused to consider that issue the first time around, but now they might. None of that helps the men themselves, of course. They've been in jail over two years now, stuck in hellholes. For them it's like Hitler's Germany." He rolled a cigarette and offered it to Henriette, then made another for himself. "What's next for you?" he asked.

"I want to be an anthropologist," she said, inhaling for the first time all summer and then blowing out smoke through her nose like a dragon. It seemed impossible that she would ever be a working social scientist. "But I'm not in any hurry." Air seemed to blow through her words the way the breeze might lift her skirt if she twirled.

"What kind of work have you been doing here with Izzy?" Harold rose to refill their glasses.

"Working with an informant," said Izzy. "She's good with people." Henriette clung to praise and drank more, seeking to wash away her possibly fatal error. The conversation circled round to the ever ready topics of academics and departmental politics. Betty retired to the bedroom, and Henriette put her feet up on the couch and leaned back against one armrest. This is going to be fun, she thought. Get rid of the wives and get drunk with the husbands.

"The economics department at the university is leaning further and further right," said Harold. "I have to get out of there." He loosened the top button of his shirt.

"Anthropology's just the same," said Izzy. "You should stick around here. We have fine conversations far from the high mucky-mucks at the University. Henriette knows what I'm talking about." She nodded agreement. As the evening wore on the laughter got louder, and Henriette felt like a lynchpin, enabling the men to enjoy each other's performance just by being herself, listening and smoking and occasionally interjecting a wry remark. Thesis proposal and exams, ghosts and parents had never seemed so far away. About midnight, Izzy went to join Betty.

"Let's go for a walk," said Henriette, wanting to defer the sober dawn. "The desert's beautiful at night." Outside Harold looked up and exclaimed at the sky full of stars, so much more brilliant than in the city, while a soft, warm wind lifted Henriette's hair. She swayed and stumbled a little on the rough ground, and Harold took her elbow, then slipped his hand into hers. You should stop this right here, she told herself, but she wasn't really listening. A band had already started to play in her head, quiet and remote at first, then getting louder and louder. The music obliterated all the troubles that awaited her, letting her forget herself as she had just now with Izzy and Harold, yet lifting her up as the indispensable center of everything, the one who made all connections possible. Harold dropped her hand, then lifted his to her curls, raising them and letting them fall, just like the warm desert wind.

"You're beautiful, all grown up," he said. They often said things like that, the boys in the band, and she always smiled appreciation, knowing they wouldn't touch her. Now they were tuning up, and she cleared her throat, preparing to sing.

Since jazz stepping's become all the rage
It's even gotten to the old birdcage,
Say, my canary's got circles under his eyes.

Her deep contralto voice resonated throughout her body so that every nerve and muscle seemed to sing, a delicious sound that filled her and reached from her puny self up to the stars, while her fingers and toes warmed with alcohol, and Harold's caress gave sleepy pleasure. She paused between verses. "You've got a fine voice," said Harold. They walked a few steps in silence. "I heard your man Dilly visited. Are you going to marry him?" Dilly, she thought with a stab, the man who had not and might never understand what she'd seen at the funeral.

"Marry?" asked the girl with the band. Brass and drums upped the tempo, and she took up her song, hips shimmying gently as she sang, mic in hand, in front of the band. Her voice came straight and passionate from the heart, her thin body transparent.

He used to whistle a prisoner's song
But now he does snake hips the whole day long
Say, my canary's got circles under his eyes.

"Where do you sleep?" asked Harold, arm now around her shoulder, fingers tucking her hair behind her ear. Wordless, she pointed back to the garage, feeling warm and safe. Nothing could touch her, and no one could hurt her, the white girl in front who sings with the band. "Marry?" she asked again. Bermuda, the telling, the thesis proposal, exams, her marriage, her violation: all vanished as she sang the night out. Singing and singing her song without end, dancing the mic and danced by the music, the girl out front who is backed by the band. She'd sleep on the bus, head on a brown shoulder, then wake in a new town and go out for coffee, enjoying the looks, some shocked and some friendly, of people who'd just seen the girl with the band. She smiled and wrinkled her nose. "Marry? Oh no, I don't think so." She stumbled and laughed as he guided her back to the bus, where two could just fit on the narrow bunk, and the engine's rumbling could drown out her dreams.

WHEN SHE AWOKE IN THE morning, Harold was up and in the house, and the only sign that he'd been in her bed was a smell of tobacco and whisky. The sheets stuck to her skin, and she curled in disgust, equally furious with him and herself. She was a stupid, goodfornothing slut, and he was a motherfucking sonofabitch. She didn't want to get up. Her hangover was nothing to joke about but a sign of illness of body and mind, a foretaste of death, which she once again yearned for and hoped would come soon. The adobe house, her typewriter, even the desert and the infinite sky all turned flat and opaque, denying her vision. Good, she thought, with bitter irony. If the funeral was nothing but branches and words, then nothing bad could happen to Charlie. Her mind spun, and she closed it. She stayed in bed until Izzy and Harold had left for the reservation.

"Are you OK?" asked Betty when Henriette stumbled into the house, late.

"Just hungover," said Henriette

"Harold said he slept well in his sleeping bag under the stars," said Betty. Henriette spent the day nursing her misery and typing notes, wanting desperately to take back the previous night, to promise fidelity that no one had yet questioned, resolving that Dilly must never know. She tried to blame the event on booze, on shame, or on Harold, but she couldn't think further about how or why it had happened. The prospect of marriage felt like a door slammed in her family's face, adulthood like a tunnel ending with the grave, and childhood a closet full of unfinished business.

JUST BEFORE THE DANIELS AND Henriette left Tularosa for Chicago, a letter arrived from Dilly. It was only a few scrawled lines, signed with a big X. He'd labeled the X "his mark," as though he were illiterate. Henriette frowned at this feeble attempt at humor, probably the end to a long night of drinking. The next morning he'd added a sober and sardonic note: "About midnight life's burden got too heavy to carry, and I laid it at the feet of Jesus, falling into a profound slumber in my own beddy-bye." He signed it, "Feeling punk, your Dallying Dildo."

Alarmed, she wrote him back: "A little tight is fun, but I don't want you getting swacked every night. Please take care." Maybe she'd upset him by refusing to say a clear "yes" to marriage, intimidated by the tumbling letters of telling. And maybe some impossible telepathy had whispered her secret infidelity in his sleeping ear, where it would fester, an abiding suspicion, until one day he woke up to the truth. Maybe some equally impossible ghost had told him of her violation of taboo. She'd never know, and the possibilities were terrifying. Consequences of her actions were closing in, and she looked around like a cornered rodent for a safe place where she could step aside and watch.

Chapter 28

Henriette and her parents boarded the elegant, five-deck Queen of Bermuda at the Furness Terminal in New York. The three settled into their outside stateroom on the "B" deck. Henriette would sleep in an upper bunk with Mother below, while Father had a single bed on the other side of the small room. He'd paid one hundred and twenty dollars for round trip passage for three, all meals included, and private toilet and shower made this room especially luxurious. The boat was outfitted with wireless telegraphy, but telegrams would be way too expensive, and Henriette resigned herself to sailing the ocean without communication.

Father unpacked jar after jar of pills, lining them up on a shelf, and Henriette was alarmed at his worsening condition. She hoped there was a doctor on board. She unpacked bathing suits, dresses for dinner, and long gowns for dancing, and then went swimming in the mosaic-lined pool, sun reflecting off the brilliant azure-and-green tiles. The salt water soothed her as she floated on her back, staring at passing clouds in a bright blue sky. Filled with conflict about the funeral, her two violations, and the impossibility of writing a thesis, she rehearsed the Telling. After drying herself and dressing, she began to explore the boat, locating its talking-picture salon and big dance hall, while her typing fingers imagined Mother's outraged response:

H-o-w-c-o-u-l-d-y-o-u? Standing on the forward deck with wind in her face, she tried to remember the beetle's iridescent perfection and struggled to regain that transparent vision, but all she saw was railing and churning water, tempting her to throw herself in and take the parents with her.

The second day out the boat encountered a big Atlantic storm with gales up to seventy-five miles per hour. Mother got seasick and took to her bed, along with many of the other passengers. At mealtime, Mother still too sick to eat, Father and Henriette went to the near-empty dining saloon, draped with silk and lacquered scarlet, decorated with ornaments of Chinese jade and silver. Artie Shaw and his New Music whistled quietly while attentive waiters worked, jaunty notes playing under the clank of dishes and spoons. With few to serve, they brought British specialties followed by little savory alternatives to dessert that delighted Henriette's salt-loving tongue: individual marrow custards and tiny pigeon tarts, molds of tomato aspic with hard-boiled eggs and chives and round blue cheese biscuits with bulls eyes of fig jam. She would fatten up for Dilly.

Eating alone with Father, Henriette felt special, while she sensed uneasily that something unsaid and sad lay between them, something older than her engagement and rotten, like fermenting fruit. To her surprise, a vast plain of regret opened inside her. Maybe this step really was a mistake. Who had ever adored her without question except her unpredictable and dear, dangerous father? They seemed to be connected by an unknowable, subterranean stream.

"I noticed all those jars of pills," she said.

"Yes, I try to avoid excitement, and I take diuretics and blood pressure drugs. They relieve some symptoms." He paused. "My heart is failing."

"Why didn't you tell me earlier?" asked Henriette. The specter of Nadine rose inside her, gone forever. It might be now or never, if she and Father were going to talk. "Has it been hard for you, being married to Mother?" she asked.

'Hard?" he asked. "Life is hard. Mother saved my life. She discovered me when we were both struggling students of Jenkin Lloyd Jones, and she led me from the shtetl's pleading superstition into the modern land of justice, reason, and decency." At that last word Henriette looked at him sideways to see if he knew he was sugarcoating the truth, but he seemed oblivious. "Didn't you find her harsh and unbending? Did she give you the love that everyone needs?"

"Love is expressed in more ways than one," he said, stern. "Your mother gave me children, a household, a life that supported me. Thus I was able to succeed in the world, keep food on the table, and give you and your brothers all that you've had. Like this trip." Here Henriette almost laughed, the trip being the last-ditch trap the parents had set for her before her final escape. "You fought late at night," she said. "I listened when I was a child."

"I'm sorry," he said, and reached out, but she withdrew her hand before he could touch it. "I've always loved you as much as one person can love another." Yes, adoration without question. There was a price to pay for that, and Father was never going to acknowledge the price she'd paid. Within her plain of regret, a yearning for some sort of connection appeared, too strange to think about, and she resolved to leave it unexamined. Nothing must interfere with her getting out — it was now or never.

On the Queen of Bermuda's last day before arrival, the sea was calm, and Mother came up on deck with Henriette, head wrapped in a silk scarf as protection against the wind. Henriette let the wind ruffle her hair as they watched the birds that indicated land was near, leaning together on the railing.

"I have something to tell you," said Henriette, clenching her jaw to control her chattering teeth. "Dilly and I are going to get married." Mother frowned and looked confused.

"What? That's impossible. You certainly are not."

"But I am."

Mother turned to face Henriette, feet planted apart, back to the wind, as fixed in her direction as the steamship itself. "We forbade you to see him." Behind Mother's bulk birds flew, glorious white against blue sky. "What would you live on? The salary of a poor graduate student? Professors don't make money — they live on learning." She sniffed.

"We'll get by," said Henriette. One furious and determined but gen-teel mother, she told herself, was nothing compared to a violent, hate-filled crowd or a name with power to kill. "Dilly's got a research grant that includes a cabin on the Klamath Indian Reservation."

"That barbarian will have guns in the house."

"Some people do.

"He shoots animals," said Mother. "You've been raised in a civilized household. How can you give that up?" Words fell like blows, then edged towards pleas as the rock-hard voice turned brittle and began to shatter. "You're making a terrible mistake. Think about it, and you'll change your mind." She turned back to the rail, and then snapped back to Henriette. "And don't tell Father, poor man. It would kill him."

Feeling a noose slip around her neck, and convinced that the gun issue was just an excuse to tie her more tightly, Henriette was utterly undone. She fled to the stateroom, where she quickly changed, then went to the pool and jumped in. There the splash of her arms and legs muffled the sound of her weeping as she swam angry laps, and the water of the pool absorbed her tears. The power of the parents was a mystery. Exhausted, she climbed out, went to the Ladies Writing Salon and wrote to Dilly: "Please keep me safe in a small house away from the world."

AT DINNER IN BERMUDA'S HOTEL Inverurie, Father turned to her, eyes sad and almost begging while his wide mouth delivered words it seemed the eyes could not believe. "You mustn't do what you're thinking of." So Mother had commandeered control of that information. "How did things go this far without our knowledge?" he asked.

"I don't believe you really care that Dilly hunts," said Henriette. "You just don't want me to have a life of my own."

"You leave me to handle everything," said Mother, speaking for Father and indicating him with a glance. "I need your support." Somehow Mother managed to be ironclad and pitiful at once.

"You never even noticed I existed," said Henriette. "Remember Mrs. Witherspoon?" Henriette trembled to think what she'd started.

"Of course." Mother frowned at her lamb chop, which she began to dissect. "What about her?" Father ate in silence, while Henriette's dinner remained untouched on her plate.

"Remember the day I went with you to Lincoln Center, to help out?" If she could get Mother to acknowledge the significance of Mrs. Witherspoon's long-ago surprise — a daughter? — history might rewrite itself, transforming Henriette into Mother's companion in womanhood.

"No," said Mother. "I don't remember you ever helping out." Nothing would be solved here, and escape was the only solution. She'd already left three times: to the dorm, to Scottsboro, to the desert. This final escape should be easier.

"So that's settled," she said, with an awkward little smile. "I am getting married." And she waited to see what they would do next.

"Has Dilly told his parents?" asked Mother. Henriette nodded "yes" though she didn't know.

"What do they think about him marrying a Jewish girl?"

Henriette had no intention of repeating Dilly's parents' confusion of Unitarian with Anarchist. "They can't tell a Jew from any other kind of person," she said. "There are no Jews in their town and no Negroes."

"A boy with neither culture nor future," said Mother. Henriette felt a glimmer of confidence that she could stand up to her parents, and they would survive. "Still, if you're determined to marry you must at least have a proper wedding. We can have it at the house. You should get married on the date of our anniversary," and she looked at Father, who nodded without smiling.

"I have to talk to Dilly first," said Henriette, but she was glad to acquiesce, considering any concession a small price to pay for their acceptance of the fact. "You'll have to finance it," she said. "Dilly's parents can't help out."

"We'll pay for the wedding," said Father. "But no more allowance after that."

"Dilly won't have more than his research grant."

"Think about what you'll have to give up," said Mother. Henriette imagined giving up nice clothes and celery soup and jazz on the Victrola, and she didn't care, but telling Dilly that the parents would definitely cut her off — that would be hard. Maybe they would change their minds.

After breakfast Henriette began a letter to Dilly on hotel stationary, eager to tell him "yes." She wouldn't tell Dilly that the bitchoids rejected him. "I've told them," she wrote, "and we can get married." She turned the paper over and drew two connected hearts and three daisies, then labeled it "hearts and flowers," in case her drawing failed to speak. "Mother wants it to be on their anniversary in November," the letter continued. "Do you mind? Don't worry, they'll pay for the wedding." She left a space, then added, "Nothing seems to touch me very deeply in the way of trouble," while the terrors of a thesis without a topic, exams far from a library, loss of allowance, and potential dangers to herself and Charlie swam in a murky moat around her castle of unconcern.

THE FIRST THING HENRIETTE DID on arrival in New York was to mail her letters to Dilly. She received his response in Chicago. "We can get married whenever you want," he wrote. "The date doesn't matter. Weddings are for the masnpas anyway." Delighted by his coinage, she wrote back: "What I really want is to marry you as soon as I can and not bother writing up my notes until I'm good and ready." Now back in touch with the news, Henriette learned that one of the Scottsboro boys had been tried and convicted a third time and another a second. Both were sentenced to death, the sentences suspended. Leibowitz asked that the remaining trials be postponed, as the issue of jury selection had gained some traction and insured appeal. To the citizens of Alabama it was unimaginable that a Negro might sit on a jury, but people all over the world were questioning the justice of that. So all the young men of Scottsboro were back on death row, and Henriette wondered if protesting had done any good at all. She'd wait to see what the Alabama Supreme Court would do with the latest appeal.

SOON AFTER HER RETURN, HENRIETTE lay on a couch in Dr. Whitson's office and watched fish swim back and forth in their tank. Brilliant orange and blue and fickle as they darted from one side to the other, they seemed blissfully ignorant of what went on in this room. They'd never tell, so why should she? She'd begun to think maybe that night in the desert had never happened. Speaking it would make the whole thing real.

Dr. Whitson took her seat. "I'm getting married," said Henriette.

"Oh," said Dr. Whitson. "Good news?" Henriette wanted to say yes, it's good news but creates a problem about money, thesis proposal, and exams, but all she could think of was one despicable night in August. She was silent a minute. Dr. Whitson waited.

"Dilly and I wrote letters all summer," Henriette burst out. "Love is so much easier on paper!"

Dr. Whitson murmured agreement. "What happens when you meet?"

Henriette thought of Dilly's arrival in Tularosa, how glad she'd been to see him, how he'd failed to understand her Apache experience, and how undeserving she'd turned out to be.

"I don't feel good enough for him," said Henriette, voice breaking. "When he gets jittery or drinks too much, I make him out sick to make me feel better, but really he's normal and stable and strong."

"Perhaps you are afraid of contaminating something you love," said Dr. Whitson. "You see yourself as damaged, and you fear taking something fine and beautiful and good and making it into something like yourself." Oh yes, thought Henriette. You don't know the half of it. But she was glad to have the words, "damage" and "contamination." She sat up and turned to face the doctor. "I've learned one thing: those ties that kept me trapped at home bound the parents as much as me. Once I said in no uncertain terms that I was leaving, they let the hunting issue go, got down off their principled high horse, and turned to grumbly wedding planning. They said they'd cut off my allowance, but I think they might change their minds."

The doctor smiled and this time Henriette didn't have to guess at her expression. "It seems you've discovered that your parents are people, not superhuman powers, just people struggling with the conditions in which they find themselves, good but faulty humans. Perhaps we're truly through."

THE WEEK BEFORE THE WEDDING, Dilly arrived back in town. He and Henriette had long been looking forward to seeing *Mädchen in*

Uniform, the German film released in 1931 and just now making its way to the U.S. Henriette watched for Dilly's arrival in the living room window of the Oak Park house, wanting to have him to herself before he intersected with the parents.

She slid into his flivver, and they leaned over the gearshift for a big hug and kiss, then pulled back to look at each other and assess what difference the previous weeks had wrought.

"You're filling out. You look snazzy, and we're going to get hitched," said Dilly, exuberant.

"Signed, sealed, and delivered. But we still have to get through the ceremony."

"We should plan that."

"Oh God," said Henriette, sighing. "The clan is gathering with Reverend Jones tomorrow night. Attendance is required. Let's not think about it until then."

"Twenty-three skidoo, or we'll be late," said Dilly, and the car peeled out.

They drove to the South Side, where the University's Doc Films showed the picture, and afterwards they went to Jimmy's. Sitting on rickety wooden chairs, they ate meatball sandwiches and drank 3.2 beer in the smoky atmosphere. "Can you believe books and letters and even notes were forbidden in that school?" asked Henriette, struck by the movie.

"*Ja*," said Dilly. "*Streng verboten*," mimicking the headmistress' iron voice. "'Through discipline and hunger we will be strong again.' Almost seems like a prediction of Hitler's rise."

Red sauce from the juicy sandwich dripped down Henriette's chin, and she grabbed napkins from the bar for both of them. "But they couldn't stop the girls from putting photos of movie stars in their lockers."

"Wasn't it funny that the girls turned to English to describe the lure of the stars?" Dilly observed. "Remember when one asked, 'How do you say what the movie stars have?' and the answer was 'sex appeal,' in English?" He went to the bar and ordered two more beers, asking the bartender how soon he thought they'd be able to serve the real stuff.

"Any day now," said the bartender. "Repeal is on the way." Henriette raised an imaginary glass to the bartender, saluting his vision of the future. Dilly brought the drinks back to the table.

"Germany was so progressive, to make that movie about a girl in love with her teacher, when we're banning *The Children's Hour* here in Chicago. Even though it's more about rumor-mongering than Lesbianism. They were way ahead of us until Hitler," said Henriette.

"They were," said Dilly. "That was the atmosphere Katya talked about, social and artistic freedom, cabarets like the Tingeltangel."

"Why do those broadminded views blow everyone's wig? Two dames moving their bodies — that's all it is," said Henriette, though to her it was much more. She found the movie's glowing close-ups of enraptured student and teacher compellingly beautiful, but didn't let herself think about what further intimacies the images implied. Dilly shook his head, looked slightly embarrassed, and clucked disapproval of censorship.

THE NEXT DAY THE GREENBERG family gathered to meet with Reverend Jones. He would preside at the wedding, Mother's choice, of course. "Just family," she'd said, making it clear that Dorothy was not welcome at this meeting. The group sat in the living room, Father looking frail and Carl and Russell tense and impatient. Henriette slouched on the couch, her thin body almost concave, while Mother stood and showed how chairs would be rearranged and where the couple would stand to make their vows.

"Have you considered a reading?" asked Reverend Jones. Henriette as a child had often looked up at the Reverend's big white beard and thick, wavy hair, when he came to dinner or visited their summer cottage on the St. Lawrence River. Tall, calm, and kind, his presence always quieted conflicts at home, and Henriette looked forward to his visits. He took out a copy of Kahlil Gibran's *The Prophet* and handed it to Henriette, reaching down to her on the couch. "You've always had an ear for poetry," he said. "See if you find something in here." Henriette took the book and opened it. A lot of it she knew by heart. She handed the book back to the Reverend, resigned to its familiar words.

"Guess you'll be married before me after all," said Carl to Henriette. "Are you ready?"

"Henriette's dress is almost done," said Mother, as though he had spoken to her.

"Yes," said Henriette to Carl, speaking from the depths of the couch, her one word sounding as though it echoed across a field of snow. Then she sat forward. "I spent the day with a werewolf, mouth full of pins, who took in Mother's dress to fit me."

"That's not what I was asking," said Carl.

"What would you like me to wear?" Dilly asked Mother. "I don't have the full soup-and-fish."

She looked him up and down. "Anything inconspicuous will do."

"What about music?" asked Reverend Jones.

"No music," said Henriette. "It's to be a simple wedding. No attendants. No music. I like it one way or the other. Hot or cold. But not in the pot nine days old." Reverend Jones looked a little confused, and Mother guided him and Father into the dining room for tea and biscuits. The young people relaxed.

"Would you have wanted music?" Henriette asked Dilly.

"I like music," he said. "But the wedding's for the masnpas, remember?"

"How could I miss that?" she said, and picked up the book again.

"Welcome to the family," said Carl to Dilly. "Don't let Mother sink her teeth into you or you'll never get away. Look at Father, hounded and har-ried and trod upon. You have to stand up to her." He said goodbye and left.

"Have you been OK?" Henriette asked Russell.

"Yes," he said. He was silent for a bit and looked uncomfortable, as though framing what he was about to say. "I don't think you under-stand that Carl is lying about who and what he is."

"What do you mean?" asked Dilly, taken aback.

"His plan to marry," said Russell. "The whole thing's a disguise."

"I though it was part of his plan to save the world," said Henriette, getting up to stand in front of the fireplace.

"It is," said Russell. "But he has to save himself first."

"Do you mean. . .?" she asked, staring hard at him.

"Yes," said Russell. "He's no different from me." Dilly looked from one to the other, questioning.

"Wait and see," said Russell. "That marriage will explode in a hun-dred pieces," and he popped his clasped hands apart, spreading the fingers. All were silent for a moment, as though they were watching the pieces settle to the ground.

"Carl can't be queer," said Dilly. "I lived with him for two years."

"You never did notice much," said Henriette to Dilly.

Dilly ignored her jab. "You have to take a person on his own terms."

"That's hard when a person doesn't know what his own terms are," said Russell, sounding more and more like Carl.

HENRIETTE WALKED DILLY OUT TO his car, fall wind growing chilly.

"Our wedding is beginning to sound expensive to me," said Dilly. "You know I can't help pay for it."

"No one expects you to. The parental figures want it their way, and they can pay for it. But I'm giving up hope that they'll change their minds and help us after we're married."

"They won't?" asked Dilly, voice rising, turning to look at Henriette.

"Probably not. They're funny birds." She tried to sound unconcerned, but her voice shook. Life without much money would be a struggle, but nothing compared with the duplicity Carl would face if he went ahead with his marriage. Henriette remembered the strange and coded conversation she'd had with them the day she met Dorothy: open marriage, both men and women, common unhappiness. Henriette couldn't begin to think about what this entailed or what kind of catastrophic consequences might ensue.

Then Dilly kissed her on the lips and walked slowly around the car, waved once more, and drove away. That wasn't too bad, she thought. Maybe there was more than one reason she chose a boy with a gun. Now they would be truly free and could start from scratch, without the burdens of the past. They would shed civilization's shackles and step out into a free and unsullied land, like the Indians envisaged after the Ghost Dance had wrought its transformation. Maybe the world's multiple layers would open up to her again. Hunting, fishing, gathering, kinship, myth, ritual, art: they would strip away pretense and start with essentials, planting the seeds of culture and cultivating them, making a life among the shoots and flowers and some day harvesting the fruit.

Chapter 29

Everyone agreed the wedding was beautiful. Bride's and groom's guests arrived all at once, tumbling out of the cold November day and crowding into the warm house, shrugging out of coats in the hallway and handing them to a hired maid, who layered them over her arms and lugged them up the formal curved stairway before descending gracefully, as though she were the matron of the house; then bustle and eddy of introductions as the groom's family met members of the bride's and vice versa, slowly sorting themselves out into right and left sides of the living room, squeezing between the crowded rows of chairs set up for the event; then sitting, sighing, and pulling out a square or flowered handkerchief in anticipation of wedding tears.

The bride wore her mother's white velvet dress with countless tiny buttons down the back, nipping her slender waist above her hips. A white veil covered her tense face and softly sculpted, thick black hair. The groom wore his suit: a three-piece, gray pinstripe with a golden chain looped into the pants pocket, where a hidden watch insured continuity from grandfather to father to son. The couple stood before the fireplace while the portly Reverend read from *The Prophet*. A bubble of laughter began to wrinkle Henriette's eyes and threatened to escape from her mouth as she thought about the spaces in together-ness prescribed by that text. No, not for her. Everything together and everything new — that would be her marriage. Then silently she asked Grandma Bertha for an old-country blessing, complete with fiddle-accompanied song.

The Father of the bride delivered her to the groom, face grim, and the Reverend led the couple in reciting their scripted vows. The mother of the bride dabbed at her eyes, and the father patted the mother's hand, while the parents of the groom stared straight ahead at the ceremony and kept their hands to themselves. The wedding couple exchanged plain gold bands, and the groom raised the bride's veil for a dainty kiss, followed by a big hug. Everyone applauded and then moved into the dining room, where the left-siders exchanged distant pleasantries with those who'd sat on the right. A sparkling crystal punch bowl held a big block of ice, fruit juice, and ginger ale, while a candle warmed a casserole called "the lion and the lamb." A specialty of Mrs. William Vaughn Moody, it combined creamed chicken livers, scallops, shrimps, and clams with crisp little biscuits the size of a quarter. "No thank you," said the guests from Kitichara, who formed separate clusters around the groom's mother and father. All helped themselves to finger rolls stuffed with creamed chicken and slices of the bride's white cake and groom's black fruitcake, prepared by Mrs. Moody's Home Delicacies Association and thus exempt from family competition.

Had Henriette's German ancestors looked down, they would have marveled at the new-world, suburban ice palace that had replaced the chuppah, the glass crushed underfoot, the singing and the carrying of the bride and groom in uplifted chairs, the rattling of the chandelier. Sickened by shellfish as well as the cream mixed with chicken, they would have avoided the main course and settled for punch and dessert. Grandma Bertha would have looked with pity at Father, her loyal and burdened source of support, about to be torn from his beloved daughter. Missing the traditional wedding music, dancing, and prayers, she herself might have skipped with glee on the soft carpet, plopped down on the overstuffed sofa, and exalted in the walls and warmth that kept the chilly day at bay. Dilly's French ancestors would have applauded the reading from *The Prophet* but added a word about wine at Cana and lamented its absence here, while his Irish ones would surely have spiked the punch.

The couple stood like figures on a wedding cake to receive the guests, who offered handshakes to the groom, congratulating him on his acquisition, and kissed the bride, stealing a little nibble of the prize. As the guests began to leave, the mother spoke to the daughter. "You must come back tomorrow for breakfast. You can pack up then." But the bride was beginning to thaw. She would not look at Father, whose heart might be visibly breaking, his face a cracked mirror of his heart. A lifetime of fearful anticipation — what would happen to him if she actually left home? — was reaching its culminating moment, and little frozen crystals in her fingers and toes were relaxing their grip. Capillaries opened and blood surged in the vessels, making her cheeks bloom with desire for the groom, so it was all she could do not to jump and shout, "Hurrah! I'm out!" The groom had already loaded the car with essentials, and someone or other would have to pack and send the rest. She hurried upstairs and pulled her dress over her head in one sweeping gesture, buttons be damned, wriggled into a woolen travel-ing dress, tied on a jaunty scarf, and ran down the stairs.

"Good-bye, good-bye, good-bye" she cried. Grabbing the groom's hand, she flew out the door and never looked back.

Now time lengthened and spread for the couple like the vast stretch of territory they would traverse by car. Dilly's plan was to head for New Orleans, for seafood and jazz, and Henriette relished his spontaneity, traveling without reservations, dawdling and enjoying the increasing warmth. Worry released its grip on Henriette, and her eyes searched Dilly's face from the side as he drove, exploring the mystery of him with luxurious ease.

Approaching Memphis, Henriette recalled the train trip she'd taken, alone and frightened, in search of Nadine. Finding her had been a triumph, but for what? Nadine had survived less than a year and the case dragged on, the Scottsboro boys still in jail, waiting to hear from the Alabama Supreme Court. Henriette knew Dilly wanted freedom for the young men as much as she, but doubted he'd ever recognize the collusion of legal system and prejudice that guaranteed the young men's continued entrapment among juries, judges, and courts. She pushed the thought from her mind to enjoy her freedom, her married status, and Dilly's attention, while her misspent night in Tularosa remained firmly locked out of memory's reach. Likewise, the dangers invoked by a name.

In Memphis Dilly bought a great sack of barbecued spareribs at a rib shack and brought them back with two bottles of beer to their room in a roadside motel. He set the food on a small table and pulled up two chairs.

"Taste this," he said, tearing off a single rib and holding it up to her mouth. She tested the sauce with the tip of her tongue, then sucked on the end and sank her teeth into the meat, ripping it from the bone.

"It's delicious," she said. "Better than anything you get in Chicago. Remember the first time we ate together? At the Chinese place on 55th Street?"

"How could I forget?" he said, unloading ribs from the bag and opening the beer. They smiled as their eyes locked, and the complicated years since they'd met seemed to straighten into a smooth, inevitable pathway. They clinked bottles together and drank. Filled with enthusiasm for the food, the day, and each other, they ate until hands and face were covered with red, sticky sauce and then laughed at the mess.

"Don't touch anything," said Dilly. "Let's both just get in the shower." Hands held away from bodies, they went to the shower and removed clothes with fingertips, then climbed in together. The water streamed down over both, uniting them in the downpour.

"What in the hell did *The Prophet* say about not eating from the same loaf?" asked Henriette, soaping her hands and face.

"I forgot," said Dilly. "Maybe share the toothpaste but not the brush." Laughter bubbled through the water.

"How about share the water but not the shower?" Henriette suggested. Dilly took the soap, tapped her shoulder to signal her to turn, and began to wash her back.

"Sounds like share the sleep but not the bed," said Dilly. "Why'd we let him read that anyway?"

"The masnpas, remember? It probably fit their marriages." She turned back to him, and they embraced under the streaming water. "We're going to do everything differently, right?"

"Of course," said Dilly. "We're *tabula rasa*. We'll make it all up as we go."

"Invent culture from scratch," said Henriette, giddy at the thought and thrilled to think Dilly might give her the power to erase the past. They climbed out of the shower and stood dripping and drying themselves. Henriette ran a comb through her short hair, and they climbed naked into bed. Safe in the married nest, Henriette cast about for images to draw her away from the feeling of rot at the core of pleasure. *Ecstasy*— Lamarr swept up on a cloud of rapture without the basement of body parts. *Lady Chatterley*'s naked stonemason, erection adorned with flowers. Molly Bloom's "Yes I will yes." If she couldn't quite become any of these characters, they could surely help her to bury the girl with the apple. Her arms, legs, words, and thoughts disappeared into escalating passion, and she heard herself cry out as a storm cloud broke, rain poured down, and thunder rumbled and echoed over and over until it subsided to silence. Her limbs returned to her, followed by words, as she peeled herself from Dilly. No apple smells. No nausea.

"That was great," said Dilly, brushing sweat from her forehead. She lay still, thinking. Was it normal for her mind to roam this way?

MEMPHIS GAVE WAY TO MISSISSIPPI. One morning they stopped at a small café with a gas pump out front.

"Look," said Henriette as they stretched their legs, indicating with her head restrooms marked "colored" and "white." Inside Dilly ordered fried eggs for both of them, accepted an offer of grits, refused coke, and ordered coffee. "Did you see?" asked Henriette.

"This is Huey Long country," said Dilly. "Let me tell you about the poll tax and the grandfather clause." He proceeded to detail the voting laws of Mississippi, and Henriette grew impatient at his endless recitation of facts. The waitress delivered food, and Henriette wondered how long Dilly would stay in his lecturing mode. He scooped up his egg yolk before it could smear on the plate, still talking, and Henriette saw years stretching out in front of them like ties on a track, each one a collection of details that Dilly would recite to her. "You aren't listening, are you?" he asked.

"I know all that," she said. "And I'm proud I did at least something to protest that travesty of a trial, even if it did no good."

"And maybe some harm," said Dilly. "How many people know what you did?"

"Nadine, but that doesn't matter any more. And I told Izzy and Betty." She had no intention of ever mentioning Harold Overstreet's name again. "That's all." Henriette shrugged. Protest was a luxury of her unmarried days, and Dilly's storehouse of facts would earn them the warmth and food on which they'd both depend. "Have you noticed that everyone here drinks coke for breakfast? Look!"

IN NEW ORLEANS' FRENCH QUARTER they rented an apartment for a week and immersed themselves in the city, drinking café au lait and eating beignets at the Café du Monde; walking among the elegant stone houses of the above-ground cemeteries; riding an excursion boat on Lake Pontchartrain; and always hearing jazz, whether stumbling onto the somber, syncopated sounds of a funeral procession or joining the late-night hijinks of a club on Bourbon Street. Every night they made love, Henriette's mind dancing among images. One night she found herself with several men in a police van, their freed hands unscrewing the bare bulb and moving in on her, raising her skirt, shivers of fear seasoning lust. Surely such thoughts were not normal. And yet. Not normal, perhaps, but wild, wicked, and wonderful.

At the end of the week, their money began to run out. It was time to head for Oregon, for their cabin in the woods, and get back to work. Now they drove harder, taking turns at the wheel every hundred miles. The air got dryer and the vegetation more sparse as they climbed out of the low country, crossed a corner of Texas, and continued through Oklahoma to the high plains of the Panhandle. As they gained altitude in Colorado, snow-capped peaks appeared in the distance, and mountain air refreshed them. Soon the arid, rocky landscape of southern Wyoming gave way to the moonlike canyons and craters of northern Idaho. Crossing the border into Eastern Oregon, they passed through the Nez Perce reservation.

"This is where the Nez Perce fought the war of 1877," said Dilly. "Forced to leave their homelands less than sixty years ago." His fingers began to play an agitated melody on the steering wheel, and his foot pressed on the accelerator, urging the car forward like a horse.

"Something happens when a people is pushed to its limit, a whole community threatened with extinction. Something rises up in them, and I've got to find out what it is and how it works."

"The Ghost Dance?" she asked.

"Yes, as different from Snyder's Prophet Dance as dream from doctrine. Snyder imagines the dance existing earlier in pure form, uncontaminated by European influence. But how could he expect to find data free of acculturation when Indians had been trading with Europeans for over a hundred years? I don't give a damn about purity. I'm interested in how people cope. Those Indians who fought for survival had experienced disaster. The Ghost Dance of that time was part of their adaptation, no matter how much it may have been influenced by Christianity or Shaker cults or French traders or anyone else. The Ghost Dance is a near-miraculous feat of resistance, and I've got to find and talk to people who were there and took part." Dilly's passion for resistance and revival felt akin to her own need to know what Charlie knew, even if Dilly were a better participant-observer than she and more circumspect about native taboos.

"Maybe that spirit of resistance is a part of human nature," she responded with enthusiasm. "The Ghost Dancers thought the world was ending. The Apache feel that way when someone dies."

Dilly turned to smile at her. "People rally when the end seems near."

"The Ghost Dance saved some tribes, at least for a while, and the shaman saves the Apache from ghost sickness. They're both powerful," said Henriette.

"Powerful. Like community is powerful. But not superhuman. We have to walk that line."

"If only you could have seen what I saw," she said. But she knew that could not be.

BARREN DESERT GAVE WAY TO mountains and then desert again as they continued west. Soon they were in the deeply forested Cascade Range, and Henriette marveled at the height and width of the trees, the ubiquitous moss and vines, and the relative warmth, for now it was late November. Dilly knew this country and took on the role of guide, pointing out the Sprague River, Klamath Lake, and the town of Klamath Falls, where they stopped to pick up supplies with the last of their money, keeping track of the cost with pencil and paper: kerosene, canned milk, coffee, sugar, potatoes, and smoked meat that would keep without refrigeration. They picked up mail at the post office, headed north to the tiny town of Chiloquin, and continued on to the wood-land cabin provided for them by Dilly's research grant. Dilly opened the door, and they stared at a cold, empty room. "Maybe I should have gotten it set up before you came," he said.

"It'll be OK," said Henriette, standing in the middle of the barren room and wondering where to begin. She looked around. The cabin consisted of one good-sized all-purpose room and a sleeping alcove with a double bed. A pump at a sink provided water, and an outhouse stood out back. A large wood stove served for cooking and heating.

"I'll make a fire right away," said Dilly, "and then we can start unpacking." Soon Dilly had a fire spitting pitch in the stove while Henriette unloaded the car: blankets and pillows for the bed, pots and pans for the stove, her old Secor # 2 typewriter, a few essential dishes. The dresses, skirts, and city shoes in her suitcase seemed useless in this new environment, but they'd have to wait for Dilly's next check to get some country clothes.

"Letter for you," said Dilly, looking through the mail. Henriette recognized Izzy's cramped handwriting and sat to open the envelope, while Dilly continued unloading. "Thought you'd want to know," she read to herself. "Your friend Charlie Kenasy dropped dead two days ago. Heart attack, they said. Lots of Apache men have high blood pressure, and these things happen." Henriette's own heart began to flutter and pound, as though trying to escape her chest, and she gasped.

"What's that?" asked Dilly.

"Charlie Kenasy. My informant. He died." She scanned the room in a panic, wondering if ghosts would emerge from the walls. The walls themselves seemed to soften and buckle. Her breath came fast and jerky.

"You're pale," said Dilly. "You're shaking. I thought you weren't that close to him."

"I wasn't," she said, hand on her throat. She told Dilly what she'd done, and tears of shame and fear ran down her face. "I couldn't help myself. I wanted so badly to know what he knew, to see what he saw." He sat down beside her, glanced at the letter, and took both her hands.

"Of course you regret your mistake," he said. "But be clear: speaking a name cannot cause a death, to Charlie or you or anyone else. Ghost sickness can't kill. Heart attacks happen. We both know that." She nodded quickly, still breathing too fast but relieved to encounter his sensible reason. But she didn't believe him. She didn't know what she believed, but she knew she was possibly guilty of causing a death, and the death that had happened weighed on her mind and her chest like evidence, an undeniable fact that each viewed differently, a splintery wedge between them. And she couldn't help but be frightened.

"I might get sick," she said, avoiding the terms that would seem superstitious to Dilly: owl and darkness and ghost.

"Remember when Nadine died, and you wished it were you? I told you one death can't substitute for another. Charlie and you were different people, with different bodies and histories and lives." Maybe that's how they would divide up the world, Henriette thought: facts for him, unlikely connections for her.

Tangible tasks kept her occupied in the days that followed, but she was haunted by grief about Charlie and regret for the role she had played or not played in his death. She felt herself return to the funeral's underworld, an interior where the subjugated territories retained their chthonic power. Images of the infernal stormed her mind: the hard baked dirt of the burial ground; the crying, orphaned baby; the grinning faces of the gravediggers; the terrified mourners; the irrelevant white preacher; the shaman; and the branches. Now Charlie as well as Bertha and Nadine were on the other side, along with Finn, and Charlie's death had apparently propped open the door. The view from Klamath was different from the one in Tularosa, but she was glad to know the open passage was not forever closed to her.

Chapter 30

After the Christmas-New Year holiday, Dilly began meeting with the Agent, who introduced him to possible English-speaking informants. Each day he came home and relayed his impressions to Henriette. He'd discovered the small camps where the Indians lived until mid-January, when the weather turned cold, and he'd gotten to know a kid who showed him how to fish with a net, while the boy's mother gathered seeds at a distance. The father was away on a hunt and the grandmother in the camp, in their tent. Dilly asked to meet her and thus came to know Cora, a woman with "a face like a horned toad and a voice like an enraged buzzard," as he said, his voice slowing into its storytelling lilt. Wrapped in a shawl, she'd rocked back and forth on a small stool and welcomed company.

Within a month Dilly got to know her extended family. "I like the way these Indians do things," he said to Henriette one afternoon, warming himself at the wood stove. She poured tea for both of them. "No 'please' or 'thank you.' No bourgeois politeness. Just simple, direct acts and words. And under that a vast, complex network of relationships and beliefs that includes earth, sun, moon, animals, and plants as equal partners in everything they do."

"I got close to that network in Tularosa," she said. "I hope it thinks well of me."

"Belief doesn't make a thing real. I have to learn the secret of the community's survival when the odds were all against them. That was real."

"Remember your rule: 'some secrets should stay that way,'" she said.

"There's nothing to fear here," he said, and she hoped it was true.

DILLY REPORTED TO THE UNIVERSITY of Chicago by mail every so often to discuss his work with his advisors, and the department secretary wrote back, including news and gossip in her letters. One day in January, frost crackling on the muddy ground, he picked up the mail. Back in the warm cabin, he opened a thick envelope, set aside some manuscript pages, and began to read the letter.

"Remember Harold Overstreet?" he asked Henriette. "Friend of Carl's, economist? He married a white woman in September, couldn't get a job teaching in a white university or a black one. They've gone off to Europe, where he's got a good job. Isn't that nifty?" A fury sour as stomach acid welled up from Henriette's gut to her throat and broke right through her impassive face, twisting it into a mask of spite. "That's rich," she said, voice sharp and savage. "It's so cute." She grabbed a broom and began sweeping with a vengeance.

"Jesus Christ!" exclaimed Dilly. "Did I say something?"

Henriette jabbed the floor with her broom, reaching under the stove and into all the cabin's corners. "It's nothing to do with you. I've known him since I was sixteen." Her voice ferociously controlled. Face livid. Her breath came fast, but she spoke slowly. "He is to me a cock-sucking son of a bitch and always will be. I may as well admit it. I hate his guts."

Dilly stared at her. "Any time an academic can get a job, it's good news. Why would you hate him?" She held her breath, hoping he wouldn't interrogate her. She swept until every crumb on the floor was collected, gathered the dust into a dustpan, and dumped it in the garbage. When she looked up, her face had returned to its normal state,

and Dilly shrugged a question, looking at her, then turned to the manuscript pages, reading. Over the next few days Henriette frequently
caught Dilly watching her, perhaps checking to see if she would explode again. Slowly her outburst faded into the accumulating collection of things they agreed tacitly not to discuss, and she grew confident
that her secret was safe.

LATE IN JANUARY DILLY CAME home to say that someone had been
inquiring about them at the Agency. "Wanted to know where we were
living. Black beard, tall, might have been drinking. Name of Lucky. Is
that anyone you know?"

"Good God!" said Henriette. "How did he find us, and what on
earth is he doing here? I met him the year before I started college, old
friend of Carl's."

"How would he know we were in Oregon?"

"Maybe Carl told him." She felt cornered. "He's a newspaperman.
He finds things out." Like he'd found out about the party she'd thrown
for demonstrators at the Oak Park house and turned up, uninvited.

"I'll tell the Agent to send him on out," said Dilly. "Anyone who's
come this far to see us deserves a drink and a meal."

"I'm not sure about that," said Henriette, eager to avoid Lucky but
unwilling to fill Dilly in on details. "He's a brash, unpredictable, hostile person." Dilly's hospitality prevailed, and a few days later Lucky
knocked on the door, looking thinner and more haggard than Henriette
remembered, with shaggy hair and pants too short for his long legs.

"I'm down on my luck," said Lucky, after a few pleasantries. "I lost
my job with City News, and freelance journalism can't keep you alive.
I hit the road in search of friends. I need money." Henriette gulped to
think he'd come all this way for what they didn't have, and marveled at
his ability to make her feel guilty.

"We don't have any," said Dilly. "We're living on the land, hunting and fishing. My small grant pays just for necessities." Lucky downed his drink in one swallow and tapped his glass for more. The couple exchanged glances, and Dilly poured him another finger. Lucky stood and began to pace.

"She owes me," he said, pointing to Henriette. "Your smarty-pants sleaze."

"Hey, wait a minute," said Dilly. "Henriette's my wife." But Lucky didn't stop to listen.

"She dropped me. She gave me her bo-dy," he said, separating the syllables "her vir-gin-i-ty, and then cut me off. She's a cock tease, and my life's been on the skids ever since she left."

"Jesus!" said Henriette, aghast, while Dilly looked from one to the other. "That's crazy. I don't owe you anything." What had she ever done to encourage Lucky or to make him hate her?

"You left me high and dry," he said, pointing a finger at her. "Little bitch."

"You can't talk like that in here." Dilly stood up. "Shut up or get out."

Lucky crouched down and addressed Henriette face to face. "I warned you," he said. "I told you how hard-up I was, and you paid no attention. I told you how Betsy was staying in St. Louis, though she knew her husband wouldn't take her back."

"Who the hell is that?" asked Henriette, but Lucky went on talking, even as Dilly interrupted.

"I told you to shut up," said Dilly, louder, moving closer

"Sandra had stopped returning my calls." Lucky's head jerked up and down while his eyes remained fixed on Henriette, and his voice babbled on, singsong and ironic. "Susan never called, and if I called her it entailed some responsibility — such was the condition of our parting. I'd never been completely transported by Lois, and Phyllis was only fourteen. And you snubbed me, told me to leave you alone."

While Lucky focused on Henriette with whacky intensity, Dilly retrieved his gun from a drawer and put it in his pocket. "

You're nuts," said Henriette. "You can't be here." She slipped out of her chair and went to stand just behind Dilly. Lucky's eyes followed. "You're a hypocrite," she said, voice starting to break. "I told you once that you were the damned lousiest man this side of the Rockies. You're the lousiest man in the world."

"Now wait just a minute," he said, addressing Dilly, voice slower and cooler. "I know some things about your little whore. She attended rallies and hung out with Communists all through school. I can spread that around — I'm a newspaperman, we share news — and keep you from getting a job all your life."

"You're insulting my wife," said Dilly. "And threatening me. I accept neither." His hands shook as he took the gun out of his pocket. "Now walk out that door and out of these woods and never come back." The moment froze as an old fantasy of Henriette's sprang to life. Dilly's hairy arm raised, his big hand clenched into a fist, and cowering below him, one of the beefy boys with peanut butter breath who'd teased him as a child. The fist lowered, a rifle in the hand, the crosshairs fixed not on tomorrow's dinner but on Lucky. That image now fused with another: Dilly facing a mob in a dark alley, whole body rotating like the turret of a tank, pale light reflecting from the apologetic palms of would-be attackers. Lucky stared at the gun barrel. "I'll alert the tribal police that you are a dangerous person," said Dilly. "And you won't be allowed on the reservation again." Lucky grabbed his coat and stamped out the door. The room seemed to breathe, and seconds began to pass.

Henriette burst into tears, and Dilly held her until they abated. "I don't understand," he said. "Do you?"

"I slept with him once, when I was seventeen," said Henriette, glad to confess her less treacherous act. "Ever since, I've regretted it. It was horrible. Whenever I run into him, he seems obsessed and angry, talking lewdly about his conquests and blaming me for all his woes. I never thought he'd find us here."

"We'll be safe," said Dilly. "The tribal police will look out for us. But his threat to spill the beans about your protests — that could do some real damage to my prospects."

"I think you scared him. Maybe he'll forget about it," said Henriette, hoping it was true.

IN THE DAYS THAT FOLLOWED, she reflected on Lucky's threat. She was still proud of her trip to Alabama. Had she known that the case would drag on and on through the years of her marriage, that only one of the nine black men would survive to make a life, marry, and tell his story to the world, she might have doubted the worth of her journey. She could not have imagined that the Alabama Supreme Court would repeatedly confirm the young men's convictions, though she would have felt justified by the U.S. Supreme Court's landmark decision the next year, this time ruling that segregation of juries was a violation of due process, a decision first set in motion by Leibowitz's insistence that Negroes be called "Mister." And she would have taken grim pleasure in Leibowitz' change of heart about the fairness of southerners. "If you could see those bigots whose mouths are slits in their faces, whose eyes pop out at you like frogs, whose chins drip tobacco juice... you would not ask how they could do it," he said.

But she would have despaired when a Jackson County grand jury, with one black man on it, reindicted the defendants, and more trials and convictions followed. One of the men would escape to die in another jail; one would serve in the army, then shoot and kill his wife and himself; one would be accused of another rape and acquitted. Alabama would drop charges against two of the men who'd been twelve and thirteen, and two who'd been blind or seriously ill at the time of the alleged event. Paroles would be repeatedly refused, given, violated; pardons would be denied. The only one who survived to live out his life fought for his pardon and received it, from Governor Wallace, forty-five years after the train crunched gravel in Paint Rock, Alabama. Had Henriette known any of this in the months she lived at Klamath, her shaky faith in people might well have been shattered. Perhaps it was, for in later years she remained drawn to the dark promise of final rest, the last act of her play, and as her elders and contemporaries passed, she saw herself progressing from the balcony of a theatre to the main floor and up to the front row, not sad to know that she would be the next to take center stage, with no Busby Berkeley to transport her from the theatre to cinematic realms.

But the Klamath months were Henriette's honeymoon. As the days began to lengthen and warm, she took on Dilly's preferences. She began to share his drink of bourbon and branch before dinner, overcoming her dislike of the harsh taste, and she cooked whatever he shot or caught. She learned to gather berries and mushrooms in the woods, and Dilly taught her to avoid the deadly Amanita. As she read and commented on his notes in the evening, she imagined herself becoming an anthropologist by proxy. Her own exams and fragmentary notes from Tularosa became an annoyance that she dismissed with contempt for requirements and degrees. She had left her parents and was here with Dilly, and that was more important than anything. She took pride in her ability to stretch out rabbit with potatoes and rutabaga towards the end of the month, as they waited for Dilly's grant check to come.

Sometimes, when Henriette was alone in the cabin, her fear of Lucky's threatened repercussions gave way to a sweet nostalgia for her days of rallies and parades, and she sang a Wobbly anthem, crooning in a low, gentle tone:

Longhaired preachers come out every night

And they tell you what's wrong and what's right.

If you ask them for something to eat

They will answer in voices so sweet

You will eat, by and by

In that glorious land above the sky, way up high!

Work and pray, live on hay,

There'll be pie in the sky when you die.

Then she'd shout the final line: "That's a lie," thinking of her life on the left with Nadine, goose bumps rising at the memory of all they'd risked in Alabama.

As the tones of her song and her shout died away, she'd shed a few tears for Nadine, then open her mind to images of the trip. Safely tucked into memory, the event had acquired a patina of daring that worked its way into her sex life, seasoning lust with risk. Beneath her plaid Pendleton shirt and her bulky corduroys hid a powerful queen, a naked Nefertiti, the Egyptian profile connected to delicate breasts, slim waist, and thick thatch of public hair. No beggar she! Dilly loved the willing partner she'd become in bed, even if he didn't see the connection with her bravery and disapproved of her former alliances. Her union was with Dilly, though her thoughts were all her own. As she worked around the cabin during the day, she longed for him to come home.

In the evening she would greet him with a warm, full-body hug, and when she brought him his drink, she'd sit in his lap. Soon they'd meander to the bedroom, alone with each other and no one around for miles. The woods were so marvelously private! Even the squirrels scampering on the roof couldn't see or hear them. Owls hooting in the dark reminded her that anything could happen, but she felt safe in Dilly's arms. With no one to criticize, Henriette let go of all her categories. Out the window and into the wild flew "chaste" and "vulgar," "mature" and "immature." With a little shout of triumph, she'd roll on top.

Afterwards they'd lie together, and Henriette would hum her Wobbly lullaby. Maybe some day she'd sing that song to her children. Children? She hadn't thought about that before, but surely they were expected, perhaps inevitable. She'd found a new grounding for her life, not searching the psyche or seeking radical social change but feeling the sway of wind, rain, wood, and fire. Now she could add her free and fecund body to that list. If her belly began to swell, that would be one more facet of nature with which she would gladly contend.

Chapter 31

In May, a telegram was delivered to the Agency and carried to Dilly and Henriette's front door by the Agent himself. Father had died. Tantrum and attack had alternated, weakening his heart, until finally it failed. Dilly rushed to comfort and support Henriette, taking her in his arms and holding her tight. He would borrow money for her to go home, would drive her to Portland and put her on the train. She could stay as long as necessary, should go ahead and mourn. Henriette backed away from his embrace, pale and scared. "I'm not going back," she said.

"When someone dies you make the trip," Dilly said. "Attend the wake and funeral, eat hot dish with the other mourners. All that helps."

"I got out once, and I'm staying out. If I go back I might never leave."

"Of course you'll leave," said Dilly. "We're married. You'll stay a little while and then come back." Henriette sank into a chair and began playing with a salt shaker, blank and silent, sprinkling a few grains on her palm and licking them up. She looked at Dilly as though he were a stranger. Apparently he expected her to grieve the loss of her father, and she didn't. Her loss was something much more devastating, though she couldn't exactly name it. It was like a loss of hope, hope for something truthful and honest that now could never be. Dilly couldn't possibly understand.

What had she imagined with Father alive? Some sort of confrontation, perhaps, some straight words spoken with forthright eyes, some untangling of love and anger. Henriette's eyes were dry, but she felt vital fluids flowing from her body into the universe, leaving her limp, as though she'd finally become the airy bag of skin she'd once wished to be, hovering just outside the solid world. Her family had been a tightly wound ball of string, but now the string had been cut, and the whole was unspooling. She would not give up the healthy web she was just now weaving to sacrifice herself among those frayed, confusing threads, especially when the one person to whom she needed to connect was gone. The ties that bound had been loosened, and Father, like Grandma Bertha, like Nadine and Charlie, had disappeared into the unchangeable past. The more Henriette felt like kicking and screaming, the quieter she got.

She began staying in bed while Dilly rose, dressed, and went to talk to Cora and her family. The past seeped up through the present, and her own untold transgression in Tularosa festered and bubbled. Sometimes she wished Dilly weren't so unsuspecting. On bad days she thought he might even have secrets of his own — she was sure his mother did. Sometimes she thought of having it out, but no, Dilly believed in secrets well kept, and she'd come to agree with him.

One day he came home at noon, found her in bed, and sat down beside her.

"Sometimes I'm afraid Lucky will come back while you're out," said Henriette.

"You don't have to worry. The tribal police have the law on their side, and Indians fully understand avoidance."

He lay down on top of the covers. "Cora and I are going deeper. When she stops talking, I know she's traveling to the past, and I wait." He fidgeted with the blanket, gripping and releasing. "Today she closed her eyes and seemed almost to sink into a trance." His voice grew slow, not launching into a story but traveling somewhere far away. "She said the Ghost Dance promised them new heavens and a new earth. They danced for four days and four nights to bring back the dead, and when she talked about it she seemed to see the ancestors, with no clear demarcation between herself and them. It gave me goose bumps." Henriette covered his hand with hers, suspecting Cora had seen the open passage.

Could this be what they had come here for, driving two thousand miles and settling in the wilderness? Could Dilly be discovering, in the not-so-distant past of a not-so-different people, a truth about his own life, a truth more important than who gets what, when, and how? She didn't know, but she remembered the puzzle of his "laying his troubles at the feet of Jesus" when he'd had too much to drink — of course he hadn't really meant it, any more than they meant "Jesus Christ!" when they shouted in the woods — but she wondered just what he had meant and whether Cora was opening a door for him that he had never more than nudged.

Apprehensive but energized by Dilly's account, Henriette scrambled out of bed and made sardine sandwiches, seeking to dispel the cobwebs in her head or find a way to say what couldn't be said. If Cora and Dilly were having conversations with the dead, maybe she could do that too.

A few weeks later, after Dilly had left for the reservation, Henriette crawled out of bed, found one of his blank notebooks, and took it back under the covers with her. She began to write a letter to Father, then tore it up. She looked around at the dresser and chair covered with clothes dropped at the end of the day and the square window with its view of a madrone tree outside, reddish bark peeling. Walking over to the window, she inspected the tree more closely. Even in winter the leaves were bright green and shiny, and the curly bark made her want to go outside and strip it. Underneath she could see the trunk, silky smooth and silvery. Standing at the window, she began to draw, trying to depict the contrasting textures of the view. Peeling bark, smooth trunk. Bright green, cushiony moss. And dangling moss, airy and lime green. Each plant living and dying uniquely, like the beetle, like herself, and each one overflowing with its own reality. Perhaps an ancient rabbi whispered in her ear that one could not "pray in vain" about the past, or maybe Bertha tapped her shoulder with a gentle reprimand, but suddenly she knew that the world up to now could not be changed. Done was done, and no way could Dilly disagree with that. Perhaps a price had been paid. Then, bit by bit, as though she were waking from a dream, the world here and now opened, as unencumbered as the funeral's open passage. She stepped into it, unafraid.

She returned to the bed and began to paint the scene in words. The words seemed to open a hole in the page, an interesting space where the warmth and solid hope of her life with Dilly could meet the desolation of the gray and muddy winter, brushing up against the varied vegetation that grew unstoppably, faint light sifting through the rich tangles. Each tree, leaf, and creature was at her disposal to say what she needed to say. Here was a space like the one through which the shaman had traveled: one that was neither black nor white, a space where telling and not telling could meet and forge something new. She remembered May Day on Haymarket Square, almost two years before. Warm breeze. White lace dress blowing against her legs. She, the Spirit of Haymarket, reciting Vachel Lindsay's words to the crowd: "Sleep softly...eagle forgotten...under the stone." When had she turned from glorious words to the study of upright apes? Words like Lindsay's became acts. Could prickle skin. Topple monarchs. Raise the dead. She mustn't forget.

She tucked her feet into slippers, shrugged into a robe, and walked into the cabin's main room, where her old typewriter sat on the table, and then ran her hand over the keys and smiled to think of all the detailed field notes she'd fed it in Tularosa. It must have gotten indigestion. She thought of her first night at college, when she'd awakened in a panic, fearing she might not be able control the flow of words through the machine, fearing she might lose control of the telling. But she was older now, and she could surely try.

Perhaps her poem could be a private letter to Father. In a poem, love and hate and anger could tussle together in a sort of code, so no one would know what she really was saying, and she could safely hide between the words. She fetched her notebook from the bedroom and rolled a sheet of paper into the machine, then began to rearrange words and lines, trying different orders. The growling of her stomach told her that she'd spent the morning writing. Feeling good, she pulled the paper from the machine and tucked it into the notebook, then put the notebook into a cupboard, out of sight.

She kept her pastime hidden for a few weeks. One day Dilly walked in just after she'd put it away, and she hurried to make their favorite Limburger cheese and onion sandwiches for lunch.

"Your eyes look bright," he said. "I think you're feeling better, even chipper." They sat at the table and began to eat.

"I am," she said. "I've been making some notes. Not notes, you know, I mean nothing from Tularosa, just writing some stuff."

"Oh?" he asked.

"I don't know where it's going," she said.

"That's OK," he said. "Remember, no rush. No rush to get back to your notes and your thesis." She took a big bite of sandwich and chewed in silence, relieved. He wasn't going to ask what she was writing or why, and he wasn't going to ask to see it. If she had to show her unformed work to anyone, even Dilly, it would mean exposure, and exposure might explode the chrysalis in which the words were just beginning to touch the edge of feelings, and feelings to bleed back, coloring words.

TIME BEGAN TO FEEL ENCHANTED, without beginning or end, like a single note that sings itself forever. Henriette and Dilly settled down with bourbon and branch. "Cora's kids were small," Dilly began, "when game got scarce and food ran out. Her friends and relatives died, children too. The dead outnumbered the living, and unburied bodies piled up. Everyone hungry. The natural world betrayed them, stolen. Then across the plains and over mountains came the Ghost Dance, spreading from tribe to tribe. The dance promised that the earth would open and swallow the thieves." He spread his big hands, looking down as though into a deep crevasse. "In spring, when the grass was high, the earth would be covered with new soil, burying the enemy." He clapped his hands shut. "All Indians who danced the Ghost Dance would be taken up into the air and suspended there." He lifted his hands, as though carrying them. "Then they would be replaced, with the ghosts of their ancestors, on the new earth." His hands floated downwards, gentle as rain, as though replacing tiny Indians on their own land. Henriette reached over and took Dilly's hand, hearing a catch in his voice and seeing his eyes shine and almost spill.

"It's a story of salvation," she said, attracted but also afraid of his emotion, like when he'd sung "God damn your eyes" at the party long ago, hands shaking with uncontrollable rage. She stood up and took the lid off a pot on the stove, gave it a stir, and moved it to a cooler spot. A savory smell drifted out, covering the caramel smell of bourbon. "They were pushed to the edge, and they thought it would save them. It obviously didn't," continued Dilly. He waved his hand to indicate the reservation beyond the window. "All Cora's brothers and sisters died. But in a sense it did save the community — they're still here, even if they live like serfs." He brushed what might have been moisture from his eyes. "You were right about the Agent. The Agent *is* the enemy."

"But you need him, and you use him. Without him you wouldn't be here."

"They are bastards at heart. Remember the story about the Indian who kept a fox on a leash to steal chickens? One more lie to make Indians seem savage."

"Yes, ridiculous." They were silent while Henriette filled bowls with rabbit stew, thick with salt pork and soured cream. She cut bread, and they carried the bowls to the table and sat.

"There's something here, in this land and in this people, something I don't understand," said Dilly. "I want it." His voice became intense, rising and remaining on a single fevered pitch. "I want it the way a starving man wants food or a drowning man needs air, and I'm going to stay here and breathe it in as long as I can."

"I know what you mean," said Henriette. Dilly sniffed the stew, took up a spoon, and began to eat. "Delicious," he said. "Tender and rich. Your two-day marination paid off." Sounds of blowing, slurping, and chewing.

It seemed Dilly had found a new love. Not a literal rival, like Katya, not a drinking pal and intellectual idol, like Hankton. Dilly had room for so many loves in his big heart that Henriette feared the others would squeeze her out. And would it always be like this, with new loves wedging between them? Her imagination stopped there, unable to fathom the havoc a whimpering infant might create in the space between her and Dilly. But that was a long ways off. For this special time, Cora and the tragedy of her youth filled Dilly's imagination. Perhaps the various characters Henriette brought to their bed each night would soon be joined by guests of Dilly's own.

ON A CHILLY MORNING EARLY in the New Year, they got in the flivver and headed down Dead Indian Memorial Road to Grants Pass, the nearest sizable city, for a break.

"What a god-awful name for a road," said Henriette.

"Jesus, yes," said Dilly. In a restaurant they ate steak and a big salad, food they'd been missing all winter, then looked for a movie. *Gold Diggers of 1933* had made its way to Oregon, and they were delighted to find another Warner Brothers production with dance by Busby Berkeley. Berkeley's impish staging thrilled them again, but this time Dilly kept his arm tight around Henriette's shoulder while a realistic theatre setting showed a couple "Petting in the Park." Then the camera exploded the scene to reveal every kind of couple, from animals to babies, paired up in different locations. Four tiers of lovely ladies disrobed in silhouette, ogled by a conniving baby. A parade of chorus girls revealed their faces one by one, singing, "You're in the money now," one girl breaking into pig Latin and making a joke out of their tenuous employment. Each of these scenes seemed to stand the Depression on its head, carefree in the middle of the struggle. The final number, "Forgotten Man," used Roosevelt's term to mourn the homeless veterans of the Great War. Widowed women sang, "Remember my forgotten man/You put a rifle in his hand." The men marched in rain, recalling the trench warfare they'd endured, carrying the dead and wounded. Then they stood in line for coffee and sandwiches. The song ended with a triumphal military parade arcing above the stage, recalling the veterans' occupation of Pennsylvania Avenue, marching for their bonuses, and their routing by MacArthur, his cavalry and tanks. This march had helped bring Roosevelt to the presidency, despite its shame, casualties, and deaths. The song's recognition of the forgotten moved Henriette to tears. She recalled Vanzetti's words, spoken near the end of his life: "Never in our full life could we hope to do such work for... men's understanding of man, as now we do by accident." Happy days might really be on their way.

They drove back to Chiloquin, talking about the complex swirling of chorus girls with neon-lit violins and speculating on how a musical could end on such a tragic note and still feel upbeat.

ONE DAY, SITTING AT THE typewriter, Henriette remembered the story she'd wanted to write about the funeral in Tularosa, "Liberty Country." The hard, baked dirt. The owl's cry. Her sense of being watched. The shaman and the branches. The images stormed her mind, seeking the life they'd had on that first day, and she struggled to hold them at a distance. Writing was like opening a mineshaft to the possible in all its murky horror.

Then a tune from another time, long before, curled up like smoke to remind her that once she'd felt the strength to look hopelessness in the face. At the Sunset Café, the long, brave exploration of Louis Armstrong's trumpet had probed all the corners of despair, and Henriette had followed it, the music giving her courage. And "Forgotten Man" had done the same. "Wouldn't it be great to have some music in the cabin?" she asked.

"Wonderful idea," said Dilly. "I'll buy a phonograph with my next check, and we can send for our records." That evening Henriette wrote Mother to send her collection of jazz, and soon the records came. Shortly thereafter, Dilly found a used guitar at a shop in Chiloquin and applied his knowledge of music to teach himself to play. He discovered the mountain ballads, love songs, and union songs collected by Alan Lomax. Here was something they could agree to sing together: "Look for the Union Label," her alto voice harmonizing with his bass. Dilly sang other things he might not say, like a song about a Swedish-American organizer framed on a murder charge and shot by a firing squad, long before Sacco and Vanzetti. His voice was slow and dreamy. "I dreamed I saw Joe Hill last night./Alive as you and me./Says I but Joe you're ten years dead./I never died says he." Henriette sang along, thinking of Nadine, the tune accumulating power and weight. Both the ILD and the N-double-A were still fighting to free the Scottsboro Boys when they weren't fighting with each other, and Henriette envisioned Nadine working for a united front, pointing out the uselessness of quarreling over methods. "Don't be a bunch of stumble bums," she'd say, and make them laugh at themselves. "From San Diego up to Maine/In every mine and mill/ Where workers strike and organize/It's there you'll find Joe Hill." The tune made Henriette's throat ache but did not strangle her voice, and both sang with full, free voices. Then, quietly, "It's there you'll find Joe Hill." The notes faded away.

On Henriette's best days, life with Dilly felt like a return to her old sense of a Golden Age, a time before trouble, when now was always. She'd felt a seed of that hope the first time they'd slept together, back in Chicago, as though the world could be healed, and now the seed had sprouted and blossomed. Unlike her first home, which smothered her voice, the cabin in Chiloquin taught her to speak, and sometimes it seemed that everything she'd once found polluted about herself was bathed in cleansing light. On other days, her violations of taboo and of faithfulness returned to haunt her, and she realized she'd have to live with imperfection. Then her doubts about goodness in people seemed like a painful but abiding truth. She thanked whatever gods might be for the safe house of Dilly, for the man who would never leave her with nothing and no one.

Sounds of jazz filled the cabin as summer came to the woods, mingling with the birdsong and breeze that flowed through the open windows. Burlap curtains framed the windows and logs sized for warming, roasting, or broiling were stacked by the front door. Henriette's beloved cast iron frying pan sat on the stove, ready to fry potatoes or simmer a stew, and Dilly kept the knives sharp with a steel that hung on the wall. Close-woven Indian baskets with intricate diamond designs held everything from matches to mail. "Nobody knows you when you're down and out," Henriette belted out, singing along with Bessie Smith, the forest as receptive to her voice as it was to sounds of sex.

Henriette had discovered wild mint in the woods and transplanted some to a plot by the front door, where it thrived and spread in a clean-scented tangle, and she clipped and chopped and cooked with it. Savory smells of browned fish and mint often lingered overnight in the cabin, greeting her and Dilly in the morning. Little by little, Henriette began to go deeper into the sights and sounds and smells of the funeral, the building blocks of "Liberty Country." On paper she set the scene, creating a nest for death and diggers and endurance. She felt more zestful than ever before, and rejoiced to discover connections between the world she observed and described and the feelings they could evoke and represent. Always solicitous, Dilly was glad to see her happy and never questioned her abandonment of anthropology. Now when he talked about the Ghost Dance, she glowed as much as he, thinking of the story growing inside her, already taking form on the page.

Fomite

A fomite is a medium capable of transmitting infectious organisms from one individual to another.

"The activity of art is based on the capacity of people to be infected by the feelings of others." Tolstoy, *What Is Art?*

Writing a review on Amazon, Good Reads, Shelfari, Library Thing or other social media sites for readers will help the progress of independent publishing. To submit a review, go to the book page on any of the sites and follow the links for reviews. Books from independent presses rely on reader to reader communications.

For more information or to order any of our books, visit
http://www.fomitepress.com/FOMITE/Our_Books.html

The Way None
of This Happened
Mike Breiner

The Moment Before an Injury
Joshua Amses

Nothing Beside Remains
Jaysinh Birjépatil

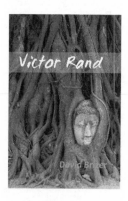

Cycling in Plato's Cave
David Cavanagh

Victor Rand
David Brizer

Summer on the
Cold War Planet
Paula Closson Buck

Fomite

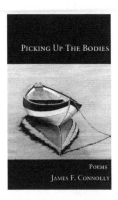

Picking Up the Bodies
James F. Connolly

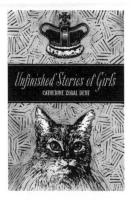

Unfinished Stories of Girls
Catherine Zobal Dent

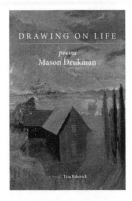

Drawing on Life
Mason Drukman

*Foreign Tales of
Exemplum and Woe*
J. C. Ellefson

Free Fall/Caída libre
Tina Escaja

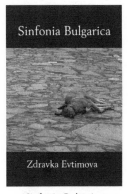

Sinfonia Bulgarica
Zdravka Evtimova

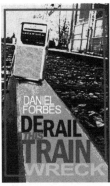

Derail Thie Train Wreck
Daniel Forbes

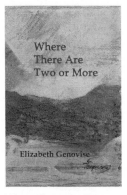

*Where There Are Two or
More*
Elizabeth Genovise

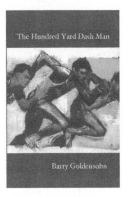

*The Hundred Yard
Dash Man*
Barry Goldensohn

Fomite

*When You Remeber
Deir Yassin*
R. L. Green

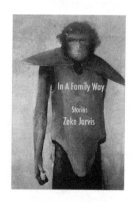

In A Family Way
Zeke Jarvis

Thicker Than Blood
Jan English Leary

*A Guide
to the Western Slopes*
Roger Lebovitz

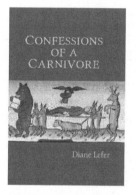

Confessions of a Carnivore
Diane Lefer

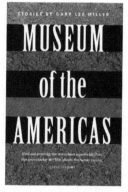

Museum of the Americas
Gary Lee Miller

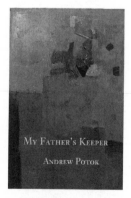

My Father's Keeper
Andrew Potok

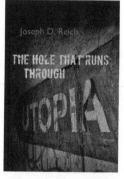

*The Hole That Runs
Through Utopia*
Joseph D. Reich

Companion Plants
Kathryn Roberts

Fomite

Rafi's World
Fred Russell

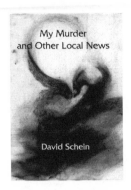

My Murder
and Other Local News
David Schein

Bread & Sentences
Peter Schumann

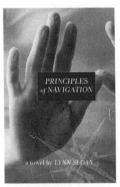

Principles of Navigation
Lynn Sloan

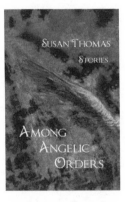

Among Angelic Orders
Susan Thoma

Everyone Lives Here
Sharon Webster

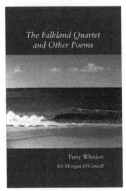

The Falkland Quartet
Tony Whedon

The Return of
Jason Green
Suzi Wizowaty

The Inconveniece
of the Wings
Silas Dent Zobal

Fomite

More Titles from Fomite...